Alexander Thom und Co.

The Local Government Board for Ireland

The eleventh report with appendices

Alexander Thom und Co.

The Local Government Board for Ireland
The eleventh report with appendices

ISBN/EAN: 9783742806130

Manufactured in Europe, USA, Canada, Australia, Japa

Cover: Foto ©Andreas Hilbeck / pixelio.de

Manufactured and distributed by brebook publishing software
(www.brebook.com)

Alexander Thom und Co.

The Local Government Board for Ireland

ANNUAL REPORT

OF

THE LOCAL GOVERNMENT BOARD

FOR IRELAND,

BEING

THE ELEVENTH REPORT UNDER "THE LOCAL GOVERNMENT BOARD (IRELAND) ACT," 35 & 36 VIC., c. 69;

WITH

APPENDICES.

Presented to both Houses of Parliament by Command of Her Majesty.

DUBLIN:

PRINTED BY ALEX. THOM & CO., 87, 88, & 89, ABBEY-STREET,

THE QUEEN'S PRINTING OFFICE.

To be purchased, either directly or through any Bookseller, from any of the following Agents, viz.:

Messrs. Hansard, 13, Great Queen-street, W.C., and 32, Abingdon-street, Westminster;

Messrs. Eyre and Spottiswoode, East Harding-street, Fleet-street, and Sale Office, House of Lords;

Messrs. Adam and Charles Black, of Edinburgh;

Messrs. Alexander Thom and Co., or Messrs. Hodges, Figgis, and Co., of Dublin.

1883.

TABLE OF CONTENTS.

A 2

DISPENSARY HOUSES ACT.

LOCAL GOVERNMENT ACTS AND PUBLIC HEALTH ACT.

DEPARTMENTAL ARRANGEMENTS.

APPENDIX.

APPENDIX A.—ORDERS, CIRCULARS OF INSTRUCTION, AND CORRESPONDENCE UNDER THE POOR LAW ACTS.

I. ORDERS.

II. Circulars, &c.

APPENDIX B.—Circulars of Instruction and Correspondence under the Medical Charities Act and Vaccination Acts.

Circulars.

APPENDIX C.

Orders and Instructional Circulars under the Local Government Act and the Public Health Act.

I. Circulars.

APPENDIX D.—Tables connected with Poor Relief and Expenditure.

APPENDIX E.—Tabular Returns in connexion with Relief under the Medical Charities Act.

Index.

ANNUAL REPORT

OF THE

LOCAL GOVERNMENT BOARD FOR IRELAND,

BEING

THE ELEVENTH REPORT UNDER "THE LOCAL GOVERNMENT BOARD (IRELAND) ACT," 35 & 36 VIC., CAP. 69.

TO HIS EXCELLENCY JOHN POYNTZ, EARL SPENCER, K.G., &c., &c., &c.,

Lord Lieutenant General and General Governor of Ireland.

Local Government Board,
Dublin, 11*th April*, 1883

MAY IT PLEASE YOUR EXCELLENCY,

WE, the Local Government Board for Ireland, submit to your Excellency this our Eleventh Annual Report under the statute 35 & 36 Vic., cap. 69, entitled "The Local Government Board (Ireland) Act, 1872," relating to our proceedings up to the 31st March, 1883.

POOR RELIEF.

1. We submit, in the first place, in continuation of similar returns in previous Annual Reports, a summary of weekly returns of persons relieved, in the workhouse and out of the workhouse, for fifty-two weeks from the week ended 11th February, 1882, to the week ended 3rd February, 1883, both inclusive; and we give, in illustration of these and previous returns, the two indoor and outdoor diagrams,* so as to afford a comparison of the fluctuations which have occurred in each year for the last seven years.

* See diagrams facing p. 30.

SUMMARY of Weekly Returns of Persons relieved in Unions in Ireland, from the week

Week ended Saturday.	Relieved in the Workhouse.													
	Able-bodied.			Orphan Children under 15 years of age.	Sick in Workhouse Hospitals.			All other Classes.			Total Number in Workhouses.	Average Weekly Cost per head for Maintenance and Clothing.	Deaths.	
	Males.	Females.	Total.		Fever Patients.	Other Cases.	Total.	Males aged 15 and upwards.	Females aged 15 and upwards.	Total.			No. in the Week.	Weekly rate of Mortality per 1,000.
1865.												s. d.		
Feb. 11,	[illegible]	[illegible]	[illegible]	[illegible]	[illegible]	[illegible]	[illegible]	[illegible]	[illegible]	[illegible]	[illegible]	[illegible]	[illegible]	[illegible]
18,	[illegible]	[illegible]	[illegible]	[illegible]	[illegible]	[illegible]	[illegible]	[illegible]	[illegible]	[illegible]	[illegible]	[illegible]	[illegible]	[illegible]
25,	[illegible]	[illegible]	[illegible]	[illegible]	[illegible]	[illegible]	[illegible]	[illegible]	[illegible]	[illegible]	[illegible]	[illegible]	[illegible]	[illegible]
Mar. 4,	[illegible]	[illegible]	[illegible]	[illegible]	[illegible]	[illegible]	[illegible]	[illegible]	[illegible]	[illegible]	[illegible]	[illegible]	[illegible]	[illegible]
11,	[illegible]	[illegible]	[illegible]	[illegible]	[illegible]	[illegible]	[illegible]	[illegible]	[illegible]	[illegible]	[illegible]	[illegible]	[illegible]	[illegible]
18,	[illegible]	[illegible]	[illegible]	[illegible]	[illegible]	[illegible]	[illegible]	[illegible]	[illegible]	[illegible]	[illegible]	[illegible]	[illegible]	[illegible]
25,	[illegible]	[illegible]	[illegible]	[illegible]	[illegible]	[illegible]	[illegible]	[illegible]	[illegible]	[illegible]	[illegible]	[illegible]	[illegible]	[illegible]
April 1,	[illegible]	[illegible]	[illegible]	[illegible]	[illegible]	[illegible]	[illegible]	[illegible]	[illegible]	[illegible]	[illegible]	[illegible]	[illegible]	[illegible]
8,	[illegible]	[illegible]	[illegible]	[illegible]	[illegible]	[illegible]	[illegible]	[illegible]	[illegible]	[illegible]	[illegible]	[illegible]	[illegible]	[illegible]
15,	[illegible]	[illegible]	[illegible]	[illegible]	[illegible]	[illegible]	[illegible]	[illegible]	[illegible]	[illegible]	[illegible]	[illegible]	[illegible]	[illegible]
22,	[illegible]	[illegible]	[illegible]	[illegible]	[illegible]	[illegible]	[illegible]	[illegible]	[illegible]	[illegible]	[illegible]	[illegible]	[illegible]	[illegible]
29,	[illegible]	[illegible]	[illegible]	[illegible]	[illegible]	[illegible]	[illegible]	[illegible]	[illegible]	[illegible]	[illegible]	[illegible]	[illegible]	[illegible]
May 6,	[illegible]	[illegible]	[illegible]	[illegible]	[illegible]	[illegible]	[illegible]	[illegible]	[illegible]	[illegible]	[illegible]	[illegible]	[illegible]	[illegible]
13,	[illegible]	[illegible]	[illegible]	[illegible]	[illegible]	[illegible]	[illegible]	[illegible]	[illegible]	[illegible]	[illegible]	[illegible]	[illegible]	[illegible]
20,	[illegible]	[illegible]	[illegible]	[illegible]	[illegible]	[illegible]	[illegible]	[illegible]	[illegible]	[illegible]	[illegible]	[illegible]	[illegible]	[illegible]
27,	[illegible]	[illegible]	[illegible]	[illegible]	[illegible]	[illegible]	[illegible]	[illegible]	[illegible]	[illegible]	[illegible]	[illegible]	[illegible]	[illegible]
June 3,	[illegible]	[illegible]	[illegible]	[illegible]	[illegible]	[illegible]	[illegible]	[illegible]	[illegible]	[illegible]	[illegible]	[illegible]	[illegible]	[illegible]
10,	[illegible]	[illegible]	[illegible]	[illegible]	[illegible]	[illegible]	[illegible]	[illegible]	[illegible]	[illegible]	[illegible]	[illegible]	[illegible]	[illegible]
17,	[illegible]	[illegible]	[illegible]	[illegible]	[illegible]	[illegible]	[illegible]	[illegible]	[illegible]	[illegible]	[illegible]	[illegible]	[illegible]	[illegible]
24,	[illegible]	[illegible]	[illegible]	[illegible]	[illegible]	[illegible]	[illegible]	[illegible]	[illegible]	[illegible]	[illegible]	[illegible]	[illegible]	[illegible]
July 1,	[illegible]	[illegible]	[illegible]	[illegible]	[illegible]	[illegible]	[illegible]	[illegible]	[illegible]	[illegible]	[illegible]	[illegible]	[illegible]	[illegible]
8,	[illegible]	[illegible]	[illegible]	[illegible]	[illegible]	[illegible]	[illegible]	[illegible]	[illegible]	[illegible]	[illegible]	[illegible]	[illegible]	[illegible]
15,	[illegible]	[illegible]	[illegible]	[illegible]	[illegible]	[illegible]	[illegible]	[illegible]	[illegible]	[illegible]	[illegible]	[illegible]	[illegible]	[illegible]
22,	[illegible]	[illegible]	[illegible]	[illegible]	[illegible]	[illegible]	[illegible]	[illegible]	[illegible]	[illegible]	[illegible]	[illegible]	[illegible]	[illegible]
29,	[illegible]	[illegible]	[illegible]	[illegible]	[illegible]	[illegible]	[illegible]	[illegible]	[illegible]	[illegible]	[illegible]	[illegible]	[illegible]	[illegible]
Aug. 5,	[illegible]	[illegible]	[illegible]	[illegible]	[illegible]	[illegible]	[illegible]	[illegible]	[illegible]	[illegible]	[illegible]	[illegible]	[illegible]	[illegible]
12,	[illegible]	[illegible]	[illegible]	[illegible]	[illegible]	[illegible]	[illegible]	[illegible]	[illegible]	[illegible]	[illegible]	[illegible]	[illegible]	[illegible]
19,	[illegible]	[illegible]	[illegible]	[illegible]	[illegible]	[illegible]	[illegible]	[illegible]	[illegible]	[illegible]	[illegible]	[illegible]	[illegible]	[illegible]
26,	[illegible]	[illegible]	[illegible]	[illegible]	[illegible]	[illegible]	[illegible]	[illegible]	[illegible]	[illegible]	[illegible]	[illegible]	[illegible]	[illegible]
Sept. 2,	[illegible]	[illegible]	[illegible]	[illegible]	[illegible]	[illegible]	[illegible]	[illegible]	[illegible]	[illegible]	[illegible]	[illegible]	[illegible]	[illegible]
9,	[illegible]	[illegible]	[illegible]	[illegible]	[illegible]	[illegible]	[illegible]	[illegible]	[illegible]	[illegible]	[illegible]	[illegible]	[illegible]	[illegible]
16,	[illegible]	[illegible]	[illegible]	[illegible]	[illegible]	[illegible]	[illegible]	[illegible]	[illegible]	[illegible]	[illegible]	[illegible]	[illegible]	[illegible]
23,	[illegible]	[illegible]	[illegible]	[illegible]	[illegible]	[illegible]	[illegible]	[illegible]	[illegible]	[illegible]	[illegible]	[illegible]	[illegible]	[illegible]
30,	[illegible]	[illegible]	[illegible]	[illegible]	[illegible]	[illegible]	[illegible]	[illegible]	[illegible]	[illegible]	[illegible]	[illegible]	[illegible]	[illegible]
Oct. 7,	[illegible]	[illegible]	[illegible]	[illegible]	[illegible]	[illegible]	[illegible]	[illegible]	[illegible]	[illegible]	[illegible]	[illegible]	[illegible]	[illegible]
14,	[illegible]	[illegible]	[illegible]	[illegible]	[illegible]	[illegible]	[illegible]	[illegible]	[illegible]	[illegible]	[illegible]	[illegible]	[illegible]	[illegible]
21,	[illegible]	[illegible]	[illegible]	[illegible]	[illegible]	[illegible]	[illegible]	[illegible]	[illegible]	[illegible]	[illegible]	[illegible]	[illegible]	[illegible]
28,	[illegible]	[illegible]	[illegible]	[illegible]	[illegible]	[illegible]	[illegible]	[illegible]	[illegible]	[illegible]	[illegible]	[illegible]	[illegible]	[illegible]
Nov. 4,	[illegible]	[illegible]	[illegible]	[illegible]	[illegible]	[illegible]	[illegible]	[illegible]	[illegible]	[illegible]	[illegible]	[illegible]	[illegible]	[illegible]
11,	[illegible]	[illegible]	[illegible]	[illegible]	[illegible]	[illegible]	[illegible]	[illegible]	[illegible]	[illegible]	[illegible]	[illegible]	[illegible]	[illegible]
18,	[illegible]	[illegible]	[illegible]	[illegible]	[illegible]	[illegible]	[illegible]	[illegible]	[illegible]	[illegible]	[illegible]	[illegible]	[illegible]	[illegible]
25,	[illegible]	[illegible]	[illegible]	[illegible]	[illegible]	[illegible]	[illegible]	[illegible]	[illegible]	[illegible]	[illegible]	[illegible]	[illegible]	[illegible]
Dec. 2,	[illegible]	[illegible]	[illegible]	[illegible]	[illegible]	[illegible]	[illegible]	[illegible]	[illegible]	[illegible]	[illegible]	[illegible]	[illegible]	[illegible]
9,	[illegible]	[illegible]	[illegible]	[illegible]	[illegible]	[illegible]	[illegible]	[illegible]	[illegible]	[illegible]	[illegible]	[illegible]	[illegible]	[illegible]
16,	[illegible]	[illegible]	[illegible]	[illegible]	[illegible]	[illegible]	[illegible]	[illegible]	[illegible]	[illegible]	[illegible]	[illegible]	[illegible]	[illegible]
23,	[illegible]	[illegible]	[illegible]	[illegible]	[illegible]	[illegible]	[illegible]	[illegible]	[illegible]	[illegible]	[illegible]	[illegible]	[illegible]	[illegible]
30,	[illegible]	[illegible]	[illegible]	[illegible]	[illegible]	[illegible]	[illegible]	[illegible]	[illegible]	[illegible]	[illegible]	[illegible]	[illegible]	[illegible]
1866.														
Jan. 6,	[illegible]	[illegible]	[illegible]	[illegible]	[illegible]	[illegible]	[illegible]	[illegible]	[illegible]	[illegible]	[illegible]	[illegible]	[illegible]	[illegible]
13,	[illegible]	[illegible]	[illegible]	[illegible]	[illegible]	[illegible]	[illegible]	[illegible]	[illegible]	[illegible]	[illegible]	[illegible]	[illegible]	[illegible]
20,	[illegible]	[illegible]	[illegible]	[illegible]	[illegible]	[illegible]	[illegible]	[illegible]	[illegible]	[illegible]	[illegible]	[illegible]	[illegible]	[illegible]
27,	[illegible]	[illegible]	[illegible]	[illegible]	[illegible]	[illegible]	[illegible]	[illegible]	[illegible]	[illegible]	[illegible]	[illegible]	[illegible]	[illegible]
Feb. 3,	[illegible]	[illegible]	[illegible]	[illegible]	[illegible]	[illegible]	[illegible]	[illegible]	[illegible]	[illegible]	[illegible]	[illegible]	[illegible]	[illegible]

ended 11th February, 1883, to the week ended 3rd February, 1883, both inclusive.

[illegible]						No. of Persons [illegible]		No. of Blind and Deaf and Dumb [illegible]		[illegible]								Total [illegible]
[illegible]			[illegible]			[illegible]				[illegible]		[illegible]		[illegible]			Total [illegible]	
[illegible]	[illegible]	[illegible]	[illegible]	[illegible]	[illegible]	[illegible]	[illegible]	Blind.	Deaf and Dumb.	No. of Cases.	No. of Persons.	No. of Cases.	No. of Persons.	Males.	Females.	Total.		
[illegible]	[illegible]	[illegible]	[illegible]	[illegible]	[illegible]	[illegible]	[illegible]	[illegible]	[illegible]	[illegible]	[illegible]	[illegible]	[illegible]	[illegible]	[illegible]	[illegible]	[illegible]	[illegible]

2. The following tables represent, in figures, the maximum, minimum, and average daily numbers shown in each diagram for the whole series of seven years:—

RELIEF IN WORKHOUSE.

—	Maximum Number.	Date.	Minimum Number.	Date.	Average Daily Number.
1876–77, .	48,469	11 March, 1876	38,789	26 August, 1876	43,225
1877–78, .	51,720	9 February, 1878	40,179	1 September, 1077	44,876
1878–79, .	54,216	8 February, 1879	42,960	24 August, 1878	47,994
1879–80, .	59,591	31 January, 1880	47,421	23 August, 1879	51,946
1880–81, .	60,341	21 February, 1880	47,162	4 September, 1880	53,796
1881–82, .	58,508	12 February, 1881	47,183	10 September, 1881	52,772
1882–83, .	56,045	6 February, 1883	46,196	9 September, 1882	50,569

OUT-DOOR RELIEF.

—	Maximum Numbers.	Date.	Minimum Numbers.	Date.	Average Daily Number.
1876–77, .	33,976	25 March, 1876	29,076	7 October, 1876	31,620
1877–78, .	37,103	9 February, 1878	30,963	6 October, 1877	33,517
1878–79, .	41,900	8 February, 1879	33,541	14 September, 1878	36,274
1879–80, .	47,418	7 February, 1880	35,602	11 October, 1879	38,639
1880–81, .	93,167	5 February, 1881	46,308	2 October, 1880	60,823
1881–82, .	90,805	12 February, 1881	51,437	3 October, 1881	60,196
1882–83, .	64,041	8 February, 1883	53,856	14 October, 1882	58,835

3. In our Report for the year 1882 we noticed the fluctuation in the number of persons who received relief in the five previous years, and we observed that the number, which had been increasing in each successive year since 1877, and which reached the maximum in 1881, began to decline in 1882, and that there was a decrease in the number of workhouse inmates, as well as in those on Out-door relief, during that year as compared with the previous year.

We are now glad to be able to report a continued improvement in the same direction, the average daily number of workhouse inmates in the last year, ended February, 1883, having been less by 2,208 than in the previous year, and the average daily number on Out-door relief having diminished by 1,361.

4. But while these statistics indicate that there was a gradual improvement in the condition of the poor during the past two years, and up to the Autumn of 1882, unfavourable reports reached us towards the end of that year as to the state of the potato crop in some of the western districts in Ireland;

we had, however, reason to believe that the representations made to us as to the extent of the destitution existing, or likely to arise, were in many instances exaggerated, but we entertained no doubt that, owing to a deficient potato crop, there would be unusual poverty during the winter in particular localities, and an increased number of applications for relief. We therefore thought it right to address the Guardians of Unions in which distress was apprehended, and to point out to them that it was of the utmost importance that they should be prepared to meet any degree of pressure on the workhouse which might be likely to occur, by making provision beforehand of ample stores of bedding and clothing, and by placing all the unoccupied wards of the workhouse in good and habitable order.

We also called the attention of the Guardians to the necessity of so limiting the area of each relief district that the Relieving Officer would be easily accessible to all the poor persons residing in it, and we instructed our Inspectors to make inquiries and to report whether the arrangements in this respect were satisfactory in each Union under their charge. The letters to Boards of Guardians, above referred to, will be found in the Appendix.*

5. In consequence of these communications additional Relieving Officers were appointed in several Unions, and the necessary steps were taken to secure that the machinery for the distribution of relief was in efficient working order.

6. We also obtained authority to employ temporarily two additional Inspectors, in order that the Unions in which exceptional distress prevailed might have constant attention, and that we might be able to obtain prompt information on any matter calling for inquiry. Major Bonbe Fox and Dr. Woodhouse, who had both been employed as Temporary Inspectors in the year 1860, were selected for this duty.

7. In the month of December we received from the Under Secretary to the Lord Lieutenant a letter† communicating the views of Her Majesty's Government with respect to the measures which should be taken for the relief of the destitute poor in the Unions in the west of Ireland in which exceptional distress might prevail, and stating that the Government had, after full consideration of all the circumstances, determined to rely solely upon the administration of relief through the ordinary channel provided by law, viz, the Boards of Guardians, as they were satisfied that no machinery so efficient as that of the Guardians could be devised for the distribution of relief.

It was, however, anticipated that in some Unions the poor-rates which the Guardians would be able to make and levy during the present year might not be sufficient to meet the exceptional expenditure thrown upon them, and it was intimated to us that when such was proved to be the case, and when we were satisfied that the want of funds did not arise from neglect in enforcing the collection of rates, the Government would be prepared to empower Boards of Guardians to borrow at once such sums as might be necessary to meet the temporary pressure on

* See Appendix, pp. 61 to 67. † See Appendix, pp. 65 6.

their resources, and to obtain afterwards the necessary legislative sanction to such proceedings.

8. In some few Unions the Guardians have been obliged to obtain advances from their treasurers, and up to the 31st of March, the following loans have been sanctioned:—

In Belmullet Union,	£1,000.
In Killala "	500.
In Newport "	1,000.

The resources of the Unions in other places have been found sufficient up to the present to meet the charges for relief, but it is probable that further loans will be required during the summer months. We are of opinion, as we stated to your Excellency in our Report of the 13th ultimo, that great poverty exists in particular localities, but that the destitution is not widespread and general, and we consider that the administration of the relief which may be afforded under the Poor Law is sufficient to cope with the distress which exists or may be apprehended.

9. On the 31st ultimo there was vacant accommodation in the workhouses in Ireland for about 36,220 persons, while in the Province of Connaught, and in the Counties of Donegal, Clare, Kerry, and West Cork, which contain the poorest Unions in Ireland, there was room in the workhouses for over 15,230.

10. The following is a Statement showing the Number of Persons in the Workhouse and on Out-door Relief, in each week since the 1st of January last; and in the corresponding weeks of the year 1882:—

Year 1883.				Year 1882.			
Week ended	Number of Persons			Week ended	Number of Persons		
	In Workhouse.	On Out-door Relief.	Total.		In Workhouse.	On Out-door Relief.	Total.
January 6,	52,748	61,186	114,085	January 7,	53,731	58,348	112,089
" 13,	54,597	61,974	116,571	" 14,	54,421	55,737	110,148
" 20,	54,709	61,870	116,579	" 21,	54,380	58,162	112,542
" 27,	54,167	62,341	116,508	" 28,	54,311	58,634	112,947
February 3,	56,045	64,011	120,056	February 4,	54,893	56,214	111,007
" 10,	56,631	64,468	120,960	" 11,	54,480	56,521	111,076
" 17,	56,618	63,387	120,160	" 18,	54,807	60,961	115,768
" 24,	56,572	65,998	122,570	" 25,	54,760	61,190	116,046
March 3,	54,570	65,060	121,610	March 4,	54,775	61,780	116,098
" 10,	55,518	65,975	121,398	" 11,	54,469	61,684	116,153
" 17,	54,768	65,119	119,886	" 18,	54,529	61,585	116,013
" 24,	54,490	64,998	119,488	" 25,	53,506	60,512	114,018
" 31,	54,347	62,707	117,054	April 1,	57,096	60,873	118,169

11. Since the date of our last report we found it necessary to make orders authorizing outdoor relief to the able-bodied classes in only three Unions, viz., Waterford, North Dublin, and Wexford.*

The order in Waterford remained in force for only fifteen days, and was issued in consequence of the prevalence of infectious disease in the workhouse; in the other two Unions the orders were issued on account of insufficient room in the workhouses, and the order in each case only continued in force for one month.

* See Appendix, p. 42.

12. The following is a tabulated account of admissions to the workhouse during the last year, ended 29th September, in comparison with those of the twenty-three preceding years:—

Year ended 29th September.	Number of Paupers in Workhouses at the commencement of the Year.	Numbers of Persons admitted during the Year.						Number of Births in the Workhouses during the Year.	Total number of Persons relieved in the Workhouses during the Year.	Number of Deaths in the Workhouses during the Year.
		Number admitted in Sickness.				Number admitted who were not sick.	Total number admitted during the Year.			
		Suffering from Fever or other contagious Disease.	Suffering under other Diseases.	Suffering from accidental Injury.	Total number admitted in Sickness.					
1859,	[illegible]	[illegible]	[illegible]	[illegible]	[illegible]	[illegible]	[illegible]	[illegible]	[illegible]	[illegible]
1860,	[illegible]	6,107	[illegible]	[illegible]	[illegible]	[illegible]	[illegible]	[illegible]	170,840	9,677
1861,	[illegible]	[illegible]	[illegible]	[illegible]	[illegible]	[illegible]	[illegible]	[illegible]	[illegible]	[illegible]
1862,	[illegible]	[illegible]	[illegible]	[illegible]	[illegible]	[illegible]	[illegible]	[illegible]	[illegible]	[illegible]
1863,	[illegible]	[illegible]	[illegible]	[illegible]	[illegible]	[illegible]	[illegible]	[illegible]	[illegible]	[illegible]
1864,	[illegible]	[illegible]	[illegible]	[illegible]	61,684	[illegible]	[illegible]	[illegible]	[illegible]	[illegible]
1865,	[illegible]	[illegible]	41,168	[illegible]	[illegible]	[illegible]	[illegible]	8,751	[illegible]	[illegible]
1866,	[illegible]	[illegible]	[illegible]	[illegible]	[illegible]	[illegible]	[illegible]	[illegible]	[illegible]	[illegible]
1867,	[illegible]	[illegible]	46,170	[illegible]	[illegible]	[illegible]	[illegible]	[illegible]	[illegible]	[illegible]
1868,	[illegible]	[illegible]	[illegible]	[illegible]	[illegible]	[illegible]	[illegible]	[illegible]	[illegible]	[illegible]
1869,	[illegible]	9,876	[illegible]	2,411	[illegible]	[illegible]	[illegible]	9,110	[illegible]	[illegible]
1870,	[illegible]	[illegible]	[illegible]	[illegible]	[illegible]	[illegible]	[illegible]	[illegible]	[illegible]	[illegible]
1871,	[illegible]	3,719	[illegible]	[illegible]	[illegible]	[illegible]	[illegible]	[illegible]	[illegible]	[illegible]
1872,	46,071	10,813	[illegible]	3,310	[illegible]	[illegible]	165,745	[illegible]	[illegible]	11,046
1873,	[illegible]	6,235	43,741	[illegible]	[illegible]	[illegible]	[illegible]	[illegible]	[illegible]	[illegible]
1874,	61,148	6,196	[illegible]	[illegible]	[illegible]	[illegible]	[illegible]	2,014	[illegible]	[illegible]
1875,	[illegible]	[illegible]	[illegible]	[illegible]	[illegible]	[illegible]	[illegible]	1,750	[illegible]	11,476
1876,	[illegible]	[illegible]	[illegible]	[illegible]	[illegible]	[illegible]	[illegible]	1,645	[illegible]	[illegible]
1877,	[illegible]	[illegible]	[illegible]	[illegible]	[illegible]	[illegible]	[illegible]	1,702	[illegible]	[illegible]
1878,	[illegible]	[illegible]	[illegible]	[illegible]	[illegible]	[illegible]	[illegible]	1,725	[illegible]	[illegible]
1879,	[illegible]	[illegible]	[illegible]	[illegible]	[illegible]	[illegible]	[illegible]	[illegible]	[illegible]	[illegible]
1880,	[illegible]	[illegible]	[illegible]	[illegible]	[illegible]	[illegible]	[illegible]	[illegible]	[illegible]	[illegible]
1881,	[illegible]	[illegible]	46,104	2,101	[illegible]	[illegible]	[illegible]	[illegible]	[illegible]	[illegible]
1882,	[illegible]	7,073	[illegible]	[illegible]	[illegible]	[illegible]	[illegible]	[illegible]	[illegible]	[illegible]

It will be observed from the above that a decrease of 1,502 has taken place in the total number admitted in sickness during the year, and a decrease of 27,783 in the number admitted who were not sick, while there was an increase of 450 in the number suffering from fever or other dangerous contagious disease.

13. The following is a statement of the result of the Weekly Summaries of In-door Relief, showing the average daily number of recipients of relief for each of the thirty-one years ended 29th September, 1882:—

Average Daily Number in receipt of Relief during the year, Average Number of Deaths per Week, and Rate of Mortality.

Year ended 29th Sept.	Estimated Population.	Able-bodied.			[illegible]	Sick in Workhouse Hospitals.			All other Classes.			[illegible]	Deaths in Week.		[illegible]
		[illegible]	[illegible]	[illegible]		[illegible]	[illegible]	[illegible]	[illegible]	[illegible]	[illegible]		[illegible]	[illegible]	
1852.	[illegible]	[illegible]	[illegible]	[illegible]	[illegible]	[illegible]	[illegible]	[illegible]	[illegible]	[illegible]	[illegible]	[illegible]	[illegible]	[illegible]	[illegible]
1853.	[illegible]	[illegible]	[illegible]	[illegible]	[illegible]	[illegible]	[illegible]	[illegible]	[illegible]	[illegible]	[illegible]	[illegible]	[illegible]	[illegible]	[illegible]
1854.	[illegible]	[illegible]	[illegible]	[illegible]	[illegible]	[illegible]	[illegible]	[illegible]	[illegible]	[illegible]	[illegible]	[illegible]	[illegible]	[illegible]	[illegible]
1855.	[illegible]	[illegible]	[illegible]	[illegible]	[illegible]	[illegible]	[illegible]	[illegible]	[illegible]	[illegible]	[illegible]	[illegible]	[illegible]	[illegible]	[illegible]
1856.	[illegible]	[illegible]	[illegible]	[illegible]	[illegible]	[illegible]	[illegible]	[illegible]	[illegible]	[illegible]	[illegible]	[illegible]	[illegible]	[illegible]	[illegible]
1857.	[illegible]	[illegible]	[illegible]	[illegible]	[illegible]	[illegible]	[illegible]	[illegible]	[illegible]	[illegible]	[illegible]	[illegible]	[illegible]	[illegible]	[illegible]
1858.	[illegible]	[illegible]	[illegible]	[illegible]	[illegible]	[illegible]	[illegible]	[illegible]	[illegible]	[illegible]	[illegible]	[illegible]	[illegible]	[illegible]	[illegible]
1859.	[illegible]	[illegible]	[illegible]	[illegible]	[illegible]	[illegible]	[illegible]	[illegible]	[illegible]	[illegible]	[illegible]	[illegible]	[illegible]	[illegible]	[illegible]
1860.	[illegible]	[illegible]	[illegible]	[illegible]	[illegible]	[illegible]	[illegible]	[illegible]	[illegible]	[illegible]	[illegible]	[illegible]	[illegible]	[illegible]	[illegible]
1861.	[illegible]	[illegible]	[illegible]	[illegible]	[illegible]	[illegible]	[illegible]	[illegible]	[illegible]	[illegible]	[illegible]	[illegible]	[illegible]	[illegible]	[illegible]
1862.	[illegible]	[illegible]	[illegible]	[illegible]	[illegible]	[illegible]	[illegible]	[illegible]	[illegible]	[illegible]	[illegible]	[illegible]	[illegible]	[illegible]	[illegible]
1863.	[illegible]	[illegible]	[illegible]	[illegible]	[illegible]	[illegible]	[illegible]	[illegible]	[illegible]	[illegible]	[illegible]	[illegible]	[illegible]	[illegible]	[illegible]
1864.	[illegible]	[illegible]	[illegible]	[illegible]	[illegible]	[illegible]	[illegible]	[illegible]	[illegible]	[illegible]	[illegible]	[illegible]	[illegible]	[illegible]	[illegible]
1865.	[illegible]	[illegible]	[illegible]	[illegible]	[illegible]	[illegible]	[illegible]	[illegible]	[illegible]	[illegible]	[illegible]	[illegible]	[illegible]	[illegible]	[illegible]
1866.	[illegible]	[illegible]	[illegible]	[illegible]	[illegible]	[illegible]	[illegible]	[illegible]	[illegible]	[illegible]	[illegible]	[illegible]	[illegible]	[illegible]	[illegible]
1867.	[illegible]	[illegible]	[illegible]	[illegible]	[illegible]	[illegible]	[illegible]	[illegible]	[illegible]	[illegible]	[illegible]	[illegible]	[illegible]	[illegible]	[illegible]
1868.	[illegible]	[illegible]	[illegible]	[illegible]	[illegible]	[illegible]	[illegible]	[illegible]	[illegible]	[illegible]	[illegible]	[illegible]	[illegible]	[illegible]	[illegible]
1869.	[illegible]	[illegible]	[illegible]	[illegible]	[illegible]	[illegible]	[illegible]	[illegible]	[illegible]	[illegible]	[illegible]	[illegible]	[illegible]	[illegible]	[illegible]
1870.	[illegible]	[illegible]	[illegible]	[illegible]	[illegible]	[illegible]	[illegible]	[illegible]	[illegible]	[illegible]	[illegible]	[illegible]	[illegible]	[illegible]	[illegible]
1871.	[illegible]	[illegible]	[illegible]	[illegible]	[illegible]	[illegible]	[illegible]	[illegible]	[illegible]	[illegible]	[illegible]	[illegible]	[illegible]	[illegible]	[illegible]
1872.	[illegible]	[illegible]	[illegible]	[illegible]	[illegible]	[illegible]	[illegible]	[illegible]	[illegible]	[illegible]	[illegible]	[illegible]	[illegible]	[illegible]	[illegible]
1873.	[illegible]	[illegible]	[illegible]	[illegible]	[illegible]	[illegible]	[illegible]	[illegible]	[illegible]	[illegible]	[illegible]	[illegible]	[illegible]	[illegible]	[illegible]
1874.	[illegible]	[illegible]	[illegible]	[illegible]	[illegible]	[illegible]	[illegible]	[illegible]	[illegible]	[illegible]	[illegible]	[illegible]	[illegible]	[illegible]	[illegible]
1875.	[illegible]	[illegible]	[illegible]	[illegible]	[illegible]	[illegible]	[illegible]	[illegible]	[illegible]	[illegible]	[illegible]	[illegible]	[illegible]	[illegible]	[illegible]
1876.	[illegible]	[illegible]	[illegible]	[illegible]	[illegible]	[illegible]	[illegible]	[illegible]	[illegible]	[illegible]	[illegible]	[illegible]	[illegible]	[illegible]	[illegible]
1877.	[illegible]	[illegible]	[illegible]	[illegible]	[illegible]	[illegible]	[illegible]	[illegible]	[illegible]	[illegible]	[illegible]	[illegible]	[illegible]	[illegible]	[illegible]
1878.	[illegible]	[illegible]	[illegible]	[illegible]	[illegible]	[illegible]	[illegible]	[illegible]	[illegible]	[illegible]	[illegible]	[illegible]	[illegible]	[illegible]	[illegible]
1879.	[illegible]	[illegible]	[illegible]	[illegible]	[illegible]	[illegible]	[illegible]	[illegible]	[illegible]	[illegible]	[illegible]	[illegible]	[illegible]	[illegible]	[illegible]
1880.	[illegible]	[illegible]	[illegible]	[illegible]	[illegible]	[illegible]	[illegible]	[illegible]	[illegible]	[illegible]	[illegible]	[illegible]	[illegible]	[illegible]	[illegible]
1881.	[illegible]	[illegible]	[illegible]	[illegible]	[illegible]	[illegible]	[illegible]	[illegible]	[illegible]	[illegible]	[illegible]	[illegible]	[illegible]	[illegible]	[illegible]
1882.	[illegible]	[illegible]	[illegible]	[illegible]	[illegible]	[illegible]	[illegible]	[illegible]	[illegible]	[illegible]	[illegible]	[illegible]	[illegible]	[illegible]	[illegible]

14. We here continue from last Report a form of table exhibiting for the last thirty-three years the per-centage in each successive year of the several classes of workhouse inmates as compared with the whole number—

CLASSIFIED RETURN of the Number of Inmates of Workhouses in Ireland, on the first Saturday of January; and the per-centage of the several classes on the total Number of Inmates.

First Saturday of January.	Inmates not in Hospital.				Inmates in Hospital.	Total Number in Workhouses.	Per-centage on Total Number.				
	Able-bodied.		Children under 15 years of age.	Other inmates.			Able-bodied.		Children under 15 years of age not in Hospital.	Other classes not in Hospital.	In Hospital.
	Males.	Females.					Males.	Females.			
4 Jan., 1851	26,174	63,238	91,189	16,077	[illegible]	[illegible]	10·7	24·1	40·4	6·6	16·0
3 " 1852	16,164	37,[illegible]	76,[illegible]	11,404	36,073	[illegible]	9·3	22·4	45·5	7·0	15·8
1 " 1853	10,[illegible]	30,[illegible]	63,414	10,678	[illegible]	[illegible]	[illegible]	[illegible]	44·7	7·0	[illegible]
7 " 1854	6,[illegible]	21,[illegible]	47,792	8,736	[illegible]	104,[illegible]	[illegible]	[illegible]	[illegible]	8·4	21·0
6 " 1855	6,197	16,[illegible]	34,[illegible]	[illegible]	[illegible]	[illegible]	7·0	17·1	[illegible]	[illegible]	[illegible]
5 " 1856	4,646	13,7[illegible]	27,[illegible]	7,777	[illegible]	73,347	6·3	19·0	37·7	10·7	[illegible]
3 " 1857	3,513	8,[illegible]	19,177	6,611	16,071	46,[illegible]	6·4	18·5	41·2	12·6	[illegible]
2 " 1858	1,881	6,337	14,[illegible]	6,237	16,[illegible]	40,[illegible]	[illegible]	[illegible]	31·7	13·9	[illegible]
1 " 1859	2,347	6,[illegible]	12,[illegible]	6,467	15,[illegible]	41,[illegible]	5·1	15·8	[illegible]	14·6	[illegible]
7 " 1860	3,151	6,791	11,707	7,[illegible]	14,[illegible]	43,[illegible]	3·1	15·7	[illegible]	17·4	34·7
5 " 1861	3,[illegible]	7,[illegible]	11,[illegible]	8,075	16,[illegible]	47,[illegible]	[illegible]	[illegible]	[illegible]	17·9	[illegible]
4 " 1862	3,486	9,101	16,[illegible]	9,311	17,[illegible]	[illegible]	[illegible]	16·7	[illegible]	17·6	[illegible]
3 " 1863	4,[illegible]	9,641	16,730	11,175	18,431	[illegible]	6·7	16·1	[illegible]	18·6	[illegible]
2 " 1864	3,[illegible]	9,[illegible]	17,170	11,[illegible]	18,[illegible]	[illegible]	6·1	14·9	[illegible]	19·5	[illegible]
7 " 1865	3,[illegible]	8,[illegible]	16,[illegible]	12,101	19,[illegible]	[illegible]	5·7	[illegible]	[illegible]	[illegible]	[illegible]
6 " 1866	3,001	8,[illegible]	14,[illegible]	11,[illegible]	17,[illegible]	[illegible]	[illegible]	[illegible]	[illegible]	21·1	[illegible]
5 " 1867	3,016	7,[illegible]	13,[illegible]	11,[illegible]	17,[illegible]	[illegible]	[illegible]	[illegible]	[illegible]	[illegible]	[illegible]
4 " 1868	3,[illegible]	7,[illegible]	[illegible]	12,[illegible]	16,[illegible]	[illegible]	5·1	[illegible]	[illegible]	[illegible]	[illegible]
2 " 1869	3,531	7,[illegible]	13,546	13,[illegible]	16,[illegible]	[illegible]	5·1	[illegible]	[illegible]	[illegible]	[illegible]
1 " 1870	3,[illegible]	6,[illegible]	14,[illegible]	13,725	16,[illegible]	53,[illegible]	6·0	11·[illegible]	[illegible]	[illegible]	31·4
7 " 1871	3,[illegible]	5,[illegible]	13,[illegible]	13,[illegible]	16,[illegible]	[illegible]	4·9	11·6	[illegible]	24·1	[illegible]
6 " 1872	2,[illegible]	4,197	13,431	13,[illegible]	16,[illegible]	48,[illegible]	4·6	10·7	[illegible]	[illegible]	[illegible]
4 " 1873	2,[illegible]	5,117	[illegible]	12,[illegible]	17,[illegible]	[illegible]	4·7	10·9	[illegible]	[illegible]	[illegible]
3 " 1874	2,[illegible]	5,[illegible]	12,1[illegible]	12,777	18,[illegible]	[illegible]	[illegible]	10·1	[illegible]	[illegible]	[illegible]
2 " 1875	2,[illegible]	5,1[illegible]	12,1[illegible]	[illegible]	17,318	[illegible]	4·7	10·4	[illegible]	[illegible]	[illegible]
1 " 1876	2,[illegible]	4,[illegible]	10,974	11,[illegible]	16,[illegible]	[illegible]	[illegible]	[illegible]	[illegible]	[illegible]	[illegible]
6 " 1877	2,167	4,[illegible]	10,[illegible]	11,[illegible]	16,161	[illegible]	4·6	[illegible]	[illegible]	[illegible]	[illegible]
5 " 1878	2,[illegible]	4,[illegible]	11,[illegible]	12,[illegible]	16,[illegible]	[illegible]	[illegible]	[illegible]	[illegible]	[illegible]	[illegible]
4 " 1879	2,[illegible]	5,[illegible]	11,[illegible]	13,[illegible]	17,[illegible]	[illegible]	[illegible]	9·1	[illegible]	[illegible]	[illegible]
3 " 1880	3,[illegible]	6,[illegible]	13,1[illegible]	16,[illegible]	[illegible]	[illegible]	6·1	10·0	[illegible]	[illegible]	[illegible]
1 " 1881	3,[illegible]	5,[illegible]	[illegible]	14,[illegible]	[illegible]	[illegible]	[illegible]	[illegible]	[illegible]	[illegible]	[illegible]
7 " 1882	3,[illegible]	4,[illegible]	11,410	13,[illegible]	19,[illegible]	[illegible]	[illegible]	[illegible]	21·2	[illegible]	[illegible]
6 " 1883	3,[illegible]	5,1[illegible]	11,[illegible]	16,[illegible]	[illegible]	[illegible]	6·1	[illegible]	[illegible]	[illegible]	[illegible]

15. We hereunto subjoin a tabular statement showing from month to month the number of "night lodgers," a term corresponding to "casuals" in England, for the past twelve months, in continuation of a similar Table in last Report.

RETURN of NIGHT-LODGERS or CASUALS relieved.

Week ended	Number relieved during the week.				Number in Workhouses at close of the week.			
	Males.	Females.	Children under 15.	Total.	Males.	Females.	Children under 15.	Total.
4th March, 1882, .	2,300	840	442	3,582	272	136	93	501
1st April, " .	2,739	577	498	3,814	258	172	53	483
6th May, " .	2,263	631	517	3,411	317	109	101	527
3rd June, " .	2,550	963	517	4,030	347	170	98	615
1st July, " .	1,815	1,073	530	3,418	238	174	117	529
5th August, " .	1,239	566	429	2,234	183	125	103	411
2nd September, " .	1,269	465	373	2,107	163	91	73	327
7th October, " .	1,325	524	404	2,253	190	120	90	400
4th November, " .	1,223	433	320	1,976	216	120	92	428
2nd December, " .	1,161	431	284	1,876	190	114	74	378
6th January, 1883, .	1,755	499	391	2,645	311	140	112	563
3rd February, " .	1,811	477	363	2,651	271	191	90	552
3rd March, " .	1,092	554	415	2,061	222	118	71	411

16. As part of the statistics, which are brought up very nearly to the date of this Report, the following table exhibits in the accustomed form:—

CLASSIFICATION of Causes of Death in Workhouses, from 21st January, 1882, to 20th January, 1883.

Causes of Death.	In the four Weeks ended														Previous Year.
	18th Feb.	18th March.	15th April.	13th May.	10th June.	8th July.	5th Aug.	2nd Sept.	30th Sept.	28th Oct.	25th Nov.	23rd Dec.	20th Jan.	Total.	
Age, . .	272	311	288	274	140	272	180	180	189	177	189	257	281	3,441	3,461
Apoplexy, .	5	6	5	10	7	4	4	6	6	5	10	15	7	90	116
Asthma, . .	11	6	4	9	5	4	3	6	3	5	4	6	13	79	61
Atrophy, .	80	73	97	94	73	61	62	70	77	68	69	165	154	1,063	1,087
Brain Disease, .	29	35	41	35	31	28	34	21	34	31	33	49	45	416	460
Cancer, . .	13	23	14	18	26	11	25	14	13	18	20	27	23	225	243
Childbirth, .	–	2	2	2	3	3	–	–	–	–	–	–	1	13	8
Cholera, . .	–	–	–	–	–	–	–	–	1	–	2	–	1	4	–
Consumption, .	67	79	101	99	70	78	71	76	64	62	54	101	71	951	973
Convulsions, .	15	21	9	19	8	16	14	10	8	19	11	14	15	163	201
Croup, . .	4	8	7	5	1	–	–	3	3	1	8	–	4	44	18
Diarrhoea, .	31	62	33	31	27	33	19	13	35	19	21	17	23	365	353

CLASSIFICATION of Causes of Death in Workhouses, from 21st January, 1882, to 20th January, 1883—*continued.*

Causes of Death.	18th Feb.	18th March.	15th April.	13th May.	10th June.	8th July.	5th Aug.	2nd Sept.	30th Sept.	28th Oct.	25th Nov.	23rd Dec.	20th Jan.	Total.	Previous Year.
	In the four Weeks ended														
Dropsy,	12	13	[illegible]	11	14	17	10	[illegible]	17	[illegible]	13	[illegible]	15	[illegible]	[illegible]
Dysentery,	6	3	4	5	0	4	2	2	1	3	1	3	2	37	47
Dyspepsia,	1	1	–	1	–	–	1	3	–	–	2	2	4	19	31
Epilepsy,	5	6	8	5	8	7	6	5	6	4	9	7	12	[illegible]	73
Fever,	[illegible]	[illegible]	57	47	71	[illegible]	43	[illegible]	47	[illegible]	[illegible]	37	42	586	552
Gangrene,	2	6	4	6	2	3	1	2	5	4	1	9	6	41	[illegible]
Heart Disease,	[illegible]	43	34	[illegible]	41	37	[illegible]	[illegible]	[illegible]	41	43	[illegible]	[illegible]	[illegible]	[illegible]
Hooping Cough,	5	–	–	4	1	3	7	1	1	1	4	3	10	[illegible]	[illegible]
Inflammation or other diseases of Bowels,	10	7	6	6	1	7	[illegible]	10	[illegible]	3	13	31	7	117	171
Kidneys,	16	11	6	4	11	4	17	5	8	17	13	5	14	141	[illegible]
Liver,	5	7	8	11	9	6	8	1	6	1	4	5	5	[illegible]	[illegible]
Lungs,	[illegible]	187	244	165	146	110	81	123	[illegible]	116	151	[illegible]	[illegible]	2,027	2,317
Measles,	18	4	5	3	6	1	8	1	7	5	1	13	2	[illegible]	[illegible]
Paralysis,	45	16	19	[illegible]	24	24	[illegible]	19	18	27	[illegible]	[illegible]	[illegible]	278	[illegible]
Pleurisy,	1	2	4	2	1	5	–	–	–	2	2	9	–	[illegible]	[illegible]
Rheumatism,	17	11	11	10	13	6	5	5	1	7	4	18	4	[illegible]	[illegible]
Scarlatina,	6	5	7	2	4	2	1	2	7	3	9	8	4	[illegible]	70
Scrofula,	8	10	18	11	11	16	11	8	8	6	4	7	4	114	115
Small-pox,	20	16	8	3	9	7	1	1	–	2	5	–	–	76	64
Ulcer,	4	7	3	2	6	7	–	4	2	8	10	1	5	[illegible]	[illegible]
Other Diseases,	31	16	34	34	42	36	[illegible]	47	40	[illegible]	[illegible]	[illegible]	[illegible]	[illegible]	401
Total,	917	[illegible]	[illegible]	[illegible]	[illegible]	727	[illegible]	[illegible]	844	767	834	1,277	[illegible]	11,272	–
Previous year,	[illegible]	1,032	1,179	946	777	[illegible]	670	[illegible]	531	[illegible]	[illegible]	815	854	–	11,247

The total number of deaths in the workhouses in the fifty-two weeks comprised in the Table has been 11,272. In the corresponding Table in the last Annual Report the total number of deaths was 11,247; so that there has been an increase of 25 deaths, as compared with the number last year.

Deaths by fever were 586, as against 552; by lung disease, 2,027, as against 2,317; and deaths by small-pox 76, as against 64 in last year.

ORPHANS AND DESERTED CHILDREN.

17. The number of orphans and deserted children out at nurse from the Workhouses in Ireland, under the provisions of the Act 39 and 40 Vic., c. 38, extending the legal age from 10 years to 13 years, on the 3rd February last was 2,308, an increase of 59 over the number in the preceding year.

Seed Supply.

18. With respect to the repayment of loans under the Seed Supply Act, we alluded in our last report to the further indulgence accorded to Boards of Guardians by the Local Government Board Amendment Act, 1881, in regard to the payment of the instalments of this debt. The payments during the past year have been fairly satisfactory; the amount advanced to Boards of Guardians under the Seed Supply Act, after crediting the Unions with the sums refunded, was £598,306 10s. 0d., and of this £284,685 10s. 3d. was paid up to the 31st of March, leaving £313,620 14s. 0d. due on that date.

Emigration.

19. Our proceedings in carrying out the Emigration clauses of the Arrears of Rent (Ireland) Act, up to the month of November last, were fully described in our letter to the Under-Secretary of the 18th of that month, of which a copy is annexed.*

We also append† a report which we received from Major Gaskell, one of the members of the Emigration Committee, detailing the result of a visit made, in pursuance of our directions, to the United States and to Canada, with the view of ascertaining the prospects of persons emigrating to those countries, and for the purpose of making arrangements for their reception on arriving there.

Since the month of November the desire on the part of the Boards of Guardians of the poorer Unions to have their Unions scheduled under the Act has increased considerably, and 43 Unions, or parts of Unions, have been scheduled accordingly.‡ The selection of emigrants is now proceeding rapidly, and the poor throughout the west of Ireland are very desirous to take advantage of the provisions of the Act; in many cases they are willing to contribute towards the expense of their emigration by providing their own outfit, and sometimes a small sum in cash. More than 21,000 persons have applied to be allowed to emigrate from 29 of the Scheduled Unions.

Mr. Tuke's Committee have undertaken the arrangements for the emigration of persons from five electoral divisions in Belmullet Union, and five in Clifden Union, in addition to those mentioned in our letter above referred to, and that Committee are now actively engaged in carrying out the emigration from thirty electoral divisions situated in the Unions of Belmullet, Clifden, Newport, and Oughterard.

Two Committees have also been formed in the county Kerry for similar purposes, the funds required in each case, in excess of the Government grant, being provided from private sources.

The pressure of work which has devolved on the Emigration Committee in assisting Boards of Guardians to select emi-

* See Appendix, p. 151. † See Appendix, p. 170.
‡ See list, Appendix, p. 191.

grants has been such as to render it necessary to increase the number of members. Three gentlemen have accordingly been added to the Committee, and Sir Robert Jackson, Mr. W. S. Wall, and Mr. John Ross-of-Bladensburg have been selected for that duty.

20. We now continue the series of recent statistics by repeating, with one additional year, the table showing the number of persons assisted by Boards of Guardians to emigrate under the provisions of the Irish Poor Relief Acts, exclusive of those assisted under the Emigration clauses of the Arrears of Rent (Ireland) Act, above referred to—and the cost incurred for that purpose in each year, that is to say, for now thirty-three years past, ended on the 25th of March.

EMIGRATION under the Act 12 & 13 Vic., c. 104, sec. 26, dated 1st August, 1849.

Period.	Amount authorised to be expended by Boards of Guardians. £	s.	d.	Number of Persons assisted to Emigrate. Men.	Women.	Children under 15 years of age.	Total.
Aug., 1849, to 25 Mar., 1851,	11,161	14	11	541	1,244	787	2,572
Year ended 25 March, 1852,	21,019	3	4½	790	2,644	943	4,377
" " 1853,	14,617	8	11½	493	2,316	1,115	3,924
" " 1854,	12,146	17	6	483	1,272	946	2,701
" " 1855,	24,363	5	2½	138	2,847	759	3,744
" " 1856,	3,615	6	5	84	283	463	830
" " 1857,	2,719	15	1	71	368	363	802
" " 1858,	4,177	10	1½	66	468	405	939
" " 1859,	2,033	10	0	37	270	180	487
" " 1860,	1,729	18	9	43	179	141	363
" " 1861,	1,463	19	11	44	178	125	347
" " 1862,	526	17	4	17	73	33	123
" " 1863,	2,433	16	8	41	317	139	497
" " 1864,	4,770	4	6	123	501	245	869
" " 1865,	2,510	17	11	93	316	437	846
" " 1866,	3,425	9	11	180	380	560	1,120
" " 1867,	2,023	10	0	66	228	459	753
" " 1868,	1,963	9	6	71	285	463	819
" " 1869,	1,839	13	6	71	205	439	715
" " 1870,	1,839	19	4	49	219	449	717
" " 1871,	2,268	9	11	48	220	493	761
" " 1872,	2,094	5	10	84	223	289	596
" " 1873,	1,364	14	5	44	173	334	551
" " 1874,	2,246	3	9	67	325	474	866
" " 1875,	1,247	15	1	58	169	381	608
" " 1876,	891	6	6	34	97	228	359
" " 1877,	456	17	4	13	71	116	200
" " 1878,	530	4	7	18	46	84	148
" " 1879,	451	1	5	34	83	128	244
" " 1880,	731	5	1	55	91	147	293
" " 1881,	6,033	18	6	210	558	546	1,314
" " 1882,	4,311	2	9	258	834	403	1,495
" " 1883,	4,293	16	3½	513	634	489	1,636
Total, . . . £	145,814	4	11¾	4,636	17,770	14,120	36,526

FINANCIAL STATISTICS OF YEAR ENDED 29TH SEPTEMBER, 1882.

21. We now proceed to the statistics arising out of the accounts of the Unions for the year ended 29th September, 1882.

We deal in the first place with Poor Relief Expenditure.

Year ended 29th September.	Net Annual Value.	Poor Rate lodged.	Poor Relief Expenditure during the Year.						Paupers relieved.			
			In-Maintenance and Clothing.	Out-door Relief.	Cost of Relief to Blind and Deaf and Dumb Asylums and Extra (?)	Salaries and Rations of Officers.	All other Expenses.	Total.	In Workhouses.	Out-door.	In Blind and Deaf and Dumb Asylums.	Total.
	£	£	£	£	£	£	£	£				
1882,	13,854,[illegible]	1,161,57[illegible]	68[illegible],11[illegible]	18[illegible]	11,[illegible]	1[illegible]	17[illegible],[illegible]01	[illegible],4[illegible]	[illegible]	181,[illegible]	79[illegible]	[illegible]
1881,	13,7[illegible]	1,0[illegible]	[illegible]	1[illegible]	11,[illegible]	1[illegible]	17[illegible]	[illegible]	[illegible]	[illegible]	77[illegible]	[illegible]
Increase,	84,925	70,1[illegible]	718	–	–	704	2,603	2,355	–	–	19	–
Decrease,	–	–	–	1,474	196	–	–	–	60,601	91,8[illegible]	–	154,841

From the above table it will be seen that there has been an increase of £718 in "in-maintenance and clothing;" an increase of £704 in "salaries and rations of officers," and an increase of £2,603 in "all other expenses," making a total increase of £4,025, from which is to be deducted a decrease of £1,474 in "out-door relief" and a decrease of £196 in the "cost of relief for deaf, dumb, and blind," being a total decrease of £1,670, leaving a net increase of £2,355.

TREASURY SUBSIDIES.

22. The following is a statement of the Parliamentary Grant for Medical and Educational purposes, and for Salaries under the "Public Health (Ireland) Act," for the year ended 25th March 1882:—

	Amount allowed for the Year.		
	£	s.	d.
Medical purposes, . . .	74,925	18	8
Educational purposes, . . .	10,341	3	10
Total for Medical and Educational purposes, . . .	85,267	2	6
For Salaries under Public Health Act, . . .	14,237	8	9
Total, . . .	99,504	11	3

The total amount allowed under the Parliamentary Grant for Medical and Educational purposes for the year ended 25th March, 1882, namely, £85,267 2*s.* 6*d.*, is £2,431 0*s.* 0*d.* more than the amount for the previous year.

The amount of Salaries under Public Health (Ireland) Act, namely, £14,237 8*s.* 9*d.*, is £521 0*s.* 10*d.* more than for the previous year.

Expenditure for all purposes for Twenty-one Years past.

[illegible] Statement of the Annual Collection and Expenditure of Poor Rates for twenty-one years, ended on the 29th September, [illegible], showing the Net Annual Value of Property rated, the Amount of Poor Rate collected, and the Expenditure under the Poor Relief and Medical Charities Acts, &c. for each year ended 29th September, from [illegible] to [illegible], inclusive.

[illegible]

Collection and Expenditure.

Hence it will be seen that while the total expenditure of Poor Rates, for all purposes, viz.: relief, medical relief, burial-grounds, registration of births, deaths, and marriages, sanitary measures, expenses under Superannuation Acts, payments under Cattle Disease (Animals) Acts, and under National School Teachers Act, was, in 1881, £1,251,017, making a poundage of 1s. 9¾d. on the valuation, the expenditure in 1882 for those purposes was £1,255,978 being an increase in the total expenditure of £4,350 and making a poundage of the expenditure on the valuation of 1s. 9¾d.

The current Sanitary Expenditure for the year was £51,345 in comparison with £43,918 in the previous year.

Medical Charities Act, and Vaccination Acts.

24. We next submit to your Excellency the report of our proceedings under these Acts of Parliament for the year ended 30th September, 1882.

The annexed table exhibits, in the usual form, the progress and fluctuations of the medical relief afforded under the Medical Charities Act, for each year of the twelve years ended 30th September, 1882, in each province, and for the whole of Ireland.

The cases are distinguished, as usual, into those prescribed for at the Dispensaries, and those attended at the patients' houses, each class of cases occupying a separate column.

In Ulster there has been a decrease of 4,026 cases prescribed for at the Dispensaries, and a decrease of 1,494 of those attended at their own houses.

In Munster there has been a decrease of 6,914 cases prescribed for at the Dispensaries, and of 3,007 of those attended at their own houses.

In Leinster there has been a decrease of 1,143 cases prescribed for at the Dispensaries, and an increase of 3,488 of those attended at their own houses.

In Connaught there has been a decrease of 1,955 cases prescribed for at the Dispensaries, and a decrease of 1,706 of those attended at their own houses.

The last three columns in the Table show a decrease of 17,357 cases for all Ireland, including both classes, as compared with previous year.

It will be seen by the particulars in our annual Report for 1882, that there had been a net decrease of 76,918, in the number of cases throughout Ireland in 1881, as compared with the previous year, and it is satisfactory to observe that there was a further decrease in the cases for the year 1882.

[Table.

[illegible]

[illegible]	[illegible]			[illegible]			[illegible]			[illegible]			[illegible]		
	[illegible]	[illegible]	[illegible]	[illegible]	[illegible]	[illegible]	[illegible]	[illegible]	[illegible]	[illegible]	[illegible]	[illegible]	[illegible]	[illegible]	[illegible]
	(1.)	(2.)	(3.)	(4.)	(5.)	(6.)	(7.)	(8.)	(9.)	(10.)	(11.)	(12.)	(13.)	(14.)	(15.)
[illegible]	[illegible]	[illegible]	[illegible]	[illegible]	[illegible]	[illegible]	[illegible]	[illegible]	[illegible]	[illegible]	[illegible]	[illegible]	[illegible]	[illegible]	[illegible]
[illegible]	[illegible]	[illegible]	[illegible]	[illegible]	[illegible]	[illegible]	[illegible]	[illegible]	[illegible]	[illegible]	[illegible]	[illegible]	[illegible]	[illegible]	[illegible]
[illegible]	[illegible]	[illegible]	[illegible]	[illegible]	[illegible]	[illegible]	[illegible]	[illegible]	[illegible]	[illegible]	[illegible]	[illegible]	[illegible]	[illegible]	[illegible]
[illegible]	[illegible]	[illegible]	[illegible]	[illegible]	[illegible]	[illegible]	[illegible]	[illegible]	[illegible]	[illegible]	[illegible]	[illegible]	[illegible]	[illegible]	[illegible]
[illegible]	[illegible]	[illegible]	[illegible]	[illegible]	[illegible]	[illegible]	[illegible]	[illegible]	[illegible]	[illegible]	[illegible]	[illegible]	[illegible]	[illegible]	[illegible]
[illegible]	[illegible]	[illegible]	[illegible]	[illegible]	[illegible]	[illegible]	[illegible]	[illegible]	[illegible]	[illegible]	[illegible]	[illegible]	[illegible]	[illegible]	[illegible]
[illegible]	[illegible]	[illegible]	[illegible]	[illegible]	[illegible]	[illegible]	[illegible]	[illegible]	[illegible]	[illegible]	[illegible]	[illegible]	[illegible]	[illegible]	[illegible]
[illegible]	[illegible]	[illegible]	[illegible]	[illegible]	[illegible]	[illegible]	[illegible]	[illegible]	[illegible]	[illegible]	[illegible]	[illegible]	[illegible]	[illegible]	[illegible]
[illegible]	[illegible]	[illegible]	[illegible]	[illegible]	[illegible]	[illegible]	[illegible]	[illegible]	[illegible]	[illegible]	[illegible]	[illegible]	[illegible]	[illegible]	[illegible]
[illegible]	[illegible]	[illegible]	[illegible]	[illegible]	[illegible]	[illegible]	[illegible]	[illegible]	[illegible]	[illegible]	[illegible]	[illegible]	[illegible]	[illegible]	[illegible]
[illegible]	[illegible]	[illegible]	[illegible]	[illegible]	[illegible]	[illegible]	[illegible]	[illegible]	[illegible]	[illegible]	[illegible]	[illegible]	[illegible]	[illegible]	[illegible]
[illegible]	[illegible]	[illegible]	[illegible]	[illegible]	[illegible]	[illegible]	[illegible]	[illegible]	[illegible]	[illegible]	[illegible]	[illegible]	[illegible]	[illegible]	[illegible]

Vaccination.

26. In the following table are shown the number of cases of vaccination in each year from 1855 to 1882; the compulsory Act having been passed in 1864:—

Table.

	Number of Cases of Vaccination.		Number of Cases of Vaccination.
Year ended Sept. 30th, 1855, .	46,711	Year ended Sept. 30th, 1869, .	125,672
" " 1856, .	84,131	" " 1870, .	140,220
" " 1857, .	47,855	" " 1871, .	178,889
" " 1858, .	54,964	" " 1872, .	252,484
" " 1859, .	140,411	" " 1873, .	138,678
" " 1860, .	107,305	" " 1874, .	139,487
" " 1861, .	90,258	" " 1875, .	137,340
" " 1862, .	89,665	" " 1876, .	114,487
" " 1863, .	108,810	" " 1877, .	117,679
" " 1864, .	101,610	" " 1878, .	133,045
" " 1865, .	189,142	" " 1879, .	125,911
" " 1866, .	137,124	" " 1880, .	147,828
" " 1867, .	125,741	" " 1881, .	118,557
" " 1868, .	131,426	" " 1882, .	132,825

The next table presents the record of the vaccinations performed at the Dispensaries and Vaccination Stations since 1864, distinguishing the cases of children born since January, 1864, from those of persons born before that time, the former being liable to, the latter exempt from, compulsory vaccination.

Totals for Ireland of Number of Cases of Vaccination performed during the Years ended September 30th.

Years.	Cases of Children born since January 1st, 1864.	Other Cases.	Totals.
1865,	97,160	71,982	169,142
1866,	104,730	32,391	137,124
1867,	107,473	18,268	125,741
1868,	118,613	12,813	131,426
1869,	117,912	7,760	125,672
1870,	135,057	5,162	140,220
1871,	139,043	40,836	178,889
1872,	142,662	109,822	252,484
1873,	119,319	19,354	138,673
1874,	119,237	20,250	139,487
1875,	119,675	17,665	137,340
1876,	112,459	1,998	114,457
1877,	115,190	2,489	117,679
1878,	122,149	10,896	133,045
1879,	116,427	9,484	125,911
1880,	138,410	9,418	147,828
1881,	109,993	8,563	118,557
1882,	116,411	16,414	132,825

The following table contains a summary of the total number of cases of vaccination during the year ended 30th September, 1882, the cases being classified under the headings, "under one year old when vaccinated," "above one year old when vaccinated," and "other persons."

—	Children Born since 1st January, 1864.		Other Persons.	Total.
	Under one year old when Vaccinated.	Above one year old when Vaccinated.		
Total of Ireland, . .	92,384	22,127	18,414	132,925

27. The following is a return of the number of Births registered and of the number of Children Vaccinated in each of the 6 years ending with 1882 :—

Year.	Births Registered.	Children Vaccinated.
1877,	139,848	116,090
1878,	134,117	122,149
1879,	135,286	118,437
1880,	128,086	136,418
1881,	125,840	140,[illegible]
1882,	122,715	108,[illegible]

Vaccine Department.

28. During the year ended 31st of March, 1883, 3,326 applications have been received from Medical Officers of Workhouses and Dispensaries, and other public institutions, from Military Medical Officers stationed in Ireland, and from private practitioners, for lymph, and 17,391 points, and 2,042 tubes charged with lymph were distributed. During the same period 1,920 vaccinations have been performed at the Stations in Sackville-street, and York-street, Dublin.

We have received two reports from the Secretary of the Vaccine Department, detailing the results of the vaccination of infants with bovine lymph, obtained from Dr. Warlomont, of Brussels. The reports will be found in the Appendix.

SMALL-POX.

29. The number of deaths in workhouses from small-pox, and the number of cases of the disease treated by Dispensary Medical Officers for each of the last nineteen years are given in the following table:—

DEATHS in WORKHOUSES from SMALL-POX, and NUMBER of CASES of SMALL-POX treated by DISPENSARY MEDICAL OFFICERS.

Deaths in Workhouses from Small-pox.		Number of Cases of Small-pox treated by Medical Officers of Dispensary Districts.	
PERIOD, 52 Weeks ended	Number of Deaths.	PERIOD, 52 Weeks ended	Number of Cases.
11th February, 1865, . .	145	30th September, 1864, . .	1,985
10th February, 1866, . .	39	30th September, 1865, . .	2,600
9th February, 1867, . .	9	30th September, 1866, . .	579
8th February, 1868, . .	5	30th September, 1867, . .	165
6th February, 1869, . .	8	30th September, 1868, . .	155
5th February, 1870, . .	1	30th September, 1869, . .	37
4th February, 1871, . .	16	30th September, 1870, . .	41
3rd February, 1872, . .	452	30th September, 1871, . .	779
1st February, 1873, . .	677	30th September, 1872, . .	10,217
31st January, 1874, . .	110	30th September, 1873, . .	636
30th January, 1875, . .	112	30th September, 1874, . .	661
29th January, 1876, . .	41	30th September, 1875, . .	481
27th January, 1877, . .	9	30th September, 1876, . .	29
26th January, 1878, . .	19	30th September, 1877, . .	117
25th January, 1879, . .	254	30th September, 1878, . .	1,259
24th January, 1880, . .	112	30th September, 1879, . .	1,844
22nd January, 1881, . .	97	30th September, 1880, . .	863
21st January, 1882, . .	64	30th September, 1881, . .	114
20th January, 1883, . .	76	30th September, 1882, . .	479

The following table shows in each Province the quarters of the year when the disease most prevailed:—

SUMMARY of SMALL-POX cases attended by Dispensary Medical Officers during the year ended 30th September, 1882,—taken from their quarterly Returns.

PROVINCES.	Quarter, 31st Dec., 1881.	Quarter, 31st Mar., 1882.	Quarter, 30th June, 1882.	Quarter, 30th Sept., 1882.	Total.
Ulster, . . .	76	170	62	11	321
Munster, . . .	28	53	31	19	166
Leinster, . . .	–	4	1	2	7
Connaught, . . .	6	8	–	–	13
Total Ireland, .	112	241	84	37	479

The deaths in workhouses in 1882, are more by twelve than the number in 1881. The number of cases treated in Dispensary Districts under the Medical Charities Act being 365 more than in the previous year.

The return above given of the cases in the several provinces shows that the disease was most prevalent in the province of Ulster.

The following table shows the Unions where the disease principally appeared, so far as is shown by the Dispensary Returns for the year 1882:—

Union.	Quarter ended 31st March.	Quarter ended 30th June.	Quarter ended 30th Sept.	Quarter ended 31st Dec.	Total
Armagh, . . .	82	6	—	—	86
Belfast, . . .	118	27	10	5	155
Clonmel, . . .	—	8	14	2	24
Waterford, . . .	66	30	1	-	97

Fever in Dispensary Districts.

30. The following is a return of the number of cases of fever reported as attended by the Medical Officers of Dispensary Districts during each of the eighteen years ended 30th September, 1882, beginning with 26,566 cases of attack in 1865, and ending with 8,389 in 1882:—

Year ended	Number of Cases.	Decrease per Year.	Increase.
1865,	26,566	-	-
1866,	22,287	4,279	-
1867,	18,975	3,312	-
1868,	17,400	1,575	-
1869,	16,880	516	-
1870,	15,744	1,158	-
1871,	15,574	170	-
1872,	15,604	-	30
1873,	14,456	1,148	-
1874,	14,424	30	-
1875,	13,280	1,144	-
1876,	11,646	1,634	-
1877,	11,396	250	-
1878,	10,945	451	-
1879,	10,879	-	54
1880,	11,211	-	372
1881,	9,710	1,499	-
1882,	8,389	1,324	-

There were 2,554 cases of scarlatina treated by Medical Officers of Dispensary Districts in 1882, against 3,782 in 1881, being a decrease of 1,228.

31. The next table gives the expenditure under the Medical Charities and Vaccination Acts for the last twelve years, ended 29th September, 1882.

MEDICAL CHARITIES EXPENDITURE, Years ended 29th September.

Year.	Ulster.	Munster.	Leinster.	Connaught.	Total.
	£	£	£	£	£
1871,	36,361	38,863	41,181	19,311	135,005
1872,	39,896	41,978	42,480	18,694	141,648
1873,	38,896	40,031	42,051	18,185	139,170
1874,	40,834	39,623	41,983	19,015	140,872
1875,	39,833	40,039	41,743	19,848	141,458
1876,	40,033	38,804	43,538	19,069	141,463
1877,	39,358	38,863	42,842	18,769	141,076
1878,	39,884	42,774	44,030	19,024	144,912
1879,	40,962	40,657	44,893	20,230	146,090
1880,	43,283	43,168	45,508	21,114	153,073
1881,	43,640	44,065	47,429	22,110	157,244
1882,	44,839	44,863	47,389	21,967	159,025

And the following shows in more detail, and under the usual heads a comparative statement of the expenditure for the two years ended September 29th, 1881 and 1882, respectively:—

MEDICAL CHARITIES EXPENDITURE.

	1881.	1882.
	£	£
1. Medicines and medical appliances,	29,093	27,767
2. Rent of Dispensary buildings,	6,385	6,539
3. Books, forms, stationery, printing, and advertising,	1,909	1,187
4. Salaries of { Medical Officers,	88,819	88,663
4. Salaries of { Apothecaries,	2,711	2,751
5. Fuel, porters, and incidental expenses,	15,891	15,603
EXPENSES UNDER VACCINATION ACTS:		
6. Vaccination fees and other expenses:—		
Fees to Medical Officers,	12,065	16,415
Other expenses,	1,054	1,159
Total,	£157,244	£159,023

PROVIDING DISPENSARY-HOUSES AND DWELLING-HOUSES.

32. In connexion with the administration of the Medical Charities Act we refer here, in continuation of our previous report, to the "Act to give facilities for providing Dispensary-houses and Dwelling-houses for Medical Officers of Dispensary Districts in certain parts of Ireland," which received the Royal Assent on the 21st of July, 1879.

A general disposition continues to be shown to take advantage of the provisions of the Act, and proceedings under it are still pending in several cases.

Since our last Annual Report certificates have been issue under the Act in the following Unions:—

Bandon	Union, ...	Templemartin Dispensary District.
Cork	"	Carrignavar " "
Lurgan	"	Lurgan " "
Macroom	"	Clonmoyle " "
Swinford	"	Kilkelly " "

Local Government Acts.

Provisional Orders, &c.

33. Since the date of our last Report we have issued the following provisional Orders:—

Date.	Place.	Purpose.
3rd April, '82. .	Town of Ballymena, .	Transferring jurisdiction over certain matters from the Grand Jury of the County of Antrim to the Ballymena Urban Sanitary Authority.
3rd April, '82. .	Town of Lurgan, .	Transferring jurisdiction over certain matters from the Grand Jury of the County of Armagh to the Lurgan Urban Sanitary Authority.
8th April, '82, .	Borough of Clonmel, .	Settling differences and adjusting certain matters of account between the Grand Jury of Tipperary (South Riding) and the Corporation of Clonmel.
17th April, '82. .	Town of Bangor,	Authorising the Urban Sanitary Authority to purchase and acquire, but only by agreement, certain lands required for additional works for the better supply of gas, and other matters.
16th May, '82. .	Ballina Union, .	Empowering the Guardians to put in force the provisions of the Lands Clauses Acts with respect to certain lands required for the Ballina Waterworks.
16th May, '82, .	Town of Queenstown	Order with respect to the Queenstown Waterworks.
17th May, '82. .	Ballymoney Union, .	Order with respect to the Ballymoney Waterworks.
17th May, '82. .	City of Dublin, . .	Order with respect to the making of a new street in Dublin.
18th May, '82. .	Larne Union, .	Order with respect to the Larne Waterworks.
19th May, '82, .	City of Londonderry, .	Order with respect to the Londonderry Waterworks.
20th May, '82, .	Ennis Union, . .	Order with respect to the Drumcliff Burial Ground.
23rd May, '82, .	Banbridge, . .	Authorising the formation of the "Banbridge Burial Ground United District."
22nd Dec., '82, .	Limerick, . . .	Empowering the Urban Sanitary Authority to put in force the provisions of the Lands Clauses Acts with respect to lands required for the Limerick Waterworks.
21st Feb., '83, .	Town of Listowel, .	Constituting the town and District an Urban Sanitary District.

We approved of the adoption of the provisions of the Towns Improvement (Ireland) Act, 1854, in the Towns of

Listowel, . .	on the 24th April, 1882.
Tralee, . .	„ 16th June, 1882.
Warrenpoint, . .	„ 18th July, 1882.

and fixed the number of Commissioners to be elected at twenty-one in the case of Tralee, and twelve in the cases of Listowel and Warrenpoint, respectively.

In the following cases we have received petitions for provisional Orders, but the proceedings preparatory to the issue of the Orders have not yet terminated:—

Towns of Fermoy, Carlow, and Thurles.—To transfer certain powers from the Grand Juries to the respective Urban Sanitary Authorities.

Tralee.—To amend the provisional Order of 1880, with respect to the levy of a special rate of 2*s.* in the pound.

Rathmines and Rathgar.—To put in force the provisions of the Lands Clauses Acts with respect to the making of a new street and other matters.

Killarney.—A similar petition with respect to the Killarney waterworks.

Warrenpoint.—To constitute the town an Urban Sanitary District.

Bye-Laws.

34. Bye-laws have been submitted to and confirmed by us as follows:—

County Louth, (exclusive of Borough of Dundalk.)	Regulating the use of locomotives upon highways.
Dublin City, . . .	Slaughter-houses and Abattoir.
Magherafelt Union, .	Common lodging-houses.
Waterford City, . .	Keeping of animals.
New Ross Town, . .	Prohibiting use of locomotives upon the "New Ross Bridge."
Drogheda Town, . .	Regulating public markets.
Cork City, . . .	Regulating traffic over Parnell bridge and the approaches thereto.
Banbridge Town, . .	Common lodging-houses.
Newry Union, (Warrenpoint Town.) . .	Hackney-carriages, boats, and slaughter-houses.

Consent has been given to the establishment of a butter market in the town of Clonmel, and to the alteration of days for holding fairs in the towns of Midleton and Tuam.

Burial Grounds.

35. Orders have been made and gazetted prohibiting further interments in the burial grounds named hereunder:—

1. The graveyard attached to the White Abbey in the Parish of Kildare, Naas Union.
2. The Church graveyard in the Town of Enniskillen.

These Orders were made subject to certain exceptions mentioned therein, and we retain power to grant licenses for burial in certain cases, from time to time, if it should appear to us expedient to do so.

PUBLIC HEALTH.

36. Our Report upon Public Health is continued from the 26th and subsequent paragraphs of the last annual Report, in which details were given of the operations in regard to sewerage and water-supply, under the provisions of the Public Health Act, 1878, in continuation of the detail of proceedings under the Act of 1874.

The extent of the operations relating to sewerage and water-supply is still in some degree measured in Rural districts by the number of the Orders under seal, fixing the area of charge for each such operation, together with the loans borrowed for these purposes through the Public Works Commissioners.

In the year 1875–76 the number of such Orders was 79; in 1876–77 it was 89; in 1877–78 it was 122; in 1878–79 it was 117; in 1879–80 it was 126; in 1880–1 it was 103; and in 1881–2, 79. From 25th March, 1882, to the 25th March, 1883, the number of additional Orders of Charge has been 83, issued to 59 different Unions.

On the whole, therefore, 798 Orders, fixing areas of charge for sewerage or water-supply, or both, have been issued during the last eight years.

These Orders have been applied for by 157 different Boards of Guardians out of 163 acting for Rural Sanitary Districts.

The preceding statements relate to Rural Sanitary Districts only, Orders fixing areas of charge not being applicable to Urban Sanitary Districts, inasmuch as in such districts all sanitary expenses are chargeable upon funds levied from the whole district.

LOANS.

37. In both Urban and Rural Sanitary Districts a considerable part of the expenditure on sewerage and water-supply is carried out by means of loans which, on the recommendation of the Local Government Board, are issued to the Sanitary Authority in each case by the Public Works Commissioners for Ireland.

In the year ended 31st March, 1876, loans were so recommended to the extent of £37,584; in the following year to the further amount of £41,085; in the year ended 31st March, 1878, to the amount of £62,056; in the year ended 31st March, 1879, to the amount of £124,464; in the year ended 31st March, 1880, to £292,824; in the year ended 31st March, 1881, £199,252; in the year ended 31st March, 1882, £202,374, making a total of £959,629, in the course of the seven years.

The following is a List of Loans sanctioned by the Local Government Board, Ireland, from the 31st March, 1882, to the 31st March, 1883.

LIST of LOANS sanctioned by the LOCAL GOVERNMENT BOARD, IRELAND, from the 31st March, 1882, to the 31st March, 1883.

Name of Sanitary District.		Amount.			Purpose.	Date of Sanction.
		£	s.	d.		
Armagh,	Urban, .	1,760	0	0	To complete Waterworks.	21st February, 1883.
Ardee,	Rural, .	1,909	0	0	Main Drainage & Sewerage.	22nd February, 1883.
Athlone,	do., .	50	0	0	Fencing Burial Ground.	5th April, 1882.
Ballinasloe,	Urban, .	125	0	0	Plans of Sewerage and Waterworks.	23rd June, 1882.
Ballymoney,	Rural, .	400	0	0	£150, New Cemetery. £250, Enclosing Old Cemetery.	6th February, 1883.
Ballyshannon,	do., .	150	0	0	Main Sewer, Well, &c., Belleek.	22nd April, 1882.
Banbridge Burial Board,		1,000	0	0	Burial Ground.	19th December, 1882.
Bangor,	Urban, .	6,000	0	0	Waterworks.	3rd April, 1882.
Do.,	do., .	3,000	0	0	Purchase of Gas Works.	6th Sept., 1882.
Belmullet,	Rural, .	58	0	0	Fencing Burial Ground.	1st December, 1882.
Clonmel,	Urban, .	8,000	0	0	Fencing Cemetery at Clonmel.	8th March, 1883.
Downpatrick,	Rural, .	60	0	0	Water Supply, Ballinahinch.	7th June, 1882.
Drumcondra,	Urban, .	489	15	8	Sewerage.	22nd February, 1883.
Dublin,	do., .	1,500	0	0	Pumping Station, North Lotts Drainage.	24th April, 1882.
Do.,	do., .	12,000	0	0	Plunket-street Area Improvement Scheme.	28th Nov., 1882.
Dungannon,	Rural, .	8,500	0	0	Sewerage Works.	17th July, 1882.
Ennis,	do., .	800	0	0	Burial Ground.	9th January, 1883.
Enniskillen,	Urban, .	700	0	0	Supplemental Water Pipe.	18th April, 1882.
Fermoy,	do., .	15,000	0	0	Waterworks.	18th January, 1883.
Glin,	Rural, .	550	0	0	Sewerage Works, Shanagolden.	9th January, 1883.
Kilkeel,	do., .	800	0	0	Rostrevor Waterworks.	25th October, 1882.
Kilrush,	do., .	40	0	0	Calpry's Well.	18th April, 1882.
Kinsale,	Urban, .	1,500	0	0	Waterworks.	8th April, 1882.
Larne,	Rural, .	250	0	0	Drainage, M'Garel Cemetery.	10th January, 1883.
Do.,	do., .	5,000	0	0	Waterworks.	8th March, 1883.
Listowel,	do., .	143	0	0	Sewerage Works, completion of.	17th March, 1883.
Loughrea,	do., .	110	0	0	Burial Ground purposes.	5th October, 1882.
Milford,	do., .	130	0	0	Rathmullan Waterworks.	6th Sept., 1882.
Navan,	Urban, .	1,610	0	0	£1,530, Sewerage Works. 480, Balance of Loan for Town Hall.	2nd May, 1882.
Do.,	do., .	850	0	0	Flagging purposes.	20th June, 1882.

LIST of LOANS sanctioned by the LOCAL GOVERNMENT BOARD, IRELAND, from the 31st March, 1882, to the 31st March, 1883—*continued.*

Name of Sanitary District.		Amount.			Purpose.	Date of Sanction.
		£	s.	d.		
Newtownards,	Urban, .	1,000	0	0	Markets accommodation.	22nd August, 1882.
Queenstown,	do., .	500	0	0	Water Supply, Small's Well.	25th Nov., 1882.
Rathkeale,	Rural, .	100	0	0	Waterworks, Pallaskenry.	20th April, 1883.
Do.,	do., .	450	0	0	Sewerage Works, Additional Loan.	31st October, 1882.
Roscommon,	do., .	115	0	0	Pump at Four Roads.	28th April, 1882.
Scariff,	do., .	161	0	0	£106, Pump at Scariff. £55, Pump at Tomgraney.	4th December, 1882.
Do.,	do., .	60	0	0	Pump at Killaloe.	26th February, 1883.
Skibbereen,	do., .	13	0	0	Additional Loan, Baltimore Water Supply.	9th June, 1882.
Tuam,	do., .	1,800	0	0	Cemetery at Tuam.	8th August, 1882.

The total amount of the loans included in the above list is £66,954, which, added to the previous sums, constitutes a total of £1,026,583 for the eight years in question.

This expenditure, which is independent of disbursements from the current rates for the same purposes, relates mainly to the cost of structural works for water-supply and sewerage.

The amount of sanitary expenditure in Rural Sanitary Districts amounted in the year ended 29th September, 1882, to £51,345 in comparison with £48,918 in the preceding year.

ARTIZANS AND LABOURERS' DWELLINGS IMPROVEMENT ACT, 1875.

38. In paragraph 28 of the Report for 1882, an account is given in continuation of previous accounts, of the steps which had been taken in Dublin, and Cork, under the Artizans' Dwellings Act up to that time.

The Act is legally applicable to only five places in Ireland, namely, Dublin, Belfast, Cork, Limerick, and Londonderry.

We have obtained the following information respecting these projects in course of being carried out, from the officers of the following Local Authorities:—

DUBLIN:

PLUNKET STREET AREA.

It will be seen from the paragraph of last year's Report, above referred to, that the arbitrator in the matter of property rights in this area was about to hear any objections that might be made to the draft awards as published, and the final result was that the sum to be paid to the owners of the property amounted to £19,067 2s. 10d.; the original estimate for the purchase of the site having been £12,470.

The actual cost of the undertaking was found to be considerably in excess of what had been estimated, and accordingly the Municipal Council made application to the Local Government Board for sanction to an extension of the original loan for the Scheme, by £12,000.

The Artizans Dwellings Committee are now in possession of the greater part of the property, and are engaged in pulling down a large number of houses, hoping, within a few months, to have the area cleared.

Coombe Area.

With regard to the Coombe Area Improvement Scheme, the Artizans Dwellings Company, to whom it was leased for a lengthened period at an annual rent of £200, have completed the erection upon it of 211 houses and cottages, which are at present populated by over 1000 persons. The roads, squares, and footpaths in this area have all been asphalted.

Cork.

Since 31st March, 1882, the greater part of the improved area No. 1, under the Artizans Dwellings Improvement Scheme, has been leased by the Corporation to the Improved Dwellings Company (Limited), who have erected thereon about fifty new dwelling-houses, in accordance with plans approved by the Corporation, and these dwellings are now ready to be let. No proposal has been received for the remainder of the ground cleared in this area.

In connection with the area No. 2, some of the condemned dwellings have been compulsorily removed, under Justices' order, as dangerous; and negotiations have been entered into with the owners of other premises, with a view to the purchase of their interests, if possible, by agreement.

No progress has been made with any of the other five areas. No advances of money have been obtained from the Board of Works since the 31st March, 1882, in connexion with this Scheme.

No steps have been taken under the Act during the year in the three other urban districts to which it applies, namely: Londonderry, Limerick, and Belfast.

Departmental Arrangements.

89. We have, since the date of our last Report, been deprived of the services of our Secretary, Mr. Banks, who was obliged to retire from ill-health, having served in this department for more than forty-six years, and we desire to place on record our sense of his ability and devotion to his duties, from which the public service has derived so much advantage. The office of Secretary was conferred on Mr. Wodsworth, who had been Assistant-Secretary since 1874, and Mr. Brenan, one of our first-class clerks, was promoted to the position of Assistant-Secretary.

One of our auditors, Mr. Collot, having resigned, the vacancy thus caused has been filled up by the appointment of Mr. Byrne, one of the first-class clerks.

We have no other changes in the department to report to your Excellency.

We have the honour to be,

Your Excellency's obedient Servants,

G. O. TREVELYAN.
HENRY ROBINSON.
R. G. C. HAMILTON.
CHARLES CROKER-KING.
GEORGE MORRIS.

APPENDIX

TO THE

ELEVENTH ANNUAL REPORT

OF

THE LOCAL GOVERNMENT BOARD FOR IRELAND.

APPENDIX A.

ORDERS, CIRCULARS OF INSTRUCTION, AND CORRESPONDENCE UNDER THE POOR LAW ACTS.

I.—ORDERS.

No. 1.—General Order for Elections to supply Vacancies in Boards of Guardians for year ending 25th March, 1883.

To the Guardians of the Poor of the several Unions named in the Schedule hereunto annexed; to the Returning Officer and other Officers in each of the said Unions respectively, and to all other Persons whom it may concern:

Whereas by reason of default of election, disqualification, resignation, refusal to act, or otherwise, the proper number of Guardians does not exist in the Unions, Electoral Divisions, Wards and Districts thereof mentioned in the Schedule to this Order; and it is expedient for the due administration of the Laws for the Relief of the Poor that such vacancies should be supplied.

Now Therefore, under the authority of the Statute made and passed in the Second Year of the Reign of Her present Majesty, Queen Victoria, entitled "An Act for the more effectual Relief of the Destitute Poor in Ireland," and of the several Acts in force amending the same, and providing for the execution of the Laws for Relief of the Poor in Ireland, we, the Local Government Board for Ireland, do hereby Order and Direct that—

1. The Returning Officer of each of the Unions in the said Schedule mentioned shall proceed in the manner and according to the form prescribed in the Order regulating the Election of Guardians now in force in such Union, for the Election of a Guardian or Guardians to supply the present vacancy or vacancies in the number of Guardians required in the several Electoral Divisions, Wards and Districts named in the said Schedule against the name of the Union to which he is Returning Officer.

2. The Returning Officer shall give Notice of the Election to supply such vacancy or vacancies, in the Form of Notice hereunto annexed. And such Notice shall be posted in the usual places for posting such Notices, in the Electoral Division or Divisions respectively, for which the Election is to be held; and a copy thereof shall be sent by post, to each of the Justices resident in the Division, or qualified to be Ex-Officio Guardians in respect of property situate therein.

3. The days on which the proceedings set forth in the said Election Order are to take place, shall be the following; that is to say:—

The day for publishing Notice of the Election, shall be the	16th of May, 1882.
The last day for receiving Nominations of Candidates for the Office of Guardian shall be the . . . but no Nominations shall be received after the hour of 3 o'clock in the afternoon of that day.	23rd of May, "
The day for forwarding the List of Candidates shall be the	26th of May, "
The day on which the Voting Papers shall be distributed in the event of any contest, shall be the and, if necessary, the following day.	7th of June, "
The day on which the Voting Papers shall be collected, shall be the . . . . . and, if necessary, the following day.	9th of June, "
The day for making the Return of Guardians elected, shall be the	13th of June, "

or any day (not being Sunday) after the said Thirteenth day of June, not later than the Twentieth day of June next. But if in any Union no more Candidates for each Electoral Division, Ward or District, be named in the List of Persons nominated than the number of Guardians to be elected for the same, the Returning Officer of such Union may make the Return of the Election on any day after the day for making up and forwarding the List of Candidates, and before the Thirteenth day of June; or if, after forwarding the said List, the number of Candidates, by reason of resignation or otherwise, be reduced to the number of Guardians to be elected, the Returning Officer may make the Return on any day after the day on which the number shall have been so reduced as aforesaid, and before the said Thirteenth day of June.

4. The cost of providing the Notice of the Election, and any other Forms required to be procured for use in such Election, and any other Expenses necessarily attending the Election, except the expenses incurred in respect of Voting Papers, shall be charged to the Electoral Division or the Electoral Divisions in common, as the case may be, for which the Expense may be required to be incurred; and the cost of providing, distributing and collecting Voting Papers, where it may be necessary to issue such Papers, shall be charged to the respective Divisions for which they may be required.

SCHEDULE.

Names of Unions.	Names of Electoral Divisions and Ward or District for which an Election is to be held.	Number of Guardians now to be elected.	Names of Unions.	Names of Electoral Divisions and Ward or District for which an Election is to be held.	Number of Guardians now to be elected.
ABBEYLEIX, . .	Clash, . . .	One.	ENNISKILLEN, .	Dough, . .	One.
BALLYCASTLE, .	Drumeallagh, .	One.	GALWAY, . .	Killannin, .	One.
BALLYMONEY, .	Dervock, . .	One.	GLENTIES, . .	Innishkeel and Kilgoly District, .	One.
BALLYSHANNON, .	Belleek, . . Castlecaldwell, .	One. One.	KILKENNY, .	Kilkenny Electoral Division:— St. Mary's Ward, Ballybeagh, . Outrath, . Dunmore, . .	 One. One. One. One.
BANBRIDGE, .	Lawrencetown, . .	One.			
BANTRY, . .	Ahil, . .	One.			
BAWNBOY, . .	Drumreilly, South,	One.			
BELMULLET, .	Knockadaff, . . Muingnabo, . .	One. One.	KILLADYSERT, .	Kilchreest, . .	One.
BORRISOKANE, .	Borrisokane, .	One.	LURGAN, . .	Tullylish, . .	One.
BOYLE, . .	Altagowlan, . .	One.	MACROOM, . .	Macloneigh, .	One.
CARRICK-ON-SHANNON,	Creeve, . . .	One.	MAGHERAFELT, .	Maghera, . .	One.
CARRICK-ON-SUIR,	Carrick-on-Suir, . Tullahought, .	One. One.	MOUNTBELLEW, .	Kilgallan, . . Lackan, . .	One. One.
CASHEL, . . .	Golden, . . Kilpatrick, . .	One. One.	PARSONSTOWN, .	Drumcullen, . Knockbarron and Letter District,	One. One.
CELBRIDGE, .	Celbridge, . .	One.	ROSCOMMON, .	Drumdaff, . .	One.
CLIFDEN, . .	Derrycunlagh and Derrylea District,	One.	SKIBBEREEN, .	Cloghdonnell, . Garrane, . .	One. One.
CLONMEL, . .	Clonmel, . .	One.	SWINEFORD, .	Cloonmore, . . Swineford, . .	One. One.
COOTEHILL, . .	Drum, . . .	One.			
DUBLIN, SOUTH, .	South City Division: Mansion House Ward, . .	One.	THOMASTOWN, .	Knocktopher, .	One.
			URLINGFORD, .	Bawnlick, . .	One.
DUNFANAGHY,	Ards, . . .	One.	WATERFORD, .	Waterford Electoral Division:—Custom House Ward, . .	One.
DUNGARVAN, .	Keereen, . .	One.			
ENNIS, . .	Furroor, Killaniv, and Kiltark District, . . .	One.			

FORM OF NOTICE.

NOTICE.

———UNION.

Election of [a Guardian *or* Guardians] of the Poor to supply [a vacancy *or* vacancies, *as the case may be*,] in the Board of Guardians of the above Union, for the year ending the 25th of March, 1883.

I, the undersigned, Returning Officer of the above-named Union, do hereby give Notice, that—

1. An Election of [a Guardian *or* Guardians] is to be held for the [Electoral Division, *or* Electoral Divisions, *or* undermentioned Electoral Divisions, Ward or Districts *as the case may be*] in the ——— Union; and the number of Guardians to be elected for such Divisions, Ward or District is as follows:—

For the Electoral Division of   Guardians

[*The Names of the Electoral Divisions and the Number of Guardians to be here inserted, as well as the amount of Qualification where it is different for different Divisions.*]

2. Any male person of full age, not expressly disqualified by law, who is entitled, under the provisions of the Acts for the Relief of the Destitute Poor in Ireland, to Vote at Elections of Guardians in the said Union, and who shall

have been liable under the last made Rate to pay or contribute Rate in respect of property of the net annual value of not less than   Pounds, [*or the amounts above stated respectively,*] in his occupation, or for which he is rated as Owner or Immediate Lessor within the said Union, or who is entitled to vote in respect of net rent payable to his receipt in the said Union, of that amount, or who is entitled to vote in respect of Tithe Rent Charge payable to his receipt from property within the Union, of that amount, will be eligible as a Guardian for any Electoral Division [Ward *or* District, *as the case may be*] above-named. But no person being in Holy Orders, or being a regular Minister of any religious denomination, is eligible as a Guardian: and no person who has been convicted of felony, fraud, or perjury—and no person who has been adjudged to be liable to any forfeiture for having provided, furnished, or supplied for his own profit any materials, goods, or provisions for the use of any Workhouse, or for having been concerned in furnishing or supplying the same, or in any Contract relating thereto—is capable of being elected or appointed or of acting as a Guardian.

3. No Occupier rated to the Poor Rate will be entitled to vote in that capacity unless he shall have paid all Poor Rates previously made and assessed upon him, except such as shall have been made or become due within Six Calendar Months immediately preceding such voting; and no Owner or Immediate Lessor who is rated under the provisions of the Act 6 & 7 Vic., c. 92, secs. 1 & 4, or of the Act 12 & 13 Vic., c. 91, sec. 63, or of the Act 12 & 13 Vic., c. 104, sec. 10, will be entitled to vote in respect of the property for which he is so rated, unless he shall have paid all the Rates made and assessed upon him in respect of such property, except such as shall have been made, or become due within six calendar months immediately preceding such voting.

4. No Ratepayer will be entitled to vote in respect of any property not in his actual occupation, or in respect of any interest equivalent to Profit Rent arising out of property occupied by him, unless he shall, one calendar month at the least previous to the first day hereinafter named for collecting Votes, have delivered to the Board of Guardians of the Union, or to the person acting for the time being as Returning Officer, a statement in writing of his name and address, and the description and local situation of the property in respect of which he claims to vote, specifying in Cities, Towns, and their Suburbs, having Streets and other Roadways, the Name of the Street or Roadway, and the Number of the House or Tenement, if any, and the Parish in which the property is situate, and in other places the Barony, Parish, and Townland, so that the property may be ascertained and identified with reasonable certainty, together with the nature of the interest of the Ratepayer therein, and its net annual value over and above all rents payable by him, and the amount of rent payable to him, and the names of the Tenants or Occupiers by whom Poor Rates have been deducted from such rent, and such claim to vote must be executed in the presence of a Justice of the Peace.

5. Any Ratepayer in respect of property not in his actual occupation, may, by writing under his hand, appoint any person to Vote as his Proxy; but such Proxy must, one calendar month previous to the day on which he shall claim to Vote, have given to the Board of Guardians or the Returning Officer, a statement in writing of his own name and address, and also the name and address of the Ratepayer appointing him such Proxy, and the description and local situation of the property in respect of which he claims to Vote as Proxy, specifying in Cities, Towns, and their Suburbs, having Streets and other Roadways, the Name of the Street or Roadway, and the Number of the House or Tenement, if any, and the Parish in which the property is situate, and in other places the Barony, Parish, and Townland, so that the property may be ascertained and identified with reasonable certainty, together with the nature of the interest of the Ratepayer therein, and its net annual value, over and above all rents payable by him, and the amount of rent payable to him, and the Names of the Tenants or Occupiers by whom Poor Rates have been deducted from such rent. The Proxy must also give an original or attested copy of the writing appointing him such Proxy, and the claim to vote must be executed in the presence of a Justice of the Peace. No person can vote as a Proxy for more than twenty owners of property in any one Electoral Division or Ward, unless he be a Steward, Bailiff, Land Agent or Collector of Rents for the owners of property for whom he may be appointed to vote.

6. Nominations of Guardians for any Electoral Division [Ward *or* District,] above-named must be made by Ratepayers entitled to vote in the Division [Ward *or* District], according to the form prescribed by the Poor Law Commissioners, printed copies of which form may be had on application to me; and such Nominations will be received by me at , and will be receivable on and after the date of this Notice, up to the hour of five o'clock in the afternoon of the day of ; but no nomination will be valid if received after that time, or before the issue of this Notice; or if the Nominator shall not have paid all the Poor Rates previously made and assessed upon him, except such as shall have been made or become due within the Six Calendar Months immediately preceding the nomination.

7. If any person put in nomination for the office of Guardian in any Electoral Division [Ward *or* District, *as the case may be*], above-named shall tender to the Returning Officer his refusal in writing, to serve such office, the Election of such person is to be no further proceeded with for such Division [Ward *or* District]; and such writing will be received by me at the place above named.

8. If more than the above mentioned number of Guardians be duly nominated for any Electoral Division [Ward *or* District,] above-named, I shall cause Voting Papers to be delivered on the day of , and if necessary on the following day, to the address in the Electoral Division Ward [*or* District] of each Ratepayer and Proxy qualified to Vote, which Voting Papers will contain full instructions as to the mode of Voting; and on the day of and if necessary on the following day, I shall cause such Voting Papers to be collected.

9. On the day of and following days, I shall attend in the Board Room of the said Union, at the hour of 10 o'clock in the forenoon; and I shall thereafter proceed to ascertain the number of Votes given for each Candidate.

10. Every person entitled to vote, who shall not have received a Voting Paper, on either of the days appointed for delivering the same, may on application in person to the Returning Officer, on the days appointed for the collection of the Voting Papers, receive a Voting Paper, and fill up the same in the presence of the Returning Officer, and then and there deliver the same to him. And if in any case a Voting Paper duly issued shall not have been collected on the proper days, through the default of any of the persons employed by the Returning Officer for the collection of Voting Papers, the Voter may, in person, deliver the Paper to the Returning Officer on or before the day of

11. If any person knowingly and fraudulently, and with the intent of giving a greater number of Votes than he is by law entitled to give, tender or forward to the Returning Officer a false statement of the grounds on which he claims to Vote, or to give additional Votes; or forge, falsify, or knowingly or fraudulently alter after signature, any paper containing a statement of Claim to Vote, Proxy, Nomination, or Vote for the Election of Guardians, or refusal to serve the Office of Guardian; or conspire to forge, falsify, or so alter any such Paper; or knowingly tender or forward to the proper Officer any such Paper forged, falsified, or so altered as aforesaid; or wilfully suppress, carry off, destroy, or deface any Statement of Claim to Vote, Proxy, or Nomination of a Candidate for the Office of Guardian, after the same has been duly signed; or in like manner suppress, carry off, destroy, or deface any Voting Paper after the same has been issued by the Returning Officer; the Person so offending is liable to a penalty of Ten Pounds, recoverable by distress and sale of the offender's goods, or to Imprisonment for three months, on complaint and conviction before two Justices of the Peace.

18 (Name of Returning Officer)————————

Returning Officer for the Union.

Sealed with our seal, this Twenty-ninth day of April, in the year of Our Lord One Thousand Eight Hundred and Eighty-two.

(Signed), HENRY ROBINSON.
CHARLES CROKER-KING.
COWPER. GEORGE MORRIS.

I, FRANCIS THOMAS DE GREY, EARL COWPER, Lord Lieutenant-General and General Governor of Ireland, do hereby approve this Order.

By command of His Excellency,

T. H. BURKE.

No. 2.—GENERAL ORDER Assessing upon CONTRIBUTORY UNIONS under the National School Teachers Act, their respective proportions of Results Fees for the year ending 31st March, 1883.

To the GUARDIANS of the POOR of the several Unions named in the Schedule to this Order; to the TREASURER of each of such Unions; and to all persons whom it may concern:

WHEREAS We, the Local Government Board for Ireland, have received from the Commissioners of National Education an Estimate for the year ending the 31st day of March, 1883, of the full amount payable as Results Fees in respect of Pupils attending the National Schools in each of the Unions which have become contributory Unions, under an Act passed in the Thirty-ninth year of the Reign of Her present Majesty, Queen Victoria, entitled "An Act to provide for additional Payments to Teachers of National Schools in Ireland:"

AND WHEREAS the Unions which have become contributory under the said Act are those of which the Names are placed in the first column of the Schedule hereto:

AND WHEREAS by the said Act it is enacted that the Commissioners of National Education shall require the Local Government Board in every year to provide a sum equal to one-third of such full amount payable as Results Fees as aforesaid, and that the said Local Government Board shall thereafter provide such sum in the manner by the said Act prescribed; and the Local Government Board have received from the Commissioners of National Education a requisition to provide, in the year 1882–83, a sum equal to one-third of such full amount aforesaid:

AND WHEREAS it is by the said Act further enacted—"Upon the receipt of every such estimate the Local Government Board shall by an Order under their Seal assess upon each contributory union a sum equal to one-third of the full amount payable as results fees in respect of pupils attending the National schools in such contributory union, and shall transmit a copy of such order to the guardians and likewise to the treasurer of such contributory union, stating the amount so assessed on such contributory union."

AND it is further enacted that "forthwith on the receipt of such order by the treasurer of any contributory union he shall, out of the funds then lying in his hands to the credit of the guardians of such union, or if there shall be then no sufficient assets, out of the moneys next received by him and placed to the credit of such guardians, pay over the amount so assessed on such contributory union to the Bank of Ireland, to be there placed to the credit of the Commissioners of Education to a separate account, to be entitled "The Results Fees Account:" and that the guardians of such contributory union shall in their account with the electoral divisions of such contributory union debit each electoral division with its proportion of the said amount according to the net annual value for the time being of the property rateable to the rates for the relief of the destitute poor in each such division:"

AND WHEREAS it is provided by the said Act that if in any financial year the sum provided by the Local Government Board in respect of any contributory union exceeds the amount required for the purposes of the Act in such year in respect of such contributory union, such overplus shall be carried to the credit of the next following financial year, and in such last-mentioned year only such sum shall be raised by assessment on such contributory union as shall be necessary in addition thereto to make up the sum which would in the ordinary course under the said Act be required to be provided by the Local Government Board in respect of such contributory union in such next following year;

AND WHEREAS we have received from the Commissioners of National Education a statement of the surplus of previous assessments, as set forth in the fourth column of the Schedule hereto:

NOW THEREFORE, in pursuance of the powers vested in us by the said Act, We do hereby assess upon each of the unions named in the first column of the Schedule hereto the amount set opposite to its name in the fifth column, such sum being equal to one-third of such full amount payable as Results Fees as aforesaid by such Union, as set forth in the second column of the said Schedule, less the amount of surplus of previous assessments as set forth in the fourth column.

SCHEDULE.—CONTRIBUTORY POOR LAW UNIONS.

Name of Union.	Full Amount of Results Fees payable to the Teachers of National Schools situated in Union. (Estimated.)			Amount equal to one-third of the full amount of estimated Results Fees.			Surplus of previous Assessments.			Amount assessed on each Union, being one-third of the full amount of estimated Results Fees less amount of Surplus of previous Assessments.
1st Column.	2nd Column.			3rd Column.			4th Column.			5th Column.
	£	s.	d.	£	s.	d.	£	s.	d.	£
Ballyvaghan,	302	4	3	100	14	9	40	14	9	60
Belfast,	13,823	1	6	4,607	13	10	607	13	10	4,000
Castlecomer,	957	13	3	319	4	5	59	4	5	260
Cavan,	2,902	1	6	967	7	2	67	7	2	900
Clogheen,	1,602	7	6	534	2	6	134	2	6	400
Clonakilty,	2,100	0	0	700	0	0	—			700
Donaghmore,	350	14	9	116	18	3	66	18	3	50
Downpatrick,	2,563	9	3	854	9	9	129	9	9	725
Dungannon,	1,677	7	6	559	2	6	159	2	6	400
Enniskillen,	1,591	3	0	530	7	8	0	7	8	530
Irvinestown,	940	10	3	313	10	1	113	10	1	200
Kells,	1,163	4	3	387	14	9	87	14	9	300
Larne,	1,776	5	3	592	1	9	92	1	9	500
Lisburn,	2,529	6	9	843	2	3	43	2	3	800
Mallow,	1,740	0	0	580	0	0	—			580
Milford,	701	9	6	233	16	6	133	16	6	100
Navan,	1,184	17	0	394	19	0	144	19	0	250
Newry,	2,733	5	6	911	1	10	161	1	10	750
Strabane,	1,693	7	6	564	9	2	64	9	2	500
Trim,	1,072	10	3	357	10	1	77	10	1	280

Sealed with our Seal, this Eighteenth day of May, in the year of Our Lord One Thousand Eight Hundred and Eighty-two.

(Signed), HENRY ROBINSON.
CHARLES CROKER-KING.
GEORGE MORRIS.

SPENCER,

I, JOHN POYNTZ, Earl Spencer, Lord Lieutenant-General and General Governor of Ireland, do hereby approve this Order.

By Command of His Excellency,

R. G. C. HAMILTON.

No. 3.—General Order assessing the amount payable by each Union under the Contagious Diseases (Animals) Act.

To the Guardians of the Poor of the several Unions named in the Schedule hereunto annexed; to the Treasurer of each of such Unions, and to all Persons whom it may concern.

Whereas, by an Act passed in the Forty-second year of the Reign of Her present Majesty, Queen Victoria, entitled "An Act for making better provision respecting Contagious and Infectious Diseases of Cattle and other Animals, and for other purposes," it is among other things enacted that on receipt of the Certificate of the Chief Secretary or Under Secretary to the Lord Lieutenant of Ireland to the effect that a sum equivalent to a certain Poundage, to be specified in such Certificate, on the net annual value of the property in all the Unions in Ireland, is required for the purposes of the Act, the Local Government Board shall, by Order under their Seal, assess that sum on the several Unions, in proportion to the net annual value of the property therein, and the said Board shall transmit copies of the Order to the Guardians and to the Treasurer of each Union:

And Whereas by the said Act it is further enacted that on receipt of such Order, the Treasurer of each Union shall out of the Union funds, pay over the amount assessed on the Union to the Bank of Ireland, to be placed to the General Cattle Diseases Fund, and the Guardians of each Union shall debit the several Electoral Divisions with proportions of that sum, according to the net annual value of the property therein:

And Whereas it is provided by the said Act that no larger sum shall be levied under the said Act at any one time than shall be equivalent to a poundage of One Halfpenny in the Pound on the net annual value of the property in all the Unions; nor shall any larger sum be levied under the said Act in the whole than shall be equivalent, taken with any money before the commencement of the said Act carried to the Cattle Plague Account, to a poundage of Fourpence in the Pound on the net annual value of the property in all the Unions:

And Whereas a Certificate under the hand of the Chief Secretary to the Lord Lieutenant, bearing date the Third day of June, One Thousand Eight Hundred and Eighty-two, has been received by Us, the Local Government Board for Ireland, in which it is certified that a sum of Fourteen Thousand Three Hundred and Forty Pounds Four Shillings and Three Farthings sterling, being equivalent to a rating of One Farthing in the Pound on the net annual value of the property in all the Unions in Ireland, is required for the purpose of the said Act:

Now Therefore, in pursuance of the provisions of the said Act, We, the Local Government Board for Ireland, do hereby assess the said sum of Fourteen Thousand Three Hundred and Forty Pounds Four Shillings and Three Farthings, upon the several Unions in Ireland, in proportion to the net annual value of the property in each Union according to the Valuation thereof now in force as follows; that is to say, we assess upon each Union the amount set opposite to its name in the Schedule hereunto annexed.

SCHEDULE.

Union.	Amount Assessed. £	s.	d.
Abbeyleix,	70	7	2¼
Antrim,	180	16	9¼
Ardee,	88	6	1½
Armagh,	214	1	3¼
Athlone,	99	2	9¼
Athy,	115	11	2
Bailieborough,	41	19	2¼
Ballina,	81	8	11¼
Ballinasloe,	81	14	9¼
Ballinrobe,	69	18	0¼
Ballycastle,	46	4	10
Ballymahon,	64	12	6
Ballymena,	185	3	11½
Ballymoney,	86	18	2¼
Ballyshannon,	89	19	11¼
Ballyvaghan,	20	14	0¼
Balrothery,	99	19	1½
Baltinglass,	76	18	2
Banbridge,	167	2	1
Bandon,	77	0	9¼
Bantry,	59	13	4¼
Bawnboy,	41	11	2¼
Belfast,	782	10	10
Belmullet,	11	7	7¼
Borrisokane,	48	13	6¼
Boyle,	76	16	4
Cahersiveen,	23	16	11¼
Callan,	78	1	5¼
Carlow,	153	11	0¼
Carrickmacross,	82	13	10½
Carrick-on-Shannon,	80	6	10¼
Carrick-on-Suir,	63	14	9
Cashel,	111	19	11
Castlebar,	48	10	10
Castleblayney,	78	17	7¼
Castlecomer,	33	15	8¼
Castlederg,	27	8	5¼
Castlerea,	75	14	6
Castletown,	12	14	10¼
Cavan,	118	1	9¼
Celbridge,	119	17	11
Claremorris,	44	8	5¼
Clifden,	16	16	4
Clogheen,	46	17	0¼
Clogher,	38	16	10¼
Clonakilty,	55	0	1¼
Clones,	60	0	1¼
Clonmel,	74	17	11
Coleraine,	107	1	9
Cookstown,	65	5	6¼
Cootehill,	73	17	1
Cork,	864	4	0
Corrofin,	21	5	6¼
Croom,	66	4	9
Delvin,	54	12	2
Dingle,	29	16	9¼
Donaghmore,	42	16	8¼
Donegal,	38	1	1
Downpatrick,	185	6	2¼
Drogheda,	120	6	6¼
Dromore, West,	65	8	7¼
Dublin, North,	897	15	4¼
Dublin, South,	687	6	4¼
Dundalk,	111	6	7¼
Dunfanaghy,	12	1	5¼
Dungannon,	96	11	11¼
Dungarvan,	86	3	2¼
Dunmanway,	84	12	11
Dunshaughlin,	110	2	6
Edenderry,	99	14	0¼
Ennis,	77	7	9¼
Enniscorthy,	118	6	2
Enniskillen,	111	0	5¼
Ennistymon,	88	10	4¼
Fermoy,	108	8	7¼
Galway,	62	0	1
Glenamaddy,	53	2	6
Glenties,	21	4	10¼
Glin,	20	16	4¼
Gorey,	83	15	10¼
Gort,	44	16	9¼
Gortin,	20	9	4¼
Granard,	69	6	6¼
Inishowen,	40	15	10¼
Irvinestown,	51	2	7¼
Kanturk,	80	11	4¼
Kells,	100	4	8¼
Kenmare,	20	5	8¼
Kilkeel,	45	9	7¼
Kilkenny,	104	8	9
Killadysert,	28	0	1¼
Killala,	21	7	8¼
Killarney,	79	11	2
Kilmacthomas,	84	15	6¼
Kilmallock,	149	14	8
Kilrush,	64	17	11¼
Kinsale,	63	5	9¼
Larne,	103	8	9¼
Letterkenny,	69	9	0
Limavady,	79	8	8¼
Limerick,	804	11	10½
Lisburn,	181	17	4
Lismore,	51	16	1¼
Lisnaskea,	60	9	11¼
Listowel,	55	6	5¼
Londonderry,	188	5	8¼
Longford,	63	16	1¼
Loughrea,	79	7	11¼
Lurgan,	149	14	7¼
Macroom,	62	4	6
Magherafelt,	96	9	11¼
Mallow,	110	10	5¼
Manorhamilton,	45	6	8¼
Midleton,	96	9	2¼
Milford,	31	4	1¼
Millstreet,	20	2	5¼
Mitchelstown,	51	4	5¼
Mohill,	41	16	9¼
Monaghan,	99	19	4¼
Mount Bellew,	45	8	1¼
Mountmellick,	106	15	1
Mullingar,	164	17	9
Naas,	180	0	4¼
Navan,	102	16	8¼
Nenagh,	98	5	8¼
Newcastle,	84	19	6¼
Newport,	15	8	9¼
New Ross,	108	19	6
Newry,	175	15	6
Newtownards,	148	12	8¼
Oldcastle,	65	5	0¼
Omagh,	98	14	0

SCHEDULE—*continued.*

Union.	Amount Assessed. £	s.	d.	Union.	Amount Assessed. £	s.	d.
Oughterard,	15	12	4½	Thomastown,	69	0	8½
Parsonstown,	107	8	8¼	Thurles,	94	4	8¼
Portumna,	66	19	0½	Tipperary,	168	17	0½
Rathdown,	278	14	8¼	Tobercurry,	45	9	1½
Rathdrum,	133	8	7½	Tralee,	90	1	8½
Rathkeale,	58	10	8	Trim,	118	12	4¼
Roscommon,	67	8	7½	Tuam,	80	8	3¼
Roscrea,	74	9	5	Tulla,	84	17	0
Scariff,	95	16	0½	Tullamore,	96	13	7½
Shillelagh,	52	8	1½	Urlingford,	47	13	8½
Skibbereen,	48	8	9¼	Waterford,	189	8	8¼
Skull,	16	15	8	Westport,	83	10	11
Sligo,	109	18	9¼	Wexford,	112	10	1½
Strabane,	101	4	11¾	Youghal,	62	16	1½
Stranorlar,	81	10	6				
Strokestown,	81	8	8½	Total,	£14,840	4	0¾
Swineford,	49	10	8½				

Sealed with our Seal, this Nineteenth day of June, in the Year of Our Lord One Thousand Eight Hundred and Eighty-two.

(Signed),

HENRY ROBINSON.
CHARLES CROKER-KING.
GEORGE MORRIS.

SPENCER.

I, JOHN POYNTZ, EARL SPENCER, Lord Lieutenant-General and General Governor of Ireland, do hereby approve this Order,

By His Excellency's Command,

W. S. B. KAYE.

No. 4.—GENERAL ORDER for regulating the Meetings and Proceedings of BOARDS of GUARDIANS in IRELAND, and the Appointment and Duties of UNION OFFICERS.

To the GUARDIANS of the POOR of the several Unions named in the Schedule hereunto annexed, and the OFFICERS of such Unions; and to all others whom it may concern:

WE, the Local Government Board for Ireland, in pursuance of the authorities vested in Us, by an Act passed in the Second Year of the Reign of Her Majesty, Queen Victoria, intituled, "An Act for the more effectual Relief of the Destitute Poor in Ireland," and by the other Acts in force for the Relief of the Poor in Ireland, and amending the said Act, and by the Local Government Board (Ireland) Act, 1872, do hereby rescind so much of every Order heretofore issued by the Poor Law Commissioners, or the Commissioners for administering the Laws for Relief of the Poor in Ireland, or the Local Government Board for Ireland, to the several Unions named in the Schedule hereunto annexed, and now in force, as is in any way affected or altered by the Regulations herein contained, except so far as the same may have authorised the making of any Contract not yet executed, or the appointment of any of the existing Officers, or the giving and receiving of securities for the performance of their duties;

And We do hereby Order, Direct, and Declare, with respect to each and every of the Unions named in the said Schedule, as follows :—

MEETINGS OF THE GUARDIANS.

ARTICLE 1.—No Guardian shall act in virtue of his Office, otherwise than as a member, and at a meeting of the Board of Guardians, legally assembled.

Provided, however, that in cases where the consent of a majority of the total number of the Guardians of a Union, or where the consent of the Guardian, or of a majority of Guardians, of any Electoral Division, is required by the said Acts, it shall be lawful for any Guardian to give his consent otherwise than at a meeting of the Board of Guardians.

Provided, also, that this Article shall not be construed to apply to cases in which the said Acts, or any Orders of the Local Government Board may specially authorize a Guardian to act otherwise than at a meeting of the Board of Guardians.

ARTICLE 2.—The Guardians shall, upon the day of the week, and the hour of the day, and at the place already appointed for holding the Ordinary Meetings, hold an Ordinary Meeting, once at the least in every week, for the execution of their duties; and may, when they think fit, change the period, time, and place, with the consent of the Local Government Board previously had and obtained; provided, however, that if they shall think fit, the Guardians may, with the previous consent of the Local Government Board, appoint more than one day in each week for the transaction of the ordinary business of the Union.

ARTICLE 3.—The Guardians shall, after every annual or general election of Guardians for the Union, elect out of the whole number of Guardians a Chairman, Vice-Chairman, and Deputy Vice-Chairman, who shall respectively continue to hold their offices until the election of a Chairman, Vice-Chairman, and Deputy Vice-Chairman, following the next annual or general election of Guardians shall take place, unless they shall previously die, resign, become incapable, or be disqualified, by ceasing to be Guardians of the Union. Notice of the election of a Chairman, Vice-Chairman, and Deputy Vice-Chairman shall be given to each Guardian by the Clerk to the Guardians, in the Form A hereunto annexed, and shall be sent by the Clerk to every Guardian on the day on which he receives from the Returning Officer the certified copy of the return of the election of Guardians, or on the day following. The election of a Chairman, Vice-Chairman, and Deputy Vice-Chairman shall take place at the first ordinary meeting of the Guardians at the usual hour of meeting, provided that three clear days shall elapse between the day on which the Clerk to the Guardians receives the copy of the Return of the election, and the day of the Guardians' first ordinary meeting; but if three clear days shall not elapse between the day on which the Clerk to the Guardians receives the copy of the Return of the Election and the day of the Guardians' first ordinary meeting, the election of a Chairman, Vice-Chairman, and Deputy Vice-Chairman shall take place on the day of the Guardians' second ordinary meeting, at the usual hour of meeting.

ARTICLE 4.—If a Chairman, Vice-Chairman, or Deputy Vice-Chairman die, resign his office, or become incapable or disqualified to act as Chairman, Vice-Chairman, or Deputy Vice-Chairman before the expiration of his term of office, the Guardians shall, within one month after the occurrence of the death, resignation, incapacity, or disqualification, and not sooner than seven days after such vacancy shall have been notified to the Guardians at an ordinary meeting of the Board elect some other Guardian to such office, as the case may require. Notice of the election to fill the vacancy shall be given to each Guardian by the Clerk to the Guardians at least three days before the election shall take place; but no *ex-officio* Guardian shall be deemed to vacate such office at the period prescribed by law for the selection of *ex-officio* Guardians, if he continue to act as *ex-officio* Guardian at and after such period according to law.

Article 5.—If three Guardians be not present at any meeting, an entry of that fact shall be made in the Minute Book by the Clerk to the Guardians, and the time for holding such meeting shall be deemed to have expired as soon as the said entry shall have been made. But one hour at least shall be allowed to elapse from the time fixed for the commencement of the Meeting before such entry shall be made, and the Clerk to the Guardians shall report the fact of such failure of attendance to the Local Government Board on the following day.

Article 6.—If three or four or more Guardians be present at any Ordinary Meeting, such three, or the majority of such four or more Guardians, may adjourn the same to the day of the next Ordinary Meeting, or to some other day previous to the next Ordinary Meeting.

Article 7.—An Extraordinary Meeting of the Guardians may be summoned to be held at any time, upon the requisition of any two Guardians, addressed to the Clerk to the Guardians. Every such requisition shall be made in writing, according to the Form B hereunto annexed; and no business other than the business specified in the said requisition shall be transacted at such Extraordinary Meeting. Provided that an Extraordinary Meeting shall be summoned by the Clerk to the Guardians, on being required by the Local Government Board to summon such meeting.

Article 8.—Notice of every such Extraordinary Meeting, and notice of every change in the period, time, or place of holding any Ordinary Meeting, and notice of the adjournment of any Meeting shall be given in writing to every Guardian. Every such notice shall be respectively according to the Forms C, D, and E, hereunto annexed, and shall be given or sent by the Clerk to every Guardian; or left at his place of abode two days, if practicable, before the day appointed for the meeting to which it relates; but if any case of emergency should arise, requiring that an Extraordinary Meeting of the Guardians should immediately take place, notice shall nevertheless be given to as many of the Guardians as may be practicable, and they, or any three of them, shall meet at the ordinary place of meeting, and take such case into consideration, and may make an Order or Orders thereon.

PROCEEDINGS OF THE BOARD.

Article 9.—At every Meeting the Chairman, or in his absence the Vice-Chairman, or in his absence, the Deputy Vice-Chairman, shall preside; and if, at the commencement of any Meeting, the Chairman, Vice-Chairman, and Deputy Vice-Chairman be absent, the Guardians present shall elect one of themselves to preside at such Meeting as Chairman thereof, until the Chairman, Vice-Chairman, or Deputy Vice-Chairman, as the case may be, may take the chair. In case the office of Chairman, Vice-Chairman, or Deputy Vice-Chairman, shall be vacant at the commencement of any meeting, such vacancy shall be deemed to be equivalent to the absence of such officer for the purposes of this Article.

Article 10.—Every question at any Meeting of Guardians shall be determined by a majority of the votes of the Guardians present thereat and voting on the question; and when there shall be an equal number of votes on any question, such question shall be deemed to have been lost; but no act of any Meeting of the Guardians shall be valid unless three Guardians at least be present, and if no greater number of Guardians be present, unless they shall all of them concur therein; and all such votes shall be given openly, and not by ballot or in any other secret manner.

ARTICLE 11.—The Presiding Chairman shall be entitled to give one vote upon each question that may be submitted to the Guardians; but he shall not, under any circumstances, be entitled to any additional vote or casting vote.

ARTICLE 12.—No resolution previously agreed to or adopted by the Board of Guardians shall be rescinded, altered, or amended (except in pursuance of an order, regulation or request of the Local Government Board), unless some Guardian shall have given to the Board fourteen days' notice of a motion to rescind or alter such resolution; and such notice shall be in writing, and shall be forthwith entered on the Minutes by the Clerk, who shall, within seven days after such entry, forward a copy of the same to each Guardian.

Provided always that this regulation shall not extend to any resolution which relates only to the admission into, or the discharge from the workhouse of any destitute person, or to any decision of the Guardians arising on their examination, approval, or correction of the register of persons relieved.

ARTICLE 13.—The Guardians may, from time to time (as occasion may require), appoint a Committee to consider and report on any subject or matters referred to them, and the Guardians shall name one member of every such Committee to be chairman of the same; and such Committee may meet at such times and places as to them may seem convenient; but no act or decision of any such Committee shall be deemed to be the act of the Board of Guardians unless the same shall have been reported to and expressly adopted by the said Board.

ARTICLE 14.—At every ordinary meeting of the Guardians, the business (including any business which may have been adjourned from a previous meeting) shall be conducted in the following order:—

1stly.—The Minutes of the last Ordinary Meeting, and of any other Meeting which may have been held since such Ordinary Meeting, shall be read to the Guardians and signed by the Chairman presiding at the Meeting at which such Minutes are read; and an entry of the same having been so read shall be made in the Minutes of the day when read.

2ndly.—The Guardians shall examine and approve or correct (if necessary) the Register Book of persons admitted into and relieved in the Workhouse, and the Out-door Relief Register; and such Register Books, when so examined and approved or corrected, shall be signed by the Chairman and countersigned by the Clerk.

3rdly.—They shall receive and consider the Report of the Clerk or other Officer upon the execution of all orders made by the Board at such previous meeting, or any preceding meeting; and shall give such further directions thereon as may appear necessary.

4thly.—They shall examine the Clerk's Accounts, the Treasurer's Book of Receipts and Payments, the Accounts of the Collectors of Rates, the Accounts and other Books of the Master of the Workhouse, the Medical Officer's Weekly Return Book, the several Relieving Officers' Accounts, and the Accounts which may be required to be kept by any other Officer in the Union; and shall see that such of them as are required to be authenticated by the Clerk are duly authenticated and signed by him; and they shall thereupon direct such cheques to be drawn on the Treasurer, and such orders to be made on Contractors as may appear necessary to provide for the relief of the destitute poor in the Workhouse, and by the Relieving Officers in their several districts; and every such cheque or order shall be signed by the presiding Chairman and two Guardians, and countersigned by the Clerk.

5thly.—They shall consider and decide upon, and give the necessary directions respecting all provisional admissions into the Workhouse since the last Ordinary Meeting of the Guardians.

6thly.—They shall take into consideration the Report of any District Committee of Guardians appointed under an order of the Local Government Board to receive and examine applications for relief; and they shall further consider all applications for relief, and the particulars recorded in regard to each case in the Application and Report Book of each Relieving Officer, and shall decide whether any, and, if so, what relief or further relief should be granted in each particular case, in pursuance of the laws for the relief of the poor; and the decision of the Board shall be forthwith recorded in the said books, to be authorized by the signature or initials of the presiding Chairman in the columns respectively provided for that purpose.

7thly.—They shall consider the Report of the Master of the Workhouse, and order the discharge of such persons as appear to be no longer proper objects of relief in the Workhouse of the Union.

8thly.—They shall examine the Reports of the several Officers, and the Report of the Visiting Committee of the Workhouse, and make such orders thereon respectively as may appear to them fitting and expedient.

9thly.—They shall take into consideration all letters addressed by the Local Government Board to the presiding Chairman or to the Clerk of the Union, and all other correspondence relating to the business of the Union; and the receipt and substance of such letters or communications, with such directions as the Board may give thereon, shall be recorded on the minutes.

10thly.—They shall, subject to the approval of the Local Government Board, determine the kind of work to be performed by the persons admitted into the Workhouse, and give all needful directions concerning the management and discipline of the Workhouse of the Union, and the providing of furniture and stores, and other articles.

11thly.—They shall proceed to examine and select from amongst the candidates presenting themselves before them competent persons to fill any vacancy or vacancies that may exist amongst the Officers, whom the Guardians are legally empowered to appoint, due notice having been previously given of such election, as hereinafter provided.

12thly.—They shall transact any business connected with the administration of the laws for the relief of the poor in the union, and consider any resolution proposed by any Guardian relating to the business of the union, but not having immediate reference to the business previously under their consideration, due notice having been given thereof, if necessary, as hereinbefore provided in Article 12; and the business so transacted and the Guardians' decision on such proposed resolution shall be recorded on the Minutes of their proceedings.

13thly.—The Presiding Chairman shall receive, and shall cause to be read aloud by the Clerk, and entered upon the Minutes, any notice for the election of a Union Officer, or any notice of any resolution relating to the business of the union intended to be proposed at any future meeting of the Guardians.

14thly.—They shall transact any business arising under the Medical Charities Act.

15thly.—They shall transact any business arising under the Public Health (Ireland) Act, 1878.

16thly.—They shall transact any business arising under the Contagious Diseases (Animals) Act, 1876.

No matter or question shall be brought forward at the Meeting until all the business of the meeting comprised in the foregoing order of proceeding shall first have been disposed of.

Provided, however, that the Guardians shall be enabled, with the consent of the Local Government Board previously obtained, to make a rule in regard to the order of their proceedings, different from that hereinbefore laid down: and any such rule shall, when approved by the Local Government Board, have the same effect as the order contained in this Article, and shall not be rescinded or altered by the Guardians without fourteen days' notice, nor without the consent of the Local Government Board.

Provided also, that when it shall appear to them necessary, the Guardians present at any meeting shall be enabled to depart, at such meeting, from the order of the proceedings hereinbefore laid down, or laid down in their general rule on the subject, provided that the proposal to depart from such order of proceedings shall not be adopted unless all the Guardians present concur therein and vote therefor.

And provided also, that whenever the Guardians shall have appointed more than one day in each week for their ordinary Meetings, they shall apportion the business to be transacted at each such Meeting in such manner that the same business shall invariably be transacted upon one of the days fixed for the Meeting of the Guardians; and whenever it is herein provided that any act shall be performed at each ordinary Meeting of the Guardians, such provision shall be interpreted to mean such day of weekly meeting as shall be appointed by the Guardians for that purpose.

CONTRACTS.

Article 15.—All Contracts to be entered into on behalf of the Union, relating to the maintenance, clothing, lodging, employment, or relief of the poor, or for any other purpose relating to, or connected with, the general management of the poor, shall be made and entered into by the Guardians.

Article 16.—The Guardians shall require Tenders to be made in some sealed paper for the supply of all provisions, fuel, clothing, furniture, or other goods, or materials, the consumption of which may be estimated, one month with another, to exceed ten pounds per month, and also of all furniture, or materials, or other articles, the cost of which may be reasonably estimated to exceed ten pounds in a single sum.

Article 17.—Any work or repairs to be executed in the Workhouse, or the premises connected with the Workhouse, or any fittings to be put up therein, which shall respectively be reasonably estimated to exceed the cost of twenty pounds in one sum, shall be contracted for by the Guardians, on sealed Tenders, in the manner prescribed in Articles 15 and 16.

Article 18.—Notice of the nature and conditions of the Contract to be entered into, of the last day and hour on which Tenders will be received, and the day on which the Tenders will be opened shall be given in some newspaper circulating in the Union, and in such other manner as the Guardians may direct, not less than ten days previous to the last day on which such tender shall be received: and no tender shall be opened by the Clerk, or any Guardian or other person, before the day specified in such notice, or otherwise than at a Meeting of the said Guardians.

Article 19.—When any Tender shall be accepted, the party making the Tender shall, in pursuance of these regulations, enter into a Contract, in writing, with the Guardians, containing the terms, conditions, and stipulations mutually agreed upon; and whenever the Guardians shall deem it advisable, the party contracting shall, in like manner, find one or more surety or sureties, who shall enter into a bond in such penalty as the Guardians shall think fit, conditioned for the due performance of the Contract.

Article 20.—The Contracts shall be in such form as the Local Government Board may, from time to time, prescribe or approve, if any form shall have been prescribed or approved for that purpose by the Local Government Board.

Article 21.—Provided always, that if from the peculiar nature of any furniture, provisions, goods, materials, or fittings to be supplied, or of any work or repairs to be executed, it shall appear to the Guardians desirable that a specific person or persons be employed to supply or execute the same, or that they should be purchased without requiring sealed Tenders, as hereinbefore directed, it shall be lawful for the Board of Guardians, with the consent of the Local Government Board first had and obtained, to enter into a contract with such person or persons as may be deemed best qualified to supply or execute the same, and to require such sureties and securities as are specified in Article 19, or to purchase such furniture, provisions, goods, materials, or fittings, in such other manner as the Local Government Board may direct or sanction.

RELIEF BY WAY OF LOAN.

Article 22.—Any relief in the Workhouse, or the cost price thereof, which the Guardians shall, after due consideration of the circumstances of the case, think fit to give by way of Loan, shall be given by way of Loan, and shall be recoverable as such under the provisions of the said first-recited Act.

ORDERS FOR PAYMENT OF MONEY.

Article 23.—The Guardians shall pay every sum amounting to three pounds or more, by a distinct and separate cheque or order, which shall be drawn upon the Treasurer of the Union, and shall be signed by the presiding Chairman of the Meeting and two other Guardians present thereat; and shall be countersigned by the Clerk to the Guardians.

APPOINTMENT OF PAID OFFICERS.

Article 24.—The Board of Guardians shall, as soon as may be requisite, and from time to time hereafter upon the occurrence of any vacancy, appoint fit persons to perform respectively the duties specified by the Rules and Regulations of the Local Government Board, in force at the time, to be the duties of the following officers:—

1. Clerk to the Guardians.
2. Treasurer of the Union.
3. Medical Officer of the Workhouse.
4. Master of the Workhouse.
5. Matron.
6. Porter.
7. Schoolmaster.
8. Schoolmistress.

And shall appoint such Assistants as the Board of Guardians, with the consent of the Local Government Board, shall deem necessary for the efficient performance of the duties of the said several Officers;

And the Guardians shall further appoint as many Relieving Officers as the Local Government Board shall from time to time require or approve; and shall assign to such Relieving Officers such Electoral Division or Divisions, or such parts thereof, as the Local Government Board may direct or approve;

The Board of Guardians of any Union shall, subject to the approval of the Local Government Board, appoint from time to time such and so many persons as they may deem expedient to collect and levy the Rates made on the several Electoral Divisions of the Union, and shall assign to such Collectors such Electoral Division or Divisions as the Local Government Board may approve.

ARTICLE 25.—The officers so appointed to or holding any of the said offices, shall respectively perform the duties required of them in such manner as may be prescribed by the General Regulations of the Local Government Board in force at the time, or by any special Order which may be made by the Local Government Board from time to time, affecting any particular Union and the Officers thereof, and shall discharge all such other duties conformable with the nature of their respective offices, as the Board of Guardians may lawfully require them to perform.

ARTICLE 26.—The Board of Guardians may, from time to time, with the consent of the Local Government Board previously obtained, and after fourteen days' notice shall have been given to the Board by a Guardian, of a motion for such purpose, make any change in the division of the Union into Districts for the Collection of the Poor Rate, or in the Districts of Relieving Officers.

MODE OF APPOINTMENT.

ARTICLE 27.—Every Officer and Assistant to be appointed under this Order shall be appointed by a majority of the Guardians present at any Meeting of the Board, in the manner directed in Article 10; and every such appointment shall, as soon as the same shall have been made, be reported to the Local Government Board by the Clerk to the Guardians.

ARTICLE 28.—No appointment of any Officer or Assistant shall be made under this Order, unless notice that such appointment will be made shall have been given and entered on the Minutes at one of the two Ordinary Meetings of the Board next preceding the Meeting at which the appointment shall be made, and unless an advertisement giving notice of such appointment shall, by the direction of the Guardians, entered on their Minutes, have appeared in some public paper, at least seven days before the day on which such appointment shall be made.

Provided that this regulation shall not apply to the appointment of any person who may, subject to the approval of the Local Government Board, be employed temporarily to act as an officer or assistant.

QUALIFICATIONS OF OFFICERS.

ARTICLE 29.—No person shall be appointed by the Guardians as a Collector of Poor Rates or Relieving Officer who is engaged in retail trade of any kind.

ARTICLE 30.—If the Master and Matron be respectively husband and wife, and one of them should be dismissed by order of the Local Government Board, or should otherwise vacate his or her office, the other shall not be qualified to hold his or her office of Master or Matron, as the case may be, after such dismissal or vacating of office.

ARTICLE 31.—No person shall hold any office under this Order, who shall not have reached the age of twenty-one years.

ARTICLE 32.—Provided always that the Guardians may, with the consent of the Local Government Board previously obtained, but not otherwise, dispense with any of the conditions specified in Articles 29, 30, and 31.

Article 33.—The qualifications of every Medical Officer hereafter to be appointed shall be as follows, that is to say:—

No. 1. He shall have obtained a Degree in Medicine, or a Diploma or Licence to practise Medicine, from some College or other Body that may be authorised to grant a Diploma or Licence to practise Medicine in Great Britain or Ireland, or he shall be a Licentiate of the Apothecaries' Hall, Dublin, and he shall also have obtained a Diploma in Surgery or a Licence to practise Surgery from some College or other Body that may be authorized to grant a Diploma or Licence to practise Surgery in Great Britain or Ireland, and also a Certificate from some Board or Court of Examiners, or other Body duly authorised to grant the same, of his possessing a competent knowledge of Midwifery.

No. 2. He shall have reached the age of twenty-three years.

Provided, that under special circumstances affecting the particular Workhouse for which the appointment is made, that part of the above qualification which requires a separate Medical Certificate or Diploma may be dispensed with by the Local Government Board if they shall deem it necessary to do so.

Provided also, that the foregoing Regulation shall not apply to any person holding the office of Medical Officer of the Workhouse at the date hereof, either in respect to his present appointment or any future appointment to the said office.

And provided also that this regulation shall not apply to any person who shall at any time previously to his appointment as Medical Officer of a Workhouse, have held office in any Union in Ireland, either as Medical Officer of a Workhouse, or Medical Officer of a Dispensary District, having been duly qualified for such office at such previous time.

Article 34.—No person shall be appointed to the office of Master, Matron, Relieving Officer, Schoolmaster, Schoolmistress, or Porter, under this Order, who will not agree to give one month's notice previous to resigning the office, or to forfeit one month's amount of salary, to be deducted as liquidated damages from the amount of salary due at the time of such resignation.

Salaries of the Officers.

Article 35.—The Board of Guardians shall pay to the several Officers and Assistants appointed to or holding any office or employment under this Order, such salaries or remuneration as the Local Government Board may, from time to time, direct or approve.

Provided always that, if no such remuneration or salary be expressly assigned to the Treasurer, the payment for the services of such Treasurer, shall be deemed to be the profit arising from the use of money from time to time left in his hands.

Article 36.—The salary of every Officer or Assistant appointed to or holding any office or employment under this Order, shall, subject to the regulations in Article 34, and to the obligation to account to the Auditor, be payable up to the day on which he ceases to hold such office or employment, and no longer; but no Officer having been suspended by the Board of Guardians, in pursuance of Article 40, and who shall without the previous removal of such suspension be dismissed by the Local Government Board, or by the Board of Guardians, shall be entitled to any salary from the date of such suspension.

Security of Officers.

Article 37.—The Board of Guardians shall require every person appointed, or to be hereafter appointed, to the offices of Treasurer, Clerk, Master, or Matron of the Workhouse, and every assistant employed therein in any office of trust, and every Relieving Officer and Collector of Rates, to give a Bond in such penal sum as the Guardians shall think fit, with two sufficient sureties, not being Guardians of the Union, conditioned for the due and faithful performance of the duties of the office; and shall, from time to time, call upon such Officers to supply a fresh Surety in place of any such Surety who may die, or become a Guardian, or become bankrupt or insolvent, or be released from his obligation: and every such Officer shall give immediate notice to the Board of Guardians of the death, insolvency, or bankruptcy of either of his Sureties, and shall, when required by the Guardians, in pursuance of the above regulation, supply a fresh Surety in the place of any Surety previously supplied by him.

Provided that if it shall seem fit to the Board of Guardians, not to require that the Treasurer, being a Banker or a partner of a firm engaged in Banking, should execute a Bond with Sureties as aforesaid, it shall be lawful for the Guardians, unless specially directed by the Local Government Board to require such Security, to dispense with the execution of such Bond by such Treasurer.

Article 38.—The Board of Guardians shall provide for the safe custody of all Bonds given in pursuance of the Regulations of the Local Government Board and so always that no Bond given by any person shall remain in the custody of such person himself; and the Guardians shall, once in every year (that is to say, at the Audit next after the 25th day of March), cause every person having the custody of Bonds given by any Officer of the Union, or by any Contractor for supplies, to produce such Bonds to the Auditor for his inspection; and the fact of such inspection and any defects apparent in the said Bonds, shall be reported by the Auditor to the Board of Guardians.

Continuance in Office and Suspension of Officers: Supply of Vacancies.

Article 39.—Every Officer appointed to or holding any Office under this Order shall, subject to the provisions of Article 40 of this Order, continue to hold the same until he die, or resign, or be removed by the Local Government Board, and every Porter or Assistant may be dismissed by the Board of Guardians without the consent of the Local Government Board; and every such death or resignation, and every such dismissal, and the grounds thereof, shall be reported to the Local Government Board.

Article 40.—The Board of Guardians may, at their discretion, suspend from the discharge of his duties any Union Officer except the Clerk, Chaplain, or Treasurer, and shall forthwith report such suspension, together with the cause thereof, to the Local Government Board, and if the Local Government Board shall remove such suspension, such Officer shall remain and continue to discharge his duties; but if the Local Government Board shall decide not to remove such suspension, the Board of Guardians may, on being informed of such decision of the Local Government Board, dismiss such Officer.

Article 41.—If any Officer or Assistant, appointed to or holding any Office under this Order, be at any time prevented by sickness or accident, or other sufficient reason, from the performance of his duties, the Guardians may appoint a fit person to act as his temporary substitute and may, subject to the approval of the Local Government Board, pay him a reasonable compensation for his services; and every such appointment shall be reported to the Local Government Board by the Clerk to the Guardians as soon as the same shall have been made.

Provided always that except under the provisions of this Article, or with the special permission of the Local Government Board first had and obtained on the application of the Board of Guardians, every Officer shall perform his several duties in person, and shall, on no account, entrust the same to a deputy.

Article 42.—If a Medical Officer be temporarily incapacitated from performing his duties, he shall, if practicable, recommend to the Guardians a Medical Practitioner qualified as hereinbefore provided in Article 33, competent to perform his duties during such temporary incapacity, and the Guardians shall employ such Medical Practitioner if they deem it advisable, or appoint temporarily some other Medical Practitioner possessing the necessary qualifications.

Article 43.—The Vice-Chairman, Deputy Vice-Chairman, or some Guardian to be appointed by the Board of Guardians, may perform any of the duties assigned to the Clerk until any vacancy in the office shall have been filled, or until a substitute be appointed in the case of the Clerk's absence through sickness, accident, or other sufficient reason, as provided for in Article 41.

Article 44.—No Workhouse Officer, who may have been dismissed by any Order of the Local Government Board, shall, after such dismissal, remain upon the Workhouse premises, or enter therein for the purpose of interfering in the management of such Workhouse, unless the said Local Government Board shall consent to his subsequent appointment to an office in such Workhouse, under the provisions of the said first-recited Act.

Duties of the Clerk to the Guardians.

Article 45.—The duties of the Clerk to the Guardians shall be:—

No. 1.—To attend all Meetings of the Board of Guardians; to keep punctually Minutes of the proceedings at every Meeting, and to record therein all the particulars which are required by this or any other Order of the Local Government Board to be so recorded; to enter the said Minutes in a Book, and to submit the same, so entered, to the presiding Chairman at the succeeding Meeting, to be authenticated by the signature of such Chairman, as a true record of the proceedings of the Board; and also, if required by the Board of Guardians, to attend and assist in the proceedings of all Committees appointed by the Guardians, and to act as Clerk to such Committees.

No. 2.—To provide at the cost of the Union, all Forms or Books of Accounts, Minutes, or other Books, as required of him by the Regulations of the Local Government Board, or relating to the business of the Board of Guardians, and to keep the same, together with all Bills or Accounts, Letters, or other documents, relating to the business of the Union, in a place of safe keeping; to have custody of the keys by which access to such Books and Documents is obtained; and from time to time to produce all such Books, Documents, and Vouchers for the same, together with the Bonds of any Officers or Contractors which may be in his custody, to the Auditor of the Union, at such place and time, and in such manner, as may be required by such Auditor, or by the Regulations of the Local Government Board in force at the time.

No. 3.—To peruse and conduct the correspondence of the Board of Guardians according to their directions; and to preserve the same, and all orders of the Local Government Board, and Letters received, together with copies of all Letters sent by direction of the Guardians.

No. 4.—To receive all requisitions of Guardians for Extraordinary Meetings, and to summon such Meetings accordingly as well as Extraordinary Meetings which he may be required by the Local Government Board to convene, and to prepare, sign, and send all notices required to be given to the Guardians, by any order of the Local Government Board.

No. 5.—To keep, and punctually enter up, the Out-door Relief Register; and at each ordinary Meeting of the Guardians, to produce such Out-door Relief Register, together with the Workhouse Register, for the examination, correction, or approval of the Guardians; to submit the same, when so approved or corrected, to the Chairman for his signature, and thereupon to countersign the same.

No. 6.—To produce at each ordinary meeting of the Guardians the Ledger Account of the Union, together with such other accounts as he is required to keep; and also the Treasurer's Book of Receipts and Payments, and to submit the same to the Board of Guardians for their examination, such examination to be attested by the signature or the initials of the presiding Chairman.

No. 7.—Once at least in each fortnight, and, if the Guardians shall so require, once in each week, and at the hour, and on the day, not being the day of Meeting of the Guardians, which the Clerk shall appoint, to examine the Collecting Book, the Rate Receipt Check Book, and Rate Receipt Abstracts, which shall then be produced to him by each Collector of Poor Rates appointed by the Guardians in the Union, and likewise the Treasurer's Receipts for all Lodgments made by such Collector since the last examination of his Accounts; and in examining such accounts the Clerk shall compare each counterpart from which a receipt has been detached with the corresponding entries in the Collecting Book and the Rate Receipt Abstract, and see that the sum for which the Receipt was issued has been duly brought to account in each of those books; and he shall ascertain, and authenticate by his signature or initials the correctness of the entries in those books, as well as of the sums total carried forward into the Weekly Balance Sheet of Collectors' Receipts and Lodgments.

No. 8.—At the next meeting of the Guardians, after every such examination of a Collector's Accounts, to lay before the Board of Guardians a copy of the Weekly Balance Sheet of Collectors' Receipts and Lodgments for each Electoral Division in the district of such Collector; and in case any Collector shall neglect to attend for such examination, or fail to produce his Accounts as required, to record such omission on the Minutes of the Guardians at their next meeting.

No. 9.—Previously to each ordinary meeting of the Guardians, to examine the Accounts required to be kept by the Master of the Workhouse, or by the Assistant Master or other Officer appointed to keep the Accounts of any Auxiliary Workhouse or Fever Hospital in the Union; and also to examine the Clothing Accounts, the Medical Officers' Books, and the Out-door Relief List, and Weekly Receipt and Expenditure Book of each Relieving Officer in the Union, and to ascertain the correctness of the entries made in such books, and to authenticate the same, if accurate, by his initials, and to report any inaccuracies which he may find in such Accounts to the Board of Guardians, and record such report on the Minutes of their proceedings.

No. 10.—To make up and produce at each ordinary meeting of the Board of Guardians the Abstract of Out-door Relief Lists for the week then last concluded.

No. 11.—To prepare for signature by the Guardians all cheques lawfully drawn on the Treasurer of the Union, and all orders lawfully made on Contractors or other Tradesmen, and to record in the Minutes of proceedings of the Guardians the amount of each cheque on the Treasurer, and the name of the person in whose favour it has been drawn by the Guardians, and all orders given in favour of the Master of the Workhouse and the Relieving Officers.

No. 12.—To communicate all orders and directions of the Local Government Board, or of the Board of Guardians, to the Officers or other persons to whom they may be addressed; and, so far as may be requisite, to give instructions for the prompt and correct execution of all such orders and directions, and to examine and report on such execution, or on any neglect or failure therein which may come to his knowledge.

No. 13.—To prepare, immediately after every ordinary Meeting of the Board of Guardians, a copy of the Minutes of such Meeting, and of every Meeting held since the last ordinary Meeting, and punctually to transmit the same to the office of the Local Government Board, or to the Inspector of the District, as he may be directed.

No. 14.—To prepare and transmit all answers or returns as to any question or matter connected with, or relating to the administration of the laws for the relief of the poor in the Union, or to any other business of the Union, which the Local Government Board or any Inspector may lawfully require from the Board of Guardians or from himself.

No. 15.—To give such assistance as the Board of Guardians may properly require in making or copying any Valuation to be prepared or revised under lawful authority for the Assessment to the Relief of the Poor of hereditaments within the said Union, and in making or copying the Rate to be made thereon.

No. 16.—From time to time to provide, at the charge of the Union, all necessary Rate Books, and, so far as he may be able, to fill up the same accurately with the several particulars required by law, in conformity with the Valuation in force at the time, and to permit, at all reasonable times, any person affected by any Rate for the Relief of the Poor, to inspect the Rate Books and Valuation on which such Rate shall have been made, and to take copies or extracts therefrom, as provided by law.

No. 17.—To prepare all written Contracts and Agreements to be entered into by any parties with the Guardians, and to see that the same are duly executed; and to prepare all Bonds or other Securities to be given by any of the Officers of the Union, and to see that the same are duly executed by such Officers and their Sureties, and that they are, from time to time, renewed, as occasion may require; and in case of the failure of any such persons duly to complete such Bonds or Securities, to give notice to the Guardians, and record the fact on the Minutes of their proceedings.

No. 18.—Previously to the 29th September in each year, to ascertain whether the number of Justices qualified under the first recited Act to be ex-officio Guardians in the Union and resident therein, does or does not equal the number of Elective Guardians eligible for the Union: and in case the number of such Justices exceeds or is less than the number of Elective Guardians, to take the necessary steps for the due selection or completion of the proper number of ex-officio Guardians, according to the provisions of the law in that behalf, and according to any instructions that may have been, or may hereafter be issued by the Local Government Board for the purpose; and to furnish to the Local Government Board from time to time a list of the ex-officio Guardians for each year. And if, in the preparation of such list, any question arises proper for the decision of a meeting of Justices to be held within fourteen days after the 29th of September in any year, in pursuance of the 24th section of 1 & 2 Vic., c. 56, the Clerk shall give due notice, in writing, to all Justices qualified to act as ex-officio Guardians resident in the Union, of the time and place appointed for them to meet for the purpose of deciding such question or appointing ex-officio Guardians, if circumstances should render such appointment necessary.

No. 19.—To receive and preserve all Statements of Claim to vote in the Election of Guardians and appointments of Proxies, made in pursuance of the 84th Section of the said first-recited Act, and to enter the particulars of any such Statements and appointments not already entered into the Register Books of Statements and Claims directed to be provided for that purpose; and, if not appointed Returning Officer, to assist the said officer when appointed in all matters relating to the Election of Guardians.

No. 20.—When appointed Returning Officer by the Local Government Board to conduct duly and impartially, and in strict conformity with the Regulations in force at the time, the annual or any other Election of Guardians.

No. 21.—To observe and execute all lawful orders and directions of the Board of Guardians applicable to his office.

Duties of the Treasurer.

Article 46.—The Duties of the Treasurer shall be :—

No. 1.—To receive all moneys tendered to be paid to the Board of Guardians, and to place the same to their credit, and to give a receipt in the form prescribed by the Local Government Board to the Collectors of Rates, whenever any of them shall pay to the Treasurer money to the credit of the Board of Guardians.

No. 2.—To pay out of any moneys for the time being in his hands belonging to the Board of Guardians all orders for money which shall be drawn upon him on behalf of such Guardians, and shall be signed by the presiding Chairman and two other of such Guardians at a meeting of the Board, and shall be countersigned by the Clerk, or the person for the time being acting as the Clerk, as and when the same shall be presented at the house or usual place of business of the Treasurer.

No. 3.—To keep in a book to be provided for that purpose, entitled the Treasurer's Book of Receipts and Payments, an account under the proper dates of all moneys received and paid respectively by him as such Treasurer, to be submitted to the Board of Guardians at each ordinary Meeting.

No. 4.—To submit the above-mentioned account to the Auditor at the periods of Audit, duly notified, in pursuance of the Regulations of the Local Government Board in force at the time.

Duties of the Collectors of Rates.

Article 47.—The following shall be the duties of the Collectors of Rates :—

No. 1.—From time to time to fill up and prepare a Collecting Book, or abstract of any rate made for the district for which he is constituted or appointed Collector, or any part thereof; to fill up all receipts required to be given, and to keep all books required to be kept by the orders of the Local Government Board, or other lawful authority, and make all returns which relate to the collection of the Rates for the relief of the Poor within his district.

No. 2.—To collect, with due diligence, all moneys payable on account of such Rates for the District for which he may be so constituted or appointed Collector, and to give receipts to all persons from whom he may receive any rates in the form prescribed by the Local Government Board, which shall be supplied to him by the Clerk of the Union, and to take all lawful and proper steps for enforcing the payment of any Rates not duly paid.

No. 3.—To give receipts for Poor Rates from the Receipt Check Books, as numbered and initialed and delivered to him by the Clerk of the Union, and to give no other receipts for Poor Rates whatever, on pain of dismissal from his office, and prosecution for the penalties which he may incur by Statute for a breach of this regulation; and to issue such receipts in regular succession, and in the order of their respective numbers.

No. 4.—To pay over to the Treasurer of the Union, on account of the Board of Guardians, weekly, or oftener if required, and whenever the sum in his hands shall amount to £50, all moneys collected by him, and to take a receipt from the said Treasurer for every such payment in the form prescribed by the Local Government Board.

No. 5.—To keep the Rate Receipt Check Books, and Rate Receipt Abstracts, in the form required by the Local Government Board, and duly to fill up the entries required to be made therein, with regard to all sums collected by him.

No. 6.—To attend the first Meeting of the Guardians which shall be held in every month, with the several Books which he is required to keep, and to lay before them, in a book to be especially kept for the purpose, a summary of the state of his collection, together with the receipts of the Treasurer for all sums paid in during the preceding month.

No. 7.—To submit his Collecting Book, Rate Receipt Check Books, and Rate Receipt Abstracts, to the Clerk of the Union for examination, once at the least in every fortnight, and if the Guardians shall so require, once in every week, at the hour and on the day, not being the day of meeting of the Guardians, which the Clerk shall appoint for that purpose; and at the same time to produce to the Clerk the Treasurer's Receipts for all Lodgments made by him since the last examination of his Accounts.

No. 8.—To return every Receipt Check Book, from which all the receipts shall have been detached, to the Clerk of the Union forthwith.

No. 9.—To attend every meeting of the Board of Guardians which he shall be specially required to attend.

No. 10.—To attend the Returning Officer on the days appointed for examining Nomination Papers and the Votes given at any election of Guardians of the Union, with the Collecting Book, and to assist such Officer in examining the qualification of persons nominated for the office of Guardian, or making Nominations, and the validity of the Votes.

Duties of Relieving Officers.

Article 18.—The duties of every Relieving Officer shall be:—

No. 1.—To attend all ordinary Meetings of the Board of Guardians, and to attend all other Meetings when summoned by the Clerk.

No. 2.—To attend at such places in his District, at such times of the day, and on such days in the week as the Board of Guardians shall, from time to time direct, for the purpose of dispensing relief, and of receiving applications for relief.

No. 3.—To receive all applications for relief made to him within his District, and forthwith to examine into the circumstances of every case, by visiting the home of the applicant, and by making all necessary enquiries into the state of health, the ability to work, the condition, the family, and the previous earnings, and other means of such applicant, and to report the result of such inquiries, in the prescribed form entitled the Application and Report Book, to the Board of Guardians at their next ordinary Meeting; and also to visit all persons in receipt of out-door relief whose relief is made necessary by temporary sickness at least once in each week, and all other persons in receipt of out-door relief at least once in each month, and to report concerning same at the next ordinary Meeting of the Board of Guardians, or as the Board of Guardians may direct.

No. 4.—In every case of sudden and urgent necessity, to afford such provisional relief to the destitute person as shall be requisite in the manner provided by law; that is to say, either by an order of admission to the Workhouse or Fever Hospital of the Union, provided there be room therein respectively, and by conveying any destitute poor person thereto, if necessary; or by affording such poor person immediate and temporary relief in food, lodging, medicine, or medical attendance, until the next ordinary Meeting of the Board of Guardians.

No. 5.—To report to the Board of Guardians at their next ordinary Meeting, all cases in which he shall have given provisional relief, and the nature and cost of the relief so afforded, in the prescribed form, entitled the Application and Report Book; and to take the directions of the Board of Guardians regarding any further relief to be afforded in every case so reported.

No. 6.—Duly and punctually to dispense the weekly allowances of all poor persons belonging to his District. Such allowances to be given as far as possible, at the home of the applicant, and in no case to be paid at a house licensed for the sale of intoxicating drinks, and to relieve all poor persons within his District, as directed by the Board of Guardians, and authorized by the signature and Initials of the Chairman of the meeting in the columns provided for that purpose in the prescribed form, entitled the Application and Report Book.

No. 7.—In the case of every Orphan or Deserted Child placed out at nurse or boarded out, and placed under his supervision by the Board of Guardians in pursuance of the General Order of the Local Government Board, dated 20th of November, 1876, to discharge the duty so assigned to him in accordance with the following regulations:—

To see the child safely given over in charge to the person whom the Guardians shall have selected for the purpose.

To pay, by advance or otherwise, as the Guardians shall direct, but not less often than by monthly payments, the sums granted from time to time by the Guardians for the maintenance of the child, from the funds placed at his disposal by them for that purpose.

To cause such child, if not already successfully Vaccinated, to be Vaccinated by the Medical Officer of the Dispensary District in which the place of residence shall be situate.

To visit such child once at least in every month, and also when any special occasion shall arise for so visiting it, and to report in writing immediately thereafter to the Board of Guardians on its health, cleanliness, and treatment, together with such other particulars as the Guardians shall at any time require.

To see that the child, when of sufficient age to attend school, attends the nearest National School or other public School, and remains there during the ordinary school hours, and to annex to his Report to the Board of Guardians the teacher's certificate of the child's attendance, which is required by the said General Order of the 20th November, 1876, to be given to the Relieving Officer each month.

In the event of the death of such child, to take steps for burying it, according to the directions of the Board of Guardians applicable generally to such cases.

No. 8.—To keep a separate, full, and true account of all sums and articles dispensed by him for or on account of the relief of each poor person in the District for which he shall be appointed to act, in the prescribed form, entitled the Out-door Relief List.

No. 9.—To keep a separate, full, and true account of all sums or articles received by him from the Board of Guardians, and expended or dispensed by him on the account of each Electoral Division in his District, or the Union at large, as the case may be, in the prescribed form, entitled the Weekly Receipt and Expenditure Book, and to balance the same weekly.

No. 10.—To present the prescribed Books of Accounts, severally entitled the Out-door Relief List, and Weekly Receipt and Expenditure Book, to the Clerk for his inspection and authentication, before every ordinary Meeting of the Board of Guardians, and to the Board of Guardians at such Meeting.

No. 11.—In no case to take credit in his Accounts, or enter as paid or given, any money or other articles which shall not have been paid or given previously to the taking of such credit, or the making of such entry.

No. 12.—To make out at the end of each half-year, Lists of all persons relieved at the charge of each Electoral Division, or the Union at large, in his District, in the form F hereto annexed, entitled List of Destitute Persons relieved out of the Workhouse; and to post, or cause to be posted, copies of the same in such public places as the Board of Guardians shall direct.

No. 13.—To submit to the Auditor of the Union all his books, Accounts, and Vouchers, at such place and time, and in such manner, as may be required by the Regulations in force at the time.

No. 14.—To keep a Diary, showing how he has been employed in the discharge of his duties on each day of the week, and to submit the same to the Board of Guardians at every ordinary Meeting.

No. 15.—To observe and execute all lawful orders and directions of the Board of Guardians applicable to his office.

Duties of the Officers of the Workhouse.

Article 49.—The Medical Officer, Master, Matron, Porter, Schoolmaster, and Schoolmistress, together with all Assistants appointed under this Order, shall perform all the duties set forth in any Order of the Local Government Board in force at the time, regulating the management of the Workhouse of the Union, or prescribing in any way the duties of such Officers and Assistants as aforesaid.

Duties of Warden.

Article 50.—Every Warden lawfully appointed by the Board of Guardians, in pursuance of the said recited Act, shall discharge the following duties with reference to the several Parishes, Townlands, or parts of Parishes for which he may have been so appointed:—

No. 1.—To attend the Board of Guardians at their Ordinary and Weekly Meetings whenever he may be so required; and so far as the said Guardians may lawfully require, to report to them on the state of the Poor within his Parish or District, on the increase or diminution of mendicancy therein, or on any other matters in relation to the condition of such Parish or District, on which the said Guardians may, from time to time, require information.

No. 2.—To collect and certify in writing to the Board of Guardians, when required by them so to do, any information which he may be able to obtain respecting the fact or period of the residence of any applicant for relief, within the Parish or District for which he may act.

No. 3.—To receive all applications for admission into the Workhouse, which may be made to him, by or on behalf of any destitute poor persons usually resident, or being casually within any Parish or Townland comprised within his District, and to report to the Board of Guardians, at their weekly meeting, all such applications made to him during the preceding week, together with the particulars which, on examination into the merits of each case, he shall have been enabled to collect.

No. 4.—To provide, if necessary, for the conveyance of any destitute poor person who may be unable, through old age, or infirmity of body or mind, to walk to the Workhouse, whom he shall have been directed to convey by the Board of Guardians.

Duties with Respect to the Audit of Accounts.

Article 51.—Every Officer acting under this Order, shall duly and punctually keep such Books as may be prescribed in any Order of the Local Government Board, in force at the time, for keeping and auditing the Accounts, and shall lay such Books, together with the vouchers and other necessary documents, before the Auditor, properly balanced and made up, at the time fixed for the Audit or for any adjournment thereof; and every such Officer shall, when required so to do, furnish to the Auditor or to the Board of Guardians any abstract, statement, or explanation, verbally or in writing, respecting his accounts and the items contained therein or the Vouchers relating thereto.

Explanation of Terms.

Article 52.—In this Order, the expression "The Local Government Board" means "The Local Government Board for Ireland." Whenever in describing any person or party, matter or thing, the word importing the singular number or the masculine gender only is used in this Order, the same shall be taken to include and shall be applied to several persons or parties as well as one person or party, and females as well as males, and several matters or things as well as one matter or thing, respectively, unless there be something in the subject or context repugnant to such construction.

ARTICLE 53.—Whenever in this Order any Article is referred to by its number, the Article of this Order bearing that number shall be taken to be signified thereby.

FORM A.

NOTICE OF THE ELECTION OF A CHAIRMAN, VICE-CHAIRMAN, AND DEPUTY VICE-CHAIRMAN.

To A. B., Guardian of the Poor of the —— Union.

SIR,—You are hereby informed that the Election of a Chairman, Vice-Chairman, and Deputy Vice-Chairman of the Board of Guardians for the ensuing year, will take place at the Meeting of the Board of Guardians, to be held on day, the day of , 18 , at o'clock.

Dated of , 18 .

—— Clerk to the Guardians.

FORM B.

To the Clerk to the Guardians of the —— Union.

REQUISITION FOR AN EXTRAORDINARY MEETING OF GUARDIANS.

We, the undersigned, being two of the Guardians of the Poor of the Union, do hereby require an Extraordinary Meeting of the Guardians of the said Union to be summoned, to be holden at on the day of 18 , at o'clock in the forenoon, to take into consideration [set out the motion].

Dated of 18 .

————
———— } Guardians.

FORM C.

NOTICE OF CLERK CONVENING AN EXTRAORDINARY MEETING OF GUARDIANS.

To A. B., Guardian of the Poor of the Union.

SIR,—C. D. and E. F., two of the Guardians of the Poor of the Union, have required* that an Extraordinary Meeting of the Guardians of the Poor of the said Union, at on the day of 18 , at o'clock in the forenoon, be summoned, to take into consideration [set out the motion], and you are hereby requested to attend such Meeting, at the above-named time and place.

Dated of 18 .

—— Clerk to the Guardians.

FORM D.

NOTICE OF CHANGE OF PERIOD, TIME, OR PLACE OF MEETING.

To A. B., Guardian of the Poor of the Union.

SIR,—You are hereby informed that the next Ordinary Meeting of the Guardians of the Poor of the Union, will take place at on the day of 18 , at o'clock in the forenoon, for the transaction of business; and that Meetings of the said Guardians will henceforth be held [weekly or otherwise, as the case may be] at the same place, on in every week, at the same hour in the forenoon.

Dated of

—— Clerk to the Guardians.

* Where the Meeting is convened in consequence of a requirement of the Local Government Board, the Notice may commence thus:—"The Local Government Board have required," &c., as above.

Form E.

Notice of an Adjourned Meeting of Guardians.

To A. B., Guardian of the Poor of the Union.

Sir,—This is to give you Notice, that an Adjourned Meeting of the Guardians of the Poor of the Union will be held at on the day of 18 , to take into consideration [set out the motion], which Meeting you are hereby requested to attend.

Dated of 18 .

——— Clerk to the Guardians.

Form F.

List of Destitute Persons Relieved out of the Workhouse in the ——— District, during the Half-year ended ———, 18—.

Name.	Number of dependent Members of Family.		Residence.	To what Account chargeable.	Number of Weeks during which Relief was given in the half-year.	Cost of Relief afforded.								
	Wife.	Children.				Money.			Kind.			Total.		
						£	s.	d.	£	s.	d.	£	s.	d.

——— *Relieving Officer.*

Schedule containing the Names of the Unions to which the present Order applies.

Abbeyleix,
Antrim,
Ardee,
Armagh,
Athlone,
Athy,
Bailieborough,
Ballina,
Ballinasloe,
Ballinrobe,
Ballycastle,
Ballymahon,
Ballymena,
Ballymoney,
Ballyshannon,
Ballyvaughan,
Balrothery,
Baltinglass,
Banbridge,
Bandon,
Bantry,
Bawnboy,
Belfast,
Belmullet,
Borrisokane,
Boyle,
Cahirciveen,
Callan,
Carlow,
Carrickmacross,
Carrick-on-Shannon
Carrick-on-Suir,
Cashel,
Castlebar,
Castleblayney,
Castlecomer,
Castlederg,
Castlerea,
Castletown,
Cavan,
Celbridge,
Claremorris,
Clifden,
Clogheen,
Clogher,
Clonakilty,
Clones,
Clonmel,
Coleraine,
Cookstown,
Cootehill,
Cork,
Corrofin,
Croom,
Delvin,
Dingle,
Donaghmore,
Donegal,
Downpatrick,
Drogheda,
Dromore West,
Dublin, North,
Dublin, South,
Dundalk,
Dunfanaghy,
Dungannon,
Dungarvan,
Dunmanway,
Dunshaughlin,
Edenderry,
Ennis,
Enniscorthy,
Enniskillen,
Ennistymon,
Fermoy,
Galway,
Glennamaddy,
Glenties,
Glin,
Gorey,
Gort,
Gortin,
Granard,
Inishowen,
Irvinestown,
Kanturk,
Kells,
Kenmare,
Kilkeel,
Kilkenny,
Killadysert,
Killala,
Killarney,
Kilmacthomas
Kilmallock,
Kilrush,
Kinsale,
Larne,
Letterkenny,
Limavady,
Limerick,
Lisburn,
Lismore,
Lisnaskea,
Listowel,
Londonderry,
Longford,
Loughrea,
Lurgan,
Macroom,
Magherafelt,
Mallow,
Manorhamilton,
Midleton,
Milford,
Millstreet,
Mitchelstown,
Mohill,
Monaghan,
Mountbellew,

SCHEDULE—*continued.*

Mountmellick,	Omagh,	Skibbereen,	Tralee,
Mullingar,	Oughterard,	Skull,	Trim,
Naas,	Parsonstown,	Sligo,	Tuam,
Navan,	Portumna,	Strabane,	Tulla,
Nenagh,	Rathdown,	Stranorlar,	Tullamore,
Newcastle,	Rathdrum,	Strokestown,	Urlingford,
Newport,	Rathkeale,	Swineford,	Waterford
New Ross,	Roscommon,	Thomastown,	Westport,
Newry,	Roscrea,	Thurles,	Wexford,
Newtownards,	Scariff,	Tipperary,	Youghal.
Oldcastle,	Shillelagh,	Tobercurry,	

Sealed with our Seal, this 18th day of December, in the Year of Our Lord One Thousand Eight Hundred and Eighty-two.

(Signed),

G. O. Trevelyan. Charles Croker-King.
Henry Robinson. George Morris.
R. G. C. Hamilton.

Spencer.

I, John Poyntz, Earl Spencer, Lord Lieutenant-General and General Governor of Ireland, do hereby approve this Order.

By His Excellency's Command,
R. G. C. Hamilton.

No. 5.—General Order applying the General Order of 8th August, 1879, "Sanitary Order No. III.," relating to Urban Sanitary Districts to the Town of Letterkenny.

To the Governing Body of the Town named in this Order; to the Medical Officer of the Dispensary District comprised or partly comprised therein; and to all whom it may concern:

Whereas by a General Order under our Seal, bearing date the Eighth day of August, 1879, We, the Local Government Board for Ireland, did issue Rules and Regulations under the "Public Health (Ireland) Act, 1878," for the Sanitary organization of Urban Sanitary Districts, the said General Order being numbered and described as follows;

"Sanitary Order No. III., relating to Urban Sanitary Districts."

And Whereas, since the issue of the said General Order, We have issued a Provisional Order under our Seal for the constitution of the Town of Letterkenny as an Urban Sanitary District, subject to all the Provisions of the "Public Health (Ireland) Act, 1878," affecting Urban Sanitary Districts, from and after the confirmation of the Order by Act of Parliament;

And Whereas the said Provisional Order has been duly confirmed by Parliament;

And Whereas it is expedient that the said General Order of the Eighth day of August, 1879, "Sanitary Order No. III., relating to Urban Sanitary Districts"—shall apply to and be in force in the Urban Sanitary District above named;

Now Therefore, We do hereby Order and Direct that the said General Order shall apply to and be in force in the Urban Sanitary District above named, as fully and effectually as if the name of the said Urban Sanitary District had been inserted in the Schedule to the said General Order of the Eighth day of August, 1879.

Sealed with our Seal, this Twenty-second day of December, in the Year of our Lord One Thousand Eight Hundred and Eighty-two.

(Signed),

Henry Robinson.
Charles Crorer-King.
George Morris.

Spencer,

I, John Poyntz, Earl Spencer, Lord Lieutenant-General and General Governor of Ireland, do hereby approve this Order.

By His Excellency's Command,
W. S. B. Kaye.

No. 6.—Form of Outdoor Relief Order under the provisions of "The Relief of Distress (Ireland) Act, 1880," "The Relief of Distress (Ireland) Amendment Act, 1880," and "The Protection of Person and Property (Ireland) Act, 1881," and List of Unions to which it has been issued.

Out-door Relief.

—— Union.

To the Guardians of the Poor of the —— Union; to the Clerk and other Officers of the said Union; and to all other persons whom it may concern:

We, the Local Government Board for Ireland, in pursuance of the provisions of "The Relief of Distress (Ireland) Act, 1880," "The Relief of Distress (Ireland) Amendment Act, 1880," and "The Protection of Person and Property (Ireland) Act, 1881," do hereby authorize the Guardians of the Poor of the said Union to administer relief in Food and Fuel, or either of them, out of the Workhouse to the families of persons for the time being detained under the last recited Act, whether such persons might under the Poor Law Acts have obtained relief out of the Workhouse or not, in the Union, or in any Electoral Division or Divisions thereof, from the date of this Order to the ——, or until we may, by Order under our Seal, sooner revoke this Order.

Sealed with our Seal this —— day of ——, in the year of our Lord One thousand eight hundred and——.

[Table.

TABLE showing the UNIONS in which the foregoing ORDER was declared to be in force, and the period of operation of Order in each Union (in continuation of Table in Report for 1882, Appendix A, page 30).

Union.	Period of Operation of Order.
Ballinrobe, . . .	From 27th May, 1882, to 27th June, 1882.
Cahersiveen, . . .	From 3rd April, 1882, to 3rd June, 1882.
Cork, ...	From 8th April, 1882, to 8th June, 1882.
Delvin, ...	From 22nd May, 1882, to 22nd June, 1882.
Enniskillen, . . .	From 8th May, 1882, to 7th July, 1882.
Ennistymon, . . .	From 11th May, 1882, to 10th July, 1882.
"	" 11th July, 1882, to 10th August, 1882.
Gort, ...	From 15th May, 1882, to 15th June, 1882.
"	" 26th June, 1882, to 26th July, 1882.
"	" 26th July, 1882, to 26th August, 1882.
"	" 26th August, 1882, to 26th September, 1882.
Killarney, ...	From 22nd May, 1882, to 22nd June, 1882.
Listowel, ...	From 19th May, 1882, to 19th July, 1882.
Mallow, ...	From 25th April, 1882, to 25th May, 1882.
"	" 24th June, 1882, to 24th July, 1882.
"	" 17th August, 1882, to 16th September, 1882.
Mitchelstown, . . .	From 29th April, 1882, to 29th June, 1882.
Mullingar, . . .	From 22nd April, 1882, to 22nd May, 1882.
"	" 27th May, 1882, to 27th June, 1882.
"	" 18th July, 1882, to 17th August, 1882.
"	" 18th August, 1882, to 18th September, 1882.
Nenagh, ...	From 1st April, 1882, to 1st May, 1882.
Newcastle, . . .	From 27th April, 1882, to 27th May, 1882.
Roscommon, . . .	From 18th April, 1882, to 18th May, 1882.
Tralee, . . .	From 6th May, 1882, to 8th July, 1882.
"	" 20th July, 1882, to 19th August, 1882.
Tulla, ...	From 27th April, 1882, to 27th May, 1882.

No. 7.—FORM of ORDER authorizing OUTDOOR RELIEF under Section 2 of the 10th Vic, cap. 31.

OUTDOOR RELIEF. (——— UNION).

To the GUARDIANS of the POOR of the ——— UNION; to the CLERK and other Officers of the said Union, and to all other persons whom it may concern:

WHEREAS it has been shown to our satisfaction, that, by reason of the want of room in the workhouse of the said union, adequate relief cannot be afforded therein to destitute poor persons not being persons permanently disabled, or destitute poor persons disabled by sickness or accident, or destitute poor widows having two or more legitimate children dependent on them, and it is expedient to authorize and empower the Guardians of the said union to administer relief out of the workhouse to such destitute poor persons for a limited time as hereinafter mentioned:

NOW THEREFORE, WE, the Local Government Board for Ireland, do hereby authorize and empower the said Guardians to administer relief out of the workhouse, in food, to destitute poor persons not being persons permanently disabled from labour by reason of old age, infirmity, or bodily or mental defect, and not being persons disabled from labour by reason of severe sickness or serious accident, and thereby deprived of the means of earning a subsistence for themselves and their families, whom they are liable by law to maintain, and not being poor widows having two or more legitimate children dependent on them, for the period from the date of this Order to the

AND WE do hereby make the following rules and regulations as to the granting, ordering, and giving of relief to all persons who shall be relieved by the said Guardians under the authority of this order, that is to say:—

1. Every person relieved under the authority of this Order shall be relieved in food only, and such food shall, as far as is practicable, be cooked food.

2. Every able-bodied male person relieved under the authority of this Order shall, so far as is practicable, be set to perform a task of work during eight hours at least of every day for which he receives such relief.

3. No able-bodied person who shall be in employment, nor any part of his or her family, shall receive relief as a destitute person under the authority of this Order.

AND for the more effectual administration of Relief under this Order, we do hereby authorize and direct the said Guardians to appoint so many relieving officers as shall be found sufficient from time to time, to superintend the labour of such persons as shall be set to work, in pursuance of the regulations in this Order contained, and otherwise to assist in the administration of Relief under this Order, as the said Guardians, subject to our approval, shall direct.

Sealed with our Seal, this ——— day of ———, in the year of Our Lord One thousand eight hundred and ———.

ORDER authorising OUTDOOR RELIEF under sec. 2, of 10 Vic., cap. 31.

TABLE showing the UNIONS in which the foregoing ORDER was declared to be in force.

Union.	Period of Operation of Order.
Waterford, ...	From 1st April to 15th April, 1882.
North Dublin, . . .	From 7th December, 1882 to 8th January, 1883.
Wexford, ...	From 6th February to 31st March, 1883.

II.—CIRCULARS, &c.

No. 1.—Reports from Inspectors on the prospects of the General Harvest.

Local Government Board, Dublin,
4th August, 1882.

Sir,

The Local Government Board for Ireland have received a communication from the Under Secretary to the Lord Lieutenant, in which he states that His Excellency is desirous to be furnished with information as to the harvest prospects this year, and the condition of the turf in districts where it is cut. The Board therefore request that you will be so good as to make inquiry regarding the state of the potato crop in your district, the condition of the turf where it is cut, and the prospects of the general harvest; and that you will report to them on the subject.

The Board would be glad to receive your report on or before the 24th instant, and they hope this will afford you sufficient time to procure the information required.

By order of the Board,

W. D. Wodsworth, Assistant Secretary.

To each Inspector.

Report from Mr. Armstrong.—District comprising the Counties of Cavan and Monaghan, and parts of Fermanagh and Tyrone.

Carkil, Kilskeery, 21st August, 1882.

Sir,—Referring to your letter of the 4th instant, directing me to report as to the prospects of the harvest in my district, for the information of His Excellency the Lord Lieutenant, I have the honour to state that from inquiries I have made, and from my own personal observation, I am of opinion that the early potatoes have suffered very considerably from blight; are, as a rule, very small, and not nearly as good a crop as the last two years. The later sorts of potatoes, such as Champions, are not dug as yet, nor will be for another month or six weeks. I have had a few stalks dug, by way of experiment, which showed a fair quantity of tubers of good size, and as a rule, sound.

The oat crop looks well, but will, I am afraid, be rather late.

The weather has been very bad for saving hay; most of the meadows were good and heavy—the hay on some low-lying lands were much injured by wet.

Of course there has been great difficulty in saving turf, but where the turf itself is of a hard quality, I think much injury has not been done; where it is of a soft, spongy nature I do not expect it to be of much use this year.

The accounts of the flax crop are rather indifferent.

It is utterly impossible to give authentic information so early in the season, as a great deal depends on the weather for the next two months.

I have the honour to be, sir, your obedient servant,

W. Armstrong, Inspector.

The Secretary, Local Government Board.

REPORT from Mr. R. BOURKE.—DISTRICT comprising parts of the COUNTIES of CLARE, LIMERICK, TIPPERARY, and KING'S COUNTY.

Lisnagry, Limerick, 23rd August, 1882.

GENTLEMEN,—I have to acknowledge the receipt of your letter of the 4th inst., requesting me to report upon the state of the potato crop in my district, the condition of the turf where it is cut, and the prospects of the general harvest, and to furnish my report on or before the 24th inst.

I have delayed acting upon those instructions until the last moment, as the season is later by two or three weeks than usual, and the difficulty therefore greater of forming any safe estimate of the return to be expected, from many of the crops. Moreover, there have been few summers within my recollection where the variations in temperature and the general character of the weather have changed so rapidly, and produced such remarkable effects, almost from day to day, on the appearance of the crops.

But since the receipt of your communication, I have been in correspondence with persons living in the district on whose powers of observation and calm judgment I feel the greatest reliance, and have been favoured with very full and important replies, which, applied to the opinions formed by personal examination, have enabled me to arrive at conclusions which I hope and believe will be found trustworthy. To the Chairmen of the Nenagh and Rathkeale Boards, Mr. J. J. Poe, and Mr. J. B. Hewson, as well as to the clerks of the several Unions in Tipperary, Limerick, and Clare, which comprise my district, I feel greatly indebted for their assistance, and to Mr. W. Spaight of Derry Castle, and other personal friends, I am under great obligations of the same nature.

My district (as it may be almost superfluous to mention to you) consists of the following Unions:—

In the County Limerick, five Unions with an area of 837 square miles. In the County Clare, six Unions with an area of 909 square miles; and, in the County Tipperary, three Unions in the North Riding with an area of 599 square miles.

In the entire of this area of 2,345 square miles, there is great variety of soil, a good deal of mountain and bog, and arable land of different qualities. It is only reasonable therefore, to expect that there should be serious differences in the amount of produce of the various crops and in their quality, and that no standard of comparison can be readily obtained. In my remarks, therefore, upon the harvest prospects of the present year, I have found it necessary to refer to them as applicable to two qualities of land distinguished under the heads of "poor" and "rich" lands.

Potatoes.—This crop was largely planted, and in spring presented a very satisfactory appearance, but the early summer came wet and cold, the potato got checked in growth, and where the soil was retentive there was no advance whatever in the tuber. The "champion" potato from which such excellent results proceeded last year and the year before, seemed to have lost its chief characteristics and all its vigour and robustness. As the season advanced, and the month of August brought more sunshine and higher temperature, the plants improved in appearance, and the tubers made great progress. But some crops had suffered too severely and could not altogether recover. The progress of decay in the leaves was only arrested for a time, and no advance took place in the potatoes themselves.

The result of all this has been, in my opinion, that in poor cold lands, more especially in mountain districts, there has been a total loss of about one-half of the crop, and what remains will not be of much use for human food. In the richer lands it is not so bad. There I estimate the loss from various causes at about 20 per cent. of the whole. Some of this is due to the inferiority of the crop as compared with the last two years, some to excessive moisture and absence of sun and heat, and some to disease. But this last element of mischief has chiefly affected the early kinds, leaving the champions almost uninjured. If, in the abundance of last year, the yield of potatoes might be taken at ten tons to the Irish acre, the maximum produce this year would probably not reach eight tons, reducible to three or four tons in the mountain and poor wet lands, and to six and a half tons in the better lands.

This estimated loss is, no doubt, of a very serious character, and represents to the farmer a large diminution of profit, and to the poor labouring man a great restriction in comforts. But as potatoes no longer constitute the sole or indeed the principal article of food in this class, there is no danger of absolute scarcity unless the price of corn should be augmented, and of this, happily, there is little prospect.

Turf.—As regards the supply of turf there is, in my opinion, no cause for apprehension. The quantity cut is perhaps more than usual, and a large amount is already dry and fit for use. Unless the remaining period of summer and the early part of autumn turn out exceptionally wet, all the turf ought, I think, to be saved.

General Prospects of Harvest.—In the matter of cereals the result of my observation and of the information afforded me is, that *Wheat* will be somewhat deficient in quantity and in quality. The constant wet whilst the plant was in flower greatly damaged it, and the low temperature has kept the rest of the grain small and light. In some localities the yield is stated to be 50 per cent. below the average of the last seven years, but I am disposed rather to place the loss at 20 or 25 per cent. *Oats* is everywhere a promising crop, long in the straw and with good head, but it is quite too soon to estimate with any even approximate certainty the weight of the return of grain. The same may be said of *Barley*, of which more has been sown than usual. Wheat is only grown in the good lands, and the poor and mountain districts are confined to oats alone. In ordinary seasons, the corn there is two or three weeks behind that in the lowlands, and whereas there the harvest has scarcely commenced as yet, in the mountain regions the oats are still quite green.

Green Crops.—Turnips and mangel are scarcely equal to the average of the last few years. Their success depends much on the care bestowed upon them. The season has been so productive of weeds that constant cleaning was essential to the growth of the crops, and not every farmer can afford the expense in labour which this requires. Upon the whole, however, I incline to think there will be little or no deficiency in these products.

Hay.—There has seldom been a season so favourable to the growth of meadows, and a far larger extent of land than usual has been devoted to hay. This has probably arisen from the high price of cattle, which deterred farmers from keeping up their stock to the usual amount. The meadows cut early were exposed to long rains, and the hay has not been saved in the best condition, but the later crops have been secured at a little cost and in prime state, and, upon the whole, few seasons are remembered where a larger or better crop has been saved.

Upon the whole, I see nothing in the harvest prospects of this year materially affecting the circumstances of the large farmers. Men with smaller holdings will sustain a greater relative loss—and the cottier and labouring man will probably find himself and his family a good deal pinched by the diminished produce of his potato crop. But if labour be not unduly restricted, I apprehend the workman's condition will be substantially much as it has been in better years, and if the tendency to increased wages, which is showing itself here and there, is maintained, his position should be better this year than before.

I have the honour to be, gentlemen, your obedient servant,

H. BOURKE.

The Local Government Board.

REPORT from DR. BURKE.—DISTRICT comprising the COUNTY of LONGFORD, and parts of the COUNTIES of KILDARE, KING'S COUNTY, LOUTH, MEATH, QUEEN'S COUNTY and WESTMEATH.

26, Waterloo-road, Dublin, 23rd August, 1882.

GENTLEMEN,—I have had the honour to receive your communication of the 4th inst., intimating the desire of His Excellency the Lord Lieutenant to be furnished with information, as to the harvest prospects this year, and requesting me to make inquiry regarding the state of the potato crop in my district, the condition of the turf where it is cut, and the prospects of the general harvest. With reference to which and in compliance with your instructions I beg to report that, having taken the necessary steps to obtain most reliable information, I have the honour now to submit the result thereof, together with my own views on the subject, founded on personal knowledge and observation when passing through the different portions of my district, comprising the King's, Longford, and Queen's counties, the largest portion of Meath and Westmeath, a part of Kildare, and considerable portion of Louth.

Regarding the potato crop the area of land now under cultivation with this staple article of food appears to me to be larger in extent than that of last year. Various kinds of seed have been made use of, but that relied upon generally and most extensively sown is the "Champion," the growth, maturity, and stalks of which manifest so far a very healthy abundant appearance, and, with rare exceptions, quite free from symptoms of the blight, though I have to observe that the produce will not be (in my opinion) so prolific or large as that of last year, still it may be deemed a very good and as valuable a crop, when taking into consideration that the tubers are freer from the remarkable hollowness in the centre, with which the potatoes of this species were extensively affected in 1881, Several other descriptions of seed, such as Skerry Blues, Scotch Downs, and White Rocks, have been sown. The former of which shows fair promise and appears to thrive, but as to the two latter I believe at least one-third of the crop is gone and rendered useless, both by failure and blight. However, though this may entail numerous individual losses in several detached localities, still, in my opinion, no grave apprehensions need be entertained regarding the consequences generally, considering the promising and abundant supply indicated so far by "the Champion."

As to the condition of the turf, a large quantity of such has been cut; that at an early period has been saved, and in many places has been brought home, while that cut later on, in the end of June and July, remains on the bogs, but partially saved, owing to the wetness of the latter month, and waiting for a few weeks dry weather which would leave it quite safe and fit for removal.

As to the prospects of the general harvest I have with much pleasure to observe that throughout the entire of my district, the several cereal crops, barley, oats and wheat, present a most favourable appearance; all manifest not alone excellence in quality but a more than average abundance in quantity, though somewhat backward in ripening owing to the want of heat and sun as well as the frequent bursts of wet, during the last few weeks, which it is to be hoped will cease, when I entertain no doubt the present harvest will be found to be more abundant than any we have been favoured with for the last five years.

The hay crop has been likewise good and plentiful and is now quite safe.

The mangold and turnip crops appear to be of fair average and doing well.

I am, gentlemen, your most obedient servant,

T. W. Burke, Inspector.

The Local Government Board,
Custom House, Dublin.

REPORT from Dr. BRODIE.—DISTRICT comprising parts of the COUNTIES of CORK, LIMERICK, and WATERFORD.

Cork, 22nd August, 1882.

GENTLEMEN,—I have the honour to acknowledge the receipt of your letter, dated 4th instant, requesting a report from me, for the information of his Excellency the Lord Lieutenant, as to the state of the potato crop in my district, the condition of the turf where it is cut, and the prospects of the general harvest in my district, comprising the unions of Cork, Mallow, Fermoy, Midleton, Youghal, Mitchelstown, Bandon, Dunmanway, Clonakilty, Macroom, situate in the county of Cork; Lismore, Dungarvan, Kilmacthomas, in the county of Waterford; and Kilmallock, in the county of Limerick.

On receipt of your letter of instruction I availed myself of every source from which I could derive reliable information on the subject, and now beg to submit to you the following as the result of those inquiries, and of my own personal observations, having travelled through a considerable portion of the district during the past fortnight.

CORK UNION—urban and rural.

Potatoes.—Have been severely tried by the continued rains of July. Early potatoes have proved less than half a crop, and of bad quality. The main crop, chiefly of the variety known as "champions," in well-cultivated soils will yield from one-half to two-thirds, and in high levels one-half, as compared with last year, which was the largest crop for many years in Ireland.

Turf.—A small quantity saved, but little used in this union.

Oats.—An unusually large crop.

Wheat and Barley.—Promise about an average crop.

Roots.—Promise a large crop.

Hay.—(New meadow) large crop, mostly saved in bad condition. (Old Meadow) the largest crop for many years, and the greater part saved in good condition.

Harvest.—Operations have just commenced, and will be general during the next fortnight. With fair weather, and taking into consideration the high price of cattle, the extra make and remunerative price for butter, I am of opinion that the value of this year's farm produce will compare favourably with that of 1881.

Employment.—In the urban and suburban portions of Cork union there is general sufficient employment for unskilled labour, at remunerative wages, 2s. 6d. per day. Few idle hands are to be found either in the city or environs, and the fair prospects of the harvest are likely to ensure a continuation of the present state of things.

No. of inmates in the workhouse 12th August, . . .	2,383
No. in house corresponding period last year, . . .	2,609
No. of persons in receipt of outdoor relief, . . .	3,140

At a cost of £150 17s. in money, and £7 10s. 7d. in kind.

MALLOW UNION—county of Cork.

Potatoes.—The potato crop in general is looking very well. Although showing indications of the blight, it has arrived at such an advanced stage of maturity that the injury to be sustained will not very materially affect the produce.

Turf.—In a fair condition, notwithstanding the heavy and continuous rains in the mountain districts; coal is generally used.

Oats.—Will be abundant, in the event of fair harvest weather; but in consequence of late sowing, owing to heavy rains in April, the harvest will be late.

Wheat.—In some places shows "rust," but the crop in general looks promising.

Green Crops.—Turnips and mangolds are excellent.

Hay.—An abundant crop.

FERMOY UNION—county of Cork.

Potatoes.—Though not so good as last year, which was an exceptional one, are likely to be a better crop than for years before the last. The blight, which showed itself in the early part of July, seems to have been checked by the subsequent fine weather.

Oats and Wheat.—Look healthy, and, should the present favourable weather continue, will prove to be a fair average crop.

Turf.—Coal is almost the chief article of fuel in this union; but in some mountain parts where turf is cut, the extreme wetness of portion of the summer prevented the turf from being well saved.

Green Crops.—Turnips and mangolds promise well.

Hay.—A good crop.

Harvest.—There is nothing in the present aspect of things as regards the harvest to cause uneasiness.

MIDLETON UNION—county of Cork.

Potatoes.—Compared with last year, is considered to be not much more than half a crop. The old seeds failed very early in the season. The only hope left depends on the "champions." The present price of potatoes in Midleton is one shilling per weight of 21 lbs., against sixpence last year.

Turf.—Not used in this union; coal the general article of fuel.

Oats.—Considered far superior to that of last year.

Wheat and Barley.—An average crop.

Hay.—A heavy crop; although during the saving the weather was not very favourable, yet, on the whole, there is no cause for complaint. Should the weather hold up, so as to enable the harvesting to go on satisfactorily, there is every reason to hope that the grain crop will be abundant.

MITCHELSTOWN UNION—county of Cork.

Potatoes.—There is as much (if not more) grown this year as was last year, but the yield will not be so good. Though the crop is free from disease, the tuber is small in size, owing to the constant rains in June and July. However, they are very good for eating, and it is expected there will be a sufficiency of them to last through the coming season. The description generally sown is the "champion." The potato crop of last year was the best ever remembered in Ireland, and greater than was necessary to meet the requirements, and a large quantity was appropriated for cattle feeding, so that a lesser quantity will answer in the current year.

Grain Crops.—In general, are much better than last year.

Hay.—An abundant crop.

Turf.—No public turbaries; chief articles of fuel, coal and timber. There need be no apprehension of any exceptional distress in this union during the approaching winter. High prices for cattle, and remunerative prices for butter.

No. in the workhouse, ...	203
Corresponding period last year, ...	221
On outdoor relief, ...	74
Corresponding period last year, ...	47

YOUGHAL UNION—county of Cork.

Potatoes.—A very fair crop.

Oats.—A very good crop.

Green Crops.—Promise well.

Hay.—A good crop.

Turf.—Very little used in this union.

Labour.—In good demand.

No. in the workhouse, ...	237
Corresponding period last year, ...	258

BANDON UNION—county of Cork.

Potatoes.—There appears to be but one opinion, that the potato crop is not so good as that of the previous year, the produce being small, and the disease shewing itself to some extent in the old sorts; "champions" are comparatively free from the attack.

Grain Crops.—Are all considered good.

Green Crops.—Promise to be very good.

Hay.—Is abundant and well saved.

Turf.—But little made in this union.

No. in the workhouse, ...	157

MACROOM UNION—county of Cork.

Potatoes.—The potato crop in the mountain districts has proved a failure. In the inland districts the crop, though late, will be fairly good.

Oats and wheat in the mountain districts, bad crops; in the inland portions of the union, fairly good.

Hay.—Good crop, and fairly saved.

Turf.—A great effort was made during the past few weeks of fine weather to save the turf, by which a large portion was indifferently secured, and a large portion went the other way; so that the current year's firing must be supplemented by some other fuel.

Rate of Wages.—The average rate of wages paid to labourers is from 9*s.* to 12*s.* a week

No. in the workhouse,	277
Corresponding period of last year,	290
In receipt of outdoor relief,	416
Corresponding period last year,	391

DUNMANWAY UNION—county of Cork.

Potatoes and Grain Crops.—Potato crop is likely to be a fair one, but not at all so good as that of last year; still, if the weather continues for a few weeks longer equally fine, as it has been for the past fortnight, there is every prospect of a bountiful harvest, with a crop of oats far superior to that of last year. The potatoes have increased much in size during the past fortnight.

Hay.—Has been a very heavy and abundant crop, and is now well saved.

Turf.—In consequence of the late good weather, is now quite dry, so that there can be no scarcity of firing.

KINSALE UNION—county of Cork.

Potatoes.—Early potatoes not very good; later varieties promise well. The effects of blight have considerably diminished, in consequence of the recent fine weather; selling in the market at 8*d.* per 21 lb. weight.

Oats.—A good crop, and is being out at present.

Wheat.—Not largely sown.

Barley.—Much depends on the continuance of fine weather.

Hay.—An abundant crop, and well saved.

Green Crops.—Promise well, but it would be premature to give a decided opinion at present.

Turf.—Very little used; coals principally, 17*s.* per ton delivered.

Labourers' Wages.—From 2*s.* to 2*s.* 6*d.* in the town; tradesmen, from 4*s.* to 5*s.* The prospect of the immediate commencement of the construction of a large fishery pier at a cost of £18,000 will afford much additional employment for unskilled labour during the next two years.

There need be no apprehension of any exceptional distress in this union during the coming season.

No. in the workhouse,	125
Outdoor relief,	9

CLONAKILTY—county of Cork.

Potatoes.—Are very good, so far as quality is concerned, but in quantity will not exceed one-half of last year's crop.

Oats.—A fair crop.

Wheat.—Promises to be a fair crop, but not up to the average.

Barley.—Will be an indifferent crop, owing to the heavy rains during June and July.

Green Crops.—Turnips and mangolds look well, and promise to be a fair crop.

Hay.—A good crop.

Turf.—Not much used in the union; the supply will be abundant.

Wages.—Labourers are paid 8s. to 9s. per week; permanent farm labourers receive from 3s. to 6s. per week, and, in addition, a house. No reason for apprehending that there will be any destitution among the permanent farm labourers; but some distress may probably be felt during the winter by the labourers who reside in the town, as after the harvest operations are over there will not be much employment for them.

No. in the workhouse,	284
Corresponding period last year,	289

LISMORE UNION—county of Waterford.

Potatoes.—The early crop was greatly injured by the rains of June and July. The late varieties, such as "champions," magnum bonums, promise to be a fair crop, and have up to the present resisted the disease. On the whole, it is not expected that the yield will exceed two-thirds of last year's. The present price in the market is 9*d.* per weight of 21 lbs.; the price last year at this period was 6*d.*

Oats.—Will be an average crop.

Wheat.—Will be below the average in yield, owing to the heavy rains which fell in the beginning of July.

Barley.—Not much grown in this union; will be up to the average of other seasons.

Green Crops.—Though late in making growth, owing to the cold and wet spring, will be an average crop.

Hay.—Rye-grass was a heavy crop, but was injured very much in quality by the wet weather at time of saving. Late meadows and upland hay, a heavy crop, and saved in prime condition, which will in a great measure make up for the loss in quality of the early hay crop.

Turf.—What little turf was cut is not half dried; coal is generally burned in all parts of the union.

DUNGARVAN UNION—county of Waterford.

Potatoes.—Blighted in many places, including "champions" in some localities, so that the keeping qualities of the crops are not expected to be good.

Oats.—Good beyond the average.

Wheat.—Slightly touched in some places.

Green Crops.—Very good.

Hay.—Abundant, but not of very good quality.

Turf.—This being a seaport town, turf is very little used.

KILMACTHOMAS UNION—county of Waterford.

Potatoes.—Crop seriously injured by the constant rain in the months of June and July. As compared with last year, the quantity will average about one-half.

Oats.—Promises to be a very abundant crop.

Wheat.—An average crop.

Barley.—Not grown in this locality.

Hay.—A heavy crop, all saved and secured.

Turf.—Not used, except in the immediate vicinity of turf-bogs, and to a very limited extent.

Wages.—Agricultural labourers, about 10*s.* a week.

No. in workhouse, ...	174
Last year, ...	232

KILMALLOCK UNION—county of Limerick.

Potatoes.—The early crop suffered greatly, in consequence of the constant wet weather—not half the usual yield; but the "champions," the principal potato sown, promises to be a fair crop, but not near so good as last year.

Oats.—Will be good, if there be two or three weeks more fine weather.

Wheat.—Very poor, but there is not much of it sown in the union.

Green Crops.—Are light up to the present, but they have still sufficient time to improve if we get fine weather.

Hay.—The crop was very heavy, but the quality not so very good, owing to the continued rain while saving it.

Turf.—No turbary in this part of the country.

Cattle.—Bringing fabulous prices.

Butter.—There has been a good make of butter; prices remunerative.

Wages.—Good wages at present, and plenty of work—2*s.* 6*d.* per day.

No. in the workhouse, ...	613
Corresponding period last year, ...	597

On a review of the whole surroundings in the unions under my charge, I am strongly disposed to believe, both from inquiry and my own personal observation, that there is no ground for apprehension of distress or scarcity in the coming year beyond the ordinary pressure of the necessitous classes. Every portion of my district promises more than an average good harvest, and the hopes of all classes are sanguine on this point. Although the early potatoes suffered considerably, the late varieties, "champions," magnum bonums, &c., are in excellent condition. Oats, an unusually large crop; barley, a heavy crop, but will require a continuance of fine weather, to enable it to escape lodging and discoloration. Green crops promise well in every part of my district; hay, a heavy crop, is being saved in good condition, and although a portion of the early crop suffered from the rains which fell at the time of saving, all admit that a little loss can well be borne. The want of turf will not be felt except in a portion of one of my unions, as coal is almost altogether used in the several unions in my district, and procurable at moderate prices. The farmers are getting almost fabulous prices for their cattle, and remunerative prices for their dairy produce but are not giving much employment to the labouring classes, as they manage, with the members of their families, to do the ordinary farm work.

I have the honour to remain, gentlemen,

Your obedient servant,

T. BRODIE.

REPORT from Mr. R. HAMILTON.—DISTRICT comprising the COUNTIES of ANTRIM, ARMAGH, and DOWN, and parts of LONDONDERRY, LOUTH, and TYRONE.

August 23rd, 1882.

GENTLEMEN,—In compliance with the instructions contained in your letter of the 4th inst., I have made inquiry regarding the state of the potato crop—the condition of the turf where it is cut, and the prospects of the general harvest in the several unions of my district, and I now send a statement giving the substance of the information I have received from each union—arranged by counties.

It will be seen, that the reports from all quarters represent the potato crop of this year as considerably below an average—the continuous wet during the month of July, seriously injured the crop—and in most kinds the disease appeared much earlier than usual. The "Champions," however, seem up to the present to have, comparatively speaking, escaped, and, as they are largely grown, I am in hopes the general yield may be better than is anticipated, but it is quite too soon to be able to form anything like a definite opinion on this point, as so much depends on the season—or on the weather.

The reports on the prospects of the general harvest are favourable—and, with fair harvest weather, good grain crops may be expected—but cutting has not yet generally commenced.

Turf is not much used as fuel in this district. Where it is cut, I am informed the prospect of the crop is much improved by the dry weather of this month, but a large portion of it still remains unsecured.

I have the honour to be, gentlemen, your obedient servant,

R. HAMILTON.

The Local Government Board, Dublin.

COUNTY ANTRIM.

Belfast Union.—Potato crop—Late kinds—an average—disease prevalent.

Lisburn Union.—Potato crop—below an average as regards quantity and quality—blighted in several places.

Prospects of general harvest—favourable—Green crops—good—Flax—an average crop.

Antrim Union.—Potato crop—short—especially in heavy lands—at least one-third under last year's crop. Prospects of general harvest—good—A fair supply of turf expected where it is cut.

Larne Union.—Potato crop—considerably below the average—and extensively diseased—Prospects of general harvest—good.

Ballymena Union.—Potato crop—deficient, and disease prevalent—Prospects of general harvest—fair—Turf generally saved.

Ballymoney Union.—Potato crop—deficient and disease rapidly spreading—Prospects of general harvest—fair—Turf not yet saved.

Ballycastle Union.—Potato crop—worst for many years past—Prospects of general harvest—fair in dry land—but bad in wet land—Condition of turf—unsatisfactory.

COUNTY DOWN.

Downpatrick Union.—Potato crop—inferior, and greatly blighted—Prospects of general harvest—good.

Kilkeel Union.—Potato crop—fair—Prospects of general harvest—good.

Newtownards Union.—Potato crop—fair—early kinds blighted—later kinds, still safe—Prospects of general harvest—good.

Banbridge Union.—Potato crop—deficient—General harvest—an average.

COUNTY ARMAGH.

Armagh Union.—Potato crop—below an average—Prospects of general harvest—fair.

Newry Union.—Potato crop—very deficient in quantity and in quality—Prospect of general harvest—fair.

Lurgan Union.—Potato crop—deficient in quantity and quality—The wheat crop injured by wet weather—but oat crop promises to be fair.

COUNTY LOUTH.

Dundalk Union.—Potato crop—inferior—early kind much diseased—"Champions" remain sound—Prospects of general harvest very good indeed.

COUNTY DERRY.

Magherafelt Union.—Potato crop—considerably under an average—Prospects of general harvest—favourable—Condition of turf—improved.

COUNTY TYRONE.

Cookstown Union.—Potato crop—More than one-third under that of last year—and much diseased—"Champions" remain sound—Prospects of general harvest—good in high grounds—bad in low-lying districts—A fair supply of turf now expected.

B. HAMILTON.

August 23rd, 1882.

REPORT of Mr. W. HAMILTON.—DISTRICT comprising the COUNTY of KILKENNY and parts of the COUNTIES of CARLOW, LIMERICK, TIPPERARY, WATERFORD, and WEXFORD.

Fiddown, August 22, 1882.

GENTLEMEN,—In accordance with the instructions in your letter of the 4th inst., I have made inquiry regarding the state of the potato crop in my district; the prospects of the general harvest, and the condition of the turf where it is cut; and I now beg to send herewith, abstracts of the replies, arranged by counties.

Portions of the unions are in two or three counties, in which cases, I have classed the unions in that county in which its largest area is.

There is a general concurrence of testimony, so far as it is as yet possible to judge, to the effect that, excepting under favourable circumstances as to soil, seed, culture, &c., the potato crop of 1882 will be much inferior to that of 1881, even supposing the weather henceforth to be all that is desired.

The general harvest, thus far, promises as regards the oat crop, and hay crop, to be remarkably good, notwithstanding that the early hay crop was saved under the difficulties of low temperature, and a succession of wet and sunless days, and some of it was more or less damaged. The wheat crop, if it can be saved, will be nothing particular either one way or the other; the barley crop will probably be a fair average. Green crops generally, if not very promising just now, may be much improved by fine genial weather. Grass has been very abundant.

With respect to fuel, this district is so dependent on coal and culm, that it is exceptional to find turf in any other than Thurles and Urlingford Unions, and portions of the Unions of Cashel, Clogheen, and Clonmel.

It may be worthy of question, whether, if turf were cut in the months of March and April, the chances of saving it would not be less precarious; as it was, the wet months of June and July sadly interfered with this year's supply.

I cannot conclude this report without referring to the almost unchecked growth of weeds, which, I should think, must strike any person travelling through the country, whose eyes have not become accustomed to such a serious and increasing evil.

I have the honour to be, gentlemen, your obedient servant,

W. J. Hamilton.

The Local Government Board (Ireland).

Abstracts referred to in foregoing Report.

I.—County of Kilkenny, Unions of *Callan, Castlecomer, Kilkenny, Thomastown, Urlingford.*

No. 1. What is the state of the potato crop in your locality?

The early kinds generally affected, the late kinds not nearly as good as last year; but where there has been good seed and good tillage, if the weather continue favourable there may be a tolerably good crop.

No. 2. What is the state of the general harvest as regards—

Wheat?—Wheat generally good, but in some localities, indifferent.

Oats?—A very promising crop, more than three times greater in extent than the wheat crop.

Barley?—A fairly good crop.

Green Crops, &c.?—Too many exceptions to warrant any sanguine expectations, but a good deal still depends on the weather.

No. 3. What are the prospects as to the supply of turf this season?

Urlingford Union is the only one in this county in which turf is still much used. Culm and coal are chiefly, if not exclusively, used in the other Unions. In Urlingford Union, an average supply of turf has not yet been saved.

II.—County of Tipperary, Unions of *Carrick-on-Suir, Cashel, Clogheen, Clonmel, Thurles, Tipperary.*

No. 1. What is the state of the potato crop in your locality?

The early kinds much injured by blight—the general crop does not promise nearly as well as last year; the inclement weather had an injurious effect on it. It is as yet too soon to speculate as to what the ultimate yield will be; an unusually large extent of ground was planted this year, and fine weather may yet improve the crop.

No. 2. What is the state of the general harvest as regards—

Wheat?—This crop is not very extensively grown in the S. Riding of the county Tipperary, on the whole it is not so good a crop as last year. Some of it lodged during the high winds and heavy rains—the straw generally is heavy, but, in some localities, the grain is deficient in quantity and quality.

Oats?—The oat crop in this county is nearly double the wheat and barley crop added together, it is generally represented as an excellent crop.

Barley?—This crop slightly exceeds the wheat crop in extent; in many portions of the S. Riding it is not much grown; where grown, it is generally represented as good, but there are numerous exceptions.

Green Crops, &c.?—Green crops generally late, scarcely up to an average crop in some places; where sown in good time, and well cultivated, the prospects are fair, but there are several complaints, and unless the weather be suitable there will not be as good crops of turnips, mangolds, carrots, &c., as last year. There has been abundance of grass, and the meadows were unusually heavy, but a good deal of the hay crop was saved under difficulties, and some of it was more or less injured.

No. 3. What are the prospects as to the supply of turf this season?

Thurles Union, and portions of the Unions of Cashel, Clogheen, and Clonmel, depend to some extent on turf, and this year owing to the difficulty of saving it, it is as yet generally indifferent in quality, and short in supply. Some of the poorer classes in these Unions, who have either scarcely any other kind of fuel to depend on, or who support themselves by the sale of turf, will, I apprehend, suffer, unless they can succeed in saving a late crop.

III.—County of Waterford, Union of *Waterford.*

No. 1. What is the state of the potato crop in your locality?

Not generally as good as last year. Some of the earlier kinds inferior in quantity and quality; prices much higher than last year; fair account of the champions in new ground where suitably manured and well cultivated.

No. 2. What is the state of the general harvest as regards—

Wheat?—Generally fair where not lodged, but there are some complaints of smut. The wet season has been against this crop.

Oats?—This crop is nearly four times as large as the wheat crop. It has been a good crop.

Barley?—Very little barley grown in the County Waterford, not one-twentieth part of the oat crop in extent. What there is, is generally represented as good.

Green Crops, &c.?—Where early, well tilled, and well manured, on upland ground, they are fair. Very large crop of hay, but some of it not well saved; much still depends on the weather.

No. 3. What are the prospects as to the supply of turf this season?

There is scarcely any used in Waterford Union. Even supposing that bogs were available, coals at 15s. a ton would be cheaper than turf could be produced at.

IV.—County of Wexford, Unions of *Enniscorthy, New Ross, Wexford.*

No. 1. What is the state of the potato crop in your locality?

The yield generally is inferior to that of last year. The champions are almost the only variety which appear hitherto to have resisted the disease—as yet they appear to be fairly good—but other sorts, generally represented as indifferent, and sometimes bad.

No. 2. What is the state of the general harvest as regards—

Wheat?—Not much wheat grown in this county. Generally good, but complaints in some localities of blight or smut.

Oats?—Oats a good crop and promise well so far.

Barley?—Barley a fair average crop. Largely grown in the County Wexford; last year it very nearly equalled the oat crop in extent, either of which crops was five times as great in extent as wheat.

Beans?—Very nearly 6,000 acres were under beans last year, and this year there is probably as large a crop, and a very fine one to all appearance.

Green Crops, &c.?—Very fair as yet, but some complaints of turnips and mangolds. Grass abundant, and a large crop of hay, but some of it badly saved.

No. 3. What are the prospects as to the supply of turf this season?

Coal and culm generally used in this county, scarcely any turf used.

REPORT from Dr. MACCABE.—DISTRICT comprising the COUNTIES of DUBLIN and WICKLOW, and parts of the COUNTIES of KILDARE, MEATH, CARLOW, QUEEN'S COUNTY, and WEXFORD.

Dublin, 20th August, 1882.

SIR,—In reply to your letter of the 4th instant, I have the honour to forward herewith a report upon the harvest prospects in the unions and counties in my district arranged for convenience of reference in a tabular form, and I think it well to submit a short summary as to the general results of my inspections and inquiries from Clerks of Unions, Collectors of Poor Rate, and Relieving Officers.

I beg in the first place to observe that the character of the general harvest will depend to a very great extent upon the weather from the date of this report until about the middle of September. The only counties in my district in which corn has so far been cut are Dublin, Kildare, and Wexford, and in these only to a small extent.

Potatoes.—The accounts on the whole are not favourable. The "Champions" and "Magnums" so far promise well, but the rains of July have caused premature decay of the leaves and stalks of other varieties with consequent arrest of development in the tubers, which although generally numerous are small. Blight has been reported to me from various quarters, but I have not seen any true blight. The crop I am satisfied will be very much inferior to that of last year.

Cereals, all promise well with the exception of Barley, a great deal of which has lodged in consequence of the rains of July; this is particularly the case in the Union of Athy.

Hay.—This is an unusually abundant crop. Early meadows have not been well saved. Late meadows have been properly saved. The aftergrass is exceptionally good and of excellent fattening quality.

Green Crops on the whole are good throughout my district.

Turf is expected to be scarce during the coming winter. What has been saved is not of good quality owing to rain; and during the last few weeks, when turf might have been cut under favourable circumstances, labourers have been busy on more pressing work connected with the hay and green crops.

The tabular return sent herewith presents a synopsis of the various reports received from the local observers consulted, but I have to add that my own inspections would have inclined me to express more favourable, but perhaps less trustworthy, conclusions than those embodied in the tables.

I have the honour to remain, Sir,

Your obedient servant,

F. X. MACCABE,

Local Government Board Inspector.

To the Secretary,
Local Government Board.

[TABLE.

Dublin District—Table accompanying Dr. MacCabe's Report of 20th August, 1882.

Unions.	Counties.	Potato Crop.
Dublin, North, . . .	Dublin, ...	Early potatoes a light crop, disease appearing. Late crop promises well, but shows disease.
Dublin, South, . . .	Do., ...	Fair on the whole. "Kemps" have failed. There is some disease.
Balrothery, . . .	Do., ...	Prospects of potato crop, as a rule, not favourable. "Kemps" all lost; "Scotch Downs" half lost; "Champions" show disease. Total crop below average.
Rathdown, . .	Dublin and Wicklow, . .	"Champions" good; "Kemps" light; "Scotch Downs" light and much diseased; "Magnums" light, but have escaped disease.
Athy, ...	Kildare, Queen's, and Wicklow,	"Champions" good. Other varieties fair.
Celbridge, . . .	Kildare and Dublin, . .	Every indication of *failure*. It is believed the crop will be small and inferior.
Naas, ...	Kildare and Wicklow, . .	"Kemps" and "Flounders" bad; "Champions" promise very well.
Dunshaughlin, .	Meath and Dublin, . . .	Not much disease, but tubers are small.
Carlow, .	Carlow and Queen's, . .	Potatoes much inferior to last year; not expected to exceed half a crop.
Baltinglass, . . .	Wicklow, Carlow, and Kildare,	Reports not unfavourable.
Rathdrum, . . .	Wicklow, ...	Signs of disease apparent, but, on the whole, an average crop expected.
Shillelagh, . . .	Wicklow and Carlow, . .	An average crop expected.
Gorey, ...	Wexford, ...	Potatoes are stated to be abundant and good.

(continued)

Dublin District—TABLE accompanying DR. MACCABE'S REPORT of 20th August, 1882—*continued.*

Unions.	Counties.	Cereals.	Hay Crop.	Green Crops.
DUBLIN, NORTH, .	Dublin, . .	Wheat, fair; oats, good; barley, good.	Good produce and well saved.	Good.
DUBLIN, SOUTH, .	Do. . .	All the cereals promise well.	Abundant, but some has not been well saved. Aftergrass unusually good.	Good.
BALROTHERY, .	Do. . .	Wheat, oats, and barley magnificent.	Very plentiful; a very small quantity damaged. Aftergrass unusually good.	Fair average.
RATHDOWN, .	Dublin and Wicklow.	Wheat, light; oats, good; barley, average.	A good crop, but in some instances not well saved.	Fair.
ATHY, . . .	Kildare, Queen's and Wicklow.	Cereals promise to exceed the average. Oats, magnificent. Barley has suffered by late rains and is much lodged.	Unusually large yield; quality of early crop bad owing to rain.	Good.
CELBRIDGE, . .	Kildare and Dublin.	Wheat, good; oats, remarkably good; barley, no complaints so far.	Abundant, but somewhat injured by rain.	Good.
NAAS, . . .	Kildare and Wicklow.	Wheat, good; oats, very fine; barley, very good.	Splendid crop and much is well saved. Aftergrass very fine.	Good.
DUNSHAUGHLIN, .	Meath and Dublin.	Very little tillage in this Union	A most abundant crop, but somewhat injured by wet.	Good.
CARLOW, . . .	Carlow and Queen's.	Wheat, middling; oats, good and heavy, better than for some years; barley, on the whole, fair.	On the whole good, but early hay not well saved.	Mangolds, fair; turnips, not good.
BALTINGLASS, .	Wicklow, Carlow, and Kildare.	Wheat and barley, good; oats, very good.	Very abundant, but not well saved.	Fair.
RATHDRUM, .	Wicklow, . .	On the whole the cereal crops will yield an average return.	A full crop, and most of it well saved.	Average.
SHILLELAGH, .	Wicklow and Carlow.	Up to the average. .	Good, ...	Good.
GOREY, . . .	Wexford, . .	Spring oats, bad; winter oats, fair; wheat and barley, doubtful; yield depends on weather.	Abundant, . . .	Good.

[continued.

Dublin District—Table accompanying Dr. MacCabe's Report of 20th August, 1882.—*continued.*

Unions.	Counties.	Turf.	Observations.
Dublin, North, .	Dublin, . .	Not cut in this Union. .	All depends upon the weather from this date. (15th Aug.)
Dublin, South, .	Do., . .	Where cut it is about an average.	All depends upon the weather for the next few weeks. (18 Aug.)
Balrothery, .	Do., . .	No turf bogs in this Union.	Harvest prospects very cheering if the weather holds good. (17 Aug.)
Rathdown, .	Dublin and Wicklow.	Fair; average quantity saved.	Harvest prospects, on the whole, very encouraging. (17 Aug.)
Athy, . . .	Kildare, Queen's, and Wicklow.	Cutting interfered with by rain; what is saved is inferior in quality.	Harvest has begun; all depends upon the weather for the next few weeks. (17 Aug.)
Celbridge, . .	Kildare and Dublin.	Not well saved; will be scarce and inferior.	All depends upon the weather from the 17th Aug.
Naas, ...	Kildare and Wicklow.	On the whole the reports are fair as to the quantity cut and saved.	All depends upon the weather for the next three or four weeks. (18th Aug.)
Dunshaughlin, .	Meath and Dublin.	Not cut or used in this Union.	This Union almost wholly occupied by grazing farms.
Carlow, . .	Carlow and Queen's.	Very little turf saved owing to rain.	If the weather holds good for a few weeks, I think the harvest will be better than the reports of local observers would lead one to infer. [F. M., 19th Aug.]
Baltinglass, .	Wicklow, Carlow, and Kildare.	Not well saved, . . .	—
Rathdrum, . .	Wicklow, . .	Supply rather short and in bad condition.	—
Shillelagh, .	Wicklow and Carlow.	More than an average quantity cut, but it is in a backward state and requires dry weather.	More than an average yield of all crops may be expected if the weather holds good. (17th Aug.)
Gorey, . . .	Wexford, . .	Very little turf cut in this Union.	I am disposed to think better than my informants of the harvest prospects in this Union. (F. M., 19th Aug.)

REPORT from Mr. MACFARLANE.—DISTRICT comprising parts of the COUNTIES of DONEGAL, LONDONDERRY, and TYRONE.

Gweedore, 23rd August, 1882.

SIR,—In accordance with your letter of 4th inst., stating that His Excellency the Lord Lieutenant is desirous to be furnished with information as to the Harvest prospects this year, and the condition of the Turf where cut; and that the Local Government Board wish to have a report from me, on these matters in my district, I therefore beg to submit as follows :—

My district, extending over the Counties of Londonderry and Donegal, with portions of Antrim and Tyrone, comprises great variety of soil and modes of cultivation, from the superior deep upland loam, and well drained rich alluvial lands, occupied by a most intelligent, industrious class of farmers, using the most approved modern machinery; in the Counties of Londonderry and Tyrone, and borders of Antrim, and even in portions of *Donegal*, to the heavy clays, underlying bog cut away, but generally undrained *in that county*, where a large proportion of the land under crop, is the poorest of thin peaty soils, so intermingled with stones and rocks, as to be of necessity cultivated by the spade, and this labour is not always industriously or continuously applied at the most advantageous periods; such land, when uncultivated or allowed to run out for grazing, only produces some grass and a large proportion of aquatic plants and rushes. This district having a great deal of mountain, (more or less near) the harvest prospects, under such circumstances are also varied, as they depend, not only on the actual quantity of rainfall annually, but on the number of rainy and sunless days, during the months of July and August, which also varies within comparatively short distances, according to the height and position of the neighbouring mountains, so much, that I have long since desired to have a rain-gauge at every National School and Police Barrack, to obtain some reliable statistics on such an important subject. In the rich well-cultivated lands, the Corn and Hay suffered some injury from the wet weather in July, but not to any appreciable extent. In the more remote parts, where the only corn crop is Oats, which, being lighter, and later in growth, was not thus *injured*, except where sown on wet, undrained lands, rendered colder by the extra rain, it will yield less, but all cultivators of the soil, had valuable compensation for the broken weather of July, from the *uninterrupted fine weather* which prevailed for several days *consecutively*, previous to the 12th of August, and which was taken advantage of most energetically by all classes of farmers. The Hay harvest, in the early districts was completed most satisfactorily, and it enabled those growing Clovers, and Artificial Grasses, to thresh their seeds in the field. Great progress was also made in saving turf, cut previously in the broken weather. In nearly all the district, the turf was dried and gathered into small clamps, in many places it was stacked, and a great deal has been carted home.

One energetic farmer told me he had cut, what is termed "A Second Crop" of turf, as others also might have done, who had not flax or a large hay crop to attend to. I have therefore every reason to expect there will be a good supply of turf fuel. The Potato crop alone causes anxiety from the exaggerated, and as I ascertained in some cases quite unfounded reports, as to the extent of the disease which appeared on the leaves and stalks, and with the earlier and more delicate kinds, on the tubers. Thus, Flounders, Regents, Kemps, Clusters, Skerries, Kidneys, grown for early use, have, in many places, been very much diseased, but the *general crop* which consists of *Champions*, and in Donegal, a proportion of *Lumpers*, though showing some indication of disease on the leaves, which, if it spreads to the stalk will check growth, and thus interfere with that maturity, which so much determines the quality of the potato for table use, *are not yet so affected.*

There is another kind of potato which is grown for use in April and May, when Champions are not so good to eat—viz., Brown and White Rocks. These have a percentage of disease on the tubers, but not of any extent. One man who told me he had no disease whatever yet in his Champions, had five per cent. of Rocks diseased, but said that was so trifling, and these potatoes are so good and marketable in the latter end of April and May, till the new potatoes come in, he would grow them still next year as well as Champions. As this latter potato occupies quite *five-sixths* of the land under potatoes, I made special inquiry, and, *up to this day,* I could not obtain *any distinct case of a single Champion potato having disease on the tuber,* notwithstanding the strongest assertion to the contrary. If the present wet weather continues, the disease, which in some places appears on the leaf, may go on to the stalk, and subsequently, in cold soils undrained, the tubers may become affected; but, even under such continuous adverse circumstances, I do not fear any large percentage of loss from disease with the Champion potato, which is the general crop.

The crop of potatoes last year, in the opinion of every practical farmer I have spoken to exceeded in weight and quality any potato crop for thirty years, and the oat crop was also unusually prolific. Thus, the crops of this year, which, even under the most favourable circumstances, are not likely to be so good, suffer by comparison in the estimation of the grower, especially as regards the potato, he is disappointed. Being so prolific last year, fowl, pigs, cows and horses, were fed on them, and a large quantity of these potatoes exported from Londonderry to America; and yet, at the end of the season, a large quantity kept over too long, expecting a rise in price, were thrown out rotten, as Champions do not keep well if not closely attended to. It has been suggested that some of the Champions which exhibit the appearance of disease on the leaves were the produce of seed which were selected out of pits in which the potatoes send out luxuriant buds early in the year *heated*, and thus the tubers picked out for seed were less vigorous to resist disease; but, unless this appearance of disease spreads, and goes down to the tuber with more virulence than I could at present anticipate, I have no serious apprehension of the results. It may not be out of place to remark that the high price of cattle of all kinds, ages, and sexes, appears to have a beneficial effect on the small occupier; he is now rearing all calves, instead of selling the bulls to the butcher, and only rearing the heifers. The fear of American competition, as regards a lower price for cattle, has quite passed away from the continuous high price for the young stock reared by the small occupier the last two years. I may, perhaps, add that I see a marked improvement in the appearance of the small farmer and his family. Yesterday, a steamer from Sligo to Glasgow lay to off Burtonport to receive the last contingent of men going to Scotland for the harvest; a friend with me said about forty boats were in requisition. I had previously met a large number going to Derry, to embark for the north of England, from this district, "*The lasses,*" accompanied a certain distance by friends on horseback; and they all appeared extremely clean and well dressed. Some of these had remained behind to assist in having the turf saved before thus leaving for Scotland or England to earn money wages.

I am, sir, your obedient servant,

H. J. MacFarlane,
Local Government Inspector.

To the Secretary,
Local Government Board, Dublin.

REPORT from Mr. POWER.—DISTRICT comprising the COUNTY of KERRY, and part of the COUNTY of CORK.

Killarney, 24th August, 1882.

GENTLEMEN,—In accordance with instructions conveyed in your letter of the 4th August last, I may state that I have made inquiry in my district as to the state of the potato crop, the condition of the turf where it is cut, and as to the prospects of the general harvest, and I beg to report as follows, taking each Union in my district separately:—

Listowel Union.—Potato crop variable in this Union; altogether a fair crop, but less in quantity than last year, some of the old seed giving way in the ground. Hay, a fair crop. Oats, a fair average crop. Green crops are good, all the corn crops promising; altogether a fair average harvest. Sufficient turf saved for the requirements of the winter.

Tralee Union.—Potatoes, a fair crop, but not equal to that of last year, the potatoes being small. Hay is well saved. Corn crops fair, and green crops looking well. Probably sufficient turf will be saved for the requirements of the winter.

Dingle Union.—Potatoes not so large as last year, nor so abundant in quantity, but quite as good. Hay, an average crop, the greater portion saved and in good condition. The corn and green crops promise very well, and the yield is expected to be above the average. A sufficient supply of turf.

Killarney Union.—Potato crop, below that of last year; hay well saved; oats and corn crops promising. Green crops also look well, and there is sufficient turf saved in the Union.

Cahirciveen Union.—The potato crop in this Union is variable, in some places it is inferior both in quality and quantity. In other parts of the Union, especially where champions have been sown, the crop is considered a fair average one. Corn not much grown, but what there is is very good. Oats good; and green crops satisfactory. Hay crop also good; and a sufficiency of turf saved.

Kanturk Union.—Potatoes, a fair average crop about one-third less than last year. Oats very good. Wheat and barley slightly damaged, not much sown in this district. Hay crop, unusually heavy and in fair condition. Green crops looking very well and likely to give a good return. Sufficient turf saved for the winter.

Millstreet Union.—There is a deficiency in the potato crop as compared with that of last year. The oat crop is good and equal to that of last year; wheat not so good; green crops looking well; hay crop good. Sufficient quantity of turf saved.

Kenmare Union.—A fair crop of potatoes, but not so good as last year, the potatoes being smaller. Hay well saved. Corn crops good; green crops not so favourably spoken of; turf sufficiently saved and of good quality.

Bantry Union.—Potatoes somewhat deficient in quantity, and small, considerably less than last year's crop. Wheat, oats and barley, promising; abundance of hay; and turf well saved for the requirements of the winter.

Skull Union.—The potato crop below that of last year. Corn crop may be an average one. Green crops good. Hay abundant. Turf is saved, and, with the usual addition of coal, will be sufficient for the winter.

Skibbereen Union.—The account of the potatoes in this Union not quite so promising. The potatoes are small and somewhat deficient in quantity. Oats a good crop, better than last year. Wheat—very little sown in this Union, a poor crop. Barley—good, not much sown. Green crops promising; and turf sufficient to meet the usual requirements.

Castletown-Berehaven.—It is said about one-third, if not more, of the potato crop will be lost in this Union. Hay a fair average crop. Corn crops, wheat and oats, of which there are much sown in this Union, fair. Green crops good. The turf saved will be sufficient to last through the winter, with the usual addition of coal.

In the several Unions in my District, occupying the whole of the County of Kerry and a considerable portion of West Cork, the general prospects of the harvest may be said to be favourable.

The potato crop however has shown itself variable in different localities and generally below that of last year's crop, both in quantity and quality. Where disease has shown itself, the champions appear to have resisted better than other varieties. Along the south and west coast the blight made its appearance, but the fears that were entertained have not been realized to any great extent. As to the general harvest, of course a good deal yet depends on the weather, which I am sorry to say at present is not favourable.

I am, gentlemen, your obedient servant,

W. A. Power.

To the Local Government Board.

Report from Mr. Robinson.—District comprising the County of Mayo, and part of the County of Galway.

Westport, 23rd August, 1882.

Gentlemen,—From information which I have obtained from reliable sources and from my own personal observations, I have the honour to furnish you with the following report as to the prospects of the harvest throughout my district.

The continued rains have had a marked and detrimental effect on the early potatoes, and nearly everywhere they were diseased and unfit for use. In my district, however, the proportion of this variety of potato which is planted, is an exceedingly small one, and a temporary scarcity of food among some of the poorer classes was the only result of the failure of this crop.

The Champions and other field crops, owing to the absence of warm weather, are very backward and not yet fit to be consumed.

There was very little growth of the tubers in July, and, although during the month of August they increased somewhat in size, still there has been little or no ripening weather.

In the few localities where the Champions are being dug there promises to be an average return. The crop looks healthy, though there is a little blight observable on the leaves.

At present, however, it is difficult to give any reliable information as to the probable yield. If this wet and stormy weather continues, the disease will be likely to spread, and if, on the contrary, it is succeeded by a few weeks of heat, there is every reason to believe that the crop will not be below the average.

The oat crop and other cereals generally look well throughout the country. The oats are short, but the head is well filled. The recent storms have been laying this crop in many places, but not to a very alarming extent, and if we have now a little hot weather, I think the returns of all cereals in this district will not show an unfavourable comparison with the average of other years.

There has been a fair supply of turf saved, and I do not think there are any grounds for apprehension on the score of a scarcity of fuel during the coming winter.

Just at present the condition of all the crops is somewhat critical, as so much depends on the weather during the next three weeks.

The people in most parts of my district speak gloomily enough of the prospect, some of them opining that there will not be half a crop, and others that the crop is utterly lost.

All these opinions, however, are mere surmises. The crops look well, but beyond this nothing can be said. It will be impossible before October next to lay before your Board a report on the subject which could be of much value, and until that time, too much credence should not be placed on any information on this subject which may be forthcoming.

I have the honour to be, gentlemen,

Your most obedient servant,

H. A. Robinson, Inspector.

The Local Government Board, Dublin.

Report from Dr. Roughan.—District comprising parts of the Counties of Clare, Galway, Roscommon, and Westmeath.

Maretimo, Galway, August 25, 1882.

Gentlemen,—I have the honour to acknowledge the receipt of your letter of the 4th August, informing me that you had received a communication from the Under Secretary to the Lord Lieutenant, in which he states that His Excellency is desirous to be furnished with information as to the harvest prospects this year, and the condition of the turf where it is cut, and further directing me to make inquiry regarding the potato crop in my district, the condition of the turf where it is cut, and the prospects of the general harvest, and report to you on the subject.

In accordance with these instructions I have to report that owing to the continued wet and stormy weather the yield from the potatoes will not be as good or abundant as last year's. The Champion is still ripening and only shows a very partial sign of disease, so little that it will not materially interfere with the quantity or I believe the quality. The worst reports that reach me come from Ballyvaghan Union in the County Clare, and Glennamaddy Union in the north-east of Galway.

The turf is not as dry or as well saved as could be wished owing to the incessant rains, but if the weather takes up a little the people will be able to save as much as will carry them through the winter and into spring.

The corn crop is now stacked and in well kept haggards is proof against climate.

The hay after much difficulty has been saved, and though deteriorated in quality by rain will form good wholesome food for cattle.

The green crops, including turnips, mangolds, &c., are in a very prosperous state, and will form useful articles for feeding the poor man's cattle, &c.

I have the honour to be, gentlemen,

Your obedient servant,

George F. Boughan.

Report from Major Spaight.—District comprising the Counties of Sligo and Leitrim, and parts of the Counties of Donegal, Fermanagh, and Roscommon.

Ardaghowen, Sligo, August 22nd, 1882.

Gentlemen,—I have the honour to report with reference to your letter of the 4th instant, that I have made close and careful inquiries in all parts of my district, with regard to the state of the potato crop, the condition of the turf, and the prospects of the general harvest.

All the earlier potatoes have suffered severely from blight, in many parts of my district being almost wholly destroyed, and a half crop will be a very large estimate to put down for this class.

The main hope of all now rests upon the Champion potatoes, and much will depend on the weather during the next few weeks. In the cold wet lands, and heavy clay soils, the crop was this season, necessarily very late and without some dry and warm weather now, must prove a bad one.

In light dry and gravel soils the crop was planted earlier, and here there may be an average crop, but there seems no grounds to hope that it can by any weather changes, become a bountiful one.

Oats are a good average crop in all parts of my district. Very little other cereals are grown, but where they are, they promise well.

Hay is a very abundant crop, and there is a far larger area of land in meadow this season than has perhaps been known before, particularly in the county Roscommon. This can I think be principally accounted for by the great reduction in the number of stock in the country, large tracts of land usually stocked are now almost devoid of stock, and others only half stocked.

The price of store cattle is as a consequence very high, and beyond the reach of small farmers and poor men.

As to the condition of the turf, the fine weather of the past three weeks has, in many parts of my district, averted a fuel famine. Up to that time the turf which should have been saved in May last was lying in pulp upon the ground; it is now in most places in fair condition, and with a little more dry weather I do not anticipate any scarcity.

Of course in a district such as mine the condition of the people and the crops varies very much in the different parts of it, but on the whole I am of opinion that there will not be any perceptible increase or decrease in the amount of relief it will be necessary to afford during the coming year.

I have the honour to be, gentlemen,

Your obedient servant,

George Spaight.

The Local Government Board, Dublin.

Local Government Board, Dublin,
31st August, 1882.

SIR, With reference to your minutes of the 2nd and 3rd instant, communicating the desire of His Excellency the Lord Lieutenant, that the Local Government Board for Ireland would obtain from their Inspectors, for His Excellency's information, Reports as to the harvest prospects this year, and the condition of the turf in districts where it is cut, the Board have now the honour to forward to you two copies of Reports which they have received from the several District Inspectors regarding the state of the potato crop, the condition of the turf, where it is cut, and as to the prospects of the general harvest.

By order of the Board,
W. D. WODSWORTH, Assistant Secretary.

To R. G. C. Hamilton, Esq., &c., &c.,
Dublin Castle.

No. 2.—SUPPLEMENTAL REPORTS from INSPECTORS on the GENERAL HARVEST PROSPECTS.

Local Government Board, Dublin,
8th September, 1882.

SIR,—With reference to your recent report on the state of the potato crop, the condition of the turf where it is cut, and the prospects of the general harvest, in your district, the Local Government Board for Ireland desire to acquaint you that your Report having been communicated to His Excellency the Lord Lieutenant, the Board have now received a communication from the Assistant Under Secretary requesting them to instruct their Inspectors to report again on the subject at the beginning of October.

The Board accordingly request that you will make a further Report to them on the subject, for His Excellency's information, at the beginning of the month of October.

By order of the Board,
(Signed), B. BANKS, Secretary.

To each Inspector.

REPORT from Mr. ARMSTRONG.—DISTRICT comprising the COUNTIES of CAVAN and MONAGHAN, and parts of FERMANAGH and TYRONE.

Corkil, Kilshorry, 13th October, 1882.

SIR,—Referring to your letter of the 8th ultimo, requesting me to furnish a further report on the potato crop, state of the turf, and general harvest prospects in my district, in addition to that furnished by me on the 21st August last, I have the honour to report, for the information of the Local Government Board and His Excellency the Lord Lieutenant, that I have been making inquiries and getting information from the most reliable sources in my power, and am of opinion, as a rule, that the potato crop will not be as bad a one as expected; in most districts there is not from a third to a half of the yield of last year, they are fairly sound, particularly champions, but of small size. The price is very high compared with last year. I heard of one acre being sold for £34. As a rule the people are very late in digging them. I am afraid the heavy rain on the 11th instant will not improve their condition; in some of the mountain districts in Omagh, Gortin, and Bawnboy Unions, the accounts are not so favourable, and this also applies to turf.

There has been a large amount of turf saved of very fair quality, though in some places rather wet. If the weather keeps fairly dry I think there will be an abundant supply.

There has been a very fair hay crop and generally well saved—in low-lying lands not so well; considerable damage was done both to hay and oats by the gale a fortnight ago.

The oat crop would have been an excellent one had it not been for the very bad weather, a large amount has been safely stacked, a considerable amount is still in stooks, but, I regret to say, during the last few days I have seen several fields uncut, the produce of which will be of little use.

There is very little wheat, rye, or barley grown through my district, the turnip crop varies very much in different localities.

I am informed the flax crop has been fair as a rule, but that the price is unusually low.

On the whole I do not expect any unusual distress or demand for relief during the ensuing winter or spring, but a great deal depends on the weather for the next fortnight or three weeks.

I have the honour to be, sir, your obedient servant,

W. Armstrong, Inspector.

The Secretary, Local Government Board.

Report from Mr. R. Bourke.—District comprising parts of the Counties of Clare, Limerick, Tipperary and King's County.

36, Elgin-road, Dublin, 19th October, 1882.

Gentlemen,—In compliance with the instructions conveyed in your letter of the 8th September, that I should make a further report for the information of His Excellency the Lord Lieutenant, at the begining of the present month regarding the harvest in my district, I issued circulars to the clerks of the several unions under my charge on the 2nd inst., requesting them to forward replies to certain queries then transmitted, and for that purpose to make such inquiries as might be in their power from Rate Collectors and members of their Boards.

The last of their replies has reached me within the last few days, and I think I cannot do better than forward a selection of them, which appear to me to afford very important and valuable information on the subject, under consideration; and I may add my opinion that the statements of the Union Clerks are entitled to marked attention as proceeding from men of great intelligence and experience, capable themselves of forming sound opinions and of discriminating between the opinions and reports of others.

The conclusions to be drawn from these statements would seem to be—

1st.—That the wheat crop is deficient in quantity, and rather inferior in the grain.

2nd.—That the oat crop has produced well, both as regards quantity and quality. But I must observe that the harvest was unusually late this year, and much corn was still exposed when the storm of Sunday, the 1st October, occurred, doing great damage and entailing much loss on small farmers in late and cold lands.

3rd.—That a serious loss has taken place from disease in the potato crop is unfortunately beyond doubt. It is variously estimated, but I think it is no exaggeration to place it at one-fourth. Besides the loss from disease, there has been partial failure in poor mountainy soil and in heavy clay lands, and even where the conditions of the soil were more favourable the yield is far less than last year, and below what has been the general return in ordinary years.

Regarding other crops I have nothing to add to the opinions expressed in my first report, nor has anything occurred to alter my views about the supply of turf which will probably turn out as sufficient as in ordinary years.

The harvest in general cannot, taking all produce into account, be reckoned an abundant one in my district, and the profits on farming are proportionately reduced. But there is full compensation in the value of stock of all kinds, and the abundance of well saved hay.

The comforts of the labouring classes may, here and there, be lessened by the shortness of the potato crop, but there is a promise of cheapness in flour during the ensuing winter, which is of more importance to their condition than anything else. And if I could look forward to plentiful employment for them, I should have little fears on their account. But judging from what has already taken place in the present year, there is but too much reason to apprehend that agricultural labour will be in bad demand, and the families of labourers will suffer accordingly.

I have the honour to be, gentlemen, your obedient servant,

R. Bourke.

The Local Government Board.

Nenagh Union.

Queries.	Replies.
1. Is the corn in your union generally gathered in?	Almost the entire.
2. Has the digging of the potato crop commenced?	Not yet.
3. What is your opinion regarding the yield of corn in your union, and its quality.	Wheat a fair average crop, but did not fill as well as was expected; average about eight barrels; oats an excellent crop, generally produce from fourteen to eighteen barrels an acre; barley very good, about sixteen barrels.
4. What now appear to be the actual facts as regards the potato crop—	
(*a.*) Is it considered a fair average crop as to quantity?	Yes, except in low wet lands, and in *mountain districts, a failure in those places.*
(*b.*) Are the tubers well grown and equal in size?	Well grown and good size, not so large as last year.
(*c.*) Has disease made much progress in the tuber?	Very slightly, not 5 per cent.
(*d.*) To what extent do you consider the crop has suffered from disease?	Not 5 per cent. when the crop was well grown, but (as before stated) in wet lands and mountain districts, there is NOT half a crop, and those of very bad quality.

QUERIES.	REPLIES.
5. Has the usual quantity of turf been drawn home in good condition?	Now in course of being drawn, the quality is good and plentiful.
6. Is the price of cattle high in your union or only moderate?	Cattle of all descriptions rules exceedingly high.
7. Are potatoes coming freely into market, and at what price are they being sold?	Coming in moderately; harvest work not being entirely completed; price 4*d.* per stone.
N.B.—Any additional remarks which may be considered of importance I shall be glad to get.	I have been credibly informed, since filling the foregoing answer, that there is *total failure* of the potatoes in the mountain localities of Curreeny, Kilcomina, and Abington.
	J. H. Sheehan, Clerk of Union.
	7th October, 1882.

Roscrea Union.

1. Is the corn in your union generally gathered in?	Yes.
2. Has the digging of the potato crop commenced?	Yes. The usual time being the second week in October.
3. What is your opinion regarding the yield of corn in your union, and its quality?	Threshing has not yet become general, but the previous estimate has not been materially changed—the straw being abundant, but the grain produce is rather lighter than had been anticipated. Quality.—Wheat* fair, barley inferior, oats good, but yield smaller.
4. What now appear to be the actual facts as regards the potato crop—	
(a.) Is it considered a fair average crop as to quantity?	One-fourth below the average.
(b.) Are the tubers well grown and equal in size?	The tubers are much smaller than last two years, which chiefly accounts for the lesser yield; but they are fairly equal in size, and of good quality.
(c.) Has disease made much progress in the tuber?	Disease does not appear to be making much progress.
(d.) To what extent do you consider the crop has suffered from disease?	About one-sixth of the crop has suffered from disease. The champion potato, heretofore considered so strong as to resist disease, has in several instances, been found tainted. This may be regarded as a sign of incipient weakness, or declension, and an argument for frequent renewal and change of seed.
5. Has the usual quantity of turf been drawn home in good condition?	The drawing home of turf has been delayed owing to the unsettled state of the weather, every effort being needed to secure the corn and hay crops. The home drawing of

QUERIES.	REPLIES.
	turf has now commenced, but large quantities are still in the bogs. No scarcity is apprehended, for notwithstanding the low price of coal this season, it has not been purchased to any appreciable extent.
6. Is the price of cattle high in your union, or only moderate?	High. In the last fair of Roscrea (9th October), which generally takes its tone from Ballinasloe, prices were highly remunerative. Large quantities of stock were offered, but many were taken home unsold, owners holding for still higher prices.
7. Are potatoes coming freely into market, and at what price are they being sold?	Markets not largely supplied—prices 5d. to 6d. per stone. Quality good.
N.B.—Any additional remarks which may be considered of importance, I shall be glad to get.	* Wheat I consider a fair crop, as I have above stated, though I have heard persons say the return is not such as to induce them to sow it again. This I take to be rather in consequence of the low price, than from the lightness of the crop. But as the home growth is insufficient to affect the general market, the consideration is hardly applicable here. More cheerfulness seems to prevail amongst the farming classes; and though in this union we have more arrears of rate, £920, than at this season during thirty years, this is owing to complications in the collection of seed rate, rather than to inability to pay. It is also somewhat attributable to our having struck our rates later than usual during the last three years (after 29th September), an event which we have remedied this year.

JAMES GRAY, Clerk of Roscrea Union.

13th October, 1882.

LIMERICK UNION.

1. Is the corn in your union generally gathered in?	Nearly all—except in the high lands in county Clare.
2. Has the digging of the potato crop commenced?	Not generally anywhere, but around Limerick.
3. What is your opinion regarding the yield of corn in your union, and its quality?	Yield is light. The quality is not bad, but it is far from good.
4. What now appear to be the actual facts as regards the potato crop—	

Queries.	Replies.
(a.) Is it considered a fair average crop as to quantity?	(a.) About half a crop.
(b.) Are the tubers well grown and equal in size?	(b.) All equally small. Champions are fair size.
(c.) Has disease made much progress in the tuber?	(c.) Champions now beginning to be diseased (as stated to me). Other kinds appear about one-third bad.
(d.) To what extent do you consider the crop has suffered from disease?	(d.) About one-third of crop is stated to be found diseased, as far as can be ascertained from what has been taken out of the ground.
5. Has the usual quantity of turf been drawn home in good condition?	None home yet; turf not well saved: is not well dried yet.
6. Is the price of cattle high in your union, or only moderate?	Considered high everywhere; cattle scarce; farms not fully stocked.
7. Are potatoes coming freely into market, and at what price are they being sold?	Not coming in as freely as last year; August, about thirty-six loads less than last year; September about forty loads. Where an acre would make £26 last year, it now only makes about £15. Price now from 6*d.*, to 7*d.*, a stone, this time last year from 2½*d.* to 3*d.*; this only shows a quarter crop as compared with last year.
N.B.—Any additional remarks which may be considered of importance, I shall be glad to get.	There has been no employment to signify for day-labourers either in the county or city, during the past year, except since July at the harvest; all labourers must be very badly off, should provisions run high in price during coming winter.

C. Morris Wilson, Clerk.

Limerick Union, 5 October, 1882.

Rathkeale Union.

Queries.	Replies.
1. Is the corn in your union generally gathered in?	Most of it is yet in stooks in the fields, and a quantity of oats and barley is still uncut.
2. Has the digging of the potato crop commenced?	The digging of the general crop has not yet commenced.
3. What is your opinion regarding the yield of corn in your union, and its quality?	The yield is less than a good moderate one, the grain is very soft; in all kinds; and both yield and quality are inferior to the crops of last year, the grain of the oats is not so productive as would be supposed from the great growth of straw that appeared early in the year, it generally got "lodged" and consequently the grain became deteriorated.

QUERIES.	REPLIES.
4. What now appear to be the actual facts as regards the potato crop—	
(a.) Is it considered a fair average crop as to quantity?	It was a fair average crop as to quantity, if it remained healthy.
(b.) Are the tubers well grown and equal in size?	They generally are.
(c.) Has disease made much progress in the tuber?	It has, and is making much progress.
(d.) To what extent do you consider the crop has suffered from disease?	Certainly over one fourth part up to the present time. The Champion potato is even giving way to the disease.
5. Has the usual quantity of turf been drawn home in good condition?	Half the quantity of turf of other years, has not been drawn home from the bogs. What has been drawn is tolerably well saved, but far inferior in quality to the turf of other years, though dearer; people are now going on coals more than turf.
6. Is the price of cattle high in your union, or only moderate?	Extremely high. I have no recollection of former prices being so high for any class of cattle.
7. Are potatoes coming freely into market, and at what price are they being sold?	They are not coming to market freely, they are from 6d. to 8d. a stone, an unusually high price at this season, and people who have or ought to have potatoes, are purchasing flour to a larger extent than I ever observed them before to do at this season of the year. This may go far to show that the quality of the potato in general is not good.
N.B.—Any additional remarks which may be considered of importance I shall be glad to get.	Though the present prospects of the crops are not as cheering as was expected earlier and before the bad weather played on them, yet I do not dread the visitation of any unusual distress, I can observe the people are meeting their demands better than they have done heretofore, and far more willingly, and working people have more work, one way and another though there are no special or public works going on, and the daily rate of wages is liberal.

MICHAEL FITZGIBBON,

Clerk Rathkeale Union.

5th October, 1882.

Newcastle Union.

QUERIES.	REPLIES.
1. Is the corn in your Union generally gathered in?	Yes, except a small portion grown in wet mountainous districts.
2. Has the digging of the potato crop commenced?	It has.
3. What is your opinion regarding the yield of corn in your Union, and its quality?	The produce will be light and the quality still worse, a considerable portion of the crop not coming to maturity. I do not recollect a later harvest.
4. What now appear to be the actual facts as regards the potato crop?	Deficient in quantity particularly in heavy clay lands, where about one-third of the crops failed. In light dry soils produce is barely an average, but quality good.
(*a*.) Is it considered a fair average crop as to quantity?	
(*b*.) Are the tubers well grown and equal in size?	Generally speaking very unequal in size.
(*c*.) Has disease made much progress in the tuber?	Disease has made considerable progress.
(*d*.) To what extent do you consider the crop has suffered from disease?	From one-third to one-fourth of the crop is affected at present.
5. Has the usual quantity of turf been drawn home in good condition?	Quantity less than usual and a considerable portion badly saved. Not thoroughly dry.
6. Is the price of cattle high in your Union or only moderate?	Price of cattle high.
7. Are potatoes coming freely into market, and at what price are they being sold?	Considerably less are coming into market than at same period in past years. Price 6*d*. per 14 lbs.
N.B.—Any additional remarks which may be considered of importance I shall be glad to get.	Though the occupiers will gain a considerable portion of the loss or deficiency of crops by the great increase in the price of cattle, it is to be feared there will be great increase in the number of workhouse inmates. Apart from the deficiency of crops, the farmers will likely be less disposed than ever to give employment as any year they have to purchase more provisions than usual, employment of labour almost becomes nil as far as they are concerned.

John Byrnes,
Clerk of Union.

7th October, 1882.

Croom Union.

1. Is the corn in your union generally gathered in?	No.
2. Has the digging of the potato crop commenced?	Not for storing purposes.

QUERIES.	REPLIES.
3. What is your opinion regarding the yield of corn in your union and its quality?	The corn crop is most inferior, particularly the wheat, the latter being considered the worst that has been produced for many years past, the quality is not complained of, it is the yield.
4. What now appear to be the actual facts as regards the potato crop? (a.) Is it considered a fair average crop as to quantity?	The opinion is general that the potato crop will yield not more than one-half what it did last year, it is not considered an average crop, allowing last year's to have been exceptionally good.
(b.) Are the tubers well grown and equal in size?	(b.) Tubers small and irregular in size, except on well manured land.
(c.) Has disease made much progress in the tuber?	(c.) Considerably more so than last year, but perhaps not much greater than previous (recent) years.
(d.) To what extent do you consider the crop has suffered from disease?	The complaint is general that the crop is most inferior in quantity, I am not aware that the quality is much complained of.
5. Has the usual quantity of turf been drawn home in good condition?	The wetness of the season interfered very much with the saving of turf; the quantity saved will not meet the winter demand.
6. Is the price of cattle high in your union or only moderate?	Very high, much more so than it has been for many years.
7. Are potatoes coming freely into market, and at what price are they being sold?	No; on account of this scarcity. Price 6d. per stone; could be had last year at this time for 3d.
N.B.—Any additional remarks which may be considered of importance I shall be glad to get.	The potato crop neither in quantity or quality, will bear comparison with that of last year; the belief is general that the wheat crop in this district will not pay its expenses much less leave a profit. The oat crop is fair, but selling as it is for 8d. to 9d. per stone, no farmer expects to realise the expenditure incurred in raising the crop.

ENNIS UNION.

1. Is the corn in your Union generally gathered in?	No, it is in course of being gathered in. In very few cases to my knowledge is it gathered in to be stacked in the hay-yard, but thrashed out by machine and sold out at once.
2. Has the digging of the potato crop commenced?	The oats crop is fair and for its extent yields a good return, but the wheat and barley crops are very limited.

QUERIES.	REPLIES.
3. What now appear to be the actual facts as regards the potato crop?	I regret to say they are very discouraging.
(a) Is it considered a fair average crop as to quantity?	No, it is at least one-third deficient in this Union.
(b) Are the tubers well grown and equal in size?	No, they are generally under the average size and unequal, and very disproportionate in the different kinds of soil.
(c) Has disease made much progress in the tuber?	From all I can learn it has.
(d) To what extent do you consider the crop has suffered from disease?	From the inquiries I have made I may venture to say a fourth has fully suffered.
4. Has the usual quantity of turf been drawn home in good condition?	There is a fair quantity of turf raised in remote bogs. It is not generally yet drawn home for storage. Its condition has suffered. The quantity brought for sale to this market is not as an article of fuel of as good quality for this season as formerly and will require a small mixture of wood or coal to realise its usual heating power.
5. Is the price of cattle high in your Union or only moderate?	From the inquiries I have been making I can learn the price of cattle is getting very high and I am told that a scarcity of stock in the country, has had much influence in raising the price.
6. Are potatoes coming freely into market and at what price are they being sold?	The potatoes are very scantily coming into market at present and carrying so high a price as from 5*d.* to 6*d.* per stone. However the present state of the potato market may be caused by the digging of them not being completed, and the occupation of the farmers' time in securing the other branches of the harvest.
N.B.—Any additional remarks which may be considered of importance I shall be glad to get?	Beyond the replies given above I have no other remarks of a general nature to add.

JOHN COTTER,

Clerk of the Union.

6th October, 1882.

ENNISTYMON UNION.

1. Is the corn in your union generally gathered in?	Yes.
2. Has the digging of the potato crop commenced?	Yes.

QUERIES.	REPLIES.
3. What is your opinion regarding the yield of corn, in your union and its quality?	The quality or return is not so good as last year's, owing to the unfavourable harvest weather for ripening, but on the whole the crop is not a very bad one.
4. What now appears to be the actual facts as regards the potato crop. (a.) Is it considered a fair average crop as to quantity? (b.) Are the tubers well grown and equal in size? (c.) Has disease made much progress in the tuber? (d.) To what extent do you consider the crop has suffered from disease?	The complaints of the potato crop are wide-spread and general. *Champion.*—The crop is excellent in new ground, but in broken soil much inferior to last year's. It is free from disease in black soil, in upland ground about a fourth is diseased. *Home Seed.*—The crop is extremely bad, the tubers very small and so inferior in quality as to be as a rule unfit for human food. In very many instances the crop from home seed is scarcely worth digging.
5. Has the usual quantity of turf been drawn home in good condition?	No; at the same time I don't think there will be any great want of fuel. It will be dearer than last year, the supply not being so abundant.
6. Is the price of cattle high in your union or only moderate?	The price of cattle very high.
7. Are the potatoes coming freely into market, and at what price are they being sold?	Potatoes are not coming freely into market. The price now is 7*d.* a stone, about double the price of this time last year.
N.B.—Any additional remarks which may be considered of importance, I shall be glad to get.	Green crops are not quite so good as last year, especially mangolds. The hay crop is fair but not so well saved as it was last year. JOHN O'LOUGHLIN, Clerk of Union. 7th October, 1882.

KILADAN UNION.

1. Is the corn in your union generally gathered in?	Yes.
2. Has the digging of the potato crop commenced?	Yes.
3. What is your opinion regarding the yield of corn in your union and its quality?	Something less than an average crop and quality rather inferior.
4. What now appears to be the actual facts as regards the potato crop—	
(a.) Is it considered a fair average crop as to quantity?	No.
(b.) Are the tubers well grown and equal in size?	No.
(c.) Has disease made much progress in the tuber?	Yes.

QUERIES.	REPLIES.
(*d.*) To what extent do you consider the crop has suffered from disease?	Between disease, and rot from wet, the return on the whole will be about half an average crop.
5. Has the usual quantity of turf been drawn home in good condition?	No; a sufficient quantity to meet the winter requirements is cut and saved in the bogs and if the rest of this month permits it will be drawn home.
6. Is the price of cattle high in your union or only moderate?	High, when contrasted with the prices last year, and the supply is fairly good.
7. Are potatoes coming freely into market, and at what price are they being sold.	Not yet—present market price 6*d.* to 7*d.* per stone.
N.B.—Any additional remarks which may be considered of importance, I shall be glad to get.	I fear, on the whole, the results of the harvest of the present year will fall short of a fair average. Green crops are good in this union, but not grown to any great extent.
	A. Warren, Clerk of Union.
	Kilrush, 9th October, 1882.

KILLADYSERT UNION.

1. Is the corn in your union generally gathered in?	Yes; serious damage having been done in many instances by the recent storm.
2. Has the digging of the potato crop commenced?	Not in general.
3. What is your opinion regarding the yield of corn in your union and its quality?	Corn inferior in quality and quantity, having been seriously affected during its growth and when ripening by the wet weather.
4. What now appear to be the actual facts as regards the potato crop—	
(*a.*) Is it considered a fair average crop as to quantity? (*b.*) Are the tubers well grown and equal in size? (*c.*) Has disease made much progress in the tuber? (*d.*) To what extent do you consider the crop has suffered from disease?	Potatoes are by no means an average crop, an average acre of land as compared with last year, producing little, if any more than one-third of last year's yield. Making allowance for exaggeration, the old kinds of potatoes are very seriously affected, in numerous instances they are not worth the trouble of digging, and even the "Champions" show the disease to a considerable extent.
5. Has the usual quantity of turf been drawn home in good condition?	Not all drawn home. There is no danger of a scarcity of fuel, although turf is not so well saved as in former years.
6. Is the price of cattle high in your union, or only moderate?	Prices high. Stock of all kinds scarce.

QUERIES.	REPLIES.
7. Are potatoes coming freely into market, and at what price are they being sold.	There is not at any time any extensive market in this union for potatoes, they are generally got at the Ennis and Kilrush markets; but what are being sold are according to quality from 6d. to 8d. per stone of 14 lbs.
N.B.—Any additional remarks which may be considered of importance, I shall be glad to get.	After conclusion of the harvest operations, serious want of employment will be felt by the labouring class.

ALEX. MACMAHON.
Clerk of Union.

13th Oct., 1882.

TULLA UNION.

1. Is the corn in your union generally gathered in?	No, and it suffered much damage by the storm of Sunday last, 1st inst.
2. Has the digging of the potato crop commenced?	Yes.
3. What is your opinion regarding the yield of corn in your union, and its quality?	The yield of oat crop equal to last year, wheat poor, and under yield of last year. Very little barley, quality of oats good, not so wheat.
4. What now appear to be the actual facts as regards the potato crop? (a.) Is it considered a fair average crop as to quantity?	The average yield is equal to half that of last year, though there are exceptional cases where it has been considered quite as abundant. It is a better crop than that of 1879 or 1880, but not more than half that of last year.
(b.) Are the tubers well grown and equal in size?	No, they are very disproportionate, some being unusually large, while a large per-centage of small ones cover the drill or ridge.
(c.) Has disease made much progress in the tuber? (d.) To what extent do you consider the crop has suffered from disease?	Yes, at least one-fourth of the crop has been attacked.
5. Has the usual quantity of turf been drawn home in good condition?	No, but if the present fine weather continues it soon will be.
6. Is the price of cattle high in your union, or only moderate?	Yes, very. 30s. to 40s. higher than last year's prices.
7. Are potatoes coming freely into the market and at what price are they being sold?	No market in this town, potatoes can be had from the farmers at 6d. per stone.
N.B.—Any additional remarks which may be considered of importance, I shall be glad to get.	There is great doubt and consequent gloom because of the potato crop. If the quantity at present untouched by disease remains so,

QUERIES. REPLIES.

there will be in my opinion, no great cause for alarm, but if the potatoes now being put into pits white and spotless, should get attacked, the consequences will be of that unhappy character of which we all have experience.

T. Murphy.

Clerk of Union, Tulla.

6th October, 1882.

Report from Dr. Brodie.—District comprising parts of the Counties of Cork, Limerick, and Waterford.

Cork, 30th September, 1882.

Gentlemen.—I have the honour to acknowledge the receipt of yours, requesting a further report from me, for the information of his Excellency the Lord Lieutenant, as to the "state of the potato crop," "the condition of the turf where it is cut," and the "prospects of the general harvest" in my district.

From information I have obtained from reliable sources, and from my own personal observations, I have the honour to submit the following.

Cork Union—urban and rural.

Potatoes.—Digging has commenced, and the crop upon the whole is turning out better than I anticipated.

Oats.—An unusually large crop; price very low.

Wheat.—Somewhat less than an average crop; price low.

Barley.—A heavy crop, but inferior in quality.

Roots.—Promise a fair crop.

Hay.—The largest crop for many years, a great portion saved in good condition.

Turf.—But little used in this union.

Employment.—There is in general sufficient employment for unskilled labour, at remunerative wages.

No. in workhouse, 30th September, ...	2,381.
No. in corresponding period last year, ...	2,526.
No. of persons in receipt of outdoor relief, cases 1,257; persons, ...	3,108.

Cost of outdoor relief for week, £154.

Fermoy Union.

Potatoes.—Are a good crop. The blight which threatened serious injury at first, has been checked, and the loss is scarcely appreciable. Though not so plentiful as last year (perhaps two-thirds may be the proportion), the crop will still be much better than it had been for other years previously.

Oats.—As a crop, is up to the average, the price however is lower than in previous years, being 8s. 6d. per barrel compared with 10s. 6d.

Wheat.—Not so good as in other years, owing to the great quantity of rain. The price, 20s. a barrel, as compared with 28s. to 30s. a barrel last year.

Turnips.—A splendid crop, nearly twice the produce of either of the last three years; and the green crops generally are good.

Hay.—Upland hay is very plentiful and well saved, but the ryegrass has been damaged in the saving, and falls short of other years.

Turf.—There is scarcely any cut in his union, coal almost universally used.

MALLOW UNION.

Potatoes.—Not so large or abundant as last year's crop, but in quality good.

Oats.—Generally as good as last year's excellent crop.

Wheat.—Generally good.

Turnips and Mangolds.—Very heavy crops.

Hay.—To a great extent secure, in fair condition.

Turf.—In very good condition and cheap, but not much used; coal supplied along the railway lines.

MIDLETON UNION.

Potatoes.—Champions, not planted in such quantities as last year, owing, I am told, to the fact that at the end of last season they got bad very quickly, the quality is as good, if not superior to last year; all old seeds failed.

Oats.—A good crop, but the price at present, 9s. per barrel, is rather discouraging to farmers.

Barley.—Scarcely half crop, and inferior in quality; price 17s. per barrel.

Wheat.—Not much sown, and not good this year; price 22s. 6d. per barrel, which is considered very low.

Turf.—Not used in this union; coal the general article of fuel.

Employment.—Plenty of employment in Midleton; not a man idle. Wages 2s. 6d. per day. Mechanics get from 30s. to 33s. per week.

MITCHELSTOWN UNION.

Potatoes.—Not so good as when last reported on, the produce in many places not more than half that of last year, the potato is small in size; market price 6d. per stone.

Oats.—The crop generally sown in this union has been saved and a large proportion thrashed, but the reports state there has been a fall off from last year in produce and quality; price extremely low.

Green Crops.—Generally good.

Hay.—An abundant crop.

Turf.—Where cut has been properly saved.

In-door Relief.—No. in workhouse, ...	198
" Corresponding period last year, .	230
Out-door Relief.—No. in receipt of out-door relief, cases 30; persons, . .	68
" Corresponding period last year, cases 13; persons, ...	29

DUNMANWAY UNION.

Potatoes.—The late potato crop is, with the exception of 1880 and 1881, the best they had in this union for several years.

Oats.—In area, produce, and quality, the best for many years. It is the staple corn crop of the country; price low, 5s. per cwt.

Wheat.—Is deficient in area and produce, but is of such limited growth, it is not of much consequence.

Hay.—An abundant crop, and well saved.

Turf.—Has all been saved in excellent condition.

In-door Relief.—No. in workhouse, ...		149
"	Corresponding period last year, .	140
Out-door Relief.—No. in receipt of out-door relief, cases 38; persons, ...		77
"	Corresponding period last year, cases 34; persons, ...	56

The rate of wages in and near Dunmanway and villages convenient, is 2*s.* per day at reaping and threshing corn and will continue until the corn is threshed, the usual rate of wages is 1*s.* 6*d.* per day.

Clonakilty Union.

Potatoes.—Have not improved since date of last report, fears are entertained that they will be dear and scarce during the winter.

Owing to the fine weather during the past month, the grain crops, mangolds, and turnips are much improved, and have far exceeded all expectations.

No. in workhouse, . . .	240
Corresponding period of last year,	254

Kinsale Union.

The general prospect of the harvest in this union has undergone no material change since my last report on the subject.

Potatoes.—Have proved an abundant crop, of good quality; price at present 8*d.* per 21 lbs., wholesale.

Cereals.—In general a good crop; prices low.

Labourers' Wages.—2*s.* and 2*s.* 6*d.* a day; tradesmen 4*s.* 6*d.* a day.

No apprehension of any exceptional distress in this union.

Youghal Union.

Potatoes.—Compared with last year will not be more than half a crop.

Oats.—A good crop.

Green Crops.—Where well tilled and well manured, they are good.

Wheat.—Not much grown in the district.

Labour.—In good demand; plenty of employment for all who are inclined to work.

Dungarvan Union—county of Waterford.

Potatoes.—Not a good crop, either in produce or quality. The "Champions" are black as well as the other varieties of seed.

Oats.—Very good both in produce and quality; price low, 9*s.* 6*d.* per barrel.

Wheat.—Below the average; price low.

Barley.—Below average in produce and quality.

Green Crops.—Fairly up to average.

Hay.—Abundant.

Turf.—Very little used.

Cattle.—Brought high price at last fair.

Kilmacthomas Union—county of Waterford.

Potatoes.—Since last report there has been a decided improvement in this crop as regards quantity and quality; these observations apply exclusively to the "Champions," all other descriptions have been much injured by the blight.

Oats.—A most abundant crop.

Wheat.—A fair crop, on a limited quantity sown in the union.

Barley.—Not grown in this locality.

Turf.—There are several turf bogs in the union, but, as a rule, farmers do not make turf, considering coals cheaper fuel.

Rate of Wages.—About 12*s.* per week.

In-door and Out-door Relief.—A decrease of about 20 per cent. in the in-door and out-door as compared with corresponding period last year.

LISMORE UNION—county of Waterford.

My report made, 22nd of August, of the present year regarding the state of the crops is perfectly applicable to their condition at the present time.

Potatoes.—A fair crop.

Oats.—An average crop.

Wheat.—Below average in yield.

Green Crops.—An average crop.

Hay.—Lake meadows and upland a heavy crop, and saved in good condition.

Turf.—Very little cut or saved in the locality. The use of coal general.

No apprehension of exceptional distress in this union during the coming season.

Since date of my last report, dated 22nd August, 1882, the weather has been fairly fine. Almost the entire of the green crops are now saved in good condition, with the following result:—

Wheat.—About an average crop.

Barley.—A fair crop of variable quality.

Oats.—Very abundant, in fact the best crop for many years. Farmers complain of the present low prices for grain. Oats selling 10 per cent. under last year's prices. Wheat 20 per cent. Barley, price not fully opened yet. On the other hand—

Cattle of all sorts were never so dear.

Butter.—The make is very large, and the price high and remunerative.

Hay has proved a very good crop. The great bulk of it is saved in good condition.

Roots.—An average crop. The wet month of July was much against their bulbing.

Potatoes.—Digging has commenced, and I am happy to say that the crop, upon the whole, is turning out better than was anticipated. Say about two-thirds of last season; the main crop consisting of "Champions," the quality of which is better than in any of the preceding years they were planted, the loss by disease being about 5 per cent. It has been suggested to me that too much reliance should not be placed on this variety of potato, and that every exertion should be made by those interested to *raise* and *test new varieties* of this most valuable esculent.

On the whole it may be safely assumed that no unusual distress will prevail. The harvest will be a plentiful one, and the price of provisions all likely to be low.

I have the honour to remain, gentlemen,

Your obedient servant,

T. BRODIE.

To the Local Government Board, Dublin.

REPORT from Dr. BURKE.—DISTRICT comprising the COUNTY of LONGFORD and parts of the COUNTIES of KILDARE, KING'S COUNTY, LOUTH, MEATH, QUEEN'S COUNTY, and WESTMEATH.

26, Waterloo-road, Dublin, 7th October, 1882.

GENTLEMEN,—I have had the honour to receive duly your communication of the 8th ultimo, with reference to my report of the 23rd of August last, on the state of the potato crop, the condition of the turf where it is cut, and the prospects of the general harvest; and in compliance with instructions therein contained, beg to state, both from personal observation and continued inquiries into the several subjects upon which His Excellency the Lord Lieutenant desires to be further informed, at the beginning of this month, that I see no reason to alter, with any material modification, the views entertained and expressed by me in my previous report alluded to, since the date of which we have been favoured with good and suitable weather generally. The potato crop continues, I believe, to resist fairly the efforts of "the blight," with the exception of the species mentioned—Scotch downs and white rocks principally, about a fourth of the crop of which may be deemed, in my opinion, as useless and unfit for human consumption. Large quantities of turf, cut in mid-summer and later in the season, have been saved and brought home, though a large amount still remains but partially saved on the bogs in some places; yet I think no apprehensions as to scarcity of this article of fuel need be entertained.

As regards the general harvest—oats, barley, and wheat have been all cut, show an abundant crop, and are safe; though I have to observe with deep regret that large quantities of the first named cereal are still (owing to most deplorable and wanton procrastination on the part of the farmers) left out in stacks or stooks, in the fields, as well as of the saved hay crop, which exceeds in abundance and quality that of any such for several years past.

The condition of turnips and mangels continues to be satisfactory, and I feel no hesitation in stating that throughout the entire of my district, the harvest of the present year may be classed on the whole as a very abundant and successful one.

I have the honour to be, your most obedient servant,

T. H. BURKE, Inspector.

The Local Government Board,
Custom House, Dublin.

REPORT from Mr. R. HAMILTON.—DISTRICT comprising the COUNTIES of ANTRIM, ARMAGH, and DOWN, and parts of LONDONDERRY, LOUTH, and TYRONE.

Newtownards, October 10th, 1882.

GENTLEMEN,—In reference to your letter of the 8th inst., I beg leave to inform you I have made further inquiry regarding the condition of the general harvest, and state of the potato crop in my district.

The great bulk of the harvest has now been secured—and may be considered—on the whole—a good average. There is, however, a certain proportion in the later, and mountain districts which has suffered severely from the effects of the storm of the 1st October, and the loss in these localities will be considerable.

As a general crop, the potatoes are decidedly inferior both as to quantity and quality—the "Champions" being the only variety which appears to yield a moderate return—but the people in this district are in a great degree independent of this crop as a means of subsistence.

Although the season is not one of such great abundance as last, there is good ground for believing it will be one of ordinary comfort for the poorer classes, and I see no reason for apprehending an unusual pressure for relief in any part of the district.

The farmers are receiving good prices for all kinds of agricultural produce, and there seems to be abundance of employment for labourers—besides this—the weaving trade—at which large numbers are engaged in the Counties Down, Armagh, and Antrim, is in a prosperous condition.

I annex a short abstract of the report I have had from each union in my district.

I have the honour to be, gentlemen, your obedient servant,

R. Hamilton.

The Local Government Board, Dublin.

County Antrim.

Belfast Union.—Harvest—a fair average—Potatoes—diseased and inferior.

Larne Union.—Oats—a heavy crop—Wheat under an average—Potatoes, "Champions" and "Skerries"—not much diseased—Not more than half a crop expected.

Ballymena Union.—General harvest good—Prospect of potatoes—better than was expected.

Ballymoney Union.—Harvest good—but damaged by weather—Potatoes much below average.

Antrim Union.—General harvest—not good—Potatoes—not half an average.

Ballycastle Union.—General harvest—unfavourable—Crops much damaged by storm—Potato crop very inferior.

Lisburn Union.—General harvest good—Potato crop—below an average.

County Down.

Newtownards Union.—General harvest—fair—Potato crop—inferior.

Downpatrick Union.—General harvest—good—Potatoes better than was expected.

Banbridge Union.—General harvest—fair—Potatoes, also fair.

Kilkeel Union.—General harvest—fair—Potato crop—fair.

County Armagh.

Newry Union.—General harvest—fair—Potatoes—an average crop.

Lurgan Union.—General harvest—unfavourable—Potatoes—not half a crop.

Armagh Union.—General harvest—unfavourable—much damaged by storm—Potatoes not half a crop.

County Tyrone.

Cookstown Union.—The grain crops seriously injured by storm of 1st October—Potatoes—not half an average.

County Londonderry.

Magherafelt Union.—Harvest—a fair average—Potato crop very inferior.

County Louth.

Dundalk Union.—General harvest—a fair average—Potatoes—small but sound—Crop—a fair average.

R. Hamilton.

October 10th, 1882.

REPORT from MR. W. HAMILTON.—DISTRICT comprising the COUNTY of KILKENNY and parts of the COUNTIES of CARLOW, LIMERICK, TIPPERARY, WATERFORD, and WEXFORD.

Fiddown, 2nd October, 1883.

GENTLEMEN,—In accordance with the instructions in your letter of the 8th ulto., I now beg to transmit abstracts of the replies to further inquiries which I have made in every portion of my district.

The general result is very much to the same effect as my report of the 22nd of August last.

I have the honour to be, gentlemen,

Your obedient servant,

W. J. HAMILTON.

The Local Government Board (Ireland).

I.—County of KILKENNY, Unions of *Callan, Castlecomer, Kilkenny, Thomastown, Urlingford.*

No. 1. What is the state of the potato crop in your locality?

As already stated, the early kinds were generally affected, and the late kinds not nearly as good as last year. There has been but little change since last report, if anything not so good as was then expected; but a small portion of the general crop has been raised as yet. There is a good deal of testimony to the effect, that where there was newly imported seed, and careful tillage, the yield has been abundant and the quality good; but such cases are not as general as it is to be hoped, after this year's experience, they may henceforth be. As a general rule, it may be said, that the potatoes where sound are small, and the produce very indifferent.

2. What is the state of the general harvest as regards—

Wheat?—Wheat generally promised better than it has proved; in some localities it is injured by smut, and ears are partly blind; it has not turned out a remunerative crop, especially where there was indifferent farming.

Oats?—Oats generally a very good crop. The only complaints I have heard are, its low price at present.

Barley?—Barley has not improved; it is stated to be in some localities "inferior," "light," "injured," "light and small," &c. There is not much of it.

Green Crops, &c.?—Except where early sown, on well prepared land, and carefully attended to, the general yield will probably be indifferent.

No. 3. What are the prospects as to the supply of turf this season?

Except in Urlingford Union, turf is now but little used; in portions of Urlingford Union turf is very scarce.

II.—County of TIPPERARY, Unions of *Carrick-on-Suir, Cashel, Clogheen, Clonmel, Thurles, Tipperary.*

No. 1. What is the state of the potato crop in your locality?

There has been no improvement to report since I reported in August. The Scotch Champions, as in other counties, a fair crop, smaller in size than last year, and as yet two-thirds of the produce estimated as sound. Magnum Bonums, too, well spoken of; Scotch Downs and other sorts a bad crop generally, especially in wet lands. There is the same testimony as to the value of freshly imported seed, good tillage, and carefully selected soil, without which, it seems idle to expect a good crop of sound potatoes that will keep.

No. 2. What is the state of the general harvest as regards—

Wheat?—Produce lower than was expected, quality indifferent; an unproductive and unremunerative crop.

Oats?—Generally very good; a few exceptions, but there are cases where heavy rains lodged the crop, and it did not ripen evenly.

Barley?—Barley not so good as was expected. Very little grown.

Green Crops, &c.?—There has been some improvement, but the unusual low temperature has been against green crops, and though, as elsewhere, in good and favourable soil, and where manuring and tillage have been well done, the crops are generally good and promising, I fear from the neglected look of many fields I have seen that these cases are exceptional rather than the rule.

No. 3. What are the prospects as to the supply of turf this season?

Further experience confirms what I said on this subject in my report of the 22nd of August. I fear there has been no improvement generally.

III.—County of Waterford, Union of *Waterford*.

No. 1. What is the state of the potato crop in your locality?

Potatoes are an inferior crop both in yield and quality, probably one-fourth short of last year, of course there are exceptional cases, here and there, where, with carefully selected seed, and skilful tillage, there have been good returns; in some cases on the other hand where these essentials were altogether unheeded the return has been unremunerative and disappointing.

No. 2. What is the state of the general harvest as regards—

Wheat?—About two-thirds of an average crop, of fairly good quality.

Oats?—A fine crop generally but somewhat uneven; about equal to last year in weight; but scarcely so good in quality.

Barley?—Not much grown—not quite so good as was expected when I last reported.

Green Crops, &c.?—There is a fair average promise wherever ordinary justice has been done to the land.

No. 3. What are the prospects as to the supply of turf this season?

There is scarcely any turf used in this Union.

IV.—County of Wexford, Unions of *Enniscorthy, New Ross, Wexford*.

No. 1. What is the state of the potato crop in your locality?

The yield generally inferior to that of last year. Champions have done pretty well—in some places under favourable circumstances as to seed, soil, tillage, &c., they have been represented as good and even excellent; in others, "better than could have been expected"—all other kinds, "indifferent" and even "bad,"—very little change since my report in August.

No. 2. What is the state of the general harvest as regards—

Wheat?—About an average crop.

Oats?—Black oats fair; spring and white oats not as good as was expected.

Barley?—Not so good as was expected—in many places the grain is stated to be light, small, and of inferior quality.

Green Crops, &c.?—In dry lands, well tilled, very good; there has been some improvement, but the general accounts are not good.

Beans?—A good crop.

No. 3. What are the prospects as to the supply of turf this season?

Scarcely any turf used in this Union.

REPORT from DR. MACCABE.—DISTRICT comprising the COUNTIES of DUBLIN and WICKLOW, and parts of the COUNTIES of KILDARE, MEATH, CARLOW, QUEEN'S COUNTY, and WEXFORD.

Dublin, 3rd October, 1883.

SIR,—I beg to acknowledge the receipt of your letter of the 8th September, notifying the desire of the Local Government Board that I should submit, at the beginning of October, a further report respecting the harvest prospects in my district.

In reply, I have the honour to state that since the date of my former report the weather has not been favourable, and in consequence the harvest is late this year.

With the exception of the county of Dublin, where the crops appear to be of good quality and well saved, the harvest in my district has not fulfilled the promise which the appearance of the crops held out at the date of my last report. From all other parts of my district the later accounts I have received are on the whole less encouraging than those contained in the table annexed to my former report, and the falling off is in every case attributed to the character of the season.

The following presents, I believe, a fair summary of all the additional information I have been able to obtain:—

Potatoes.—Not at all equal to last year. In well-drained and light soils not quite an average crop—in wet and heavy soils about half an average crop.

Cereals.—Wheat not so productive as last season, and in yield below the average.

Oats, the best of the cereals, in some places very good, but over all my district (except the county of Dublin, where the crops ripened early) not equal to last year.

Barley below the average, and in many barley growing districts much injured by rain.

Hay.—Abundant, but a large proportion of the crop not well saved.

Green Crops.—On the whole good.

Turf.—It has been found impossible to save the usual supply, which it is expected will fall short by about one-half.

The harvest must, I think, be regarded as below the average, but the deficiency is not sufficiently serious in any part of my district to excite apprehension respecting the prospects of the labouring classes and the poor during the approaching winter and spring.

I have the honour to remain, Sir,

Your obedient servant,

F. X. MACCABE, Inspector.

To the Secretary,
Local Government Board.

REPORT from Mr. MACFARLANE.—DISTRICT comprising parts of the COUNTIES of DONEGAL, LONDONDERRY, and TYRONE.

Londonderry, 14th October, 1882.

SIR,—As your letter of 8th September, with reference to my report of 23rd August, requests a further report this month on the state of the potato crop, the turf, and the general harvest, in my district, for the information of His Excellency the Lord Lieutenant, I would now observe—1st. The weather in September, which is of such importance where crops are late or in a mountainous region, has been unusually uncertain from wet to dry, and almost continuously damp during the month, terminating with a storm of wind on the 1st October, which for violence exceeded anything of the kind at this season of the year in my recollection.

It blew from the south with a point west, except where the conformation of the country, mountain or valley, somewhat altered its direction. A wood or plantation at the head of a glen also somewhat governed its direction, and moderated its effects. In the more exposed situations, corn and hay stacks were completely upset, and outlying stooks blown down, and in some places carried against the next hedge, or over it into the adjoining field. Large old trees were blown down which had escaped so many winter storms, when without leaves offering less resistance. The maximum force of the wind was at about three o'clock in the afternoon, and lasted only a short time, abating without rain till Monday evening, when there was a shower, succeeded by *fine weather for the rest of the week*, which was extensively and industriously taken advantage of, in gathering up the scattered corn and completing their hay harvest—September and October are the months in Donegal for saving bottom meadows—which the previous damp weather had prevented. The corn suffered from being tossed so much, but not the hay, as the tossing by the wind and fine weather after, improved its quality. Some corn, ripe but uncut, was lodged by the previous wet weather and did not lose much grain from the head, while the standing corn was quite threshed with the storm—all this will not be without some compensating results. The oat crop is, as a rule, allowed to remain too long uncut after it is quite fit, and thus during its saving some of the best corn on the head is shed and lost, while the straw generally used for fodder is much deteriorated in its feeding qualities, and encouragement will also be given to proprietors to make plantations for shelter. One small farmer told me he ought to have cut his corn several days before the storm, and that he would never again let it get so ripe before cutting.

I heard in another place that the farms on both sides of a valley, at the head of which the proprietor had taken up land for planting a wood some thirty years ago, had not suffered from the storm, and the inhabitants attributed their safety entirely to this wood, and that the name of the man who planted it would be ever respected for the future. The effect of the storm was also very variable as regards the damage done in the better portions of my district where the corn and hay had been all carted to the stackyard in good time. The sites selected being generally exposed to the south, and sheltered from the west, particularly whence rough winds are expected, the stacks in many places had thatch blown off and were otherwise tossed.

In the Gweedore and the Rosses country, in the Dunfanaghy and Glenties Unions, most of the corn had been cut and neatly thatched after being stacked, and I was agreeably surprised to find how little comparative injury had been sustained there where the crop was cut. Some had been, however, left uncut, although ripe, and it suffered severely.

The Inishowen side of Donegal and the portion of the Glenties Union to the west appeared to have received most damage. The latter portion of the week after the storm, was very much devoted to stacking and carting turf. Much that had been too damp previously was completely dried by the gale and succeeding brisk weather.

With regard to the potato crop referred to in my former report, and the potato blight which, since 1845–6, has occasionally affected this important article of food, more or less in proportion to the stage of growth the tubers had reached when disease appeared on the leaves and stalks, I don't think it has *seriously* affected the general average *quantity* or the *quality* of the crop grown this year, on the dry or properly drained and well cultivated portions of my district, in the counties Londonderry, Antrim, Tyrone, and Donegal, where Champions [have been extensively planted at a sufficiently early period of the season, and had almost attained maturity before blight on leaves indicated any check.

In the other portions of my district, the undrained clays and thin peaty soils, cold from excessive wet, where potatoes were planted too late waiting for the soil to dry by *evaporation*, the tubers had made little growth when the blight came in August, and there being no further development, these potatoes are consequently small and deficient in quality, as well as in quantity. Last year the potato crop throughout the district was far over an average, there being such exceptional dry weather in spring, that even those undrained lands were dry enough for planting at the proper time, and the effort to obtain new or fresh seed, was accompanied by the sense of its value, and the importance of having it planted early. Thus a combination of favourable circumstances resulted in a crop of potatoes considerably above what they were accustomed to, or required for home consumption, and as the surplus for sale brought low prices some carelessness was induced as to getting them planted in time this year, consequently there being only an average crop of potatoes where the Champion was planted on dry land, and even the Champion being so very deficient on wet land, it is likely that there will be high prices, and the usually larger occupier of dry land may obtain more money for the smaller surplus he has to sell, while the smaller occupier of the wet land will possibly require to have his food supply supplemented by oatmeal or Indian meal as in previous years.

The oat crop has been generally good, and over an average crop throughout the whole district even on undrained land where ordinary precaution was used in letting off the surface water during the preceding winter, and thus having the land sufficiently dry to plough and sow at the proper time. Where this was not done, and the land was sown *late*, while still wet, the oats being so slow to ripen was uncut in many places when the storm of the 1st October came and reduced the produce considerably.

The hay crop has been fairly saved even in the late parts of Donegal, and although some stacks were so much blown about by the storm it was safely gathered and no material injury was done to it. The turnips are an abundant crop also, and thus there will be a good supply of fodder for the winter; and as I have already stated there will be no dearth of fuel, a sufficient supply of turf having been fairly saved.

As nearly all these unions have mountain and lowland, and each something in common as to soil or cultivation, though differing largely in their relative proportions, I divide my district simply into dry, or properly *drained* land, with which is generally associated good cultivation, and what is wet or *undrained*, which, whether at forty feet or four hundred feet above sea level, is the line of demarkation which very much determines the reward for labour with the industrious occupier, and frequently makes all the difference between a struggle for existence and a comfortable subsistence.

I am, sir, your obedient servant,

H. J. MacFarlane,

Local Government Inspector.

To the Secretary, Local Government Board, Ireland.

Report from Mr. Power.—District comprising the County of Kerry, and part of the County of Cork.

Dublin, 2nd October, 1882.

Gentlemen,—According to instructions received from your Board, I beg to forward a further report on the prospect of the harvest in my district, consisting of the county of Kerry, and the unions of Bantry, Castletown-Bere, Skull, and Skibbereen, in West Cork.

From inquiries I have made I do not think that the crops have been injured to any extent by the weather since my last report, dated 24th September. With regard to the potato crop the reports are not so favourable, especially along the South and West Coasts. In the Castletown-Bere union the potato crop will probably be only half an average one, and the same may be said of parts of the Cahirciveen union, and other places along the coast. In the inland districts, the accounts of the potato crop are more favourable. Plenty of turf has been saved for use during the coming winter. On the whole, with the exception of the potato crop, which I think will be below the average, I think that the general harvest may be considered a fair average one.

I am, gentlemen,

Your obedient servant,

W. A. Power.

To Local Government Board.

Report from Mr. Robinson.—District comprising the County of Mayo and part of the County of Galway.

Swineford, 17th October, 1882.

Gentlemen,—In accordance with your instructions I have made further careful inquiries as to the state of the harvest and the prospects of the farming classes during the coming winter and spring.

There is a very light crop of potatoes; compared with last year I think it may be regarded as a large half crop, but the crop of 1881 was such an exceptionally heavy one that even this year's return is not much below the average, which in my district is about eight tons to the Irish acre. Last year's yield was about ten tons to the acre, and I think that the average of the present crop in this district may be reckoned at between five and six tons. Nearly every variety has now given way to the "Champion," which for about six months is a good eating potato, but it is so vigorous, that after that time it is almost impossible to prevent the growth, and it becomes strong flavoured, stringy, and unpalatable.

The oat crop is about one-eighth short in bulk of grain, but the straw is unusually long and good, and taking this into consideration I should say the crop is almost as valuable as it was last year. There is not much variation in prices, which here are always very low, as these small holdings have no barns, threshing floors, or any of the appurtenances of a properly equipped farm, and the oats are consequently either threshed on the public road or in an open yard, and hence it is difficult to buy them clean.

This crop is probably less remunerative now than it was some time ago. The term "a short crop" used to signify a high price, but at present it generally means a bad quality and low price, for now that English railways, by the magnitude of their American freight contracts, are enabled to carry imported grain at so much a lesser rate than home grown produce, the scarcity, which some time ago resulted in a proportionate inflation of prices, is now fully made up by America.

The rye-grass hay was almost everywhere spoiled in the saving, but the late hay crop was harvested in fine condition, and those who have it to dispose of are holding out for high prices.

There is an unusually good price for cattle and sheep at present, and the fluctuation in the value of pigs during the past three years is almost unprecedented. I am afraid, however, that those violent oscillations of the market must be regarded as somewhat hurtful. It is true they promote an apparent flash of prosperity for the time being, but the people are tempted to part with their breeding stock, and the trade becomes more of a speculative gambling transaction than it would be if a fair steady price was maintained.

There is a strong feeling among the people at present in favour of emigration, and unless a large number of them leave the country and a perceptible consolidation of these small holdings takes place, I fear that agriculture in my district will continue to deteriorate rather than commence to improve. The people have now contracted the habit of buying largely the artificial manures, and as they usually obtain them on credit they must take whatever is delivered to them without any analysis. It is generally a finely powdered material, and if not speedily appropriated by the crop it is washed through the land to the subsoil, and there it remains, for the people never till deep; they not only lack the horse power to do so, but more than frequently they have not the manual power, as where the farms are of insufficient size to support the family the able-bodied members are obliged to seek work elsewhere, and as the father has the turf to cut and other things to devote his time to, the women and barefooted children are left to carry out the shallow system of cultivation which is so detrimental to the land. It is a poor wretched "out-at-elbows" style of farming, this western agriculture; there is never any autumn work in the way of fencing or clearing of weeds, and beyond digging the potatoes which are required for the daily food, nothing is done from November till March.

Of late years, too, the home industries have in a great measure ceased. The draper's shop now supplies tweeds and calicoes in place of frieze and flannels they used to manufacture at home.

I believe the more advanced farmers are generally of opinion that, taking the vicissitudes of climate and bad harvests into consideration, farming in this district would be more remunerative if the whole country were allowed to get into skin, and tillage was practically abandoned for grazing. It is the intermixture of grazing and tillage which prevents agriculture improving; the profits of farming do not admit of the proper fencing of small holdings, so from November till February the cattle of each village wander about, in a heterogeneous sort of way, over everybody's holding, and no one thinks of interfering with them, but as soon as the people are beginning to turn their lands in March, then, by mutual agreements, the cattle are herded or hobbled, the fences are roughly made up, and summonses for trespass are frequent enough. But it seems almost impossible to prevent the trespassing of cattle; in fact, the whole art of herding appears to be for each man to endeavour to drive his cattle on to his neighbour's crops without being found out. Then, in order to increase the efficiency of the fences, the ditches are often dammed up so that they may be filled with water, and the result is that after heavy rains low-lying lands are swamped.

The recent storm has had a devastating effect on timber, but the damage done to the oat crop is by no means as great as the outcry would lead one to believe. The usual report current, is that the crop is utterly destroyed, or that the greater portion of it is lost, but my own observations lead me to believe that this is by no means the case.

At the time of the storm I should say that, generally speaking, half the crop of the entire country was in stooks, and of the remaining half, an equal portion was unreaped, to that properly secured in stacks. Very little injury was done to the stacks, but in unsheltered places the standing corn sustained serious damage, and the stooks suffered a good deal also.

In some localities the loss was inappreciable, and in others it was very considerable, but from all I can learn, I do not think one-eighth of the entire crop of the country has been lost.

Among the very small occupiers of land, who live always on the verge of chronic pauperism, I think that, owing to the shortness of provisions consequent on the partial failure of the potato crop, there will probably be an increased demand for relief, which however the ordinary resources of the Poor Laws will be fully able to meet.

I have the honour to be, gentlemen,

Your most obedient servant,

H. A. Robinson, Inspector.

The Local Government Board.

Report from Dr. Roughan.—District comprising parts of the Counties of Clare, Galway, Roscommon, and Westmeath.

Galway, October 8th, 1882.

Gentlemen,—I have the honour to acknowledge the receipt of your circular of the 8th of September, 1882, informing me that my report on the prospects of the harvest having been communicated to the Lord Lieutenant, the Board have received a communication from the Assistant Under Secretary, requesting the Board to instruct their Inspectors to report again on the subject at the beginning of October. In accordance with these instructions, I beg to state that from several reliable sources as well as from personal knowledge, the potato crop though far below the average of last year's crop, is more than fully equal to that produced after the introduction of the champions; the potatoes are now being sold at 4½d. per stone, and I feel satisfied that that price will not be exceeded until June next. The grain crops are excellent, especially the oats. Turnips, a crop now extensively sown, show an abundant yield; and turf, I am glad to say, is in a well saved state, being perfectly dry and in most cases has been removed from the bog to the little farmyard where it is built against the gable of the house.

I annex extracts from reports received from clerks of Unions, which can be added in a form of Appendix if the Board so desire.

I have the honour to be, gentlemen,

Your obedient servant,

Geo. F. Roughan.

Galway Union.

The potato crop is deficient and will not yield more than half last year's crop, this is owing chiefly to the fact that the people persisted in sowing the old seeds. However, no apprehension is felt, or need be felt of any thing bordering on even a scarcity of potatoes.

The condition of the turf is most satisfactory. It is well saved, and in most instances has been removed from the bog and placed in the farmyard.

Athlone Union.

The potato crop is not so luxuriant as last year, yet there will be an abundant supply of good potatoes.

The condition of the turf is good. It is quite dry and has been drawn home to the small haggards. The other crops present a fair appearance, especially the corn and turnip crops.

Portumna Union.

The potato crop this year is not quite equal to that of last year in yield or size, in truth not more than half last year's yield. The wheat crop is not equal to that of last year; a fair supply of turf has been saved.

Loughrea Union.

The yield from the potato crop will scarcely equal one half that of last year.

The supply of turf is cheap, abundant, and well saved, so that no fear need be entertained of a fuel famine. The late genial weather of the past month has rendered a great service in maturing crops, and has afforded an opportunity of carrying on successfully the harvest operations. The champion potato is still growing, and should the remainder of this month prove fine, the yield when digging will exceed former expectations. Although there is such a falling off in the supply of potatoes, as compared with last year, still the yield will fully equal the average of past years, and with an abundant supply of cereals at a low price, the poor are in no danger of suffering during the ensuing winter, and there is no probability of any pressure on the poor rates.

Glennamaddy Union.

The potato crop in this Union is scarcely half last year's yield. The failure of the potato is attributable in a great measure to the continual wet weather of June and July. Some distress may be expected in this poor Union but nothing bordering on want. A sufficient supply of turf has been saved so that no want of fuel need be anticipated.

Gort Union.

The potato crop though not as good this harvest as on last, yet it is very fair and contrasts favourably with past years in yield and quality. The turf has been saved, and no scarcity of fuel need be apprehended.

Ballinasloe Union.

The potato crop is fair, but will not equal that of last year. Turf is scarce and serious doubts are entertained that poor classes will suffer much from want of fire.

Mount Bellew Union.

The potato crop not near so good as it was last year, either in quantity or quality. The potatoes are not as good or as free from disease as last year, but as far as I can learn, the disease only extends to the old seed, and the champions remain, except in an occasional patch, untouched. No scarcity of potatoes is apprehended. The turf is in a very good state, the fine weather having done much to improve its condition, so that no dread need be felt that anything bordering on a fuel famine will be felt.

Ballyvaghan Union.

The potato crop in this Union is worse than in former years, the potatoes are small and the crop by no means plentiful. The corn crop is fair; the turnips have improved since the middle of last month, so that an average crop may be expected. The turf cutting is a late operation in this Union so that the people, instead of having their turf properly dried, are now in the month of October looking out for fine weather to save it.

Corrofin Union.

The potato crop is not as good as last year. The yield will not be more than last year's crop, and the quality is not quite so good.

The turf is in a fair state and is as well saved as usual. The other crops present a healthy appearance and the farmers seem satisfied with the yield.

Report from Major Spaight.—District comprising the Counties of Sligo and Leitrim, and parts of the Counties of Donegal, Fermanagh, and Roscommon.

Ardaghowen, Sligo, October 10, 1882.

Gentlemen,—With reference to your letter of the 8th ult., requesting a further report on the state of the crops and the prospects of the general harvest in my district, I regret much that I have to report a very marked change since the date of my last report.

The continued wet and inclement weather has retarded and injured all crops, but especially the potatoes; upon these its influence has been very fatal; the tubers, which I hoped with a term of dry and genial weather might have matured and attained their natural size, were blighted in the early stages of their growth, and the loss is now much greater than I anticipated. This is unfortunately more apparent in the districts where it will be most severely felt, viz., in the poor, mountain sides, and cold wet lands, where the holdings are small, the people more crowded, and very poor, and who had little or no manure to force the early growth.

Among this class of people I am convinced that few will have more than half a crop, and these are rotting so fast the supply will not last beyond the month of February next, and many will not have a potato left after Christmas.

I was unwilling to believe that so great a change could have taken place in the condition of this crop, and have delayed making this report in order that I might, as far as possible, test by personal examination the reports I have received from the officers of the different unions in the district.

I am now compelled to believe that this crop will prove one of the worst we have had for some years.

The only cereal grown to any extent in my district is oats; this crop promised well, but will hardly fulfil the expectations of a month since, the continued wet and absence of heat prevented the grain from filling as it should, and much retarded the ripening and harvest work. This has proved especially unfortunate this year, for a fierce gale swept over the district on the 1st October, and as much of this crop was either uncut or in stooks in the fields, causing a very serious amount of damage. I have myself seen the corn completely threshed as it stood on the ground.

Hay is an abundant crop, but as much of it was also out on the 1st inst., it has suffered severely.

Turf was cut in abundance, but has been very difficult to save, and cannot be of good quality. Much of it is still out on the bogs and cannot be got in without fine weather.

All other crops, though grown to a very small extent in my district, are a fair average.

The prices obtained for young stock, butter, &c., are and have been very remunerative, and the class of farmers who hold sufficient land and are able to produce these will, I think be fairly well off this year, but unfortunately in many parts of my district the great mass of the people, whose holdings are small, and the land very poor, are unable to raise or keep any stock except, perhaps, a pig, and they depend almost entirely on the potato crop to enable them to do so much; when this fails, in the absence of employment, they are left without any resource whatever.

I much fear that in some of the poorer parts of my district there will be great difficulty in saving sufficient potatoes for seed next year, and even if done, that it will be ill matured and bad seed.

I have the honour to be, gentlemen,

Your obedient servant,

GEORGE SPAIGHT.

The Local Government Board, Dublin.

Local Government Board, Dublin,
27th October, 1882.

Sir,

With reference to your letter of the 5th ultimo, referring to the reports made by the Inspectors of the Local Government Board in the month of August last, on the state of the potato crop, the condition of the turf where it is cut, and the prospects of the general harvest in their respective districts, and requesting that the Inspectors might be requested to report again on the subject at the beginning of October, the Board have now the honour to forward to you, for the information of His Excellency the Lord Lieutenant two copies of further reports which they have received from the several District Inspectors on the subject.

By order of the Board,

W. D. Wodsworth, Assistant Secretary.

To R. G. C. Hamilton, esq., &c., Dublin Castle.

No. 3.—Instructions relative to Apprehended Distress.

Local Government Board, Dublin,
18th November, 1882.

Sir,

The Local Government Board for Ireland desire to inform the Board of Guardians that they have received communications from some of the western districts in Ireland relating to apprehended distress, and that, while they have reason to believe that the representations as to the extent of the destitution existing, or likely to arise, have, in many instances been exaggerated, they entertain no doubt that, owing to a deficient potato crop, there will be unusual poverty in particular localities, and an increased number of applications for relief.

Under these circumstances the Board of Guardians should make such arrangements as may be necessary for the relief of the destitute poor in the manner authorised by the Laws at present in force, and should place themselves in a position to discharge duly and effectually the duties which devolve upon them in the administration of the Irish Poor Relief Acts.

It is of the utmost importance that the Board of Guardians should be prepared to meet any degree of pressure on the Workhouse which is likely to occur, by making provision beforehand of ample stores of bedding and clothing, and by placing all the unoccupied wards of the Workhouse in good and habitable order.

It would also be desirable that the Board of Guardians should take into consideration the number and extent of the relief districts in their Union, and ascertain whether the Relieving Officers are in a position to perform their important duties efficiently, and whether they are accessible to the poor persons residing in all parts of their districts. These objects cannot be attained if the relief districts be not of moderate size, and the Local Government Board hope that this point will receive the immediate and careful attention of the Board of Guardians.

In considering the probable wants of the poor in their Union during the winter season the Board of Guardians must rely on the powers vested in them by the existing Poor Law Acts which they are appointed to execute, and they should take all the steps which may appear to be necessary to enable them to administer these Acts effectually and with success.

By order of the Board,

To the Clerk, —— Union. B. Banks, Secretary.

NAMES of UNIONS to which this CIRCULAR was sent.

Athlone	Clonakilty	Kenmare	Oughterard
Ballina	Cootehill	Killadysert	Portumna
Ballinasloe	Corrofin	Killala	Rathkeale
Ballinrobe	Croom	Killarney	Roscommon
Ballyshannon	Dingle	Kilmallock	Scariff
Ballyvaghan	Donegal	Kilrush	Skibbereen
Bandon	Dromore West	Letterkenny	Skull
Bantry	Dunfanaghy	Limerick	Sligo
Bawnboy	Dungarvan	Listowel	Stranorlar
Belmullet	Dunmanway	Loughrea	Strokestown
Boyle	Ennis	Macroom	Swineford
Cahersiveen	Ennistymon	Manorhamilton	Tipperary
Carlow	Fermoy	Midleton	Tobercurry
Carrickmacross	Galway	Milford	Tralee
Carrick-on-Shannon	Glennamaddy	Millstreet	Trim
Castlebar	Glenties	Mohill	Tuam
Castlerea	Glin	Mount Bellew	Tulla
Castletown	Gort	Newcastle	Tullamore
Claremorris	Inishowen	Newport	Westport
Clifden	Kanturk		

No 4.—DISTRESS.—RELIEF DISTRICTS in UNIONS.

Local Government Board, Dublin,
20th November, 1882.

SIR,

The Local Government Board for Ireland transmit to you, herewith, a copy of a letter which they have addressed to the Boards of Guardians of the Unions situated in the Western Counties in Ireland, and which they propose to forward to the Boards of Guardians in any other parts of the country who may express their fears that exceptional distress will prevail in their Unions during the present winter and the coming spring.

You will observe that the Local Government Board have informed the Boards of Guardians that in considering the probable wants of the poor in their Unions during the winter season they must rely on the powers vested in them by the existing Poor Law Acts, which they are appointed to execute; and the Local Government Board wish to direct your immediate and careful attention to the arrangements existing in the Unions in your charge for the performance of the duties devolving on Relieving Officers.

The Local Government Board attach much importance to this subject, and they are prepared to exercise to the fullest extent, if necessary, the powers vested in them by the 4th Section of the Irish Poor Relief Extension Act, for the purpose of securing the employment of a sufficient number of Relieving Officers in every Union, who will be accessible to the poor persons resident in all parts of their respective districts.

The Local Government Board request that you will be so good as to report to them, with as little delay as possible, with reference to each Union in your charge, whether, in your opinion, the relief districts are of such a size as to enable the Relieving Officers to discharge their duties duly and effectually; whether the Relieving Officers are active and efficient men; and whether they reside at such places as to be within reach of the poor persons living in all parts of their districts.

By Order of the Board,

W. D. WODSWORTH, Assistant-Secretary.

To each Inspector.

No. 5.—INSTRUCTIONS relative to DISTRESS.

Local Government Board, Dublin,

12th December, 1882.

SIR,

With reference to the communication of the Local Government Board for Ireland, dated the 18th ultimo, on the subject of apprehended distress in certain districts in Ireland, the Board now transmit to you, for the information of the Board of Guardians, a copy of a letter which has been written by direction of the Lord Lieutenant in reply to a representation submitted to him respecting the condition of the poor in part of the Glenties Union; this letter describes the views of the Government as to the measures which should be taken for the relief of the destitute poor in Unions in which exceptional distress may prevail, and also expresses the intentions of the Government with respect to the proposals which have been submitted to His Excellency for the establishment of public works for the purpose of providing employment for the poor.

The Local Government Board have already pointed out to the Board of Guardians that in considering the probable wants of the poor in their Union during the winter season they must rely on the powers vested in them by the existing Poor Law Acts which they are appointed to execute, and the Board have now obtained His Excellency's permission to give publicity to the annexed letter, as they think it a matter of much importance that persons who may need relief should be made aware that they must not look forward to the expenditure of public money on public works, and that if they should be in want they must take advantage of and apply for the relief provided by law for the destitute poor.

The Local Government Board trust that the Guardians will not allow any delay to take place in making the arrangements which have been pointed out to them as necessary to enable them duly to discharge the duties which devolve upon them.

It would also be desirable that each Relieving Officer should be directed to attend frequently in different parts of his district for the purpose of receiving applications from persons in need of relief, and of inquiring into the circumstances and requirements of the poor, and that public notice should be given of the time fixed for his attendance at each relief station.

By order of the Board,

W. D. WODSWORTH, Assistant Secretary.

To the Clerk of the ——— Union.

[Sent to same Unions as Circular No. 3.]

Dublin Castle,

9th December, 1882.

I am directed to inform you that His Excellency has had under his careful consideration a letter which you forwarded to the Chief Secretary on the 28th ultimo respecting the existing and threatened distress in Carrick and Glencolumbkill, county Donegal.

The partial failure of the potato crop in certain districts of the West has given serious concern to Her Majesty's Government, and has led them to review carefully the existing agencies for the relief of distress, and His Excellency thinks it well to take this opportunity of stating the views of Her Majesty's Government with respect to the measures which should be taken for the relief of the destitute poor, not only in the Glenties Union, but also in other parts of the West in which exceptional distress may prevail.

Various proposals, all of them involving expenditure of public money, have been submitted to His Excellency and the Local Government Board as to the means by which the distress should be met, the most prominent of these being the establishment of works to give employment to poor persons in the districts where want exists or is apprehended.

Her Majesty's Government have given careful consideration to these methods of affording relief, but they are not prepared to adopt any of them, as they are satisfied by experience that relief works are not only extravagant and demoralising in their effects, but they often fail to aid the most necessitous.

The Government have, after full consideration of all the circumstances, determined to rely solely upon the administration of relief through the ordinary channel provided by law, viz., the Boards of Guardians, as they are satisfied that no machinery so efficient as that of the Guardians can be devised for the distribution of relief.

The Local Government Board being fully alive to the serious duty thus thrown upon the Guardians have already taken steps to secure that the machinery for the distribution of relief is in efficient working order.

They have issued a Circular to the Guardians of the Unions in which distress is apprehended calling their attention to the necessity of so limiting the area of each relief district that the relieving officer will be readily accessible to all the poor persons residing in it, and have instructed their Inspectors to make inquiries, and report at once whether the arrangements made in this respect are satisfactory in each Union under their charge.

You are, of course, aware that under the existing Poor Law Acts relief cannot be given in any Union to able-bodied men unless the Workhouse is full, or, by reason of fever or infectious disease, is unfit for the reception of poor persons, and by this principle Her Majesty's Government have determined to abide.

The Local Government Board have, in their circular letter above referred to, pointed out to the Boards of Guardians that it is of the utmost importance that they should be prepared to meet any degree of pressure in the Workhouse which is likely to occur, by making provision beforehand of ample stores of bedding and clothing, and by placing all the unoccupied wards of the Workhouse in good and habitable order.

Her Majesty's Government are fully aware of the great objection entertained by many poor persons to go into the Workhouse; but it cannot be contended that persons who are unable to procure for themselves the necessaries of life should be allowed to determine the manner in which public relief is to be afforded, nor can any just ground of complaint exist if to every destitute person the means shall be readily accessible of obtaining effectual relief.

In some Unions the Poor Rates which the Guardians may be able to make and levy during the present year may not be sufficient to meet the exceptional expenditure thrown upon them. When such is proved to be the case, and when the Local Government Board are satisfied that the want of funds does not arise from neglect in enforcing the collection of rates, the Government will be prepared to empower Boards of Guardians to borrow at once such sums as may be necessary to meet the temporary pressure on their resources, and to obtain afterwards the necessary legislative sanction to such proceeding.

No. 6.—Relief in Workhouse, to Persons in Occupation of Land.

Local Government Board, Dublin,
5th January, 1883.

Sir,

The Local Government Board for Ireland transmit to you herewith for the information of the Board of Guardians, a copy of a letter which has been addressed to the Board by direction of His Excellency the Lord Lieutenant, relating to the responsibility of Boards of Guardians in regard to the administration of relief, and the Board trust that the views expressed in that communication may receive the Guardians' careful attention.

The Local Government Board take this opportunity of informing the Board of Guardians that, in consequence of representations which they have received from different quarters, they apprehend that the provisions of the 2nd section of the Act 25 and 26 Vic., cap. 83, are not always correctly understood, and they, therefore, think it desirable that the Relieving Officers employed in the Union should make it clearly known to poor persons in their districts who are in the occupation of land, that, if destitute, they may be relieved in the Workhouse, and that the circumstance of being so relieved will not in any way affect their interests in their holdings.

By order of the Board,

W. D. Wodsworth, Assistant Secretary.

To the Clerk of the ——— Union.

[Sent to same Unions as Circular No. 3.]

Dublin Castle,
2nd January, 1883.

Sir,

I am directed by the Lord Lieutenant to acquaint you, for the information of the Local Government Board, that His Excellency has had before him certain resolutions passed by Boards of Guardians in a few of the districts where distress is apprehended, which appear to show that some of them are under a misapprehension as to their responsibility in the matter of relief.

The administration of relief does not rest with the Executive Government. It is by statute entrusted to the Boards of Guardians, and it is not competent for them to divest themselves of the obligation imposed upon them by law to provide relief for the destitute poor in their Unions.

The Executive Government fully recognise the difficulties the Guardians may have to contend with in districts where exceptional distress may prevail, but they have confidence that the Guardians will show themselves equal to the emergency, and that their local administration will not be found unable to cope with local distress.

His Excellency anticipates that the only cases in which failure could arise might be in some few of the poorest Unions in the West of Ireland, where the Poor Rates which the Guardians might be able to make and levy during the next few months might not be sufficient to meet the exceptional expenditure thrown upon them, and these cases, should any such arise, would be fully met by an extension of the powers of borrowing as described in the last paragraph of the enclosure to the Circular Letter to Boards of Guardians of the 12th ultimo.

I am, sir, your obedient servant,

R. G. C. Hamilton.

The Secretary to the Local Government
Board, Custom House.

No. 7.—Communication from Under Secretary, dated 10th March, 1883, as to Distress Existing or Apprehended in Certain Parts of Ireland.

Dublin Castle,
10th March, 1883.

Sir,

With reference to the undertaking given by the Chief Secretary in the House of Commons last night to lay upon the table a report of the state of the distress in Ireland, I am directed by the Lord Lieutenant to request that you will cause such a report to be immediately prepared, specifying the districts in which distress exists or is apprehended, and the measures which the Government have taken to meet it, such as appointing an additional Inspector for Glenties, reducing the area of relieving officers' districts, seeing that the Workhouses are in a proper state of preparation, &c.

The report should contain statistics of the Workhouse accommodation, and of the numbers now in receipt of relief both in-door and out-door in these districts compared with the numbers at the corresponding periods of previous years. It should also give information as to the existence of special disease in any of these districts, and of the steps taken to deal with it, and the opinion of the Local Government Board founded upon the reports of their Inspectors should be given as to the state of the people generally, and whether the Board are satisfied that the existing arrangements are sufficient to cope with the present and anticipated distress. This should be very clear and explicit.

It would be well also that information should, if possible, be obtained of the cost of food in these districts now as compared with the cost in previous years, and it would be well to refer to the action which the Government were prepared to take to convey food to certain districts when it was reported that owing to the recent bad weather the supply through ordinary channels was likely to fall short.

His Excellency would be glad that you should have this statistical information kept and returned to him fortnightly, and that the Local Government Board should accompany this with any general or special observations bearing upon the state of the various districts, particularly as to the means of employment, the rate of wages, and the expenditure (if any), of charitable funds for relief purposes. The fortnightly report should also include any information received from the Inspectors or other trustworthy sources as to the general physical condition of the people.

I am, sir, your obedient servant.

R. O. C. HAMILTON.

To the Secretary, Local Government Board.

REPORT from the LOCAL GOVERNMENT BOARD for IRELAND, dated the 13th day of March, 1883, in reply, with REPORTS from Inspectors of the Local Government Board, and other PAPERS enclosed therewith.

The Secretary to the Local Government Board, Dublin, to the Under Secretary to the Lord Lieutenant.

Local Government Board, Dublin,
13 March, 1883.

SIR,

I am directed by the Local Government Board for Ireland to acknowledge the receipt of your letter of the 10th instant, in which you state that the Lord Lieutenant requests that the Board will cause a report to be prepared, specifying the districts in Ireland in which distress exists, or is apprehended, and the measures which have been taken to meet it.

Representations as to distress have been received from different parts of Ireland; but the districts in which it prevails to the greatest extent are situated in the counties of Mayo, Galway, Donegal, Sligo, and Clare. The Board, however, propose to submit to His Excellency some information as to all the counties which have usually been termed the distressed districts—viz., the counties in Connaught and the counties Donegal, Clare, Kerry, and West Cork; and the Board transmit to you herewith copies of reports which have been received this day from the Inspectors having charge of unions in that part of Ireland.

The reports of the Inspectors contain such full particulars as to the state of the poor in their several districts that the Board think it only necessary to refer His Excellency to them, for the Board cannot afford any more specific or reliable information than is contained therein as to the condition and prospects of the poor in the West of Ireland. It appears to the Board that while there is, no doubt, great poverty in particular localities, the destitution is not widespread and general; and the Board adhere to the opinion that the administration of the relief which may be afforded under the poor law is sufficient to cope with the present and anticipated distress.

The Board are glad to observe that some of the Inspectors look forward to an improvement in the condition of the labouring classes from the stimulus given to farming operations by the recent fine weather.

The Board annex a return, showing the number of persons in receipt of relief in the counties above referred to, by which His Excellency will observe that while there is ample and suitable accommodation in the Workhouses for more than 28,000 persons, there are at present only 13,170 inmates, and further that, although the total number of persons now in receipt of relief exceeds the number relieved at this time last year by 6,873, it is less by 3,031 than the number relieved in March, 1881.

The Board also annex a statement of the prices of potatoes, Indian meal, oatmeal, and flour, in different parts of the West at the present time, and at the corresponding period of last year, which shows a considerable increase in the cost of the three former articles of food as compared with last year.

With reference to the existence of special disease in the distressed districts, the Board have received reports of the prevalence of fever in Dromore West Union, in the county Sligo, and in Swinford Union, in the county Mayo. In the former case, it was alleged that the disease was typhoid fever, and that the cause of the outbreak was the want of proper food, bad clothing, and insufficient covering; but, on sending a Medical Inspector to visit the place, he reported that, in his opinion, the disease was introduced, in the first instance, by a boy who came to the village suffering from the fever, and was afterwards propagated and spread through the medium of a small river running close to a house occupied by fever patients, the water of which, polluted by the washing of clothes, and by the excreta of the sick family, was made use of in its course by others who were attacked, and who were living lower down the stream.

In the case of Swinford Union, it was alleged in a newspaper report that over 30 persons were in the Workhouse hospital suffering from famine fever; but on communicating with the medical officer, he reported that there were only 19 cases in hospital, and that they were not cases of famine fever, but typhus and typhoid fever. The Board, however, thought it right to send a Medical Inspector to visit the union, and to ascertain the character and origin of the disease.

It was also alleged that fever was prevalent at Kilcar, in county Donegal; but on obtaining a report from a Medical Inspector, it appeared that there was only one case of fever in that parish.

With respect to the measures which have been taken to meet apprehended distress, the Board would, in the first instance, observe that two additional Inspectors have been employed temporarily, in order that unions in which exceptional distress exists may have constant attention, and that the Board may be able to obtain prompt information on any matter calling for inquiry.

The attention of the Board has also been directed to the area of each relief district, and additional relieving officers have been appointed where such districts have been found too large, in order that the relieving officers may be readily accessible to all poor persons residing in every part of the union. Six additional relieving officers have already been appointed in the part of Ireland referred to in this Report, and further appointments are under consideration.

It has also been pointed out to Boards of Guardians that it is of the utmost importance that they should be prepared to meet any pressure on the Workhouse which is likely to occur, by making provision before hand of ample stores of bedding and clothing, and by placing all unoccupied wards of the Workhouse in good and habitable order. Copies of the circulars addressed to Boards of Guardians on the subject of their duties in regard to the relief of the poor are hereunto annexed.

The Board were informed on some occasions that owing to bad weather a supply of food could not be conveyed to certain districts through ordinary channels, and was likely to fall short, and in such cases the services of gunboats were promptly placed at the disposal of the

Board and of Boards of Guardians by the naval authorities. Food was thus conveyed to the islands of Boffin and Innisturk from Westport, and to the island of Innishmurray from Sligo, while a gunboat was held in readiness, if required, to convey provisions to the neighbourhood of Glencolumbkill, in the county Donegal, and is now at the disposal of the Inspector of the district for any such purpose.

The Inspector of the unions in the county Mayo and Galway has also been allowed the use of a gunboat, to enable him to visit the islands on the coast, and much advantage has resulted from the assistance afforded by means of gunboats to the Board's Inspectors and to Boards of Guardians in making arrangements for the due relief of the poor on the western coast.

I have, &c.,

(Signed) W. D. Wodsworth, Secretary.

To the Under-Secretary,
The Castle, Dublin.

Report from Mr. Robinson :—District comprising County Mayo, and part of County Galway.

Ballina, 13 March, 1883.

Gentlemen,

In reply to your circular letter, received yesterday, requesting me to report as to the state of the poor in my district, I have the honour to submit the following report, and to inform you that since the commencement of the present year I have personally visited every part of my district, and made careful and exhaustive inquiries into the condition and prospects of the poorer classes.

Although there is a probability of an unusual amount of destitution in several parts of this district, still I do not anticipate that there will be anything in the nature of general or widespread distress.

For the occupiers of fairly substantial sized farms I think the present season is regarded as a profitable one, as the prices for cattle, sheep, &c., are beyond expectation remunerative, but for the very small holders who, for the first time since credit was stopped, now find themselves dependent on their own resources, without extraneous assistance, there is an immediate prospect of distress, which it is likely will lead to an increased demand for relief.

This distress, I believe, will be confined to particular localities, and will only be felt by that class of persons who live in a state of chronic poverty on holdings, the gross produce of which could not maintain them, at the best of times, from harvest to harvest. And if the crop of potatoes this year had been equal to that of last year, and if the price of provisions had been quite as low, the only difference to these people would be that they would run short of food in June instead of in April, as I apprehend many of them will now. There was no scarcity, it is true, last June, but then it must be remembered that the people at that time had not, as a rule, paid their rent or discharged their many other liabilities.

In forwarding to your Board the information demanded as to the price of provisions, &c., at present, and at the corresponding date last year, I have thought it well to quote the prices of the same articles in

March 1880, as that was the period of recent years when distress was most intense in this district; and your Board may thus be enabled to form some comparison between the present year and this trying time referred to.

UNION.	Potatoes per Stone.			Oatmeal per Cwt.		
	1883.	1882.	1880.	1883.	1882.	1880.
	d.	d.	d.	s. d.	s. d.	s. d.
Westport, . .	6½	3	6	16 8	13 8	13 8
Ballina, . . .	6½	6½	4½	14 8	16 6	13
Claremorris, .	6½	4	6	13 8	11 6	11 10½
Castlebar, . .	8	4	8	11 8	10 8	11 10
Swineford, . .	7	4	8	14 8	11 0	12 6
Ballinrobe, . .	4	3½	7	15 6	11 6	13 6
Oughterard, . .	8	5	8	16 6	11 8	14 6
Clifden, . . .	6	6	8	16 8	13 8	14 8
Newport, . . .	6	?	7	13 8	13 6	11 6

UNION.	Indian Meal per Cwt.			Flour per Cwt.		
	1883.	1882.	1880.	1883.	1882.	1880.
	s. d.	s. d.	s. d.	s. d.	s. d.	s. d.
Westport, . .	9 6	8 0	7 9	16 0	10 0	15 0
Ballina, . . .	8 9	6 6	7 6	17 8	17 8	16 6
Claremorris, . .	8 3	? ?	6 6	16 6	?	?
Castlebar, . .	8 6	7 8	6 9	16 8	?	?
Swineford, . .	8 6	6 5	7 6	16 8	17 8	15 6
Ballinrobe, . .	8 6	7 6	7 1	15 8	16 8	17 4
Oughterard, . .	9 6	6 6	7 6	16 9	16 6	16 6
Clifden, . . .	9 0	8 6	6 6	16 6	16 6	16 6
Newport, . . .	8 6	8 6	7 9	16 0	?	?

N.B.—The quotations in Newport, Castlebar, and Claremorris are Workhouse contract prices.

It will be seen from the foregoing table that although the price of potatoes was much the same in 1880 as it is now, Indian meal and oatmeal were considerably cheaper then, and this would appear to show that the circumstances of the people are even worse at the present time than they were then. Such, however, is not the case; the earnings in England were better last autumn than they were in the autumn of 1879. Cattle that in 1880 could be bought for £14 would not be sold now for £17. Sheep, which at that date would have been sold for 35s., would fetch 60s. to-day, and in addition to this high price for cattle, the remittances from America are now far beyond what they were then, or what, it is believed, they ever were before. The actual extent of these it would be difficult, of course, to ascertain, but that the money is coming in largely from America to these poor districts is a notorious and incontestable fact, and one which is easily accounted for by the large number of emigrants who left Ireland during the past two years.

The people in these vastly overpopulated and distressed localities are living in the hope that Government interference will come to their aid, and prop them up in their untenable position a little longer, and they seem also to have formed the opinion that the Government can take the place of private enterprise, and speculate in schemes of possible and impossible desirability.

I am most anxious not to minimise the distress; there is distress existing, and imminent, but it is, as I have before stated, by no means general, and it can be met by the administration of the ordinary poor law; and if there is any legislation for isolated cases of the kind, and if extraordinary measures of relief are adopted, the discontinuance of them at any time hereafter must inevitably leave this class of small tenants in the same state that they are at present.

I am, &c.,

(Signed),

H. A. Robinson, Inspector.

The Local Government Board,
Dublin.

Report from Dr. Roughan:—District comprising parts of the Counties of Clare, Galway, Roscommon, and Westmeath.

Loughrea, 19 March, 1883.

Gentlemen,

In reply to your letter, I have the honour to inform you that the distress in my unions, as far as I can learn, is not as serious as I apprehended it would be at this period. I find it quite impossible to ascertain how the poor people have struggled on up to this; the number relieved under the poor laws would not account for their ameliorated condition, so that the only means that could have tided them over their difficulties was charity given chiefly by their neighbours, and some from public benefactors. There is scarcely any credit given by the shopkeepers, and the price of provisions is much higher than at a corresponding period last year; for instance

The price of potatoes in 1883 was—

		5½d. per stone;	1882, 9½d.
Oatmeal - - - - - -	1883, 12s.	per cwt.;	1882, 14s. 6d.
Indian Meal - - - - -	1883, 7s. 9d.	„	1882, 8s. 9d.
Flour - - - - - -	1883, 16s. 6d.	„	1882, 15s. 6d.

I have, &c.,

(Signed),

George F. Roughan.

The Local Government Board.

REPORT from Dr. WOODHOUSE:—District comprising part of County Donegal.

Glenties, 13 March, 1883.

GENTLEMEN,

I have the honour of acknowledging receipt of your circular letter of the 10th instant.

In reply, I will take, *seriatim*, the three unions in my temporary charge.

In Donegal Union the circumstances of the poor are not so good as last year; employment is rather scarcer, and food is dearer. At the same time there is no general destitution.

In Glenties Union, owing to the fact that the bulk of the population are in good years but slightly removed from want, and that last harvest there was in many districts an almost complete failure of the potato crop, there are manifest signs of extreme poverty. Many of the poor have during the last three or four years been getting more deeply into debt, consequently credit is to a considerable extent stopped. Their industries which, with the aid of their farming, helped them in former years to live, are gradually failing them. The manufacture of flannel and woollen cloth for their own clothing has lessened. Their fishing has been less productive. The kelp making, owing to a cheaper substance yielding iodine, found in Chili, is unremunerative; it used to bring £6 10s. a ton, it will now bring only £3 10*s*. Wages for the knitting of stockings and gloves have been lately reduced 25 per cent., as stocking-knitting looms in Leicestershire have been so far perfected as to enable stockings to be woven by machinery almost as well as by hand. Every part of this union is affected by the decline of one or more of these industries.

Very many of the holdings are far too small, and much of the land is wretched, and wretchedly tilled, the same patches being cropped by potatoes many years in succession. The failure of this crop last year was most marked where the holdings were smallest and poorest.

In some localities, however, *e.g.*, Dungloe and the "Rosses," the younger adults go about the beginning of this month to work in the neighbouring counties of Derry and Tyrone, or in Scotland; their wages, or the credit given on account of these wages, will lessen the distress. Many all through the union have friends in America who send them money.

In other parts, *e.g.*, Glencolumbkille, the people are not accustomed to seek work elsewhere, nor will they do so; one of the most formidable difficulties of the situation is the supineness of the people themselves in apprehending and grappling with their untoward circumstances. This is most marked where charitable relief has been most freely given, *e.g.*, Glencolumbkille.

Many (more than half) have a cow, or perhaps two cows, besides some sheep, but they are not willing to sell these, as they would be expected to pay off their debts with the price. I should think nearly one-third have no animal larger than a pig.

Albeit in this poverty I do not believe that there has been any starvation.

In Dunfanaghy Union, as in Donegal, there are some who are exceedingly poor, but potatoes are far more abundant, and there is far less general poverty than in Glenties.

The prices of the following in Dunfanaghy, where your letter reached me, are :—

—	12th March, 1883.	Same time last Year.
Potatoes, ...	6d. per stone, . .	3d.
Oatmeal, ...	13s. 6d. per cwt, . .	11s. 6d.
Indian Meal, . . .	8s. 3d. " . .	8s.
Flour (best; this is most used), .	16s. " . .	16s.
Flour (second quality), . .	14s. " . .	14s.

In Glenties (from which I now write) the prices are :—

—	12th March, 1883.	Same time last Year.
Potatoes, ...	7d. to 7½d. per stone, .	4d.
Oatmeal, ...	14s. 6d. per cwt., . .	11s. 6d.
Indian Meal, . . .	10s. 6d. " . .	8s. 3d.
Flour (best), . . .	16s. 6d. " . .	16s.

I have, &c.

(Signed) STEWART WOODHOUSE.

The Local Government Board, Ireland.

REPORT from Mr. MACFARLANE :—District comprising parts of the Counties of Donegal, Londonderry, and Tyrone.

Killybegs, Monday, 12 March, 1883.

SIR,

In accordance with the request of the Local Government Board, conveyed in your letter of 10th instant, that I would furnish by this evening's post a report as to the state of the poor *generally* in my district, as far as I am able to afford information from the knowledge I possess, I beg, in reply, to state that having gone over the Donegal Unions immediately after the storm of 1st October, and from time to time since going through these unions with an anxious and friendly eye, as well as a strong sense of responsibility, making careful inquiry in various directions, and from the best sources for obtaining reliable information, up to the present hour, and except in some isolated cases which would have been best relieved in a workhouse, I have not seen or been informed of that serious destitution which has been so prominently put before the public. In fact, I would not suppose these descriptions referred to the district with which I had become so familiar. However, with a very continuous and extended experience of this class of land occupiers, and the soil and climate to be considered reaching back to the real potato failure and famine of 1846–7, I have been considering whether one board of guardians might not make provision to help extreme cases with seed potatoes, as in the Glenties Union, which has, in my mind, some exceptional claims for consideration, as they had not the full benefit of the Seed Act in getting a good quality of potato, as I stated on a former occasion. I allude to it as the only union in my district where I would feel bound to suggest something of the kind, if it could be done, as a supplement to local effort. I take leave to enclose herewith an appeal for subscriptions to aid those in what is decidedly in itself the *poorest portions* of Glenties Union, and considering how every kind of appeal in these matters has been *exaggerated*, I venture to commend its comparative accuracy. It will appear to ask seed for only about 13 per cent. of that very poor portion of Donegal, the Rosses.

In reference to the second portion of your letter, I beg to say that seed potatoes are increasing in price, but here and at Donegal good champion seed potatoes can be had at about 8*d*. a stone; last year they were so plenty as to be almost unsaleable, but could certainly be bought at 2½*d*. per stone.

Flour is rather cheaper than last year, being from 1*s*. 10*d*. to 1*s*. 11*d*. per stone, as against 2*s*. 1*d*. last year. Oatmeal 1*s*. 10*d*., much about same as last year. Indian meal is about 8*s*. 6*d*. per cwt., but is coming down in price. The contract price at Donegal Union till 1st June is 8*s*. 8*d*. It was about same last year.

This is the best port this side of Donegal, and I have just seen some Indian meal landed to go towards Glenties on carts.

I am, &c.,

(Signed), H. J. MACFARLANE,
Local Government Inspector.

To W. D. Wodsworth, Esq., Secretary,
Local Government Board, Dublin.

SEED for the Parishes of TEMPLECRONE and LETTERMACAWARD, on the North-West Coast of Donegal.

Several hundred families in the above-named parishes are in the greatest need of food and seed, and in a state verging on starvation. In the two parishes there are some 2,300 families. The potatoes kept for seed, in most cases, are sickly, not having come to maturity, and are therefore incapable of producing a healthy crop. Many will have to part with the last cow to purchase some, while it is calculated that 400 families are without stock or seed. More than £2,000 is required to procure half the quantity usually planted. The members of committee appeal for seed rather than for food;—Firstly, because they have given up in despair the idea that charity can feed the destitute till August. Let that rest on the shoulders of a responsible Government. Secondly, because the merchants, on seeing a considerable quantity of seed planted, and the prospects of an abundant harvest, would advance, on credit, more meal than could be purchased by the seed money. Up to the present the committee shrank from the humiliation of parading before the public the destitution of the district, but silence, hitherto heroic, would be culpable, might be criminal if longer persevered in. That the members of committee are firmly convinced of the destitution, a better proof cannot be advanced than the fact that at their first meeting they contributed out of their own slender means the sum of £53. Subscriptions from the charitable are hereby most earnestly solicited, which will be received and acknowledged by any member of the committee, or by the treasurer, Rev. C. M'Glynn, P.P., Dungloe, county Donegal.

MEMBERS OF COMMITTEE:

Rev. B. Walker, P.P., Burtonport.
Rev. Joseph Boyle, C.C., Lettermacaward.
William Hammond, J.P., Lackbeg.
James Sweeney, Dungloe.
Edward Boyle, Dungloe.
James O'Donnell, Kincashlagh.
Maurice Boyle, Dungloe.
Daniel O'Donnell, Dungloe.
Owen Boyle, Dungloe.
Anthony Sharkey, Dungloe.
Neal Doherty, Dungloe.

REPORT from Mr. POWER:—District comprising the Counties of Sligo, Leitrim, and Roscommon, and portion of the County of Donegal.

Dublin, 13 March, 1883.

GENTLEMEN,

In reference to your letter of the 10th March, requesting, for the information of His Excellency the Lord Lieutenant, a report as to the state of the poor generally in my district, I may state that having only lately taken the Sligo district in charge, I am unable to speak with certainty as to the state of the poor generally. I am inclined to think that there is some distress in parts of my district, perhaps more than usual this year, owing to wet weather, the partial failure of the potato crop, and want of credit. With regard to the prices of the articles mentioned in your letter, I have telegraphed to where I thought reliable information could be got, and beg to forward the replies herewith.

I am, &c.,

(Signed) W. A. POWER.

The Local Government Board.

Poor Law Office, Carrick-on-Shannon,
12 March, 1883.

SIR,

I have the honour to acknowledge the receipt of your telegram, and beg leave to forward the information required.

TABLE.

Articles.	Quantity.	Prices on 11th March, 1882.	Prices on 10th March, 1883.
		s. d.	s. d.
Potatoes, . . .	Stone, . . .	0 4	0 6½
Oatmeal, . . .	Cwt., . . .	11 6	14 0
Indian Meal, . . .	" . . .	8 0	8 8
Flour, ...	" . . .	17 0	16 0

I am, &c.,

(Signed) A. O'CONNOR, Clerk of the Union.

To W. A. Power, Esq.,
Local Government Inspector, 35, Raglan-road.

Poor Law Office, Boyle,
19 March, 1883.

SIR,

In reply to your telegram received this day, the following are the prices of articles named:—

—	1882.		1883.	
	s.	d.	s.	d.
Eating potatoes, . . per cwt.	4	6	4	0
Seed potatoes, early, . . „	8	8	9	6
Seed potatoes, late sorts, . „	3	9	5	6
Indian meal, . . . „	7	6	8	0
Oatmeal, . . . „	14	6	13	0

Flour, best, 17s. 8d. per cwt.; same price last year. Oats for seed or feeding purposes, per 28 stone, 30s.; last year, 24s.

I am, &c.,
(Signed) W. ODBERT, Clerk of Union.

W. A. Power, Esq.

Poor Law Office, Sligo,
13 March, 1883.

SIR,

In reply to your telegram of the above date, the following are the particulars requested, viz.:

Best eating potatoes, at 8d. per stone this year, 1883.
Ditto . ditto 4d. „ last year, 1882.
Oatmeal, at £12 5s. per ton, 29th September to 15th March, 1883.
Ditto £17 10s. „ „ „ 1882.
Indian meal, £9 4s. „ „ „ 1883.
Ditto £7 15s. „ „ „ 1882.

There is no flour used in this union, but the price of white bread for the same periods named for meals was 6½d. per 3 lb. loaf.

I have, &c.,
(Signed) N. PARKE, Clerk of the Union.

W. A. Power, Esq.,
Local Government Inspector, &c., &c.

REPORT from Mr. BOURKE:—District comprising parts of the Counties of Clare, Limerick, Tipperary, and King's County.

36, Elgin-road, Dublin,
12 March, 1883.

GENTLEMEN,

In compliance with the wish expressed in your letter of the 10th, I beg to submit, for the information of His Excellency the Lord Lieutenant, the following report on the state of the poor generally in my district, so far as I am able to judge of it.

The winter was unusually wet even for Ireland, and the flooded state of the land putting a stop to all farm work, allowed of but little employment being given. The price of provisions also continued high throughout the year, and firing was bad and dear. Under the circumstances the condition of the labouring classes must necessarily have been trying, but, as far as I can judge, it was not materially worse than during many past years. Such assistance as is usually afforded by the comfortable farmers and the residents of the higher classes appears to have sufficed to check destitution and keep the poor from going, in any large numbers, on the rates. No public subscriptions were, as far as I know, set going for their relief, except in large towns like Limerick, Ennis, and Nenagh, where fuel funds were collected. But the resources of the established charitable societies (such as that of St. Vincent de Paul) were largely drawn on for food and clothing.

Judging of the state of the poor by the extent of relief afforded from the rates, the winter would not seem to have been a very hard one in my district.

I find that in the first week of 1882 relief was given in the 14 workhouses with which I am connected to 4,974 persons, and in the corresponding period of the present year to 5,070, showing an increase of 96.

I have no means immediately at hand for comparing the out-door relief in the two periods; but this is of less importance, as out-door relief affords no trustworthy measure of actual distress. As a matter of fact, however, I think it may be safely assumed that the out-door relief afforded at the beginning of the year was slightly below that of the corresponding period of 1882.

During the months of January and February the numbers in the workhouses rose from 5,070 to 5,297, being an increase of 227, or about 4 per cent.; and the out-door relief went up from 7,130 to 7,665, being an increase of 535, or nearly 7 per cent.

These are, no doubt, indications of distress amongst the poorer classes, but it may be hoped that the improvement which has taken place in the weather may stimulate employment and improve their condition.

I have, &c.,

(Signed) R. Bourke.

The Local Government Board.

Report from Major Burke Fox:—District comprising part of the County Clare.

Ennis, County Clare,
13 March, 1883.

Gentlemen,

In reference to your letter of the 10th instant, No. 9013/83, requiring me to furnish a report as to the state of the poor generally in my district, I have the honour to inform you that though there has been for some time a considerable amount of distress in many parts of my district, more particularly amongst the small farmers and artisans in the towns and villages, arising from causes adverted to in my previous reports, I do not consider that it is anywhere increasing except in the Ballyvaughan Union.

In that union, I regret to say, there has been a serious increase both in the inmates in the house and in the amount expended on out-door relief. This I attribute in a great measure to the destitution prevailing in the electoral divisions of Abbey, Gleninagh, and Drumcreehy; but I would beg to observe that in these divisions there are about 700 applicants for emigration under the clauses of the Arrears Act, and should the emigration of these poor people be effected it will sensibly diminish the distress at present existing in this union.

In the other unions in my district the numbers in the house and on out-door relief remain pretty much as they have been for some weeks past, with the exception of the Killadysert Union, where the out-door relief is diminishing.

The fine weather which has set in for the last fortnight has given such a stimulus to farming operations as to cause (at least while the spring work lasts) a general demand for labour, which I confidently trust will materially decrease the distress now prevailing.

But I must add that I feel considerable anxiety about the small farmers in parts of my district, as, for instance, in the neighbourhood of Miltown Malbay, where I found many of them in such straitened circumstances as to cause me to feel grave apprehensions as to their ability to tide over the present crisis.

In accordance with your instructions I beg to forward the following return:—

Prices, 12th March, 1883:

Potatoes (seed) - - - -	8d. to 2s. per stone (14 lbs).
„ (eating) - - - -	6d. per stone.
Oatmeal - - - - -	16s. per cwt.
Indian meal - - - -	8s. 6d. per cwt.
Flour - - - - -	14s. to 16s. 6d. per cwt.

Prices, corresponding period, 1882:

Potatoes (seed) - - -	5d. to 6d. per stone.
„ (eating) - - - -	3d. per stone.
Oatmeal - - - - -	13s. 6d. per cwt.
Indian meal - - - -	7s. 6d. per cwt.
Flour - - - - -	14s. to 16s. 6d. per cwt.

I have, &c.,

(Signed) L. Loftus Burke Fox,
Local Government Inspector.

The Local Government Board.

Report from Major Spaight:—District comprising County Kerry and part of County Cork.

Skibbereen, 13 March, 1883.

Gentlemen,

I have the honour to acknowledge your letter of the 10th instant, requesting me to furnish you with a report, for the information of his Excellency the Lord Lieutenant, regarding the state of the poor generally in my district, and the prices of certain provisions in the town in which your letter might reach me.

I have, as you are aware, only just taken over this district, and have not yet had time even to see more than a small portion of it. My knowledge of it is therefore very limited, and it is impossible for me to form an accurate idea of the state of the poor generally.

From what I have seen there is no doubt a want of employment in many places, but I have as yet seen nothing of any distress which the ordinary resources of the poor laws are not fully able to cope with.

I annex a list, giving the comparative prices of the provisions, as requested, by which you will observe that flour is cheaper this year than last, in all the four places mentioned, and all the other sorts are dearer.

In this district, as far as I have been able to ascertain, the people now live principally on baker's bread and flour baked at home, which has taken the place of the meals hitherto used.

I took the prices in Skibbereen myself, and selected Cahersiveen, Tralee, and Kanturk, as typical of the rest of the districts from which I obtained telegrams this day giving the particulars contained in the return.

I have, &c.,
(Signed) George Spaight.

The Local Government Board,
Dublin.

Prices of Provisions this day in the following Towns:—

—	—	12th March, 1883.	12th March, 1882.
		s. d.	s. d.
Skibbereen,	Potatoes,	0 7 per stone.	0 6 per stone.
	Indian Meal,	9 4 „ cwt.	8 9 „ cwt.
	Oatmeal,	16 0 „ „	14 0 „ „
	Flour,	12 6 „ „	14 6 „ „
Cahersiveen,	Potatoes,	0 6 per stone.	0 5 per stone.
	Indian Meal,	11 2 „ cwt.	8 6 „ cwt.
	Oatmeal,	17 4 „ „	15 9 „ „
	Flour,	14 6 „ „	16 9 „ „
Kanturk,	Potatoes,	0 6 per stone.	0 4 per stone.
	Indian Meal,	8 9 „ cwt.	7 6 „ cwt.
	Oatmeal,	18 5 „ „	17 6 „ „
	Flour,	14 6 „ „	15 6 „ „
Tralee,	Potatoes,	0 6 per stone.	0 4½ per stone.
	Indian Meal,	9 6 „ cwt.	8 6 „ cwt.
	Oatmeal,	16 6 „ „	16 0 „ „
	Flour,	36 9 „ sack, 20 stone.	41 6 „ 20 stone.

Flour cheaper in 1883; all else dearer than last year.

Report from Dr. Brodie:—District comprising parts of the Counties of Cork, Limerick and Waterford.

Cork, 12 March, 1883.

Gentlemen,

In compliance with the instructions contained in your letter, dated the 10th instant, requesting me to furnish, for the information of His

Excellency the Lord Lieutenant, a report as to the state of the poor generally in my district, as far as I am able to afford the information from the knowledge I possess on the subject, also the prices of potatoes, oatmeal, Indian meal and flour at the present time, and the prices of the same articles at this time last year.

I have now the honour to report that having travelled through a considerable portion of my district during the past few weeks, I am glad to be able to state, as the result of my own personal observations, and the information derived from reliable sources, that no part of my district is in a different state from that described in my report of 30th September, 1882, and that, except the enforced suspension of farm operations caused by the heavy rains in the month of February, I did not observe any such want of employment as to excite apprehension respecting the prospects of the labouring classes and poor generally. It has now pleased the Almighty to bless us with favourable dry weather, and I have everywhere observed that seed-sowing and preparing the land for potato planting are now being carried on most extensively in my district, thereby affording employment to the labouring classes at fair wages, which leads me to hope that there is no ground for apprehension of distress in the coming season beyond the ordinary pressure of the necessitous classes, or of any relief being required beyond the limits of the ordinary administration of the Poor Laws. Out-door relief is freely given in several unions.

Prices of the following articles at present time:—

Potatoes - - - - - -	8d. per stone.
Oatmeal - - - - - -	16s. per cwt.
Indian meal - - - - -	7s. to 8s. 6d. per cwt.
Flour (baker's) - - - - -	14s. to 18s. per cwt.
Flour (retail) - - - - -	12s. to 14s. per cwt.

Prices at this time last year:—

Potatoes - - - - - -	4d. per stone.
Oatmeal - - - - - -	15s. 6d. per cwt.
Indian meal - - - - -	7s. 6d. per cwt.
Flour - - - - - -	13s. 6d. to 14s. per cwt.
Flour (retail) - - - - -	10s. to 14s. per cwt.

The labouring classes use very little oatmeal or Indian meal; they prefer bread made from second quality flour.

I have, &c.,

(Signed), T. BRODIE.

The Local Government Board,
Dublin.

RETURN of PERSONS in RECEIPT of RELIEF on SATURDAY, 3rd MARCH, 1883.

RETURN of the Numbers of Persons in Receipt of IN-DOOR and OUT-DOOR RELIEF on Saturday, 3rd March, 1883, and the corresponding Saturday of each of the Two preceding Years, in the under-mentioned Unions.

County and Union.	Workhouse Accommodation, as shown by existing Limitation Orders.	Workhouse Accommodation, as shown by Parliamentary Return of 7th September, 18[illegible].	Number of Persons in Receipt of Relief on 3rd March, 1883.			4th March, 1882.			5th March, 1881.		
			In Workhouse.	Out-door.	Total.	In Workhouse.	Out-door.	Total.	In Workhouse.	Out-door.	Total.
DONEGAL:											
Ballyshannon, . .	661	570	130	61	191	131	118	249	152	5	167
Donegal, . . .	481	579	120	121	241	115	106	212	182	90	272
Dunfanaghy, . .	479	287	90	—	90	87	—	87	85	—	85
Glenties, . . .	505	603	161	143	304	164	60	224	133	143	276
Inishowen, . .	667	400	148	349	497	116	728	844	194	329	523
Letterkenny, . .	655	305	131	1	132	161	9	170	140	2	142
Milford, . . .	600	500	113	3	116	97	2	99	104	6	110
Stranorlar, . . .	632	505	94	2	96	65	1	66	96	5	101
CLARE:											
Ballyvaghan, . .	374	233	219	148	377	372	98	470	372	324	696
Corrofin, . . .	442	326	185	201	386	183	127	310	129	293	422
Ennis, . . .	1,846	996	623	407	1,025	408	431	839	526	331	857
Ennistymon, . .	683	437	230	347	577	270	379	649	279	488	767
Kildysart, . .	667	606	160	293	453	133	390	524	171	290	461
Kilrush, . . .	1,411	943	336	1,647	1,983	321	985	1,306	330	1,048	1,388
Scarriff, . . .	1,224	796	176	110	286	174	25	199	205	69	274
Tulla, . . .	493	615	231	—	231	254	95	349	306	105	410
CORK (West Riding):											
Bandon, . . .	1,033	935	194	211	405	187	163	350	231	13	244
Bantry, . . .	779	468	116	44	170	113	23	136	122	19	141
Castletown, . .	403	240	170	93	263	162	78	240	168	42	210
Clonakilty, . .	667	464	296	141	437	249	31	280	220	67	287
Dunmanway, . .	591	379	161	219	379	149	125	274	173	47	220
Macroom, . . .	704	492	214	441	755	317	446	763	290	370	660
Millstreet, . .	942	469	207	427	634	281	360	641	235	434	679
Skibbereen, . .	820	406	337	401	738	357	347	704	420	294	715
Skull, . . .	391	218	94	340	434	167	219	386	96	187	283

RETURN of the Numbers of Persons in Receipt of IN-DOOR and OUT-DOOR RELIEF on Saturday, 3rd March, 1883, &c.—*continued.*

County and Union.	Workhouse Accommodation, as shown by existing Limitation Orders.	Workhouse Accommodation, as shown by Parliamentary Return of 11th September, 1880.	Number of Persons in Receipt of Relief on								
			3rd March, 1883.			4th March, 1882.			5th March, 1881.		
			In Workhouses.	Out-door.	Total.	In Workhouses.	Out-door.	Total.	In Workhouses.	Out-door.	Total.
KERRY:											
Cahersiveen,	512	607	150	[illegible]	353	125	240	336	147	200	[illegible]
Dingle,	1,274	704	717	5	290	213	3	210	204	1	[illegible]
Kenmare,	930	[illegible]	130	304	475	130	536	668	143	[illegible]	[illegible]
Killarney,	1,002	991	443	1,036	1,478	461	078	1,370	400	707	1,111
Listowel,	914	453	180	[illegible]	1,054	136	447	[illegible]	146	101	[illegible]
Tralee,	949	878	[illegible]	[illegible]	1,578	789	–	789	779	–	779
GALWAY:											
Ballinasloe,	1,151	[illegible]	179	149	418	276	15	[illegible]	376	143	[illegible]
Clifden,	[illegible]	603	153	786	610	217	447	494	[illegible]	450	[illegible]
Galway,	1,063	649	400	407	816	451	909	700	481	145	[illegible]
Glennamaddy,	497	055	148	201	476	153	279	381	183	[illegible]	[illegible]
Gort,	720	448	848	136	379	[illegible]	67	279	717	44	[illegible]
Loughrea,	819	487	165	471	[illegible]	283	276	547	196	173	[illegible]
Mount Bellew,	646	264	117	[illegible]	147	110	16	123	118	14	137
Oughterard,	[illegible]	230	60	[illegible]	183	84	40	126	89	45	134
Portumna,	670	340	160	61	237	131	67	204	151	118	[illegible]
Tuam,	805	510	799	778	1,077	250	639	009	250	[illegible]	[illegible]
LEITRIM:											
Carrick-on-Shannon,	790	470	307	[illegible]	[illegible]	377	910	[illegible]	308	970	[illegible]
Manorhamilton,	809	480	109	61	250	107	46	213	160	0	[illegible]
Mohill,	719	459	316	403	718	010	406	016	343	449	[illegible]
MAYO:											
Ballina,	1,073	447	812	177	489	224	117	341	237	1,178	[illegible]
Ballinrobe,	944	447	130	110	844	259	45	037	200	77	[illegible]
Belmullet,	008	406	110	45	801	107	172	279	158	4,330	4,474
Castlebar,	769	448	111	238	412	189	277	055	118	087	[illegible]
Claremorris,	430	379	272	280	430	164	170	334	170	248	474
Killala,	415	249	101	145	246	80	104	184	84	216	[illegible]
Newport,	488	275	108	20	101	109	40	149	08	47	[illegible]
Swineford,	755	470	075	406	480	215	191	400	050	403	[illegible]
Westport,	1,378	794	147	10	151	197	8	145	148	20	164

RETURN of the Numbers of Persons in Receipt of IN-DOOR and OUT-DOOR RELIEF on Saturday, 3rd March, 1883, &c.—*continued.*

COUNTY AND UNION.	Workhouse Accommodation, as shown by existing Limitation Orders.	Workhouse Accommodation, as shown by Parliamentary Return of 7th September, 1880	Number of Persons in Receipt of Relief on								
			3rd March, 1883.			4th March, 1882.			5th March, 1881.		
			In Workhouse	Out-door	Total	In Workhouse	Out-door	Total	In Workhouse	Out-door	Total
ROSCOMMON:											
Boyle,	486	412	276	481	757	377	423	800	379	488	870
Castlerea,	548	581	261	484	745	267	378	645	354	378	632
Roscommon,	551	411	365	337	702	312	370	682	367	313	670
Strokestown,	650	398	181	514	795	238	459	697	278	516	744
SLIGO:											
Dromore, West,	675	350	117	399	516	109	158	267	106	708	815
Sligo,	1,055	910	673	702	1,074	550	618	1,174	695	879	1,041
Tobercurry,	546	920	183	353	531	137	911	420	154	295	470
TOTALS,	48,347	38,040	15,176	17,36[illegible]	[illegible]	12,[illegible]	13,[illegible]	[illegible]	[illegible]	16,171	[illegible]

PRICES of PROVISIONS in FEBRUARY 1882 and FEBRUARY 1883.

COUNTY AND UNION.	Potatoes, per Stone.		Indian Meal, per Cwt.		Oatmeal, per Cwt.		Flour, per Cwt.	
	1882.	1883.	1882.	1883.	1882.	1883.	1882.	1883.
MAYO:	d.	d.	s. d.	s. d.	s. d.	s. d.	s. d.	s. d.
Westport,	5	6½	8 0	9 3	13 6	15 0	16 6	14 6
Ballina,	5½	6½	8 6	9 9	13 8	14 8	17 9	17 6
Claremorris,	4	6½	7 6	8 9	11 9	19 9	?	18 0
Castlebar,	4	8	7 8	8 8	10 6	11 9	?	16 6
Swinford,	4	7	9 3	9 8	14 0	14 6	17 6	15 8
Ballinrobe,	3½	6	7 6	9 0	11 6	14 0	16 6	15 0

PRICES of PROVISIONS in FEBRUARY 1882 and FEBRUARY 1883—*continued.*

COUNTY AND UNION.	Potatoes, per Stone.		Indian Meal, per Cwt.		Oatmeal, per Cwt.		Flour, per Cwt.	
	1882.	1883.	1882.	1883.	1882.	1883.	1882.	1883.
GALWAY:	d.	d.	s. d.	s. d.	s. d.	s. d.	s. d.	s. d.
Oughterard, . .	3	8	8 0	6 0	11 6	16 0	10 0	16 0
Clifden, . . .	6	8	8 0	8 0	13 8	14 6	18 0	16 0
Ballinasloe, . .								
Galway, . . .								
Glennamaddy, . .								
Gort, ...	4½	6½	7 8	8 0	13 6	14 8	18 0	21 4
Loughrea, . . .								
Portumna, . . .								
Tuam, ...								
LEITRIM:								
Carrick-on-Shannon, .	4	6½	8 0	6 0	11 8	14 6	17 4	16 6
ROSCOMMON:								
Boyle, . . .	6½	6	7 0	6 6	14 8	15 6	17 6	17 6
SLIGO:								
Sligo, . . .	4	8	7 0	8 2½	12 8	13 4	—	—
CORK:								
Skibbereen, .	4	7	5 9	9 4	14 9	16 0	20 8	18 6
Kanturk, . . .	4	4	7 0	8 9	12 8	13 8	18 8	16 6
Cork, . .	4	4	7 9	8 0	13 6	13 0	18 4 to 18 9	16 4 to 17 4
CLARE:								
Ennis, .	5	8	—	8 4	12 6	16 8	14 0 to 15 8	24 0 to 25 8
KERRY:								
Cahersiveen, . .	6	8	5 8	11 2	13 9	17 4	16 0	19 8
Tralee, . . .	5½	5	8 9	9 6	16 9	14 9	16 7	18 7
DONEGAL:								
Dunfanaghy, . .	3	6	9 0	9 6	15 0	18 0	10 8	18 6
Glenties, . . .	3	7½	8 8	10 8	12 0	15 0	20 8	18 6
Donegal, . . .	5½	6	6 8	6 6	14 8	15 8	16 8	15 6

"REPORT from DR. STEWART WOODHOUSE, in reference to the Parish of GLENCOLUMBKILLE, in the county of Donegal."

Carrick, 14 March, 1883.

GENTLEMEN,—In reply to your letter of 10th instant, I have the honour of laying before you the following statement in reference to the parish of Glencolumbkille.

The area of this parish is 32,245 acres. It contains a population of 4,139 persons, or about 730 families. Of these, a very few are supported by fishing alone; about a fourth by both fishing and farming, and the rest by farming. The only other industries are the spinning of wool, the weaving of flannel, and embroidery.

The data on which my observations are based were almost entirely afforded by personally visiting the homesteads of the people in the poorest localities. I have, however, to thank the Rev. F. W. Gallagher, the priest of the parish, the Rev. —— Thompson, the rector, several of the local traders and others, for the information that from time to time they supplied me with.

I have visited the homes of upwards of 100 families in the townlands of Cashel, Killaned, Doocy, Doonalt, Ballard, Banghert, Drim, Cloghan, Kinnacullagh, Meenaveen, Malinmore, Malinbeg, and Cappagh. These visits were paid at different times, ranging from the third week in January till yesterday. In 72 cases notes of the circumstances of the family were made at the time I saw them.

The townlands above mentioned are the poorest. In one or two of the very poorest townlands I went into every house; in the others, the houses were either taken as they came, or where a selection was made, the houses that had the most destitute appearance were preferred.

Dividing into three classes the 72 families whose statistics I noted, there were,—

Nine that have two cows or upwards, with sheep, &c.
Thirty-four that have no animal save a pig or fowl.
Twenty-nine that have a cow, or a cow and a calf, with, in some cases, sheep.

I visited about 30 other families of whose means I did not take notes, as most of them had stock, except 12 families of fishermen in Malinbeg who have neither cattle nor land, and were uniformly and wretchedly poor.

Taking into additional consideration Teelin, a poor locality inhabited by men who are partly farmers and partly fishermen, forming about one-fourth of the parish, and also the townlands that have no special claim to be regarded as distressed, the whole 730 families may be grouped as before under three heads, thus:—

One-quarter of them possess two cows, or upwards, some sheep, pigs, and a variable quantity of seed potatoes and oats.

One-third are exceedingly poor, their possessions being limited to some fowl and perhaps a pig; these have no seed potatoes nor oats.

The remainder (nearly one-half) possess a cow, or a cow and a calf, together with a pig, and perhaps a few sheep. Seed supply deficient.

Many have friends in America, some of whom send help.

As a rule the people are fairly well clad, especially those who wear clothing manufactured in the country; but amongst the younger women flimsy shawls and dresses purchased from the shops have taken the place of the more substantial materials woven by themselves.

I saw no scarcity of fuel in the houses.

The children look healthy, and there is no unusual amount of sickness.

The food consists of Indian meal stirabout, cakes made of Indian meal or Indian meal and flour, with or without milk. Along the coast fish and leak, and sometimes doolamaun, are added, but the doolamaun I have seen in houses was always intended for the pig. Very few eat potatoes; many have told me they had not a potato since Halloweve.

I believe half the people have not seed potatoes.

The causes of this poverty are twofold. One set of causes is permanent, and to a great extent irremediable; the other is special and peculiar to the past year.

Amongst the *permanent* causes may be mentioned:—

1. The small size of the holdings, when the poorness of the soil is taken into consideration. Some have settled upon ground which nature never intended for arable land. Others by sub-divisions among their families have reduced the farm to a "cow's grass," or a mere potato patch.

2. Bad Farming.—Poor as is the soil it does not get justice. Hardly anything is done in winter. Drainage should be easy, as most of the farms have a slope, but drains are very deficient. The preparing the ground for seed is postponed till spring has well begun. At the present date (14th March) there are fields intended for tillage to which nothing has yet been done. I have been told that potatoes are sometimes set only nine inches apart, resulting in a crop disproportionately small to the amount of seed. The same patch of land is planted with potatoes for successive years. Moreover the entire dependence for food supply is placed on the potato crop, oats being quite subordinate. Except grass and a few cabbages, nothing else is grown. Goats would thrive well here, but there is not one to be seen.

3. Deterioration of Climate.—Complaint is frequent that during the last five years the climate has become worse than it used to be; that the summers are colder, wetter, and stormier. I am informed that the potato crop of 1881 was scanty here, though good generally throughout Ireland.

4. Failure of Industries.—The fish are said to have become much more scarce during the past three or four years. Herrings were formerly abundant; now they have quite left the coast. The fishing gear, spite of gifts from the Fishery Inspector and Commissioners, has deteriorated.

The manufacture of flannel and of woollen cloth has greatly diminished, involving the loss of women's employment in carding and spinning.

Kelp-making has ceased; almost no kelp has been made since 1879. Whatever may have been the cause of its decline then, it could not now be revived, as owing to the discovery in Chili of a cheaper material yielding iodine, kelp is only worth £2 10*s.* a ton, whereas it used to bring £5 or £7.

The causes peculiar to the last year are:—

1. The failure, more or less general, of the potato crop, not so much from disease as from want of development. Champions failed just as much as the older varieties. The failure is attributed to the coldness of the summer, and also to high winds in July which shook the stalks, loosening the roots so that tubers did not properly form.

2. A storm on 1st October partially unroofed a number of houses, and blew away many small stacks of oats and hay, especially along the coast of Malin Glen, and the base of Slieve League. Several of the houses have not yet been repaired.

3. Lessened credit given by shopkeepers.

The Poor Law relief is as follows:—The Union Workhouse at Glenties, distant 16 Irish miles from Carrick (the chief village of the parish). This workhouse will accommodate 505 inmates; at the present date (14th March) there are 160. It is in good order, clean, and comfortably heated. The beds and bed-clothing are good, and the diet similar to if not better than the usual diet of the small farmers of the country, while the sick get special diet and extras as ordered by the medical attendant who visits daily. I have repeatedly asked numbers of the inmates if they were comfortable, and, with a few exceptions, they said they were. These exceptions all referred to the want of tobacco; they said they were comfortable otherwise. There is a separate ward for any women who have led immoral lives, so that they cannot mix with the rest. The children are all well cared and in good health with one exception, an infant that has eczema on the head, which is however very curable. There is also a Fever Hospital, a separate building with 40 beds.

The relieving officer has lived in this parish since boyhood, and is intimately acquainted with the people and their circumstances. Up till the 10th instant his relief district comprised the parish of Kilcar, and part of the parish of Killybegs as well as the parish of Glencolumbkille. In this district since the 16th December last he has attended four relief stations on fixed days every week, notices to that effect having been posted in public places. Now the greater portion of this relief district has been placed under the charge of a recently appointed relieving officer, so as to leave to the experienced officer simply the parish of Glencolumbkille (population 4,139), and one electoral division (population 531) besides. He lives within two miles of the most distressed townlands. His present relief stations and attendance days are the following:—

Carrick every Tuesday.
Malinbeg every Wednesday.
Glen (Malin) every Thursday.
Malinmore every Monday and Saturday.

These relief stations are very central as regards the distribution of the population, and are especially convenient for the poorer localities. The remotest hamlet in the parish is within three Irish miles of one or other of these relief stations, and for the most of them are much nearer.

The map of the parish here appended, traced from the electoral division map, shows the relief stations and positions of poorest places.

Belonging to the Union is a good covered spring ambulance; and the relieving officer can without difficulty procure cars for the conveyance of persons to the workhouse.

From the permanent causes above mentioned, especially the first and second, this parish is always in a state of poverty. Even a year when potatoes are abundant does not avail to lift the bulk of the people out of it. The present distress is an accentuation or exacerbation of the usual state. There are parts of Donegal which are, so far as the land is concerned, actually poorer, but the people here are more helpless. They are not accustomed nor disposed to seek employment in other countries or counties, as the inhabitants do in some other parts of West Donegal. On the 14th of last month printed notices were posted throughout this parish by an agent of Messrs. Dunbar, McMaster & Co., of the Linen Works, Gilford, County Down, offering "constant employment to hands, male and female, of 14 years old and upwards; car and railway fares paid." The agent remained two or three days here, but no one accepted the offer.

There is an inability to see that their straitened circumstances are the result of tendencies which have been long in operation, and which cannot be averted. There is consequently a tacit refusal to acknowledge that any mode of effectively dealing with these difficulties can be found except by relief works or gratuities.

Emigration is not in favour. Some have aged parents dwelling with them; with others the hard work they would have to do in America is a deterrent.

I have been frankly told by some able-bodied men that they would have to work in America in "a way that wouldn't suit them." Statements have been circulated among them that if they went their old people would be sent back by the American Government, and lastly, the priest of the parish is strongly opposed to it. Consequently hardly a family will avail themselves of the free emigration offered under the Arrears Act.

Unfortunately self-reliance has in many cases broken down. I have been asked for money by a man who acknowledged he had at the time two cows, and who in happier years would never have dreamed of begging. Nor is this a solitary instance. A plan, introduced early last month, of giving charitable aid by paying people for work done on their own farms, instead of, as previously, working elsewhere, has contributed to this. A crowd have asked me, "will you pay me for working on my own land," and then simply for money.

Crime and immorality are exceedingly rare, and I will gratefully add that by the people whose houses I visited I was uniformly received with courtesy and every disposition to oblige.

I have, &c.

(Signed) STEWART WOODHOUSE.

The Local Government Board,
Ireland.

No. 8.—Payments to National School Teachers.

Local Government Board, Dublin,
30th December, 1882.

Sir,

In pursuance of the 4th Section of "The National School Teachers (Ireland) Act, 1875," the Local Government Board for Ireland transmit to you herewith, to be laid before the Board of Guardians of —— Union, the notice which they are required by that Section to transmit, on or before the 1st day of January, to the Guardians of every union which shall not at such time be a contributory union within the meaning of the Act.

The notice now transmitted, as in the case of the notice which was transmitted on the 30th December last, requires the Guardians within forty days from the receipt thereof, to inform the Local Government Board whether, for the purpose of increasing the remuneration of the teachers of National Schools within the union, they are willing to make their union a contributory union within the meaning of the Act, and the Guardians will observe therefore that by the present notice they are now called upon in pursuance of the requirement of the Act, to decide whether they will become contributory for the year 1883-84 (that is for the year commencing on the 1st April next), and subsequent years, until the resolution to contribute be legally revoked.

The Board forwarded with their circular of the 30th August, 1875, a copy of the Act, and of various other documents relating to this subject, and they desire to refer the Board of Guardians to that circular and the documents which accompanied it, for any information which they may require before replying to the enclosed notice.

The Board have to add that the Commissioners of National Education have furnished them with an estimate of the probable amount which will be payable by the Guardians of the several unions in results fees to teachers of National Schools within the respective unions for the year 1883-84, and the liability which according to this estimate, the Guardians will incur by making their union a contributory one is not expected to exceed £

By order of the Board,

W. D. Wodsworth, Assistant Secretary.

To the Clerk —— Union.

Enclosure.

Notice in pursuance of Section 4 of "The National School Teachers (Ireland) Act, 1875," 38 and 39 Vic., c. 96.

"The Guardians of —— Union are hereby required, within forty days after the receipt hereof, to inform the Local Government Board for Ireland whether, for the purpose of increasing the remuneration of the Teachers of National Schools within the Union, they are willing to become a contributory union within the meaning of 'The National School Teachers (Ireland) Act,' (38 and 39 Vic., c. 96).

"By order of the Board,

"W. D. Wodsworth, Assistant Secretary.

"30th December, 1882."

No. 9.—Correspondence relative to the dissolution of the Carrick-on-Suir Board of Guardians.

I. Letter from Local Government Board dated 20th July, 1882.
II. Order dissolving the Board of Guardians.
III. Order for the re-election of Board of Guardians.

Local Government Board, Dublin,
20th July, 1882.

Sir,

The Local Government Board for Ireland have had before them the Minutes of Proceedings of the Board of Guardians of Carrick-on-Suir Union at their meeting on the 15th instant, and the Local Government Board regret to observe that the Guardians again adjourned without transacting the business which should have come before them on that day or the arrear of business left undone at their meetings on the 1st, 8th, and 11th instant.

The Local Government Board, under these circumstances, deem it necessary to review the recent proceedings of the Board of Guardians, and to advert to the correspondence which has taken place on the subject.

The Board of Guardians will bear in mind that a letter was laid before them on the 1st instant relating to the power possessed by the majority of the Guardians present at any meeting to adjourn such meeting, in which letter the Local Government Board stated that "if a Guardians' meeting is adjourned with the view of interfering with the transaction of the ordinary business of the Union, and if by reason of repeated adjournments of such a character the Guardians fail to discharge their duties duly and effectually, according to the intention of the Poor Law Acts, the Local Government Board would be under the necessity of dissolving the Board of Guardians, and appointing paid officers to carry the provisions of the said Acts into execution."

It appears that at the meeting on the day referred to, viz.: the 1st instant, the Chairman having declined to put a question to the meeting which was wholly unconnected with the duties of the Board of Guardians, the majority of the Guardians present voted for the adjournment of the meeting, and that the meeting was accordingly adjourned, leaving much of the ordinary business unfinished.

The Guardians adopted a similar course on the 8th instant, the 11th instant, and again on the 15th instant, and the Local Government Board have received reports from their Inspector, Mr. Hamilton, describing the business which has been neglected by reason of the repeated adjournments referred to, from which it appears that the business remaining unfinished at the meeting on the 1st instant was :—

I. The consideration of Board's letter, and sealed order under the Contagious Diseases Animals Act, 1878.

II. The adoption of a new rate—the rate books having been duly certified by the Clerk, and dated, and submitted.

III. The consideration of any Reports in the Form P received, and the disposal of the Reports of the several Sanitary Officers, and

IV. The signing of the cheques for the purposes of Outdoor Relief, and other cheques.

The Local Government Board understand that all the business above specified, together with the ordinary weekly business, was adjourned on the 8th to the 11th instant, and further adjourned on the 11th to the 15th instant, and that all the business which had thus accumulated was again postponed on the 15th instant; the Local Government Board also learn from Mr. Hamilton that no cheques have been issued for three weeks to enable the Relieving Officers to continue to administer outdoor relief, and that the Clerk of the Union has advanced to the Relieving Officers, from his own resources, the sums necessary for the purpose, the weekly amount being about £16 or £17.

On the 14th instant the Local Government Board addressed the Board of Guardians on the subject of their proceedings at their three previous meetings, and warned them that "if at their next meeting they again adjourn for reasons such as those which influenced them on the 1st, 8th, and 11th instant, and if they persist in neglecting to discharge their legitimate duties, the Local Government Board will at once take steps to place the management of the affairs of the Union in the hands of paid Guardians."

The Board of Guardians having adjourned the meeting on the 15th instant without transacting their ordinary business, and having now failed to discharge their duties at four consecutive meetings, the Local Government Board cannot avoid arriving at the conclusion that through the default of the Board of Guardians of Carrick-on-Suir Union the duties of such Board of Guardians have not been duly and effectually discharged according to the intention of the several Acts which are in force for the Relief of the destitute Poor in Ireland, and the Local Government Board therefore feel it necessary, in the exercise of their powers under the 18th Section of the Act 10 Vic. cap. 31, to dissolve the said Board of Guardians, and to appoint paid officers to carry into execution the provisions of the said Acts.

The order dissolving the Board of Guardians is transmitted to you herewith.

By order of the Board,

W. D. Wodsworth, Assistant Secretary.

To the Clerk, Carrick-on-Suir Union.

II.—Order Dissolving Board of Guardians.

Carrick-on-Suir Union.

To the Guardians of the Poor of the Carrick-on-Suir Union; to the Clerk of the said Union; and to all other persons whom it may concern:

Whereas, through the default of the Board of Guardians of the Carrick-on-Suir Union, the duties of the Board of Guardians of the said union have not been duly and effectually discharged according to the intention of the Acts in force for the Relief of the Destitute Poor in Ireland:

Now therefore, We, the Local Government Board for Ireland, do hereby, in exercise of the powers by the said Acts vested in us in this behalf, declare the said Board of Guardians to be dissolved, and the said Board is hereby dissolved accordingly.

Sealed with our seal this twentieth day of July, in the year of our Lord one thousand eight hundred and eighty-two.

(Signed), R. G. C. Hamilton,
Charles Crokee King.

III.—Order for the Re-election of Board of Guardians.

Carrick-on-Suir Union.

To the Returning Officer and other Officers of the Carrick-on-Suir Union; and to all other persons whom it may concern:

Whereas We, the Local Government Board for Ireland, did, by an Order under Seal, bearing date the twentieth day of July, 1882, declare the Board of Guardians of the Carrick-on-Suir Union to be dissolved, and did thereafter appoint Paid Officers for carrying into execution in the said union the provisions of the Acts in force for the Relief of the Destitute Poor in Ireland, as well as the "Act to provide for the better Distribution, Support, and Management of Medical Charities in Ireland," and the "Public Health (Ireland) Act, 1878;"

And whereas it appears to us expedient to direct the discontinuance in office of such Paid Officers, and the Re-election of a Board of Guardians for the said Union as hereinafter is provided:

Now therefore, in exercise of the powers vested in us, We do hereby direct the discontinuance in office of such Paid Officers in the said Union, and We do hereby Order and Direct that all Powers and Authorities of such Paid Officers shall cease and determine in the said Union on the twenty-sixth day of March next, if a Board of Guardians of the said Union shall on that day have been duly elected, otherwise on such one of the fourteen days next after the Twenty-fifth day of March next as shall be the day on which the Election of the said Board of Guardians shall be completed.

And We do hereby Order and Direct that the several proceedings directed in a General Order of the Commissioners for administering the Laws for Relief of the Poor in Ireland, bearing date the Second day of January, 1863, to be taken in each year for the Election of Guardians of the Poor in Unions in Ireland, shall be taken by the Returning Officer and others for the Election of a Board of Guardians for the said Carrick-on-Suir Union for the year ending the 25th day of March, 1884, and that the following shall be the days on which the proceedings for the said Election shall be taken respectively, that is to say:—

The day for issuing the Notice of the Election shall be the	26th	February,	1883.
The last day for receiving nominations of Guardians shall be the	5th	March,	"
but no Nomination shall be received after the hour of 5 o'clock in the afternoon of that day.			
The day for forwarding the List of Candidates shall be the	8th	"	"
The first day for issuing Voting Papers shall be the .	19th	"	"
The first day for collecting Voting Papers shall be the .	21st	"	"
The last day for applying for Voting Papers by Voters to whom they shall not have been duly delivered previously shall be the	22nd	"	"
The last day for delivering Voting Papers to the Returning Officer by Voters from whom they shall not have been duly collected previously shall be the . .	24th	"	"
And the day for making the Return of Guardians elected shall be the	26th	"	"
or one of the fourteen days next following the 25th day of March, not being a Sunday.			

And We do hereby Order and Direct that the Returning Officer shall give notice of the said Election according to the Form of Notice,

"Form B," prescribed by the said General Order, bearing date the Second day of January, 1863.

Sealed with our Seal, this Seventeenth day of February, in the year of our Lord One Thousand Eight Hundred and Eighty-three.

(Signed) HENRY ROBINSON,
CHARLES CROKER KING,
GEORGE MORRIS.

No. 10.—EMIGRATION SECTIONS OF ARREARS OF RENT ACT.

Local Government Board, Dublin,
26th August, 1882.

SIR,

The Local Government Board for Ireland forward to you herewith, for the information of the Board of Guardians, a copy of those Sections of the Arrears of Rent (Ireland) Act, 1882, which contain provisions relating to the Emigration of poor persons resident within the Union.

By order of the Board,
B. BANKS, Secretary.

To the Clerk of each Union.

SECTIONS of "ARREARS OF RENT (IRELAND) ACT, 1882" (45 & 46 VIC., Ch. 47), which relate to EMIGRATION.

"SEC. 18. From and after the passing of this Act the Board of Guardians of any union in Ireland are authorised to borrow money for the purpose of defraying or assisting to defray the expenses of the emigration of poor persons resident within their union, or any electoral division thereof, in manner provided by the Poor Law Amendment (Ireland) Act, 1849, as amended by subsequent Acts, subject to the following modifications; (that is to say),

"(1.) The provisions of the said Act in relation to the repayment of the advance by annual instalments shall not apply;

"(2.) The advances may be made by the Commissioners of Public Works out of any moneys granted to them for the purpose of loans in place of the Public Works Loans Commissioners;

"(3.) Every such advance made by the Commissioners of Public Works shall bear interest at the rate of three-and-a-half per centum per annum, or at such other rate as the Treasury may from time to time fix, in order to enable the advance to be made without loss to the Exchequer;

"(4.) Every such advance made by the Commissioners of Public Works, and the interest thereon, shall be repaid within such period from the date of the advance, not being less than fifteen years, nor more than thirty years, as the Treasury may from time to time fix.

"For the purposes of this Act the Poor Law Amendment (Ireland) Act, 1849, means the Act of the session of the twelfth and thirteenth years of the reign of Her present Majesty, chapter one hundred and four.

"SEC. 19. If at any time the Commissioners of Public Works in Ireland certify that any sum remains due to them from the Board of Guardians of any union on account of any loan or advance made under this Act, and is then payable to the Commissioners, the Local Government Board shall, by order under their seal, require the Guardians of the union to pay the sum so certified, and shall send copies of such order to the Board of Guardians and to the treasurer of the union; and thereupon the treasurer of the union shall, out of any money then in his hands to the credit of the Guardians, or if such money is insufficient for the purpose, then out of all moneys subsequently received by him on account of the Guardians, pay over the amount mentioned in the order to the Commissioners of Public Works. The Guardians of the union shall debit the several electoral divisions with such proportions of that sum as may be payable by such electoral divisions respectively.

"Sec. 20. The Treasury may, from time to time, authorize the Commissioners of Public Works to make, subject to the regulations of the Treasury, grants to the Board of Guardians of any union, or such other body or persons and on such terms as the Lord Lieutenant may approve, for emigration purposes.

"The moneys so granted shall be applied in accordance with the said regulations for the same purposes as moneys borrowed under the provisions of this Act.

"The sums granted by the Commissioners of Public Works shall not exceed one hundred thousand pounds in the whole, and the sums granted shall not exceed five pounds per each person.

"Such grants shall only be made for the benefit of the unions mentioned in the second schedule of this Act,* and of such other unions or electoral divisions as may from time to time be settled by the Local Government Board, with the consent of the Lord Lieutenant: Provided that such unions are situate wholly or in part in some county specified in the schedule to the public notice issued by the Commissioners of Public Works in Ireland on the twenty-second day of November one thousand eight hundred and seventy-nine, that is to say, the counties of Donegal, Clare, Cork (West Riding), Kerry, Galway, Leitrim, Mayo, Roscommon, and Sligo.

"Each grant shall only be made on the recommendation of the Lord Lieutenant, stating that the Lord Lieutenant is satisfied that the Guardians of the union are unable, without unduly burdening the ratepayers to make adequate provision, by borrowing under the powers conferred upon them by this Act, or otherwise, for the emigration purposes of the union, and that proper arrangements have been made for securing the satisfactory emigration of such persons.

"The money required for the purpose of grants under this section shall be paid by the Land Commission to the Commissioners of Public Works, and shall be part of the liabilities of the Land Commission, and be a charge primarily upon the Irish Church Temporalities Fund, and subject thereto, on the Consolidated Fund, in such manner as may be provided by Parliament.

"Sec. 21. The Lord Lieutenant may from time to time make provision that arrangements shall be made for securing the satisfactory emigration of persons for whom means of emigration are provided under this Act, by prescribing rules in relation to such matters, and for the employment of special agents for that purpose, and otherwise as he thinks expedient. And any grants made under this Act for emigration purposes shall be applicable to defraying the expenses of such arrangements in such manner as the Lord Lieutenant directs."

* The Unions mentioned in the Schedule are :—

Belmullet,
Newport,
Swinford,
Clifden,
Oughterard,

No. 11.—Emigration.—Arrears of Rent (Ireland) Act, 1882.

Local Government Board, Dublin,
November 18, 1882.

Sir,

The Local Government Board for Ireland acknowledge the receipt of your Minute of the 17th instant, and in accordance with the desire expressed by the Lord Lieutenant, they have now the honour to submit, for his Excellency's information, a report as to what has been done up to the present time towards carrying out the emigration clauses of the Arrears of Rent (Ireland) Act, 1882.

On the passing of the Arrears of Rent Act the Lord Lieutenant appointed a Committee, consisting of Mr. Redington and Major Gaskell, to assist in drawing up rules for regulating the emigration to be conducted under its provisions, and to inquire into the facilities which would be afforded by the governments of the various places to which emigrants might be sent, the best times of year for sending them, and the arrangements necessary for their reception and employment on reaching their destination.

The rules have now been drawn up and approved, and copies are annexed hereto.

The Committee, after putting themselves into communication with the various Colonial authorities, have furnished a report, of which a copy is annexed.

This was only a preliminary report, but it appears to show that it is to Canada that the emigrants should principally be sent. The best time for sending emigrants to that Colony is from April to October.

The result of the communications of the Committee with the authorities of the United States is embodied in a report which the Local Government Board have to-day received from Major Gaskell, a copy of which is annexed.

There is an evident desire on the part of many of the poorer unions to take advantage of the Act, and annexed is a statement showing that, in addition to the five unions scheduled by the Act, the boards of guardians of 26 unions have applied to have the whole or part of the unions scheduled.

Out of this number, 12 unions have been wholly or in part scheduled, and the applications of the remainder are under consideration.

Some of the electoral divisions are, however, so poor that it is scarcely possible, even with the extended period for repayment of loans which the Act gives, for them to borrow any money for the purpose of emigration.

The Local Government Board have applied, through the Emigration Committee, to Mr. Tuke's Committee with the view of ascertaining whether in such cases they will take the place of the guardians, and find the means necessary to supplement the maximum grant of £5 a head which the Government can give.

Mr. Tuke's Committee have now intimated their willingness to assist and co-operate with the Emigration Committee, subject to the rules made by the Lord Lieutenant, and they will undertake the arrangements for the emigration of persons from the number of electoral divisions stated in the following unions, namely:—

* Belmullet Union	8	electoral divisions.
* Clifden "	3	" "
Newport "	5	" "
Oughterard "	4	" "

* Since this letter was written Mr. Tuke's Committee have undertaken the emigration from five additional Electoral Divisions in Belmullet Union, and five in Clifden Union.

Under this arrangement the operation of the guardians and Mr. Tuke's Committee will be kept separate.

In the electoral divisions thus assisted by Mr. Tuke's Committee emigration will be met by the maximum grant of £5, supplemented by contributions from Mr. Tuke's fund, and the selection of emigrants will rest with the Emigration Committee and Mr. Tuke's Committee.

In other poor electoral divisions the emigration must be carried on by the guardians, and will be met by the maximum grant of £5, supplemented by loans or moneys raised by the guardians, and the selection of emigrants will rest with the guardians and Emigration Committee.

In divisions somewhat better off financially the Government grant will be £4, £3, or £2 a head, according to the position of the division, and the cost of emigration will be met by this contribution, together with moneys raised by the guardians for the purpose on the security of the rates, and the selection will rest jointly with the guardians and the Emigration Committee.

In electoral divisions where the whole cost can be raised by the guardians on the security of the rates there will be no Government grant, and the selection will be entirely in the hands of the guardians.

In all the above cases the emigration will be conducted subject to the provisions of the emigration rules.

The greatest care has been taken in the framing of these rules to secure that the emigrants are properly looked after. A male and female agent will be appointed both at the ports of embarkation and disembarkation to look after their comfort.

At present it is not intended to send out more than about 15 families in one ship, so as not to throw too many of them on the labour market at once, and, from all accounts the Local Government Board have, there will be no difficulty in obtaining suitable employment for as many as may be sent. Another feature of the scheme is, that whole families only, as a rule, are to be emigrated under the provisions of the Act.

No objection will be raised to boards of guardians assisting individuals who can contribute themselves, either in the shape of money or of passage tickets sent to them by their friends; but, as a rule, the Government grant will only be given in such cases where they form part of a whole family emigrating.

At the present moment one of the Emigration Committee, Mr. Redington, is visiting the unions scheduled under the Act with the Local Government Board's inspector of the district, to explain the advantages of the scheme, and the conditions attaching to Government aid.

Between the 7th and 10th instant Mr. Redington attended to meet the boards of guardians in Swinford, Westport, Newport, Clifden, and Oughterard Unions.

The guardians generally appeared to be desirous to take advantage of the facilities offered by the Act to effect the emigration of poor persons from their unions, and the guardians of Swinford, Westport, Newport, and Oughterard Unions determined to post notices through their districts inviting applications from persons wishing to be assisted to emigrate.

The greatest care will be exercised in the selection of agents, both in this country at the ports of embarkation, and particularly at the ports of disembarkation abroad. At these latter ports the emigration agents of the Colonial authorities will probably be employed, and a lady to look after the comfort of the women and children will be associated with the agent at each place.

Although, as has been stated in paragraph 5, it is to Canada that emigrants must mainly be sent, a letter has been addressed to the Colonial Office asking them to forward an application to each of the following Governments, asking if it be possible for them to provide free passages for such numbers of persons of the agricultural labourer and domestic servant class as we may desire to send to them, namely:—

Victoria,	New Zealand,
South Australia,	Cape of Good Hope,
New South Wales,	Natal, and
Queensland,	Western Australia,
Tasmania,	

In all arrangements with the guardians the Local Government Board desire to leave them as free as possible, in fact to throw upon them the whole of the work, subject only to a compliance with the rules, and the concurrence of the Committee in the selection of persons to be emigrated.

The Local Government Board, however, will at all times be ready to give the guardians the benefit of the assistance and advice of the Emigration Committee, who are required by the rules to satisfy themselves as to the adequacy of the arrangements made, and to report them in detail to the Board, whose approval of them must be obtained before the despatch of any selected emigrants.

I have, &c.,

(Signed) B. Banks, Secretary.

To R. G. C. Hamilton.

Enclosures.

A.—Rules for scheduled Unions and Electoral Divisions.

B.—Rules, under section 18, borrowing.

C.—First Report of Emigration Committee, 10th October, 1882.

D.—Report of Major Gaskell of result of Conference in London, 17th November, 1882.

E.—List of unions which have applied to be scheduled, and result up to 18th November, 1882.

A.

Emigration.—45 & 46 Victoria, Cap. 47

Rules prescribed by the Lord Lieutenant in relation to the Emigration of Poor Persons under the 18th, 19th, 20th, and 21st Sections of the Arrears of Rent (Ireland) Act, 1882.

Selection.

I.—Boards of Guardians who are desirous to borrow money to supplement the grants offered by the Government for the emigration of poor persons resident within any electoral division of their union scheduled under the 20th section of the Arrears of Rent (Ireland) Act shall prepare lists in the annexed Form (7 C). In making the selection they will be aided by the Emigration Committee acting under the Local Government Board, or one member thereof; and they shall submit such lists to the Local Government Board, with a view of obtaining the Board's consent, as provided in section 26 of 12 & 13 Vic., cap. 104.

II.—As a rule, the Government grants shall be applied to the emigration of whole families only, but individuals may, in exceptional cases, be approved; and, if females, they must place themselves under the care of a married couple approved by the guardians, or of some person appointed by them, until they arrive at their destination.

Applicants for assistance to emigrate should, in all cases, be warned not to leave their employment, nor to make any preparation to emigrate, until they shall receive notice that they have been selected. Such notice of selection shall be given to every approved emigrant as soon as possible after the decision of the approving authority shall have been made known.

Provision of Funds.

III. The treasurer of the union shall be requested to open a separate account, to be called the "Emigration Account," to the credit of which the money borrowed by the guardians for emigration purposes shall be lodged. The Government grant shall be paid into the same account, and cheques on this account shall be signed in the usual manner by the presiding chairman of any board meeting and two other guardians present thereat, and shall be countersigned by the clerk to the guardians.

If the whole number of persons for whose emigration grants are made by the Government shall not be sent out by the guardians, the grants made in respect of such persons shall be returned to the Commissioners of Public Works.

A monthly return shall be furnished to the Local Government Board by the clerk of the union, and countersigned by a member of the Emigration Committee, showing the number of emigrants who have embarked during the preceding month.

The guardians shall use their discretion in requiring applicants to contribute a portion of the cost of their emigration, and the amount of such contribution shall be paid into the emigration account.

Outfit.

IV. The guardians, in conjunction with the Emigration Committee, or one member thereof, shall see that each emigrant has at least the following outfit, subject, in the case of a child, to such modification as the Guardians, with the approval of the Emigration Committee, may direct, viz.:—

Males.	Females.
1 suit of clothes.	1 dress.
1 overcoat.	1 jacket.
2 shirts.	2 woollen petticoats.
2 pairs of socks.	2 sets of underclothing.
2 handkerchiefs.	2 pairs of stockings.
1 muffler.	2 handkerchiefs.
1 pair of boots.	1 shawl.
1 hat or cap.	1 pair of boots.
2 towels.	1 hat or bonnet.
1 brush and comb.	2 towels.
1 rug or coverlet.	1 brush and comb.
1 bag or box.	Sewing and knitting materials.
	1 rug or coverlet.
	1 bag or box.

A ship outfit shall also be provided, consisting of—

A mattress and pillow.
A knife, fork, and spoon.
A tin plate, drinking mug, and can.
1 lb. marine soap.

Embarkation Arrangements.

V. The Guardians, in conjunction with the Emigration Committee, or one member thereof, shall provide for the conveyance of the emigrants to the port of embarkation, and for their board and lodging while there. Two agents, one male and one female (man and wife if possible), shall be appointed by the Government to act under the Emigration Committee in superintending the whole of the arrangements at the port of embarkation.

Ocean Passage.

VI. The Guardians, in conjunction with the Emigration Committee, or one member thereof, shall make contracts for the conveyance of the emigrants from the port of embarkation to the country to which they are going, or shall place them at the time of embarkation in charge of the person or persons through whose agency they will be conveyed to their destination.

Reception and Disposal.

VII. Emigrants to North America shall be landed at one or other of the undermentioned ports—

New York.	Quebec.
Boston.	Halifax.*

Two agents, one male and one female, shall be appointed by the Government at each of these ports, whose duty it will be to keep the Emigration Committee informed as to the number of emigrants for whom there is a prospect of immediate employment, and as to the necessary arrangements for the conveyance of the emigrants from the ship to their destination, including their subsistence during the journey. The Emigration Committee shall satisfy themselves as to the adequacy of these arrangements, and shall report them in detail to the Local Government Board, whose approval of them shall be obtained before the despatch of any selected emigrants. The Emigration Committee shall also see that a sufficient sum of money is placed by the Guardians in the agents' hands to enable these arrangements to be carried out.

Grants to Body or Person other than Boards of Guardians.

VIII. In cases in which the Government grant may be made to any body or person other than a Board of Guardians, the selection of the emigrants shall be made by such body or person, with the aid of the Emigration Committee acting under the Local Government Board, or one member thereof, and the list of persons so selected shall be transmitted to the Local Government Board for their approval.

IX. The body or person receiving the grant shall undertake to carry out the emigration in the manner prescribed for the guidance of Boards of Guardians by Rules II., IV., V., VI., and VII.

Emigration to the Australasian and South African Colonies.

X. In the event of emigrants, selected under Rules I. and VIII., proceeding to these Colonies, the necessary arrangements shall be made by the Guardians, or other body or persons, in conjunction with the representatives of the Colonial Governments in London, and subject to the approval of the Local Government Board.

Given at Dublin Castle this 24th day of October, 1882.

By His Excellency's command,

(Signed) R. G. C. Hamilton.

Note.—Since the issue of these rules Philadelphia has been added as an additional port.—R. G. C. H., 18 Nov.

Emigration.
Union Emigration List.

Union.

List and Description of Persons whom the Guardians of the above Union propose to assist to Emigrate.

No.	Names*		Age	Whether Married or Single		[illegible]	[illegible]	[illegible]	[illegible]	[illegible]	[illegible]	[illegible]	[illegible]	[illegible]	[illegible]	[illegible]	[illegible]	[illegible]
	Christian.	Surname.		M.	S.													

* It will be convenient to arrange the names in this List so that all the persons chargeable to the same Electoral Division, or to the Union at large, and [illegible] may be placed together.

I certify that I have seen the several inmates of the Workhouse named in the above list, and that I consider them to be fit for the voyage.

(Signature) Medical Officer of the Workhouse.
Dated.

(Signature) Clerk of the Union.
Dated.

B.

EMIGRATION.—45 & 46 Vic., cap. 47.

RULES prescribed by the LORD LIEUTENANT in relation to the EMIGRATION of POOR PERSONS under the 18th section of the Arrears of Rent (Ireland) Act, 1882.

I. Boards of Guardians in non-scheduled Unions who are desirous to borrow money for emigration purposes under the 18th section of the Arrears of Rent (Ireland) Act, 1882, shall prepare lists of the persons wishing to emigrate in the annexed *Form* (7 B), and shall submit the same to the Local Government Board, with the view of obtaining the Board's consent, as provided in section 26 of 12 and 13 Vic., cap. 104.

II. The Guardians shall see that each emigrant has at least the following outfit, subject in the case of a child to such modifications as the Guardians may determine, viz. :—

Males.	Females.
1 suit of clothes.	1 dress.
1 overcoat.	1 jacket.
2 shirts.	2 woollen petticoats.
2 pairs of socks.	2 sets of underclothing.
2 handkerchiefs.	2 pairs of stockings.
1 muffler.	2 handkerchiefs.
1 pair of boots.	1 shawl.
1 hat or cap.	1 pair of boots.
2 towels.	1 hat or bonnet.
1 brush and comb.	2 towels.
1 rug or coverlet.	1 brush and comb.
1 bag or box.	Sewing and knitting materials.
	1 rug or coverlet.
	1 bag or box.

A ship outfit shall also be provided, consisting of—

A mattress and pillow.
A knife, fork, and spoon.
A tin plate, drinking mug, and can.
1 lb. marine soap.

III. The guardians shall provide for the conveyance of the emigrants to the port of embarkation, for their shipment at such place, and for their transport by sea under proper supervision to the country to which they are to proceed.

IV. The guardians shall arrange with the local emigration agent at the port of landing for the reception of the emigrants and for their subsequent disposal. A sufficient sum of money shall be placed in his hands for that purpose.

V. When emigrants embark at ports where local agents are employed by the Government, the guardians may avail themselves of the services of such agents for the purpose of superintending the embarkation and making the necessary arrangements for the subsistence and accommodation of the emigrants before embarkation; and when the emigrants disembark at New York, Boston, Quebec, or Halifax, where the Government propose to employ local agents, the guardians may avail themselves of the services of such agents to make the necessary arrangements for the conveyance of the emigrants from the ship to their destination, including their subsistence during the journey.

Given at Dublin Castle this 30th day of October, 1882.

By His Excellency's command,

(Signed) R. G. C. HAMILTON.

Emigration,
Form for Descriptive List.]

Union.

List and Description of Persons whom the Guardians of the above Union propose to assist to Emigrate.

No.	Names.*		Age.	Whether Married or Single.		Whether Husband, Wife, Son or Daughter of any other Person named in this List.	Whether Parents ...	Whether ...	[illegible]	[illegible]	Previous Occupation.	Where ...	Estimated Cost of Emigration.				Proportion ...	Proportion ... †	Remarks.
	Surname.	Christian Name.		M.	S.								Amount of Passage Money.	Outfit ...	Allowance ...	Total Cost of Emigration.			

* [illegible]

† [illegible]

I certify‡ that I have seen the several inmates of the Workhouse named in the above List, and that I consider them to be fit for the voyage.

(Signature) Dated Medical Officer of the Workhouse.

(Signature) Dated Clerk of the Union.

‡ The medical certificate will be required only in the case of Workhouse inmates.

C.

Local Government Board, Dublin,
October 10, 1883.

GENTLEMEN,—We have the honour to report that, in accordance with our instructions, we have been in communication with the Agents-General of Victoria, South Australia, New South Wales, Queensland, Tasmania, and New Zealand, and with the Emigration Agents of the Cape of Good Hope, Natal, and Western Australia. For convenience of reference we have tabulated the information so obtained and we add a few general remarks.

Australasia and South Africa.

The object of our inquiries was to ascertain what facilities are offered by the above colonies to emigrants in the way of reception at depôts before embarking and after landing, of free or assisted passage, and of opportunity for obtaining employment.

All these points we had full opportunity, thanks to introductions from the Secretary of State for the Colonies, of discussing with the representatives of the Governments of these Colonies in London, to whom we are indebted for the ready communication of all the information we sought. We regret that the particulars which we are thus enabled to give do not promise much for the end we have in view, viz., provision for emigrants from Ireland of the poorer classes; for unquestionably, in regard to climate, resources, and rates of wages, the Australasian and South African colonies compare favourably with the countries of the North American continent.

It is almost needless to state that the cost of passage to Australia and New Zealand is in all cases so high that, unless the whole, or almost the whole, of it be met by a system of free or very liberally assisted emigration, those countries are closed to emigrants under the *Arrears of Rent (Ireland) Act*, 1882.

In Queensland alone are facilities offered for any considerable amount of *free* emigration, but we were informed that the number of Irish applying for passages is at all times in excess of the proportion of that nationality allowed by the laws of the Colony.

In several of the Colonies emigration is *assisted*, and in all but Natal the *nomination* system appears to obtain. Under this system colonists nominate their relatives or friends in the United Kingdom, subject to the approval of the Agent-General in London, paying a largely reduced fare, and taking charge of the friends on their arrival. Thus the Colonial Government is relieved from all responsibility, while the benefits of select immigration are secured to the colony. But the advantages of the system are confined to the colonists and their friends at home. Under existing laws the Colonial Governments have no power to nominate, and there is no prospect of the laws being altered unless to meet an exceptional case. We are not without hope that an exception might be made in some cases in favour of agricultural labourers and women fitted for general domestic service, if approved by the Colonial authorities in London; and we recommend that a special application be addressed through the Colonial Office to each of the Governments we have named, asking if it be possible for them to provide free passages for such numbers as they shall determine of emigrants from Ireland of the above mentioned classes.

Canada.

From all the accounts which the Committee have received, oral as well as documentary, they are led to think that the Dominion of Canada offers the most hopeful field for the rural employment and settlement of large numbers of Irish emigrant farmers and labourers.

The High Commissioner for Canada was absent from London at the time of our visit, but we had an interview at Belfast with Sir C. Tupper, Minister of Railways in Canada, and Mr. Colmer, Secretary to the High Commissioner. Sir C. Tupper gave us a most encouraging account of the prospects of emigrants to Manitoba. He said that, owing to the construction of the Canadian Pacific Railway and the great amount of building work now going on in the town of Winnipeg, there is an almost unlimited demand for labour in that province. He expressed the greatest desire that the stream of Irish immigration should find its way thither, and assured us that he would aid any movement for that object by every means in his power.

Assisted passages are already offered by the Canadian Government to emigrants intending to reside in Canada, at the rate of £3 per adult to Quebec; and Sir C. Tupper held out hopes of still further assistance in the way of free railway or steamboat transport from Quebec to any destination in the Dominion. He said, however, that there is no chance of his Government making any provision for the settlement of emigrants on their arrival in Manitoba, though it is very necessary that such provision should be made. It is obvious that this cannot be done with the limited means provided by the Arrears of Rent (Ireland) Act; and unless the Canadian Pacific Railway Company, or other private association, will devise and carry out a settlement scheme in conjunction with the Land Commissioners of Ireland, or otherwise, it is a question how far emigrants should be encouraged to proceed to the North-west. In any case there is a large demand for labour in Ontario and the older provinces of Canada, caused partly by their increasing prosperity and partly by the migration of many of the inhabitants of Manitoba.

On the whole, we incline to the opinion that unless the emigrant has friends in the Far West he had better begin by taking any suitable employment that offers in the eastern provinces, whence he may work his way westward as he gets accustomed to the country and accumulates the necessary funds.

The best time of year for sending emigrants to Canada is from April to October, but we are informed that domestic servants can go out at any time with good prospect of immediate employment.

The arrangements made by the Canadian Government for the reception and disposal of emigrants, as described to us by the Secretary to the High Commissioner for Canada, seem to be very complete. There are emigration agents and depôts in eleven of the principal towns of Canada. Emigrants are supported there for a time at a moderate charge, and are advised as to the best means of obtaining employment. The Secretary to the High Commissioner, however, informs us that the demand for labour is so great that any long stay at these depôts is unnecessary. There seems little doubt that under an organized system employment could be secured for all immigrants immediately on their arrival in the country.

United States. It is likely that owing to the large number of Irish at present settled in the United States many of our emigrants will select that country as their destination. There is no doubt that a considerable amount of employment can be obtained there, and that it is an advantage to the emigrant to find himself among friends on his arrival in a new country. Unfortunately, however, the mass of the emigrants have hitherto remained crowded in the large cities of the Eastern States, instead of pushing on to rural districts further west. The moral and political evils resulting from this state of things are deplored by thoughtful men of all parties in America. It would not, therefore, be wise to encourage any large emigration of Irish to the United States unless some arrangements were made for the purpose of aiding them in proceeding to the interior and procuring suitable agricultural employment.

The best time for emigration to the United States is in spring and summer.

Excepting the Castle Garden depôt at New York, there seem to be no satisfactory arrangements in the United States for the reception and disposal of emigrants. It would, therefore, be necessary to appoint agents at the principal ports, whose duty it should be to collect information as to the demand for labour in the different parts of the States, and to assist emigrants in obtaining employment on arrival.

Mr. Tuke's committee.

The Committee have been in communication with the honorary secretary of Mr. Tuke's fund, with the view of ascertaining how far his committee will co-operate with and assist the Government in the following ways :—

1st. In the case of scheduled electoral divisions in respect to which the guardians are unable to provide any part of the cost of emigration, by undertaking the whole of the arrangements, receiving the whole of the maximum grant of *£5* per head from the Government, and

2nd. In cases in which the guardians supplement the Government grant, by providing the shipping and taking charge of the emigrants from the moment of embarkation, receiving from the guardians the actual cost of the sea passage, and a small contribution per head towards the expenses after landing.

The honorary secretary informs us, in reply, that the members of his committee are absent from London ; that having communicated with them by letter, he has no doubt that they will accept the first proposal, but that their answer to the second will somewhat depend on the report of the gentlemen who have been for some weeks making inquiries for them in America and Canada, and who have not yet returned.

The Committee feel bound, in conclusion, to put forward the recommendation which comes to them from all sides, and as the result of actual experience, that in order to secure the most satisfactory provision for emigrants, either in the United States or in Canada, the number of families sent out in each ship should be limited to about fifteen. Under the system of agency recommended in the accompanying rules the Emigration Committee will, of course, be informed when that number may be exceeded.

We beg to submit, for the consideration of His Excellency, the following rules for the purpose of securing the satisfactory emigration of poor persons under the Arrears of Rent (Ireland) Act, 1882.

We have, &c.

(Signed), C. T. REDINGTON.
W. P. GASKELL.

[TABLE.

M

1882.—Table showing the Facilities offered to Emigrants by

Colony.	Free Passages. To whom given.	Govt. Passage.	Govt. Kit.	Assisted Passages. To whom given.	Govt. Passage.	Govt. Kit.
Canada,	None, . . .	—		Agricultural labourers, Infants, 10s.; between 1 and 12 years, £2.	£[illegible].	5s.
				General labourers and mechanics. Infants, 10s.; between 1 and 12 years, £2.	£4.	5s.
				Female domestic servants.	£4.	5s.
Queensland,	To female domestic servants, from 17 to 30 years, also to families having not more than three children under 12 years.	—	£1 per head, except children under three years.	To certain trades, and labourers, with or without families. From 1 to 12 years, males £[illegible], females, £1; from 12 to 40 years, males, £4; females, £2; above 40 years, either sex, £4.	For sea kit, £1 must be paid in addition in every case, except for infants.	
New South Wales.	None, . . .	—		To farmers, labourers, mechanics, and female domestic servants selected by the Agent-General, at the same rates as nominated persons.	—	
Victoria,	None, . . .	—		None, ...	—	
South Australia.	As a rule, none; but very rarely to good female domestic servants who are unmarried.	Nil. . .		None, ...	—	
Western Australia.	None, . . .	—		None, ...	—	
Tasmania,	None. . . .	—		To labourers and their families with friends in the Colony who have expressed a desire to have them out, subject to approval by the emigration agent; also to female domestic servants up to 30 years.	The rates are the same as for nominated emigrants. See the next column.	
New Zealand	It is intended shortly to offer free passages to female domestic servants experienced in situations away from their own homes.	—		None.	—	
Cape of Good Hope.	To artizans for Government works; to farmers with some capital; to recruits for the Cape troops.	Nil, . .		None, ...	—	
Natal,	To 25 persons per month chosen by the emigration agent from among farmers, farm labourers, and others, and who are able to pay a deposit of £5 each, returnable on embarkation.	Nil, . .		To 50 families per month able to pay a deposit equal in amount to their passage money, which, however, is returned to them after embarkation. (The object of the deposit is to secure the embarkation of the emigrants, and means of support for them on landing).	£5 per adult.	

In all the Australasian Colonies the proportion of
In the reception depôt at Plymouth emigrants are

CANADA, and the AUSTRALASIAN and SOUTH AFRICAN COLONIES.

Nominated Passages.			Reception Depôt in the United Kingdom.	COLONY.
To whom given.	Cost. Passage.	Cost. Kit.		
None, ...	—		None, . .	CANADA.
From 1 to 12 years, males, £1. " " females, £1. " 12 to 40 years, males, £2. " " females, £1. Above 40 years, either sex, £4.	For sea kit, £1 in addition for all fares, excepting only infants.		Plymouth, .	QUEENSLAND.
Married couples, with or without children, up to 45 years, and single men and women to 40 years of age, are eligible.			Plymouth, .	NEW SOUTH WALES.
Fare, per adult man or woman.	£4.	sea kit		
" for female domestic servants.	£2.	is free.		
None, ...	—		None, . .	VICTORIA.
From 1 to 12 years of age, £2. " 12 to 40 years, . £4. " 40 to 50 years, . £8. Above 50 years, . . £14.	The sea kit is free to all.		Plymouth, .	SOUTH AUSTRALIA.
To nominees of colonists. .	For sea kit, £1 .		None, . .	WESTERN AUSTRALIA.
For a whole family, . £15. " single man, . . £10. " single woman, . £5.	£1 additional to each fare for sea kit.		None, . .	TASMANIA.
Families and single persons are eligible. All males over 12 pay £4 each, and all children beyond three per family must be paid for. Domestic servants get sea kit free.	Sea kit, £1 per fare, except for female domestic servants.		Plymouth, .	NEW ZEALAND.
To agricultural labourers, domestic servants (male and female), and artizans nominated by colonists.	Per fare, £3 10s. 6d., including the sea kit.		None, . .	CAPE OF GOOD HOPE.
Some free and some assisted passages are given to persons of the same classes as those mentioned in the first column ("free passages") who have been nominated by colonists, and who pay a deposit of £5 each.	Not exceeding £6 per head.		None, . .	NATAL.

Irish immigrants allowed in about 2 in 10.
Boarded and lodged free of charge about three days before sailing.

1882.—Table showing the Facilities offered to Emigrants—*con.*

Colony.	Reception Depôt in the Colony.	Aid given in obtaining Employment.	Cost of an Unassisted Steerage Passage.
			£ s. d.
Canada, . .	Depôts and agents in 11 of the principal towns of Canada.	Free railway passes are given to female domestic servants only.	6 0 0
Queensland, .	There are seven ports of landing and depôts at all. Immigrants may remain 14 days free.	Free passes up country are given.	16 16 0
New South Wales,	At Sydney, where there is a depôt for single women only. Married people and single men may be on board seven days if they wish.	Free passes up the country are given to immigrants within four days after arrival in port.	15 15 0
Victoria, . .	None, . . .	None, . . .	11 15 0
South Australia,	At Adelaide there is a home for single women, but no general depôt for immigrants.	Sometimes free passes are given to immigrants proceeding up the country.	16 16 0
Western Australia.	Depôt at Fremantle.	None, . . .	£15 to £18
Tasmania, . .	Launceston and Hobart Town are the ports. No depôts.	None, . . .	Family, £70 4s. 6d.; single, £17 5s. 6d., per adult by steamer. Family, £17 2s. 6d.; single, £16 5s. 6d., per adult per sailing ship.
New Zealand, .	Depôts at four ports, where immigrants can remain seven days, free of cost.	Many are assisted, but there is no rule.	£16 sailing ship; £21 by steamer.
Cape of Good Hope,	No depôts. Emigrants land at Table Bay or one of five other ports.	Government employés, farm settlers, and tenant farmers get free passes up the country.	£15 to Cape Town; £19 to Port Elizabeth; £16 to East London.
Natal, . . .	At Durban, where immigrants can remain seven days, paying for their food only.	None, . . .	15 0 0

The following suggestions were discussed, and omitted from the rules as belonging to detail. I think they are important details, and that in the interests of the people and the public they should not be lost sight of. I beg respectfully to submit them.

Printed notices shall be circulated in each locality in which the emigration clauses are to be brought into operation, informing the people to whom they should apply for assistance to emigrate, and as to the conditions on which assistance will be given. Notice to the people.

Applicants shall in every case be warned not to leave their employment, nor to make any preparation to emigrate, until they shall receive notice that they have been selected. Such notice of selection shall be given to every approved emigrant as soon as possible after the decision of the approving authority shall have been made known. Applicants to be warned not to leave their employment.

The assistance of the Government grant shall not be given to persons whose property, if sold, should suffice to pay the whole cost of their emigration, or who should be able to support themselves at home. Definition of "poor persons" under the Act.

(Signed) W. P. Gaskell.

10th October, 1882.

D.

Dublin, November 17, 1882.

Gentlemen,—I have the honour to report, that in compliance with your Minute of the 24th October, I proceeded to London on the 24th October ultimo to attend the meeting of the committee of Mr. Tuke's Fund, on the 25th October, to give any explanations the members of that committee might ask of the rules for emigration prescribed by the Lord Lieutenant, and to receive the reply of the committee to the proposal of your Board that they should undertake the emigration in certain electoral divisions.

The committee, having met on the 25th October, referred the rules and other papers to a sub-committee for report, and adjourned until the 7th November instant.

Having communicated to that sub-committee all the information they required, I called at the office of the United States Legation in London, in pursuance of the second instruction in the Minute of your Board above referred to, and then proceeded on short leave of absence.

On the 7th November instant I attended the adjourned meeting of the committee of Mr. Tuke's Fund, at which the proposition of your Board that the committee should take charge of the emigration in those electoral divisions pronounced unable, without unduly burdening the ratepayers, to raise funds by borrowing, was accepted, as reported in the honorary secretary's letter of the 8th November instant.

It remained for me to ascertain, in communication with the United States Legation in London, and from any other sources that offered, all the information procurable bearing upon the reception on landing, and the chances of employment, of emigrants to the United States.

The United States Chargé d'Affaires, Mr. Hoppin, in the absence of the minister, Mr. Lowell, informed me that he has been many years in England, and has no personal knowledge of agents or arrangements in connexion with emigration to the United States; neither is he in a position to supply, from any documents in the office of the Legation, the particular information which I sought. But he told me in general terms that the Federal Government of the United States confines its action with regard to immigrants to freeing their personal property from excise or customs dues.

That each State of the Union enacts its own laws on immigration, and that the municipalities at the ports of landing also make regulations on the subject.

He kindly undertook to obtain for me replies to any questions which it might become my duty to address to him officially, and which he might not himself be able to answer. Meanwhile he referred me to the editor of a newspaper, the "Anglo-American Times," which is published in London, and contains an impartial and reliable record of passing events in the United States, which deals specially with emigration to and settlement in America, and may be read with profit by all interested in these subjects.

I find that the experience of the editor, and the matter of his journal, refer chiefly to *settlement* as the object, and undoubtedly the best prospect, of emigrants to the United States, whereas it is *labour* of the commonest kinds which emigrants under the Arrears Act must look for, and that within a moderate distance of the eastern seaboard of America.

What then are the conditions which will affect such emigrants?

For the answer which I will give, so far as I am able, to that question I am alone responsible, but I beg explicitly to acknowledge my large indebtedness to members of Mr. Tuke's committee for information fully and freely given.

I think that the following points may be taken as established, viz.:—

That there is a very strong feeling in America against the importation of unsuitable people, particularly of "workhouse paupers."

That the shipping companies are bound by deed to the State authorities to re-ship all helpless or destitute immigrants whom they may have landed on the American shore.

That, although there is a large amount of common labour required in the large cities, there is a large floating population always seeking work, and that it is not the inexperienced hands who get the first offer of employment.

That even this year's emigrants are found joining in the cry "There are too many Irish here; don't send any more."

That the Irishman is not popular as an emigrant, Germans and Scandinavians being preferred.

That, nevertheless, there are chances of employment for (unskilled) families "of the right sort," and having a sufficient number of wage-earners over 13 years of age, in the manufacturing districts of the Eastern States; but that the demand for such families is limited, and cannot be estimated until the spring.

That, except in the manufacturing mills, not more than 60 per cent. of the labour lasts regularly through the winter.

That the wages of an able-bodied adult in the Eastern States is seldom less than 5*s.* a day; never less than 4*s.*

That female domestic servants, or women suitable to such work, are everywhere in demand.

That farm labour is to be had, but that the farmers always want hands able to plough and accustomed to agricultural machines, and that they will seldom take *families.*

That families, on being taken into employ, have to depend, if without means of their own, upon the employer to advance them food and furniture, the latter costing from 20 to 50 dollars, until they can earn wages, and that the consequent stoppages bear somewhat hardly upon the families at first, and give rise to complaints.

That ordinary families may earn, in the mills, from £8 per month upwards, but that rent and provisions are dear, dearer than in Canada.

The universal advice with regard to Irish emigrants is, "Put them on the land," *i.e.*, give them the means of "settling." But it is pretty certain, from experience, that the class of people who will emigrate under the Arrears Act are not, as a rule, ripe for colonization.

Wages, however, and the demand for labour, are much better in the Western States than in the Eastern; and there is good ground for the conclusion that if emigrants can be put down in the west, *i.e.*, west of Chicago, they will surely prosper.

One great object will be hereafter, by keeping down the expenses on this side, by obtaining the ocean passage at as low a rate as possible, and by making the most favourable terms possible direct with railway companies in America, *to push emigrants as far west as possible.*

The most satisfactory arrangements for the landing of emigrants in America are at New York. A brief description of those arrangements accompanies. They appear to be very complete.

I have, &c.,

(Signed) W. P. Gaskell.

To the Local Government Board.

ABSTRACT of the REGULATIONS of the STATE of NEW YORK for the RECEPTION of IMMIGRANTS at the PORT of NEW YORK, and STATEMENT of the Facilities afforded to them for obtaining EMPLOYMENT and proceeding to their Destinations.

The State Emigrant Landing Depôt at Castle Garden is the legal and compulsory place of debarkation for all steerage passengers.

The number of steerage passengers landed there in 1881 was 441,044, or by months as under, viz. :—

January, ...	8,887	August, ...	43,849
February, . . .	9,763	September, . . .	18,878
March, ...	27,798	October, ...	36,734
April, ...	58,146	November, ...	31,065
May, ...	76,781	December, ...	23,964
June, ...	59,121		———
July, ...	54,834		441,044

So that in April and June the emigrants passing through Castle Garden were 2,000 a day, including Sundays, and in May 2,500 a day.

An officer from Castle Garden boards every emigrant ship on arrival in the port.

After examination of their luggage on board by customs officers, immigrants are transferred by barge or steamboat to Castle Garden, being carefully examined as they enter, in order that it may be seen whether they are likely to become a future charge to the State. They so pass into the "Rotunda," a building capable of accommodating about 3,000 persons, and in which everything possible under the circumstances has been done to secure the comfort of the new arrivals.

In the building are found a—

Restaurant and bread stands, for supplying plain food at moderate prices, and kept open at night if necessary;

Responsible bankers to change money at current rates, without deduction;

Interpreters speaking and writing every European language (query Irish?—W. Gaskell); a

Telegraph office, and a

Railroad agency of the main lines, where immigrants may purchase tickets and register their luggage; a

Baggage delivery agency for New York city;

Licensed boarding-house keepers, wearing badges; a

Physician ready to attend to the sick, and a temporary hospital to serve until patients can be moved to *the hospital on Wards' Island*; a

Labour bureau, which found employment in 1881 for 49,745 persons, with employers all over the United States; and an

Information bureau, where immigrants inquiring for friends in America, or *vice versa*, may hear all that is known about them.

The care of the State for immigrants is shown by the following figures:—

83,372 free meals were furnished to destitute immigrants.

12,543 dollars were advanced to assist in forwarding immigrants to their friends, or to places where employment had been found for them.

913 persons were returned to Europe, while 6,627 persons were admitted to the hospital on Ward's Island.

(It is perhaps worthy of passing remark that, whereas the New York Commissioners for Emigration applied to the Legislature for 200,000 dollars to meet the expenses of the State emigrant institutions, the Legislature only appropriated 150,000 dollars for the purpose; and that therefore, as the Report of the Commissioners states, "many necessary repairs to buildings have been left undone, and contemplated improvements in the manner of receiving and protecting immigrants have had to be postponed.")

The shipping companies now pay to Castle Garden half a dollar per adult immigrant landed.

The whole of the services rendered to immigrants by the officials attached to Castle Garden are free of expense to the immigrant; and the railway agents are also required to convey their passengers, with their luggage, free of expense from Castle Garden to the railroad termini.

The floor of the Rotunda Building is open for the free use of recently arrived immigrants until ready to take their departure, and they are "requested to make use of the wash-rooms before leaving the premises."

W. P. Gaskell.

Note.—The estimate of the Emigration Commissioners, apart from the staff of the hospital establishment at Ward's Island, for the staff of the Castle Garden Landing Depôt for 1883 includes a secretary, treasurer, 18 clerks and interpreters, 5 inspectors, a resident physician, 2 hospital nurses, 1 matron, 1 janitor, 6 gate-keepers, 1 day and 4 night watchmen, &c., at salaries amounting to 40,000 dollars.—W. P. Gaskell.

E.

LIST of UNIONS from which applications to be Scheduled under the Emigration Clauses of the Arrears of Rent (Ireland) Act, 1882, have been received by the Local Government Board up to 18 Nov., 1882.

Union.	Result of Application.
Ballinasloe,	8 Electoral Divisions scheduled.
Ballyvaughan,	8 ,, ,,
Boyle,	75 ,, ,,
Cahirciveen,	All ,, ,,
Castlerea,	19 ,, ,,
Claremorris,	16 ,, ,,
Dromore, West,	9 ,, ,,
Newport,	The whole Union.
Letterkenny,	4 Electoral Divisions scheduled
Loughrea,	5 ,, ,,
Strokestown,	7 ,, ,,
Westport,	16 ,, ,,
Ballina,	Under consideration.
Ballyshannon,	
Carrick-on-Shannon,	
Galway,	
Glennamaddy,	
Ulla,	
Manorhamilton,	
Milford,	
Mohill,	
Roscommon,	
Sligo,	
Stranorlar,	
Tobercurry,	
Tralee,	

No. 12.—EMIGRATION—ARREARS OF RENT (IRELAND) ACT, 1882.

REPORT from MAJOR GASKELL of result of his Visit to AMERICA.

Dublin, 31st January, 1883.

GENTLEMEN,

I have the honour to submit for the information of His Excellency the Lord Lieutenant, the following report of my proceedings since I left Dublin on the 1st December, ultimo.

Having embarked at Queenstown that evening on board the s.s. Germanic, I landed with her 230 passengers at Castle Garden, New York, on the afternoon of the 11th December.

The objects before me were:—1. To ascertain the laws and regulations relating to Immigration at Philadelphia, New York and Boston, and to put myself in communication with the Immigration authorities at these ports.

2. To appoint Agents, in conformity with the Rules prescribed by the Lord Lieutenant; for the purposes of corresponding with my Committee, and of receiving the emigrants for whose passage we may hereafter be responsible.

3. To obtain special terms, if possible, from the principal Railroad Companies for the conveyance of emigrants to destinations inland; and

4. To inquire as to the probability of a demand next spring for unskilled labourers and their families.

I was also instructed to make arrangements, in concert with the Dominion and Provincial Governments of Canada, for the reception and distribution of emigrants to that country.

I have spared no effort to accomplish these objects in the shortest possible time, consistent with a due regard to the importance of some of the questions involved; and I cannot but acknowledge the courtesy and assistance which I have met with on all sides in the course of my inquiries. If the conclusions at which I have arrived appear to be at variance with the judgment of others, I must nevertheless claim for them that they are based upon the most recent information, communicated by practical men of high character and wide experience, living in different places and engaged in different callings, but speaking the same mind in regard to the prospects of unskilled labourers with families in the older States of America.

THE UNITED STATES.

Immigration Laws. In the United States one law, passed at the end of the last Session of Congress (3rd August, 1882), governs immigration at all the ports. Under that law Emigration Commissioners are appointed for each port by the Secretary of the Treasury on the nomination of the Governor of the State in which the port is situated. The duty of the Emigration Commissioners is specially to prevent the introduction into the United States of any convict, lunatic, idiot, or person likely to become a charge to the public. Such persons will not be permitted to land, but will be returned to their country at the expense of the owners of the vessels which may bring them; and with reference to this provision, my attention was particularly requested to the fact that the Commissioners of Emigration are everywhere on the alert to prevent the recurrence of trouble which they encountered last year in dealing with a large number of Jewish emigrants who landed in an almost destitute condition, proved unable or unwilling to work, and were eventually sent back to Europe.

In addition to the United States law above quoted, each State has laws of its own bearing upon immigration, the effect of which was explained to me to be that the Emigration Commissioners at Philadelphia, New York, and Boston respectively, have power to send back to their own country emigrants who may become a charge upon the public within twelve months of the date of landing.

The following are extracts from the Alien Passengers Law of Massachusetts :—

"Sec. 2. The State Board shall appoint one or more persons, to be approved by the Governor and Council, who shall ascertain the names of all persons not having a settlement in this Commonwealth brought into it by land or by any line of communication established for the regular transportation of passengers by water, and by whom or whose means such strangers are so brought, and also procure such further information as is practicable in order to identify them if they should hereafter become a public charge. All officers and agents of railroad corporations, and proprietors or agents of other means of conveyance shall furnish the agents of the Commonwealth, when so required, with the information above named, so far as in their power, by filling up "blanks" (blank forms), to be furnished them for that purpose. If any of said persons refuse or neglect to furnish such information when requested, they shall be punishable by fine not less than twenty dollars for each person in relation to whom the information is withheld.

"Sec. 11. If a person not having a settlement in this Commonwealth, brought into this State in the manner specified in section 2 (above), falls sick, or from any cause becomes a public charge within one year thereafter, the Commonwealth or other place incurring expenses for his support, sickness, or burial may in an action of contract recover the amount of such expenses from the corporation or party by whose means the party was brought into the State" (*i.e.*, probably the Shipping Company).

"Sec. 38. Any Justice of the Superior Court, or of a police district, or municipal court, or trial justice, upon complaint of the overseers of the poor of any place or of the State Board, in term time or vacation, may, by warrant directed to a constable or other person therein designated, cause any pauper not born or having a settlement in this State who may conveniently be removed, to be conveyed at the expense of the State to any other State, or if not a citizen of the United States to any place beyond the sea where he belongs."

At New York and Philadelphia the Emigration Commissioners are specially appointed; but at Boston the State Board of Health, Lunacy, and Charity is charged with the control of Immigration in addition to their other duties.

This Board in May, 1879, took the place of two long-existing Boards, viz. :—The State Board of Health, and the Board of State Charities; the latter having succeeded the Alien Commission which was established in 1852. Thus the State Charities of Massachusetts date back to the years succeeding the great Famine in Ireland, when thousands of emigrants were landed, in a miserably destitute and diseased condition, on the shores of New England, and at once became a public burden. The older members of the present generation in Boston speak with pride of the way in which Massachusetts rose to that occasion, but evince at the same time a certain soreness in the recollection, and anxiety lest history should repeat itself. The public and private charities of the State are to-day very highly organised, and the public mind is kept well informed as to the causes of destitution.

In the Annual Report of the State Board, dated January, 1882, I find the following remarks:—

"Immigration may now be viewed as the chief source of that supply of public poverty which yearly falls upon the State for support and aid.

* * * * * * *

"Migration and immigration directly or indirectly occasion much of the pauperism which our taxpayers are called upon to relieve.

* * * * * * *

"This evil of pauper immigration is great and increasing."

In the list attached to that Report of "Persons sent out of the State by the Superintendent of the Indoor Poor," during twelve months ending 30th September, 1881, I observe the names of twenty-five persons sent back to England and Ireland, and of three returned to Norway, Sweden and Denmark. The number returned to Europe from New York was 913.

In an interview with the Superintendent of the Indoor Poor, who also holds the office of Alien Commissioner, I learnt that he or his officer goes on board all emigrant ships, and narrowly inspects the emigrants as they land; that doubtful cases are detained for inquiry, and a bond taken from the master of the vessel for their return, if necessary; that emigrants once landed may nevertheless be returned if they become paupers; that a "pauper" has been authoritatively defined to be anyone who applies for relief within one year of landing in the country, another definition being "one who stands in need of immediate relief;" that once a person has gained a "settlement," by residing five years in one place (and if a male paying three years' taxes), he is entitled to relief from his *township*, if he needs it; that emigrants to New England seldom reside five years continuously in the same place, and therefore rarely acquire "settlements" until after a long residence in the country; that, if in need of relief, such persons are a charge upon the State at large, and the State may send them back whence they came; that the State, however, would exercise that right humanely, and never so as to "sunder family ties" (*i.e.*, individual members of families would not be "removed," but whole families might be, under certain circumstances); that the shipping companies never object to take back emigrants when requested to do so by the State authorities; that of the 1,000 inmates in the State Almshouse at Tewkesbury, a large number were, at the date of my interview, ablebodied men from the towns, chiefly Irish; and that there were probably several thousand men then out of work in Boston.

I had a long interview also with the Inspector of Charities who is also the Secretary of the American Social Science Association. He confirmed all that I had learned from his colleague, and said, in conclusion, with reference to emigrant families depending upon labour: "They will inevitably become paupers if left in the old States." These words of a trained observer of the condition of the working classes made an impression upon me which other opinions have tended to confirm.

Vaccination. The medical authorities at the ports are very strict as to vaccination. Every emigrant before being permitted to land must show a certificate of satisfactory vaccination issued by the ship's surgeon. On board the vessel in which I entered New York, fifty of the holders of such certificates were selected at random and closely examined by the port surgeon before the ship passed quarantine.

Landing of Emigrants. At New York, the legal and compulsory place of landing for all steerage passengers, passed by the Medical and Immigration Officers, is Castle Garden, an establishment which has been described in a previous report, and which is as complete and perfect in regard to the internal arrangements and the system of administration as circumstances admit of its being made. It is under the control of the Emigration Commissioners in all respects, except the provision of funds, for which the Commissioners are dependent upon the proceeds of the duty of half a dollar a head levied by the United States Customs on all alien passengers arriving and intending to remain in the United States; a duty imposed by the immigration law of August last in substitution for a toll of two dollars per head formerly collected by the State of New York, but appealed against by the shipowners, and pronounced unconstitutional by the Supreme Court of the United States. There is reason to anticipate that the new tax will not produce more than half the funds required for the maintenance of Castle Garden, and that annual applications will be necessary to the State Legislature to make up the deficiency.

An important share in the work of Castle Garden is taken by the Irish Emigrant Society of New York, whose president is one of the senior Emigration Commissioners. The society employs a chief clerk and a matron in the Labour Bureau, and one male attendant in the depot; the Commissioners and the German Emigrant Society employing other male attendants and a matron. The chief clerk of the Labour Bureau will correspond with my committee as to the employment and transmission of emigrants, who will receive from the male and female attendants in the depot all possible attention in common with other emigrants.

I had more than one opportunity of observing the process of dealing with emigrants at Castle Garden. So long as the numbers do not exceed five or six hundred there is plenty of room in the building, and the work is quickly and efficiently done; but the staff profess to be able to "handle" four thousand a day with their baggage, and often had to do so during the busy months of last year, working on Sundays and week-days alike. Half that number must, in my opinion, involve much bustle and crowding, in which women and children weak from the effects of the sea voyage, would suffer, and the duties of a matron become difficult. I therefore addressed an application to the Irish Emigrant Society, understanding from the president that it would almost certainly be entertained, requesting them to employ as assistant matron a woman whom I selected and proposed to pay, for the purpose of attending exclusively to the emigrants who may hereafter be consigned through my committee to their care; and I also requested the society to take charge of a certain sum per head for the benefit of such emigrants. The president, however, was prevented from attending the monthly meeting of the society in December, at which my application was considered; and the subject was referred to a sub-committee, whom I was unable to meet until my return to New York in order to re-embark. The question was then discussed in a spirit which I cannot describe as otherwise than friendly to myself, but I was informed that, although no difference will be made between emigrants forwarded through my committee and others, the sub-committee could not recommend their society to undertake any special office in favour of the former, in consequence of the strong feeling which exists among Irish Americans against the Government scheme of emigration. I therefore made an application to the Emigration Commissioners, requesting them to appoint as assistant matron the woman above referred to, and I hope soon to receive a favourable reply. It should be stated that the Commissioners are particular in not admitting to Castle Garden anyone not connected with their staff, or specially licensed by them.

At Philadelphia one line of steamers only, the "American," lands emigrants from Ireland. The owners of these vessels take a just pride in the completeness and comfort of their arrangements for landing and forwarding their passengers, and which they concisely and accurately describe as "a private Castle Garden." A gentleman to whose character and special fitness for the work no commendation of mine could do justice, attends on behalf of the Hibernian Society of Philadelphia to assist where assistance is needed; to advise as to lodgings; and specially to guard the interests of female emigrants. After conferences with this gentleman, with the President of his Society, and with the shipowners, Philadelphia.

I concluded that to make any change in the arrangements here would be a mistake; and I have made no additional appointment, pending the Lord Lieutenant's decision. The President of the Hibernian Society assured me that their Agent would give every attention to families, and that his kindness and judgment are all-sufficient. The Hibernian Society is absolutely unsectarian, and one of the oldest chartered institutions in the United States.

Boston. At Boston, two lines of steamships, the Cunard and the Allan, land emigrants from Ireland. In the case of the former the landing arrangements are very much on a par with those of the American line at Philadelphia; but no charitable agency supplements the efforts of the shipowners. The other line lands emigrants at a wharf belonging to a Railroad Company; and which appears to be practically open to all comers; though there are gates at a distance which might be closed, but for the passing and repassing of freight trains to and from the neighbouring wharves.

The "Charitable Irish Society" has existed in Boston for more than 100 years, but does not, as a rule, take any part in the reception of emigrants. At a meeting of the Society held just before my arrival, however, a Committee had been appointed to consider the expediency of establishing an Emigrants' Home; which is unquestionably needed, inasmuch as there is in Boston no control of lodging houses by license or inspection. Hoping to obtain assistance from that Committee in the selection of agents and in making provision for emigrants, I called upon an influential member of it, to whom I had an introduction, and explained my objects. The reply was a strong expression of personal and political conviction adverse to those objects; followed, however, by the assurance that if an Emigrant Home be established, it will probably be open to all emigrants alike.

Guided by the advice of a gentleman to whom I am much indebted for his assistance in this and other matters, I proceeded to appoint a very suitable married couple, resident in Boston, to receive emigrant families landing at that port.

Railroad fares. I regret to say that no special rates were to be obtained from any of the Railroad Companies in consequence of a recent arrangement, by which the four Great Trunk lines have agreed to be bound by one tariff, and to accept no reduction on the rates fixed by a joint committee.

Labour prospects. Inquiries everywhere made as to the probable demand for unskilled labour next spring have elicited only discouraging replies. The building of certain railroads which have in recent years been pushed westward and southward with great energy is now almost completed; and large numbers of men will be discharged during the spring and summer months. It was on these lines of railroad that I had hoped our emigrants would have been able to find both labour and land. The coal and iron industries are likely to suffer from the decrease in the demand for railroad iron. The agricultural work in the eastern and older western States is said to be fully provided for, except during the short season of harvest, when the extra labour required by farmers is supplied either by contractors or by single men who are boarded in the farmhouse. There remain the cotton and wool manufactures, as to the prospects of which discouraging opinions were also expressed; but, as their prosperity appears to me to depend in some measure on conditions as yet undetermined, I will state the result of inquiries on this subject made while I was at Boston.

The present Customs tariff presses hardly on manufacturers, who have to pay high prices for their raw material, but cannot compete with imported goods. They look for a revision of the tariff which shall adequately protect their manufactures. A Tariff Commission has revised the tariff, and reported to Congress. A Committee appointed by Congress to consider the report of the Commission are engaged in revising the reported tariff. The probabilities are that the changes which the manufacturers desire will not be made, and that their difficulties may increase rather than diminish. On the other hand it seemed reasonable to anticipate that the good wheat and cotton and fair corn crops of last summer would lead to increased demand for manufactured goods, and that the coming spring might witness a revived activity in that branch of trade in the manufacturing towns and cities of New England. I had been informed of the return of an active passenger agent to Boston, after a tour through New England, with the report that a great demand for labour was to be expected; and of one manufacturer having expressed the opinion that very possibly twenty thousand people might be so absorbed.

Employment in the manufacturing centres of New England.

A return which was shown to me, taken from the U. S. Census of 1880, gives the number of persons then employed in the cotton mills of New England as 129,239. The number engaged in the manufacture of wool would be at least half as many, while 5,922 were employed in silk factories. This would make a total of 200,000.

The "nativity" of that population is not specified, so I am unable to determine the proportion of Irish; but a manuscript return with which I was favoured by General Walker, the Superintendent of the late Census, and whom I saw, gives the following figures for the whole of the United States, viz.:—

Cotton Mill operatives,	Irish nativity,		19,732
Woollen Mill operatives,	" "		12,737
Silk Mill operatives,	" "		1,365
Carpet makers,	" "		3,234
			37,068
Besides "not specified."	" "		
Employés in manufacturing establishments,		2,649	
Mill and factory operatives,		2,127	
			4,776
			41,844

The annual Report of the Chief of the Bureau of Labour Statistics for Massachusetts, Mr. Carroll D. Wright, whom I also saw, shows, for the three chief manufacturing cities of that State in 1875, a total population of 129,944, of whom

72,754 (56·01 per cent.) were Americans.
27,896 (21·47 ") were Irish.
16,881 (12·63 ") were English, including a small proportion of Scotch and Welsh.
and 10,728 (8·26 ") were French Canadian.

other foreigners making up the total.

A further Return, in the same Report, of the operatives of the same three cities three years later, viz., in 1878, shows that of the whole number actually employed in the mills, 31,688,

11,436 (or 36·11 per cent.) were Americans.
8,321 (or 26·26 ") were Irish.
7,195 (or 22·72 ") were English, including Scotch and Welsh.
4,146 (or 13·09 ") were French Canadians.

The report adds: "These figures are probably fairly representative of the nativities at the present time (March, 1882), though the French Canadian element has undoubtedly increased largely proportionately."

The figures available do not enable me to go more closely into the matter than as above; but it is clear that there is already a large Irish population in the three cities alluded to. I visited two of the three, which are within one hour of Boston by rail, and I was struck with their cheerful aspect, and healthy situation.

Although the general population of these cities is kept up (it has, in fact, increased considerably since the year 1878); and although the great bulk of the people continue in one place, a minority are constantly changing. This is particularly the case with the French Canadians, who come and go from their homes in Canada or New Hampshire, where many have lately taken up vacated farms, as work or wages are abundant or failing. Thus vacancies occur for new hands.

Apart from the general question as to the expediency of endeavouring to transform a strictly rural people like the western Irish into mill operatives; apart, also, from the moral and physiological views of factory life, which were duly pressed upon me, the advantage of a permanent connexion between these large, conveniently-situated, and growing centres of industry, and the labour market in Ireland will be apparent, I think, upon consideration of the following statement with regard to the wages earned, together with the fact that the work is continued throughout the year. The average yearly earning per head of the operatives in each of the three cities above referred to is stated (for 1875), in the report already quoted, as 266 dollars, 340·46 dollars, and 349·25 dollars, respectively, the average for the three being 318·57 dollars, or £66 nearly. And each family should have several members employed.

As to the general question of the expediency of introducing the Western Irish people to factory life, I have it on high authority that the Irish make very good operatives, and that they have done much to build up the manufactures of Massachusetts.

With regard to the moral and physical aspects of the question, it happens that the Department of the Labour Bureau in Boston devoted several months of the year 1881 to an exhaustive and most ably conducted inquiry under six heads, viz.:—

The operatives; the mills; the cities;
The condition of the operatives, in their homes and in their employment;
The relations between the employers and the employed; and,
Opinions of leading citizens;

in the three cities above referred to. The results of that inquiry are given in the Report of the Bureau, from which I have already quoted figures. It is a long and interesting chapter, and hardly admits of condensation; but I believe that no one who studied it would hesitate to send families to two of the three cities, to the exclusion, however, of the third.

Another field of suitable employment for emigrant Irish families is suggested by an official statement, that of late years 2,000 farms in New Hampshire have been vacated by their owners for the more fertile land of the West. Many of these farms have been bought and occupied by Irishmen, who are known to have paid off their mortgages rapidly, and to be doing well. I wish much for more specific information on this subject than I was able to obtain.

A successful Irish Colony.

In connexion with it, though with reference to another part of the country, I will here glance at the history of an Irish colony, related to me by a gentleman who has known and watched it from its origin.

Some years ago, a proprietor in the north of Pennsylvania wished to get his land settled in a hilly district, just where the Alleghany mountains begin to rise. A Scotch immigrant population was introduced, but soon dispersed. A remarkable book was then written, setting forth the fertility of the soil, and an excellent English colony was brought out, having money enough to supply them with all necessaries. These also disappeared, though the township had been named "Britannia" in their honour. Next came some Irishmen, attracted by public works. They were of the poorest class of Irish labourers from the West and South of Ireland, and had been employed in building canals in the State of New York. These accepted the proprietor's offer of contracts, enabling them to acquire the ownership of land by easy payments, spread over about ten years, or to assign or sell their interest at any time subject to the same conditions; and forthwith entered upon holdings varying from twenty or thirty, to 100 acres. They were illiterate, unwashed, indolent, subject to no sanitary law. But they quickly improved. They held to their land and their religion. They imported their friends from Ireland, built schools and churches (adding organs in the latter), they constructed roads and bridges; they have sent a large surplus population to neighbouring factory towns, and there is at this moment no community in the United States more thoroughly respectable or, speaking comparatively, more prosperous.

Two other instances were mentioned to me within the actual personal knowledge of my informants, in which Irishmen have shown their determination to own rather than rent their homes, and have proved their inherent power of succeeding by great industry and self-denying thrift, where others have failed. But all three examples, be it remarked, affirm the truth of the axiom that no one gains headway in a new country until he has lived some time in it, and bought experience.

After anxious consideration of the whole question, I decided that it would be desirable to appoint an agent for New England, if I should be able to find a gentleman of Irish extraction, alike connected with the manufacturers and agriculturists around him and interested in his distressed countrymen in Ireland, who would be willing to undertake the office. On this subject I shall be able, I hope, to make a further communication after the arrival of the next mail from America. *Agent for New England.*

My purpose in going to Chicago was to ascertain if there is any organization there, private or public, for receiving and distributing emigrants destined for that limitless region called "the West." *Chicago.*

From Philadelphia it is said nearly all, from Castle Garden three-fourths, from Boston about one-fifth, of the emigrants "go West"—"the West" in each case meaning Chicago, which for cattle, grain, coal, produce of all kinds, and passengers, is the distributing centre between East and West and West and East. The cost of the emigrant railroad ticket from New York to Chicago, since the combination of the railroad lines, has been and is thirteen dollars—54s. But, I thought, if there should prove to be always a great demand for labourers at Chicago, and if an Emigrant Depot exist in which new arrivals may remain for a short time till hired, it might be desirable to send many of our emigrants there. I regret to say that there is neither Emigrant Depot nor demand for labour. Labourers arriving in any numbers, and certainly labourers with families requiring constant work for their support, would have no good chance of obtaining it just now, without going some five hundred miles further than Chicago, or 1,500 miles from New York. The journey from New York to Chicago occupies forty-eight hours, which for families, in summer, would be trying enough. But arrived in Chicago, they are not allowed to remain in the railway station. They must go on at once, or go into lodgings. On applying there to the representative of Bishop Ireland (who I had hoped to find would have made arrangements to carry forward families sent out by the Committee of Mr. Tuke's Fund to Chicago) I received in effect the following reply :—"There is no depot at Chicago, and no intention of forming one. It is a bad place for emigrants to stay at, and they ought at once to go forward to the West or North-west, and not stop till they get at least two hundred miles west of the Mississippi. If the English Government thinks proper to establish here an Emigrant Depot and staff, they will be met with the sympathy and personal assistance of Irishmen, but the initiative must come from England." I then asked a gentleman prominent in every work for the improvement of the condition of Irishmen in America, if, supposing the funds for such a depot were hereafter forthcoming, he would take charge of it. The reply was very prompt and in the negative. In fact in Chicago, as in Boston, the Irish feeling is very strongly against the Government scheme, and nothing short of a scheme of colonization would convert that adverse feeling into anything like active sympathy.

I am bound to state here that I left Chicago on the evening of the day of my arrival without waiting to see Bishop Ireland, who was expected there only two days later from St. Paul. No stronger temptation could have been held out to me to remain; since there is no man in America whom I so much wished to see, knowing, as I do, the almost superhuman work which he has done and continues to do in furthering colonization. But I had seen the Secretary of his Lordship's Colonization Society; I had heard from several persons what the aims of that Society are; I knew that the distribution of labourers is no part of their scheme (unless special arrangements had been made for placing a certain number of families for Mr. Tuke's Fund). I therefore wrote to his lordship, asking for specific information on this last point, and expressing my extreme regret that urgent necessity prevented my waiting to pay my respects to him at Chicago; and I left Chicago the same night, having seen three gentlemen thoroughly conversant with all the subjects on which I required information, having called also on the Roman Catholic Archbishop, who however was not at home.

Return *via* Philadelphia.

Returning from Chicago by way of Philadelphia, I called again on the agents of the "American" line of Steamships there, and on the President and Agent of the Hibernian Society, as well as on two gentlemen who took an active part last summer in assisting the emigrants sent out by Mr. Tuke's Fund. These two gentlemen were emphatic in their advice to me not to send families to America, declaring that ten thousand men were then out of work in Philadelphia and that prospects generally were not encouraging. They further declared that if under present circumstances a number of families were sent out, their arrival would create great excitement, of which Her Majesty's Minister at Washington would certainly hear.

I was much disappointed in not meeting in Philadelphia an Irish gentleman to whom I had written some time before, and who would have been able to give me specific information concerning a colony of 500 Irish who are settled and prospering in Montgomery, Alabama. I was obliged also for want of time to relinquish my intention of calling on the Chief of the Labour Bureau at Trenton in New Jersey, to whom however I have written asking for his latest Report. If this Report should contain any new facts I will communicate them later.

With regard to the employment of Irish in the southern and middle States, I made all the inquiries I could, but with no sufficiently definite result. It is certain, however, that the most southern States are too hot, except in mountain regions. There is also good authority for saying that the "poor whites" of those States are a miserable race, though their characteristics have improved since the abolition of slavery. It has been said also that cotton growing in Texas is the remedy for distress in Connemara. In Arkansas Bishop Ireland's Colonisation Society has recently taken up land and founded a colony in a fertile and healthy region on the Arkansas River. The special advantage claimed for this colony over the north-west, and which attaches to all the southern States is that the colonists will have the whole year to do what they must do in the north-west in five months. But the prospectus of this colony states particularly that there *is no room there as yet for labourers.* Cotton manufacturers are making great progress in North Georgia, and it is there that I hoped to have found means to send Irish families, but there was no demand for them through Castle Garden. Emigrants going there would go by steamer (special fare, 8 dollars) from New York to Norfolk, and thence by rail. I await information from an agent in that part of the country to whom I have written.

Arriving in New York again on the 19th January, I met by appointment a Sub-Committee of the Irish Emigration Society, as previously mentioned. It consisted of three gentlemen, for many years intimately and practically connected with Irish immigration to the United States. In the long discussion which ensued I made careful note of their unanimous opinion, to the following effect:—

"It is a serious thing to bring to America families who know nothing of the country, unless they have friends already here who have given undoubted proof of their wish to receive and of their ability to help them on their arrival.

"We fully understand and sympathise with the condition and the need of the people in some parts of Ireland, and if employment could be provided for them here it would be a very humane thing to bring them out. But to pre-arrange employment for them would be impossible. If any families are brought out this summer they will have to be supported, the country is so full of labour, and so many are looking out for fresh work. *It was different last year.*

"The reports at this moment are such as to make us believe that a very large number of labourers, estimated at 50,000 have been discharged from railroads lately. A gentleman called upon us to-day who has for years been connected with the building of railroads, and who has come some 1,500 miles to New York in the endeavour to secure in advance employment of that kind for 1,800 trained men whom he will discharge in the spring.

"The emigration you are engaged in, if not forced (I had protested against this expression), is abnormal, unusual, extraordinary, something more than the spontaneous natural flow which annually sets towards our shores. It must of necessity fail, unless the people are supported after they arrive. It will recoil unpleasantly on your Government.

"As to Bishop Ireland's colonies, people taken indiscriminately from Ireland will never suit. Good farmers on the other hand, with some capital would be sure to succeed, and such settlers in the west are an advantage to America. The class of emigrants you are dealing with are anything but an advantage.

"If families should arrive they will receive at Castle Garden every attention in connexion with other immigrants, but we cannot advise our Committee to undertake any special office in connexion with them.

"There are 12,000 people on the New York city charities to-day, and in Castle Garden a larger number of men seeking employment than we have had on our hands for two years at least, even in the winter, and we never had to do so much for people as we are doing for these. The latter are subsisting on half a loaf of bread and about a pint of coffee a day, which we provide."

The following morning I paid a final visit to Castle Garden to inquire of the Chief Clerk if he had any orders for families in reply to the circulars which I knew he had sent out. He had had two replies which he showed me. One from a factory which had taken *three* families last year, stating that the factory would always take Irish families when in want of hands, but could not say what they might require in the spring. The other, from a mill owner who took *four* families last year, expressed satisfaction with them as they "had learned to speak a little English and were getting on well." He would be willing to take more when he wanted them. But nothing was said of his wanting them now, or being likely to want them at any particular time.

The Chief Clerk said that no more than five families should ever be sent at one time, and that it would not be advisable for me to send even five until I should hear from him that he had applications for ten, as it would be impossible to keep places open.

He informed me further that he had applications for German families (only) from Virginia; that forty families had gone there in the last fortnight, and more were to go next week. The employers there would not take Irish.

In the Labour Bureau I found fifty-six, Irish and English, dejected-looking men, all without families, and 300 Germans. These were the emigrants of whom the Sub-Committee had told me on the previous day. I entered into conversation with the Irish. They said they certainly never would have come out if they had known the state of things. I told them that my business was emigration. They "wished I would start emigration back to the old country." I asked them what chance families would have if they came out in the spring. They said "None at all, as far as we know." I said, "What if they have friends in the country?" One man, older than the rest, and who seemed to have had some experience of America, replied promptly "*In this country every man's friend is his pocket.*" This was the latest impression I received, for I had to hurry on board the "Germanic," which sailed that afternoon, and arrived in Liverpool, without having touched at Queenstown, on the morning of the 30th January.

General Observations.

The United States. Is my information trustworthy, and to what does it amount?

I have no doubt that the main object of the officials, with whom it has been my duty to confer, was to demonstrate to me that they have the power to deal with emigrants likely to become a charge upon the public; and I feel sure that they have the power, or if not, that they could easily obtain it. It does not follow that they would exercise it, unless under pressure of political or other circumstances. But I believe that they were actuated also by the wish to give me all the general information they could. And if their information had differed from that of others, I might have hesitated to form a judgment of my own. But there has been no diversity in the opinions I have heard, no ambiguity or want of emphasis in the manner of expressing them. There appears to be throughout America a general unanimity of sentiment adverse to what is regarded as a Government scheme of emigration on a large scale. The argument that it is not strictly a Government scheme, but only the continuation and extension, with Government help and under Government supervision, of work begun by private hands, is not accepted. As a Government scheme it is and will be criticised. No doubt the sentiment with which it is regarded varies in intensity. Some look chiefly at the political side of the project, as it appears from their point of view, and these are its most pronounced opponents. Others, though influenced to some extent by political prejudice, are willing to consider its practical object of improving the prospects of people whose condition they realize and pity. A third, by far the most numerous class, without any strong political bias or personal interest in the matter, are nevertheless ready to join in the condemnation of the scheme because it does not come up to their own large and liberal ideas of what ought to be done. The suspicion that England seeks to rid herself of a burden at the smallest possible cost, is at the root of public opinion, and must never be lost sight of in estimating the prospects of families assisted to America with Government funds.

"These people are the victims of misgovernment, why should we be saddled with them?" was a remark made to me more than once by educated Americans. I quote it to show the political prejudice, and sense of an impending burden, which colour the American view of this emigration, and account for the anxiety with which its development is watched.

"There is no room for them in the Eastern States." This is a statement which it is most difficult to accept. But as it is made by men of business and practical knowledge, in all parts of the country, it must be accepted in the absence of evidence to the contrary, which I have failed to obtain. The question naturally occurs, "What has become of the 460,000 emigrants who landed at New York last year?" "Gone, perhaps, to flood an already over-supplied labour market. Our own surplus population in the Eastern cities must go West or starve," was the answer of one gentleman to that question. Having asked the Chief Clerk of the Labour Bureau at Castle Garden to prepare for me a return of the number of *families* for whom he had obtained employment last year, I received from him since the following meagre particulars:—The total number of families was 412, of whom 56 were Irish. Of these latter, 8 went to farms, and the rest to factories. Of the 8 one soon returned to New York, where the head of the family obtained employment as a carpenter.

There is seldom any difficulty in finding work for mechanics. Single women and girls are everywhere constantly in demand for domestic service. Except for factories, Irish families are not in request, Germans and Swedes being always asked for, and Irish often declined.

"Send your families to the west," was the universal prescription with which I was favoured. What does it mean? From the lips of some who have never had any experience of the west, it must be taken figuratively; but, generally, it means "colonize them, give them houses, land, implements and food for a year." As I have said in my remarks about Chicago, I hoped to have found a depot and labour bureau there; but I was disappointed. Chicago is a most busy and growing city; but it has already a surplus population. Rents are dearer there than even in New York. It is the centre of a fine agricultural country; but here, as in the Eastern States, the agricultural work is largely done by machinery, and the extra labour employed is confined to "farm hands" during a few weeks in the year. Even with regard to this extra labour, it is becoming more and more the custom for farmers to employ large contractors who travel with machines and gangs of men in harvest time.

What then is to be done? I see but little reason to expect any orders for families from Castle Garden. Will it be desirable to send out families to take the chance of employment with £5, or even £10, in their hands; I think not, unless they have friends to go to in one of the great cities, who have given proof of their wish to receive, and ability to help them on their arrival. It may be expected that such cases will be rare. Many such friends might be willing to receive a boy or girl whom they could employ; but probably few would be able to help a whole family.

To send families to the large cities, especially to New York, would, I think, involve a grave moral responsibility; so bad is the condition of the poor Irish in those cities. On this point, however, I speak from hearsay; for I could not spare time to visit the Irish quarters, either in New York or elsewhere.

If any families are sent to the United States under the above conditions, I think they should have in hand not less than £5 or £1 a head of all over five years of age, besides the amount of the railroad fare, which latter should be paid in Ireland.

After all, much must depend on the outcome of events in the course of the year. If the predictions on which I have relied be fulfilled, there will probably be a good deal of distress in America even during the summer. But it is hardly possible that they will not be fulfilled; and that fresh enterprises will be started. I have noticed, however, within the last day or two, the report of the failure of a large steel rolling mill in Chicago, by which 2,000 men are thrown out of work. The disposition of the moment is to invest capital in land and cattle rather than in manufactures.

There is no want of small employment agents in the towns and cities of America, but I was cautioned against employing them, except in Philadelphia, where there are two to whom the agent of the Hibernian Society occasionally has recourse.

In order to place any number of families in the United States a central agent is required, whose sole business should be to keep his eyes on the labour markets and principal works in the country, and to maintain a connexion with employers. In that way, if selection at home were carefully made, a constant emigration might be kept up with fair certainty of success. I am convinced from what I have seen that the emigration of families, to be successful, should be an intermittent and gradual process. The best centre for such an agency would probably be Chicago or St. Louis.

I have said that this emigration is criticised, and will be watched in America, as a Government scheme. That means, I think, that every family who lands either at New York or Boston, consigned to the agents whom it was my mission to appoint, will be an object of curious observation to many who would otherwise never have looked for them; will not improbably be "interviewed," and reported upon in the public press, by clever men ever on the look-out for a sensation, and highly skilled in the art of graphic description.

It is difficult now for the people in Ireland to realise the new country to which they ask to be sent; it will be still more difficult for them then, than it otherwise might have been, to take to the new life.

Two elements will always be required to ensure success, viz., a *hearty desire and determination to work* on the part of the emigrant, and at least so much consideration from his new neighbours as will secure for him a fair field. Under all the circumstances, stated, I cannot feel confident that those two elements will be present in sufficient strength in the case of people emigrating, not at their own, but at the Government expense.

CONCLUSION WITH REGARD TO THE UNITED STATES.

That public opinion is opposed to the emigration, and that labour prospects, so far as can be foreseen, are unfavourable; therefore a scheme, difficult under favourable circumstances, becomes impracticable; except (1) by limiting the emigration to those who have friends in America able and willing to help them, or for whom employment shall have been pre-arranged; or (2) by the establishment of a labour agency in America, with the object of distributing emigrants in the far West and South. Such an agency would probably require some kind of depot organization.

As already mentioned, I proceeded from Boston to Canada, travelling over the Central Vermont Railway to Montreal. At Montreal I saw the General Passenger Agent of the Grand Trunk Railway of Canada, Mr. Stevenson, on the subject of emigrant fares and other details, and went on, the same afternoon, to Quebec, by the line which runs along the north shore of the St. Lawrence River, arriving late at night. Canada.

On the following day I had an interview with Mr. Stafford, an Irishman, who has been for twenty years the Dominion Emigration Agent at Quebec. He explained that the ships are signalled about twelve hours before arriving at Quebec; that the emigrants are landed at Point Levi, on the south side of the river, as soon as possible; that the Customs examination and the issue of railway tickets then take place, and the emigrants start on their journey westward about six o'clock in the evening. They should reach Montreal, 172 miles, after travelling all night, about seven o'clock, A.M., and there breakfast, resuming their journey after breakfast, and being due at Toronto, 333 miles from Montreal (if going so far), about sixteen or eighteen hours later. Thus the journey from Quebec to Toronto is one of 505 miles, and occupies thirty-six hours. It is necessary, therefore, to provide for meals by the way. Quebec.

The Government depot at Quebec was burned down last year and has not been rebuilt. The shed in which the emigrants are received is like an ordinary English Railway "goods shed," with double doors at the sides and ends, which may be closed, but are generally open in the daytime. It is only an apology and a makeshift for a depot, and the least adapted of any that I saw as a place of shelter for emigrants. The Dominion Government will build a substantial depot as soon as they determine whether it should be at Quebec or Montreal. One of the details which I had discussed with Mr. Stevenson at Montreal was the necessity of breaking a long journey and the most convenient resting-places along his line of road, and I had mentioned Chicago particularly as a place where emigrants might arrive after about sixty hours travelling, and where they would be necessarily transferred from one station to another. He had replied: "Don't attempt a depot at Chicago; it is a very expensive and a very rough place. The emigrants should be 'booked through' to some place beyond Chicago, or they will be charged a great deal for the transfer of themselves and their baggage from station to station. Have your depot at Quebec." Mr. Stafford, at Quebec, is against having a depot there, and gives reasons which appear to me sound. "It must be very large, capable of holding several ship loads of emigrants at a time; for the ships often arrive in very quick succession, and if a depot existed every one would wish to use it, and, perhaps, to stay there for a time. The staff must be large; the provision of food and sanitary arrangements would be difficult. Probably an hospital and a medical staff might become necessary; whereas, if there is no sleeping Mr. Stevenson, Grand Trunk Railway of Canada. Mr. Stafford.

accommodation visible, emigrants will not think of remaining at Quebec. They land, after the monotony and confinement of a sea voyage, eager to go forward. It would be a mistake to lose that opportunity of dispersing them. There is no employment for them at Quebec; they would have nothing to do but to hang about the grog-shops, where their money would soon be spent. It would be difficult to get them away afterwards. It is a bad thing to get people into the habit of depending upon depots." I agree in the general tenor of these remarks.

Mr. Stafford informed me that the immigration last year had been large, but that the supply of labour had not overtaken the demand, and that the returns were being made up for the Annual Report then in course of preparation. He said, in course of a long conversation: "Hundreds of farmers in Ontario were without labour last year. Skilled farm hands may come any time after the 1st April, or by the first steamer to Quebec, which is advertised to leave England on the 19th April next. An agricultural labourer, with a family, would get from £40 to £50 a year, with house and vegetables and leave to cut firewood; but he should be able to plough, mow, and reap. If he could plough, he could do the rest. Boys of twelve years of age and upwards would be useful. Farms vary from 100 to 200 acres and upwards. Those who require labour are old-established farmers, many of them with spare houses, which they would keep empty rather than fill them with unsuitable people. There would not be room for a very large number. If too many came they would have to hang about the small towns and villages, and do the best they could. If they hang about the towns, the newspapers will comment unfavourably on the movement. While public opinion is favourable, it is important to keep it so. Do not send infirm or helpless people. Send intelligent families with plenty of grown-up children. About forty should be the oldest age. *Send them in small batches*" (this was emphasised). "They should bring their bedding with them. They will require landing money to buy food and furniture before the first wages become due. It is absolutely necessary, in the interests of the movement, that it should be done carefully and well. We shall know from our own agents where the best demand is, and distribute accordingly. Emigrants should be instructed to attend strictly to what is said to them by the Government agents, to listen to no other advice, and to take the very first work which offers."

These remarks of Mr. Stafford cover, I think, all the ground with regard to the kind of emigrant families who would be most welcome in Canada. If such families are selected—the parents able-bodied and the children well grown—the young women may go out to service, and the young men to almost any work they select, while the parents and younger children remain upon farms. With regard to the numbers to be sent in each ship, I understand that it will be necessary for my Committee to communicate with the High Commissioner for Canada in London.

From Quebec I returned—over the Grand Trunk Railway—to Montreal; and thence passed on to Ottawa, where I waited on Sir John Macdonald, in the absence of His Excellency the Governor-General; and had a long interview with Mr. Pope, the Minister for Emigration, the

Mr. Pope.

Secretary, Mr. Lowe, being present part of the time. Mr. Pope will be glad to see Irish emigration directing itself to Canada, and speaks with the greatest confidence of the prospects of all who come there able and anxious to work. He cannot, however, offer any special advantages to the Irish beyond those already open to all nations. Reminding me of the expense of the numerous agencies maintained by the Dominion, he said that he would not be able to recommend an extraordinary expenditure for this emigration; the circumstances being quite different to those under which the Dominion Parliament voted £20,000 for the Relief of Irish distress in 1880.

Mr. Lowe.

Mr. Lowe was also entirely in favour of the emigration; but appeared doubtful as to there being house accommodation for families. He wishes that it could be arranged to send out first one or two grown-up members of a family to make a home for the rest.

Mr. Pope referred me to Sir Alexander Galt for rates of passage money.

Sir Charles Tupper, the Minister of Railways, was not at Ottawa, though expected there daily; and as time pressed I proceeded by the night train to Toronto; arriving at 2 o'clock the following afternoon.

Toronto.

I called the same evening on Archbishop Lynch, hoping to hear that the Catholic communities in Ontario were ready to receive a certain number of emigrant families to be assisted by the Committee of Mr. Tuke's Fund. His Grace was pleased to inform me that the subject is very much in his thoughts, but that no definite arrangements had yet been announced. His Grace will welcome Irish families to his diocese; and strongly urges the importance of selecting the fittest recipients of so substantial a boon as the means of emigrating to Canada.

The Immigrant Depot at Toronto is well situated about a mile and a half out of the city, and away from the Railroad Station. The buildings belong to the Dominion Government; but the staff are appointed and maintained by the Government of the Province of Ontario; upon whom also all expenses fall in connexion with the immigrants. The kitchen department seemed admirably organised; and I am sure that all I heard in praise of the master and matron in charge of it was strictly true. But the rest of the buildings gave me the impression that they were constructed and fitted so as not to tempt immigrants to remain in them longer than they are allowed to do. The "Rules and Regulations" bear out this impression. The sleeping rooms consist of a long wooden shed about 100 × 50 feet; divided longitudinally in the centre by a wall, which is carried up to the roof. A floor carried across the building about half-way up the centre wall, completes the division into four rooms, two down, and two up-stairs. The entrances to the two floors are separate, and from both ends; so that, in case of fire, the means of exit should be sufficient. The only fittings consist of a "guard bed" platform about nine inches above the floor, on each side of the four rooms. The washing shed, which is separate from the main shed, is hardly on a par with that at Castle Garden, which I had perhaps unreasonably, but insensibly adopted as a standard, and the other conveniences are not intended for families. Practically, I should suppose, none but single men use this depot much; the single women being always sent to a lodging house reserved for the purpose, and families going to lodgings in the town.

Immigrant Depot.

In view, however, of the needs of our families, I addressed an official application to the Provincial Secretary, Mr. Hardy, asking whether, in the event of any considerable number of families arriving under the responsibility of my Committee, he would consider the propriety of causing one of the two ground-floor rooms in the main building to be set apart for them, and fitted with roll-up canvas sleeping berths, similar to those used on board the best emigrant ships. He was kind enough to say that I might expect a favourable reply. The regulations of the depot only permitting an emigrant to sleep there one night, Mr. Hardy also consented to waive that rule with reference to our families, so as to permit them to remain until they shall have had a fair offer of employment. On the sanitary matter I made an application to the Dominion Minister for Emigration.

Agents.

Regarding the appointment of agents, when at Quebec I had inquired from Mr. Stafford whether he could recommend to me a married couple, or widow, or single woman, whom I should be likely to approve of as a fit person, or fit persons, to act under him in receiving our families. He could think of no one suitable. His staff consists of four men "guardians," no matron at present. When at Ottawa, therefore, I requested the Minister for Emigration to bear in mind that it might hereafter become my duty to ask that a married couple be appointed to act on the staff, and under the orders of his agent at Quebec, at the cost of my Committee, and for the exclusive benefit of our emigrants. I suggested that it would be well if, in that case, the man were chosen with a view to his accompanying the families in the train as far as Montreal. (He could not go further and return to Quebec in time for the next ship, probably.) Mr. Pope said he would bear the subject in mind; but he was inclined to think that the Dominion Government would prefer to pay for all needful agents. The question was left open. I afterwards wrote to Mr. Pope from Toronto to the effect that, looking to the extra trouble which would be caused in case of considerable numbers of Irish families arriving, it appeared desirable that a travelling agent should be appointed to accompany them from Montreal to Toronto, that such an agent should reside at Toronto, and that the services of a person would be available whom I named, and who had been employed by the Ontario Government last year to accompany emigrants from Toronto to destinations westward. This appointment is also an open question, which may, perhaps, be referred to the High Commissioner for his opinion. If all three agents be appointed, the cost will not be less than £40 a month, whichever Government pays it. The Dominion Government already employs one travelling agent, but he would have ample occupation in attending to 500 other emigrants than ours. The Allan Line shipowners also send an interpreter with their passengers.

Immigration Office at Toronto.

Mr. Donaldson, Dominion Agent, and Mr. Spence, Ontario Agent.

I had several interviews with Mr. Donaldson, the Dominion Agent, and with Mr Spence, the Provincial Agent, for Immigration at Toronto. The former gentleman is in charge of the depot buildings, and has an office there; the latter has an office near the city. Both are old and experienced officers of their respective Governments, and I think it would have been both inexpedient and unnecessary to appoint a third Resident Agent, exclusively for the purpose of making inquiries as to employment for our families in Ontario. The Minister for Emigration expressed his willingness to make such an appointment if it should appear to me desirable. But, at the same time, he said, and requested Mr. Lowe to make a note, that all the Dominion Agents would be directed to bear in mind the possible needs of Irish families in making the customary spring rounds of their districts this year. Having made the acquaintance of Mr. Donaldson and Mr. Spence, I thought no longer of a third Agent.

The "Combined City Charities" of Toronto.

At the suggestion of Mr. Goldwin Smith, who was so kind as to call upon me, I attended a meeting of this Association of all the old established national benevolent societies in the city, Mr. Goldwin Smith being in the chair. The meeting were very anxious as to the strain upon their strength and resources, which would probably result from the introduction of a number of families without means, into the city and neighbourhood. I was closely questioned as to the kind of people that were coming, whether they can speak English, and "would the English Government support them if they don't get work."

I distinctly repudiated any and all liability on the part of the English Government, and gave the best account I could of the people, speaking of some from my own knowledge of them, and with regard to others from statistics of the thousands who go from Co. Mayo to England and Scotland annually. The Meeting appeared relieved, but chiefly by the assurance that the Provincial Government will allow the families to remain at the depot until they shall have had a fair offer of work.

The most important of these societies is that which manages the "House of Industry"—the nearest approach to an official Charity Board, I believe, in Canada. The revenue of this society for 1881 was slightly less than 11,000 dollars, including a "grant from the City Corporation" of 5,000, and a "grant from the Ontario Government" of 2,000 dollars. The other societies represented at the meeting which I attended were, St. Andrew's (1836), St. George's (1836), St. Vincent de Paul, the Protestant Benevolent, and the Women's Christian Association."

Some of the ladies present gave me the prices of common commodities, as follows, but no estimate was forthcoming of what it costs the poor to live:—

(One dollar = 4s. 2d. One cent = ½d.)

Lodging—three or four rooms, in the city—4 dollars a month.
" new emigrants' houses, west of the city, 4 dollars a month.
Coals, per ton (to last six weeks) 8 dollars.
Pinewood, per cord (= ½ ton coal as fuel), 4 dollars.
Flour 5 dol. 80 c. per barrel of 196 lbs. (24s. 2d.), about 1½d. per lb.
Bread, 13 cents per 4 lb. loaf.
Oatmeal, 6 dols. per barrel of 100 lbs., 25s.
Cornmeal, 4 dols. 50 cents ,, 18s. 9d., one penny and half a farthing per lb.
Beef, 10 to 14 cents per lb.; mutton, the same; at least 3 lbs. a day for a family.*
Butter, 25 cents per lb.; cheese, 16 cents per lb.
Eggs, 15 cents per dozen; potatoes, 4s. 2d. for 1½ bushel.
Wages for female servants begin at 5 dollars per month.

General Observations.

I do not attach much importance to calculations of the cost of living, in a case where the question is, whether a man gets the wages current in a locality, or no wages at all. Where one sees a vigorous population it is fair to assume that the wages of labour are sufficient to support life under ordinary conditions, and that assumption is amply safe in Upper Canada. If, however, the object be to compare the condition of a man in receipt of fair wages in England or Ireland with that of a man employed elsewhere, or to compare the prospects of a labourer with those of a settler in North America, an exact knowledge of all the circumstances becomes necessary, and to this I cannot profess.

But I may quote the experience of a man, Conner, whom I met accidentally in Toronto, and whom I regard as a favourable representative of the class of Connemara emigrants. His family was the last that I had been instrumental in sending out last year. He told me that he had been in regular work till Christmas, at six shillings a day, "digging a drain" in Toronto; that the work was stopped by the frost; that he had arrived too late in the season, and neither of his two boys had been able to get work; that he was paying 3½ dollars a month rent, had saved no money, and was living on credit at the provision-dealer's store. I knew him well two years ago, as a thoroughly sober, industrious, and trustworthy man, and I believe that to be his character still. He was dressed in a well-patched suit of common woollen material, and wore no gloves, though he had a pair in his pocket, and the thermometer was about zero, Fahr.

* Meat is said to be a necessity in the climate of North America.

He said, "*This is a fine healthy country. The people would do well to come out here if they come early enough to save some money before the winter.*" No doubt that is essential. Those who look forward to the winter season succeed; others suffer. But "none starve." *

The popular idea in the West of Ireland as to the climate in Canada is that it is very severe, and I must not pass the subject by lest it be said that I did so purposely. I had the advantage of going there just after New-Year's Day. The newspapers were commenting upon the unusual cold. The lowest *night* temperature which I saw reported was 36° below zero in Manitoba, 32° in Minnesota, 30° in Quebec and Montreal, but increasing westward to about zero at Toronto. Even under these circumstances I consider the climate of Ontario more healthy and less trying to those who are well clothed and housed, than that of the exposed parts of the West of Ireland; and such severe weather I was informed, lasts only a short time. The temperatures reported are always, I think, the extreme lowest at *nights*, which are very considerably modified during the day. The air is brisk and clear. The products of Ontario prove that the soil and climate together, are favourable to agriculture and fruit culture. It is only the labourer who suffers through the frost; and he must take care either to get yearly employment, or to save money while the work lasts. That work may be of various kinds. There are two railroads and two canals in course of construction, between Toronto and Ottawa, besides the Canadian Pacific Railroad work in the neighbourhood of French River, to the North. Toronto is a busy manufacturing city, as well as a considerable port, and the centre on which several railroad lines converge. Its population increased by nearly 31,000 in the decade ending 1881; or 55 per cent., and the populations of fourteen other cities and towns at nearly an equal rate. Agriculture has been stimulated by the export cattle trade, and the feeding of cattle in winter is becoming more and more general among the farmers of Ontario. On the whole it appears that it is not a passing wave of prosperity but a natural, steady, and certain progress that may be relied on as offering, in Upper Canada, a fair prospect to Irish emigrants capable of adapting themselves to new circumstances. That German competition, however, may be expected is suggested by the announcement of a line of German emigrant steamers, between Bremen and Quebec next summer. But there is room for all in the North-West, where the Germans are likely to go; while in Toronto, in addition to the two Official Immigration Agents, Irish emigrants will have the assistance, free of charge to them, of an energetic young Irishman, Mr. John Scully, an Employment and general Agent, who has access at all times to the Immigrant Depot, and is in communication with all the large contractors in Ontario.

On the day I left Toronto this gentleman informed me that he has reason to hope a small society would be formed, with the sanction of high authority, to help West of Ireland emigrants to obtain work.

Conclusion with regard to Canada.

1. The advantages offered by this country to emigrants have been detailed in a previous Report; but it is due to the Dominion Government that I should summarise them here.

The passage-money for agricultural labourers and their families is reduced to £3 per adult, and £2 for each child over one year.

There is an experienced Agent at Quebec to receive emigrants on their arrival, and to advise them as to the part of the country where labour is

* Connor got work as a track-man, or platelayer, on one of the railroads a day or two afterwards, through Mr. John Scully, mentioned above.

most required. The province of Ontario, which absorbs the greater number of emigrant labourers, is divided into five districts, in each of which there is a Government Agent, from whom emigrants will receive all reasonable assistance in their search for employment.

In every province of Canada free grants of land are obtainable, on certain easy conditions of residence and improvement. In Ontario the head of a family may obtain 200 acres, and each member over 18 years of age 100 acres, without distinction of sex. In the North-West Territory every male of 18 years and upwards may obtain 160 acres. Thus, a labourer who has gained experience in the country, and saved a little money, may acquire considerable property.

The high authority of Archbishop Lynch may be quoted for the following facts:—The Catholic Church in Canada is in a very prosperous condition. Priests and churches are to be found everywhere throughout the country; and Catholic education is on a better footing than in the United States. The Irish in Canada are among the most prosperous and loyal in the country. Canada is the freest and best governed country in the world, and the people are happy. The wages for farm hands are as good as in the United States, and living is cheaper.

2. The most westerly point considered in this Report has been Toronto, as the centre of distribution for Western Ontario.

But there is a limit to the number of families whom Ontario could absorb, and, if this limit should be exceeded by the number asking to be assisted to emigrate to Canada, it would become necessary to consider the practicability of sending families on to Winnipeg, and still further West, where great activity in all branches of labour may be expected next year.

In that case the additional cost would be at least £3 per fare; and the people would have to live in tents, which would cost from £3 to £5 each, unless a trial of colonization were resolved upon.

3. I had reason to hope that a draft scheme of that kind would be placed in my hands for submission with this report, but I have not yet received it. I had interviews in Toronto with both the Managing Directors of the Canada and North West Land Company, and was informed by one of them that, shortly before Christmas, he had attended a private conference at Ottawa, at which the Premier, the Minister of Emigration, the Minister of Railroads, the President and the General Manager of the Canada Pacific Railroad Company were present. Thus three parties—

The Dominion Government,
The Canada Pacific Railroad, and
The Canada and North West Land Company—

were well represented, and all inclined to the opinion that something might be done in order to supplement the present emigration under the £100,000 grant, with the £200,000 loan now in the hands of the Land Commissioners.

The Land Commissioners require that some company—with whose securities Her Majesty's Treasury would be satisfied, apart from the value of any land to be acquired by means of the £200,000, or any portion thereof—should become responsible for the administration of that fund, and for the repayment of principal and interest within a specified term of years.

The proposition before the above conference was that the English Government, by means of the £100,000, should deliver selected emigrants at a certain point, say Toronto; that there the operation of the gift money should cease, and that of the loan begin; that the Canada and North Western Land Company, acting either as the agents of the English Government, or independently, should build houses for the people on surveyed and selected Free Grant Lands of the Dominion Government contiguous to the land sections in their own hands, and so as indirectly to improve the value of these; that they should convey the emigrants there, and take from each head of a family a bond for the repayment of all outlay, which the Dominion Government would make a charge upon the land until redeemed.

I may here be allowed to refer briefly to a pamphlet entitled "Recent Experiences in the Emigration of Irish Families," in which the author states his conclusion, that "any Government scheme to settle large numbers of destitute Irish families in the Canadian North-west would be sure to fail." I think that too much stress may be laid upon the financial, and too little upon the social aspects of colonization. The failure of forty-five per cent. of a given number of settlers to pay their charges at the right time is a serious matter where regular dividends are looked for; but the improvement in the condition of the remaining fifty-five should not be altogether overlooked. In any scheme of colonization in which the Government would be likely to engage land worth £3 per acre would be obtained for almost nothing, and, with the improvements made upon it for the first settler, would be readily saleable to a second, in case of the first leaving it. No agent land company would be likely to undertake the expenditure of borrowed money where they did not see their way to recover it; and the amount up to £100 of all such expenditure necessary for settlement would remain a charge, not upon the settler, but upon the land.

No doubt, any colonization scheme would demand the most careful selection of emigrants, and the most prudent management throughout.

I have the honour to be, Gentlemen,

Your most obedient servant,

W. P. Gaskell.

The Local Government Board, Ireland.

No. 13—Emigration to United States and Canada.

Local Government Board, Dublin,
March 2nd, 1883.

Sir,

The Local Government Board for Ireland desire to acquaint the Board of Guardians that they have recently had under consideration a report which they have received from Major Gaskell, one of the members of the Emigration Committee, relating to the demand for labour in the United States and in Canada, and that from the information obtained on the subject there is reason to fear that emigrants to the United States may not always be able to procure suitable employment in that country; instructions have therefore been given to the Emigration Committee to take care that in determining upon the destination of persons who may be selected for emigration under the provisions of the 20th section of the Arrears of Rent (Ireland) Act, the Emigrants are not allowed to proceed to the United States unless they desire to join friends or relations there, and unless they can show that their friends or relations are in a position to put them in the way of procuring employment, and can help them to maintain themselves until they obtain such employment.

Under these circumstances it is desirable that applicants for Emigration should be made aware that if they wish to proceed to the United States they must be prepared to produce such evidence as will satisfy the Emigration Committee of the ability and willingness of their friends to assist them on arriving there.

The Local Government Board think it well to direct the attention of the Guardians to the assisted passages to Canada granted by the Canadian Government, and to state that they understand that the Canadian Government is willing to give the benefit of the assisted passages to specially approved families emigrating under the provisions of the Arrears of Rent (Ireland) Act. The Local Government Board are also informed that well organized arrangements for securing employment for Emigrants have been made in all parts of the Dominion.

It would therefore be desirable that the names of the persons about to proceed to Canada should be entered on a separate list, and that a copy of the list should be sent to the High Commissioner for Canada, to 9, Victoria Chambers, London, S.W., as soon as the lists are approved by the Local Government Board.

By order of the Board,

W. D. Wodsworth, Secretary.

To the Clerk of the —— Union.

List of Unions wholly or partly Scheduled under the Arrears of Rent (Ireland) Act, 1882.

	Electoral Divisions		Electoral Divisions		Electoral Divisions
Ballina,	13	Galway,	19	Newport,	all
Ballinasloe,	4	Glennamaddy,	15	Oughterard,	all
Ballyshannon,	15	Glenties,	all	Portumna,	4
Ballyvaghan,	9	Glin,	5	Roscommon,	2
Belmullet,	all	Gort,	7	Scariff,	6
Boyle,	23	Inishowen,	all	Sligo,	6
Cahersiveen,	all	Kenmare,	all	Stranorlar,	7
Carrick-on-Shannon,	16	Killala,	4	Strokestown,	9
Castlerea,	13	Killarney,	1	Swinford,	all
Claremorris,	16	Letterkenny,	6	Tobercurry,	11
Clifden,	all	Longford,	5	Tralee,	24
Donegal,	all	Manorhamilton,	15	Tuam,	29
Dromore, West,	11	Milford,	all	Westport,	17
Dunfanaghy,	all	Mohill,	all		
Ennis,	5	Mount Bellew,	1		

31st *March*, 1883.

No. 14.—Union Officers' Bond and Warrant.

Local Government Board, Dublin,
22nd March, 1883.

Sir,

Adverting to their former Circulars on the subject of Bonds of Union Officers, the Local Government Board for Ireland desire to state that new forms of Bond have been prepared, copies of which are enclosed for Clerks of Unions, Relieving Officers, and any other officer of the Union, except the above-named and Collectors of Rates; and the Local Government Board advise that these forms should be used in future.

An alteration has been made in the heading of the Warrant to confess Judgment attached to the bonds so as to make them in conformity with the Supreme Court of Judicature Act. A clause is inserted at the end of the Warrant, as well as the attestation, in conformity with the Debtors Act of 1872, to which attention was called in the Board's Circular of the 14th February, 1874.

Excepting in the case of Accounting Officers, it will probably rarely be found necessary to incur the expense of obtaining Warrants of Attorney to confess Judgment; but where that course is adopted the Warrant should be filed in the Court of Queen's Bench within three weeks after its date, to render it effective against the Union Officer concerned, or his sureties, in case of their future bankruptcy, and this can be done by the Solicitor usually employed by the Board of Guardians at a very trifling expense.

By order of the Board,

W. D. Wodsworth, Secretary.

The Clerk of each Union.

I.—Bond for Clerk and his Sureties.

Know all Men by these Presents, that we, are jointly and severally held and firmly bound to the Guardians of the Poor of the Union in the sum of of good and lawful money of the United Kingdom of Great Britain and Ireland, to be paid to the said Guardians, or their certain Attorney, Successors or Assigns, for which payment to be well and faithfully made we bind ourselves jointly, and each of us binds himself severally, our and each and every of our Heirs, Executors and Administrators, and every of them, firmly by these presents, sealed with our Seals.

Dated this day of , in the year of our Lord one thousand eight hundred and

Whereas, the above-bounden hath been duly appointed Clerk to the said Guardians of the Poor of the Union, and hath been required to enter into a bond with two sureties to the said Guardians of the Poor of the Union, in the penalty hereinbefore mentioned, to be conditioned as hereinafter is set forth, and hath requested the above-bounden and to join with him as such sureties in the above bond, subject to the condition hereinafter contained, to which they have assented; and the said Guardians have agreed to accept of them as such sureties accordingly.

Now the condition of this obligation is such that if the above-bounden do and shall, from time to time, and at all times hereafter, whilst he shall be employed in the said office of Clerk to the said Guardians of the poor of the Union, and until he shall be discharged therefrom by order of the Local Government Board for Ireland, or by and with their assent, shall cease and discontinue to hold the said office, of Clerk to the said Guardians of the Poor of the Union, duly and faithfully execute and discharge all the duties of the said office, as prescribed by the orders of the Commissioners for administering the laws for relief of the poor in Ireland, or by the said Board, and shall perform the same in person, except in case of absence in consequence of sickness or accident, or with the leave of the said Guardians; and if the above-bounden shall, when required so to do by the said Guardians or by the said Board, hand over or deliver up to the said Guardians, or to such person or persons as they may authorize to receive the same, all books, accounts, vouchers, papers, and writings, which may have come into his custody as Clerk of the said Guardians, or which may in any way appertain to the affairs of the said Union, or to the said Guardians; and if the above-bounden shall, while he holds the said office, diligently serve the said Guardians, and conduct himself honestly in all respects in the transaction of any business either belonging to the said office of Clerk, or entrusted to him by the said Guardians, then the foregoing bond or obligation shall be void.

Signed, sealed, and delivered by the above-bounden } (Seal.) (Seal.) (Seal.)

To , Gentlemen, Solicitors of Her Majesty's High Court of Justice in Ireland, Queen's Bench Division, or either of them, or to any other Solicitor of the same Division, or to any other Solicitor of any other Division of Her Majesty's High Court of Justice in Ireland aforesaid, Great Britain or elsewhere.

These are to authorise and appoint you, or either of you, to appear for us , or any or either of us, for the whole, jointly and severally, and confess one or more judgment or judgments, as of last Term, or of any Term or time whatsoever, after the date of these presents, with stay of execution until breach shall be made in the performance of the condition of the bond hereunto annexed, and bearing equal date herewith, in the said High Court of Justice in Ireland, Queen's Bench Division, or any other Division of Her Majesty's High Court of Justice in Ireland, Great Britain, or elsewhere, by acknowledging the action, or otherwise, upon one or more declaration or declarations, there to be filed against us, or any or either of us, by himself for the whole, at the suit of the Guardians of the Poor of the Union, upon a bond of sterling; and for your or any of your so doing this shall be your sufficient warrant and discharge.

And the condition of the said bond is such, that if the said do and shall, from time to time, and at all times hereafter, whilst he shall be employed in the office of Clerk to the said Guardians of the Poor of the Union, and until he shall be discharged therefrom by order of the Local Government Board for Ireland, or by and with their assent, shall cease and discontinue to hold the said office of Clerk to the said Guardians of the Poor of the Union, duly and faithfully execute and discharge all the duties of the said office, as prescribed by the orders of the Commissioners for administering the laws for relief of the poor in Ireland, or by the said Board, and shall perform the same in person, except in case of absence in consequence of sickness or accident, or with the leave of the said Guardians; and if the said shall, when required so to do by the said Guardians, or by the said Board, hand over or deliver up to the said Guardians, or to such person or persons as they may authorise to receive the same, all books, accounts, vouchers, papers, and writings, which may have come into his custody as Clerk of the said Guardians, or which may in any way appertain to the affairs of the said Union, or to the said Guardians; and if the said shall, while he holds the said office, diligently serve the said Guardians and conduct himself honestly in all respects in the transaction of any business either belonging to the said office of Clerk, or entrusted to him by the said Guardians, then the said bond or obligation shall be void.

And know all men by these Presents, that we the said do hereby for us, and each and every of us, by himself for the whole, and our, and each and every of our Heirs, Executors, Administrators, and Assigns, jointly and severally authorise you or any of you, to remise, release, and for ever quit claim unto the said Guardians of the Poor of the Union, all and all manner of error or errors, or misprision of error or errors, or erroneous proceedings whatsoever, that are or may be in or about the entering or obtaining the said judgment or judgments, or any other the proceedings thereupon; and for what you the said Solicitors, or any of you, shall do in the premises, this shall be to you and every of you a sufficient authority; and we have expressly named of in the county of a Solicitor of Her Majesty's High Court of Justice in Ireland, and requested him to attend on our behalf to inform us of the nature and effect thereof before executing same, and to witness the due execution hereof by us; and we acknowledge that the said has accordingly attended and informed us of the true nature and effect hereof before such execution. In witness whereof we have hereunto set our Hands and Seals the day of in the year of our Lord

Signed, sealed, and delivered by the said in the presence of me at in the county of a Solicitor of the High Court of Justice in Ireland, and I declare myself to be the Solicitor for the said and attending at their request, and having, previously to the execution of this warrant, informed them of the nature and effect thereof, I hereunto subscribe my name as such Solicitor.

Solicitor for the parties above named

(Seal.)

(Seal.)

(Seal.)

III.—Bond for Relieving Officer.

Know all Men by these Presents, That We, are jointly and severally held and firmly bound to the Guardians of the Poor of the Union, in the sum of of good and lawful Money of the United Kingdom of Great Britain and Ireland, to be paid to the said Guardians, or their certain Solicitor, Successors, or Assigns, for which payment to be well and faithfully made, We bind ourselves jointly, and each of us bindeth himself severally, our and each and every of our Heirs, Executors, and Administrators, and every of them, firmly by these Presents sealed with our Seals. Dated this day of in the year of our Lord one thousand eight hundred and

Whereas the above-bounden hath been duly appointed a Relieving Officer of the Union, aforesaid, and hath been required to enter into a Bond with two Sureties to the said Guardians of the Poor of the Union, in the penalty hereinbefore mentioned to be conditioned as hereinafter set forth, and hath requested the above bounden and to join with him as such Sureties in the above Bond, subject to the condition hereinafter contained, to which they have assented; and the said Guardians have agreed to accept of them as such Sureties accordingly.

Now the Condition of this obligation is such, that if the above-bounden do and shall, from time to time, and at all times hereafter, whilst he shall be employed in the said Office of Relieving Officer of the said Union, and until he shall be discharged therefrom by order of the Local Government Board for Ireland, or by and with their assent shall cease and discontinue to hold the said office duly and faithfully execute and discharge all the duties of the said Office, as prescribed by the Orders of the Commissioners for administering the Laws for Relief of the Poor in Ireland, or by the said Board; and shall from time to time, and at all times when required so to do, deliver to the Person or Persons authorized to require the same, a full, just, and true Account of all Moneys, Provisions, and other articles received and expended by him as such Relieving Officer, and shall verify such Account on Oath when thereunto lawfully required, and shall deliver to such Person or Persons, when required so to do, all the Books, Papers, and Writings in his custody or power, relating to his said Office or to the affairs of the said Union; and shall at all times, when required, pay such Moneys as upon the balance of any Account or Accounts shall appear to be in his hands to the Treasurer of the said Union, and deliver all stocks or Provisions or other Articles remaining in his hands to such Person or Persons as the said Guardians of the Poor of the Union shall authorize to receive the same, and shall in all other respects duly, fully, and faithfully observe, obey, perform, fulfil, and keep all the

Enactments, Laws, Rules, and Regulations contained in the Acts which are or shall be at any time in force for the Relief of the Destitute Poor in Ireland, or in any Order of the said Board, touching and concerning the Office of Relieving Officer as aforesaid; and if the said shall not commit or cause to suffer to be done or committed any act, matter, or thing whatsoever, whereby or by means whereof the said Guardians of the Poor of the Union, shall or may or can be wronged, defrauded, or prejudiced, then the foregoing Bond and Obligation shall be void.

Signed, Sealed, and Delivered by the above-bounden } (Seal.) (Seal.) (Seal.)

To Gentlemen, Solicitors of Her Majesty's High Court of Justice in Ireland, Queen's Bench Division, or either of them, or to any other solicitor of the same Division, or to any other solicitor of any other Division of her Majesty's High Court of Justice in Ireland aforesaid, Great Britain, or elsewhere.

These are to authorise and appoint you, or either of you, to appear for us or any or either of us for the whole, jointly and severally, and confess one or more Judgment or Judgments, as of last Term, or of any Term or time whatsoever, after the date of these Presents, with stay of Execution until breach shall be made in the performance of the Condition of the Bond hereunto annexed, and bearing equal date herewith, in the said High Court of Justice in Ireland, Queen's Bench Division, or any other Division of Her Majesty's High Court of Justice in Ireland, Great Britain, or elsewhere, by acknowledging the Action, or otherwise, upon one or more Declaration or Declarations, there to be filed against us, or any or either of us, by himself for the whole, at the suit of the Guardians of the Poor of the Union, upon a Bond of sterling; and for your or any of your so doing, this shall be your sufficient Warrant and Discharge. And the Condition of the said Bond is such, that if the said do and shall, from time to time, and at all times hereafter, whilst he shall be employed in the Office of Relieving Officer of the said Union, and until he shall be discharged therefrom by order of the Local Government Board for Ireland, or by and with their assent shall cease and discontinue to hold the said office, duly and faithfully execute and discharge all the duties of the said office, as prescribed by the Orders of the Commissioners for administering the Laws for the Relief of the Poor in Ireland, or by the said Board; and shall from time to time, and at all times when required so to do, deliver to the Person or Persons authorised to require the same, a full, just, and true Account of all Moneys, Provisions, and other articles received and expended by him as such Relieving Officer, and shall verify such Account on Oath when thereunto lawfully required, and shall deliver to such Person or Persons, when required so to do, all the Books, Papers, and Writings in his custody or power, relating to his said Office or to the affairs of the said Union; and shall at all times, when required, pay such Moneys as upon the balance of any Account or Accounts shall appear to be in his hands to the Treasurer of the said Union, and deliver all stocks of Provisions or other Articles remaining in his hands to such Person or Persons as the said Guardians of the Poor of the Union shall authorise to receive the same, and shall in all other respects duly, fully, and faithfully observe, obey, perform, fulfil, and keep all the Enactments, Laws, Rules, and Regulations, contained in the Acts which are or shall be at any time in force for the relief of the Destitute Poor in Ireland, or in any Order of the said Board, touching and concerning the Office of Relieving Officer as aforesaid; and if the said shall not commit or cause or suffer to be done or committed any act, matter, or thing whatsoever, whereby or by means whereof the said Guardians of the Poor of the Union, shall or may or can be wronged, defrauded, or prejudiced, then the said Bond and Obligation shall be void. AND KNOW ALL MEN BY THESE PRESENTS that we the said do hereby for us, and each and every of us, by himself for the whole, and our and each, and every of our Heirs, Executors, Administrators, and Assigns, jointly and severally authorise you or any of you, to remise, release, and for ever quit claim, unto the said Guardians of the Poor of all and all manner of error or errors, or misprision of error or errors, or erroneous proceedings whatsoever, that are or may be in or about the entering or obtaining the said Judgment or Judgments or any other the proceedings thereupon; and for what you the said Solicitors, or any of you, shall do in the premises, this shall be to you and every of you a sufficient authority; and we have expressly named of in the County of a Solicitor of Her Majesty's High Court of Justice in Ireland, and requested him to attend on our behalf to inform us of the nature and effect hereof before executing same, and to witness the due execution hereof by us; and we acknowledge that the said has accordingly attended and informed us of the true nature and effect hereof before such execution. In witness whereof we have hereunto set our Hands and Seals, the day of in the Year of our Lord

Signed, Sealed, and Delivered by the said in the presence of me at in the County of a Solicitor of the High Court of Justice in Ireland, and I declare myself to be the Solicitor for the said and attending at their request, and having previously to the execution of this warrant informed them of the nature and effect thereof, I hereunto subscribe my name as such Solicitor.

Solicitor for the parties above named.

(Seal.)

(Seal.)

(Seal.)

IV.—[BOND in the form for any OFFICER of the UNION, except the CLERK, a COLLECTOR of RATES, or a RELIEVING OFFICER.]

KNOW ALL MEN BY THESE PRESENTS, That WE are jointly and severally held and firmly bound to the Guardians of the Poor of the Union, in the sum of of good and lawful money of the United Kingdom of Great Britain and Ireland, to be paid to the said Guardians of the Poor of the Union, or their certain solicitor, successors, or assigns, for which payment to be well and faithfully made, We bind ourselves jointly, and each of us bindeth himself severally, our and each and every of our heirs, executors, and administrators, and every of them, firmly by these presents, sealed with our seals. Dated this day of in the year of our Lord one thousand eight hundred and

WHEREAS the above-bounden hath been duly appointed of

the Union aforesaid, and hath been required to enter into a bond with two sureties to the said Guardians of the Poor of the Union, in the penalty hereinbefore mentioned, to be conditioned as hereinafter is set forth, and hath requested the above-bounden and to join with him as such sureties, in the above bond, subject to the condition hereinafter contained, to which they have assented; and the said Guardians have agreed to accept of them as such sureties accordingly.

Now the Condition of this obligation is such, that if the above-bounden do and shall, from time to time, and at all times hereafter, whilst he shall be employed in the said office of of the said Union, and until he shall be discharged therefrom by order of the Local Government Board for Ireland, or by and with their assent shall cease and discontinue to hold the said office, duly and faithfully execute and discharge all the duties of the said office, as prescribed by the orders of the Commissioners for administering the Laws for Relief of the Poor in Ireland, or by the said Board, and shall perform the same in person, except in case of absence in consequence of sickness or accident, or with the leave of the said Guardians; and if the above-bounden shall, when required so to do by the said Guardians, or by the said Board, hand over or deliver up to the said Guardians, or to such person or persons as they may authorize to receive the same, all books, accounts, vouchers, papers, and writings which may have come into his custody as of the said Union, or which may in any way appertain to the affairs of the said Union, or to the said Guardians; and if the above-bounden shall, while he holds the said office, diligently serve the said Guardians, fulfilling all their lawful orders, and conducting himself honestly in all respects in the transaction of any business either belonging to the said office of of the said Union, or intrusted to him by the said Guardians, then the foregoing bond or obligation shall be void.

Signed, sealed, and delivered by the } (Seal.)
(Seal.)
(Seal.)

To gentlemen Solicitors of Her Majesty's High Court of Justice in Ireland, Queen's Bench Division, or either of them, or to any other Solicitor of the same Division, or to any other Solicitor of any other Division of Her Majesty's High Court of Justice in Ireland, aforesaid, Great Britain, or elsewhere.

These are to authorize and appoint you, or either of you, to appear for us or any or either of us, for the whole, jointly and severally, and confess one or more judgment or judgments, as of last term, or of any term or time whatsoever, after the date of these presents, with stay of execution until breach shall be made in the performance of the condition of the bond hereunto annexed, and bearing equal date herewith, in the said High Court of Justice in Ireland, Queen's Bench Division, or any other Division of Her Majesty's High Court of Justice in Ireland, Great Britain, or elsewhere, by acknowledging the action, or otherwise, upon one or more declaration or declarations, there to be filed against us, or any or either of us, by himself for the whole, at the suit of the Guardians of the Poor of the Union, upon a bond of sterling; and for your or any of your so doing, this shall be your sufficient warrant and discharge.

And the Condition of the said bond is such, that if the said do and shall, from time to time, and at all times hereafter, whilst he shall be employed in the office of of the said Union, and until he shall be discharged therefrom by order of the Local Government

Board for Ireland, or by and with their assent shall cease and discontinue to hold the said office, duly and faithfully execute and discharge all the duties of the said office, as prescribed by the orders of the Commissioners for administering the Laws for Relief of the Poor in Ireland, or by the said board, and shall perform the same in person, except in case of absence in consequence of sickness or accident, or with the leave of the said Guardians; and if the said shall, when required so to do by the said Guardians, or by the said Board, hand over or deliver up to the said Guardians, or to such person or persons as they may authorise to receive the same, all books, accounts, vouchers, papers, and writings which may have come into his custody as of the said Union, or which may in any way appertain to the affairs of the said Union, or to the said Guardians; and if the said shall, while he holds the said office, diligently serve the said Guardians, fulfilling all their lawful orders, and conducting himself honestly in all respects in the transaction of any business either belonging to the said office of of the said Union, or intrusted to him by the said Guardians, then the said bond or obligation shall be void.

AND KNOW ALL MEN BY THESE PRESENTS, that we the said do hereby for us, and each and every of us, by himself for the whole, and our and each, and every of our Heirs, Executors, Administrators, and Assigns, jointly and severally authorise you or any of you, to remise, release, and for ever quit claim, unto the said Guardians of the Poor of the Union, all and all manner of error or errors, or misprision of error or errors, or erroneous proceedings whatsoever, that are or may be in or about the entering or obtaining the said judgment, or judgments, or any other the proceedings thereupon; and for what you the said Solicitors, or any of you, shall do in the premises, this shall be to you and every of you a sufficient authority; and we have expressly named of in the county of a Solicitor of Her Majesty's High Court of Justice in Ireland, and requested him to attend on our behalf to inform us of the nature and effect hereof before executing same, and to witness the due execution hereof by us; and we acknowledge that the said has accordingly attended and informed us of the true nature and effect hereof before such execution. In witness whereof we have hereunto set our hands and seals, the day of in the year of our Lord

Signed, sealed, and delivered by the said in the presence of me at in the county of a Solicitor of the High Court of Justice in Ireland, and I declare myself to be the Solicitor for the said and attending at their request, and having previously to the execution of this warrant informed them of the nature and effect thereof, I hereunto subscribe my name as such Solicitor. Solicitor for the parties above named.	(Seal.) (Seal.) (Seal.)

APPENDIX B.

CIRCULARS OF INSTRUCTION AND CORRESPONDENCE UNDER THE MEDICAL CHARITIES ACT AND VACCINATION ACTS.

No. I.—Vaccination Certificates.

Local Government Board, Dublin,
17th May, 1882.

Sir,

The Local Government Board for Ireland desire to inform you that they have received a communication from the Registrar-General forwarding to them the opinion of the Law Officers of the Crown to the effect that, when a Medical Officer of a district is also the Registrar of Births and Deaths of such district, it is his duty when he vaccinates a person whose birth has been registered in another district to forward a certificate of successful vaccination to the Registrar of the district in which the birth was registered, and not to enter it in the Vaccination Register of his own district, which he keeps in pursuance of the provisions of Section 7 of the Compulsory Vaccination Act.

This opinion does not suggest any change in the manner in which Medical Officers of Dispensary Districts who are not Registrars are to discharge their duties under the first part of Section 5 of the Vaccination Amendment (Ireland) Act, 1879, but it will be necessary in future for every Medical Officer of a dispensary district, who is also the Registrar of such district, when he vaccinates a person whose birth has been registered in another Registrar's district, to enter the case in the Vaccination Register, Form G, which he is required to keep by Clause 8 of Article 21 of the Dispensary Regulations, instead of entering it in the Vaccination Register which is prescribed by Section 7 of the Compulsory Vaccination Act.

By order of the Board,

B. Banks, Secretary.

To the Medical Officer of each Dispensary District.

No. 2.—Annual Appointment of Dispensary Committees and Wardens.

Local Government Board, Dublin,
5th April, 1883.

Sir,

The Local Government Board for Ireland desire to call your attention to the Circular of the Poor Law Commissioners dated the 21st of March, 1862, relating to the annual appointment of Dispensary Committees and Wardens, and to the extracts from previous circulars appended thereto; and they request that you will take the necessary steps, as pointed out in the circular referred to, to place before the Board of Guardians, after the annual election, a correct list of the members of the Board entitled to be members of the respective Dispensary Committees in the union.

This ought to be done by distinct resolution and recorded on the minutes.

As soon as the Committee shall have been completed for any dispensary district, the Guardians should fix a day for the first meeting of such Committee, *for the special purpose of appointing their honorary officers for the current year*, in accordance with Articles 6 and 7 of the Dispensary Regulations, and you should give notice thereof to each member of the Dispensary Committee, in accordance with Articles 11 and 13 of the Dispensary Regulations.

A form for the Return of Officers of the several Dispensary Committees in the Union will be forwarded to you in due course.

By order of the Board,

B. Banks, Secretary.

To the Clerk of the Board of Guardians of each Union.

No. 3.—Return of Officers of Dispensary Committees.

Local Government Board, Dublin,
Sir, 8th April, 1882.

With reference to their circular of the 5th instant, relating to the annual appointment of Dispensary Committees and Wardens, the Local Government Board for Ireland enclose herewith a Form for the return of officers of the several Dispensary Committees in the Union.

In the circular above referred to, the Board recommended that as soon as the Committee should have been completed for any dispensary district, the Guardians should fix a day for the first meeting of such Committee, *for the special purpose of appointing their Honorary Officers for the current year*, in accordance with the Dispensary Regulations, and that you should give notice thereof to each member of the Dispensary Committee in accordance with those regulations; and if this recommendation has not been acted upon in the case of any dispensary district in the Union, the Board request that you will bring the matter again under the notice of the Board of Guardians.

Articles 6 and 7 of the Dispensary Regulations of 20th November, 1869, relate to the appointment of the honorary officers, and Articles 11 and 13 relate to the notice of meeting.

The Board enclose three copies of the Form, so as to enable you to make the Return in Duplicate to this Office, and to retain a copy for the use of the Board; and they request that you will procure the necessary information with the least practicable delay, and then forward your Return to this Office.

By order of the Board,

B. Banks, Secretary.

To the Clerk of the Board of Guardians of each Union.

No. 4.—Report of some Experiments Performed here with Calf Vaccine.

Vaccine Department,
Local Government Board, Ireland,
45, Upper Sackville-street, Dublin.

Having, by the direction of the Board, written to Dr. E. Warlomont, of Brussels, for some Calf Vaccine, I received from him ten points, five tubes, and one phial, containing a preparation which he calls (pomade), presumably a mixture of Calf Vaccine, glycerine, and water. This vaccine, he informed me, was the thirtieth reproduction from calf to calf, the original source being a case of spontaneous cowpox (Bordeaux, Dubreuilh, November, 1881). He also stated that he believed in the method of inserting the lymph, by making "cross scratches" on the infant's arms (such has always been the course carried out in this institution). Dr. Warlomont recommends "the vaccine pomade" and the tubes as being most reliable; the points cannot be depended on if kept for any time without being used.

The above is a short account of the material we used in carrying out the following experiments. I may also mention that perfectly *new* lancets were used, and that care was taken to choose the most healthy children for carrying on the vaccinations.

Thirty-two infants were vaccinated with Calf Vaccine; of these seven were done from points, thirteen from tubes, and twelve from "pomade," the results on the eighth day being as follows:—

Vaccinated from—

Points.	Tubes.	Pomade.
3 Natural.	4 Natural.	10 Natural.
3 1 Vesicle slow; 1 failed.	1 1 Slow; 1 failed.	1 1 Slow; 1 failed.
1 Failed.	3 Failed.	1 Absent.
	5 Absent.	

Total—17 Natural.
5 1 Vesicle slow; 1 failed.
4 Failed.
6 Absent.

The nine whose vesicles were slow or failed on the eighth day were re-vaccinated with pomade, satisfactory results following the week after. One of those absent on the eighth day returned on the 12th day, exhibiting normal vesicles; the other five absentees not having as yet returned, it may be presumed that the vaccination in each case was successful.

The general character of the vesicle on the eighth day was much the same as what one observes to follow the insertion of humanized vaccine lymph; it was plump and full, with a depressed centre and "pearly" in colour; there was either no areola, or just the faintest blush of its appearance; no flag or tumefaction of the arm. On tapping the vesicle, the lymph which slowly exuded was less in quantity and slightly more viscid in nature than that which we generally find it to be. In those cases which returned on the twelfth day we found the vesicle to be normal, and the areola much the same in extent and colour as it is usually found to be at that period of vaccination.

The apparent largeness of failure to take on the first occasion we consider due to the fact of the lymph having been mixed with glycerine, which, preventing the blood from coagulating previous to the infant's having been brought out of the room, rendered greater the liability of the lymph being removed by friction against the mother's clothes before it had time to enter the child's system.

From the vesicles formed on the eighth day after the insertion of the Calf Vaccine, we procured lymph in almost all the cases. With some of this fluid we inoculated eleven infants, in all cases the resulting vesicles on the eighth day were natural, from some of these infants we vaccinated two others, with a like result, the vesicles arising from the use of the lymph once and twice removed from Calf Vaccine, being natural on the eighth day: in some cases the vesicles formed, appeared to be a little plumper and more active than those arising from the direct use of the Calf Vaccine, and the lymph which exuded from them a little more viscid than usual.

As yet I have neither issued the Calf Vaccine or the "humanized" lymph obtained from its use, awaiting further directions from the Board in the matter.

For the information of the Local Government Board, Ireland.

Alex. Nixon Montgomery, m.k.q.c.p.i., &c., &c.,
Secretary.

6th July, 1882.

No. 6.—Further Report of some Experiments Performed here with Calf Vaccine.

Vaccine Department, Local Government Board,
45, Upper Sackville-street, Dublin,
7th March, 1883.

Since sending in to the Local Government Board my former Report on this subject, I have had some further experiments made, with the object of trying to discover for what length of time the Calf Vaccine might be kept, with an after certainty of its producing a typical vesicle.

We received the Calf Vaccine on the 17th May, 1882; on the 28th July following, from one tube, we vaccinated seven infants with the following results on the eighth day—

2 Natural.
2 Failed.
3 Infants not brought back.

We have not seen the latter three children since, so the results in their cases are doubtful.

On the 1st August, 1882, from some of the "Pulp" or "Pomade," we inoculated thirteen infants, with the following results on the eighth day—

Infants.	Vesicles.
1	Natural.
2	1 Vesicle nat.; 1 failed.
1	1 Vesicle slow; 1 failed.
9	Failed.

On the 29th December six infants were vaccinated from a tube.

6 Failed.

In all those cases that had failed to take the Calf Vaccine, we vaccinated with our own stock of lymph, with most satisfactory results.

From the above recorded facts it would appear that the longer Calf Vaccine is kept, the less likelihood there is of its producing its effect, and that after having been stored for some months, failure follows its use, even though the greatest care is taken in inoculating with it.

For the information of the Local Government Board for Ireland.

Alex. Nixon Montgomery, M.K.Q.C.P.I., &c., &c.,
Secretary.

APPENDIX C.

I.—Circulars.

ORDERS AND INSTRUCTIONAL CIRCULARS UNDER THE LOCAL GOVERNMENT ACT, AND THE PUBLIC HEALTH ACT.

No. 1.—Contagious Diseases (Animals) Act, 1878.

Local Government Board, Dublin,
26th June, 1882.

Sir,

The Local Government Board for Ireland have received from the Chief Secretary to his Excellency the Lord Lieutenant a certificate under the provisions of "The Contagious Diseases (Animals) Act, 1878," that a sum of £14,340 4s. 0¾d., being equivalent to a rating of one farthing in the pound on the net annual value of the property in all the unions in Ireland, is required for the purposes of the said Act.

It has been at the same time intimated to the Local Government Board that the Lord Lieutenant desires that the Board should take the further steps necessary for providing the funds required.

The Board have accordingly issued an order under the 83rd section of the Act, assessing the said sum of £14,340 4s. 0¾d. upon the several unions in Ireland in proportion to the net annual value of the property in each union according to the valuation thereof now in force.

It will be seen by the enclosed copy of the order that the sum assessed upon Union is £ , and a copy of the order has been duly forwarded to the Treasurer of the union for his information and guidance.

By order of the Board,

B. Banks, Secretary.

To the Clerk of the —— Union.

No. 2.—Contagious Diseases (Animals) Act, 1878.

Local Government Board, Dublin,
Sir, 20th June, 1882.

The Local Government Board for Ireland transmit to you herewith, for your information and guidance, a copy of an order under their seal which has been issued in pursuance of "The Contagious Diseases (Animals) Act, 1878," in accordance with the certificate of the Chief Secretary to his Excellency the Lord Lieutenant, that a sum of £14,340 4s. 0¾d., being equivalent to a rating of one farthing in the pound on the net annual value of the property in all the unions in Ireland, is required for the purposes of the said Act.

The Local Government Board desire to draw your attention as Treasurer of the Union, to the 83rd section of the Act, a copy of which is annexed hereto, by which you will perceive that on receipt of the order you are required out of the union funds to pay over the amount assessed on the union to the Bank of Ireland, to be placed to the General Cattle Diseases Fund. You will see by the order that the amount assessed on the Union is £

By order of the Board,

B. Banks, Secretary.

To the Treasurer of the —— Union.

Copy of Section 83 of the Contagious Diseases (Animals) Act, 1878, (41 & 42 Vic., c. 74).

General Cattle Diseases Fund.

83.—(1.) There shall be a General Cattle Diseases Fund for purposes of this Part.

(2.) Any money at the commencement of this Act standing at the Bank of Ireland to the credit of the Cattle Plague Account shall be transferred to the account of the General Cattle Diseases Fund; and that money shall, in the first instance, constitute that Fund, as if it had been raised under this Act.

(3.) The Chief Secretary may from time to time, as and when he thinks fit, certify to the effect that a sum equivalent to a certain poundage on the net annual value of the property in all the unions is required for the purposes of this Act.

(4.) Thereupon the Local Government Board shall by order under their seal, assess that sum on the several unions in proportion to the net annual value of the property therein.

(5.) They shall send copies of the order to the guardians and to the treasurer of each union.

(6.) Thereupon the treasurer of each union shall out of union funds pay over the amount assessed on the union to the Bank of Ireland, to be placed to the General Cattle Disease Fund.

(7.) The guardians of each union shall debit the several electoral divisions with proportions of that sum, according to the net annual value of the property therein.

(8.) No larger sum shall be levied under this Act at any one time than shall be equivalent to a poundage of one halfpenny in the pound on the net annual value of the property in all the unions; nor shall any larger sum be levied under this Act in the whole than shall be equivalent, taken with any money before the commencement of this Act carried to the cattle plague account, to a poundage of fourpence in the pound on the net annual value of the property in all the unions.

(9.) On receipt of a certificate of the Chief Secretary to the effect that any part of the sum standing to the General Cattle Disease Fund is not required for purposes of that fund, the Local Government Board shall, by order under their seal, assign the proportions returnable to the several unions, according to the net annual value of the property therein; and the Bank of Ireland shall, on a direction to that effect from the Chief Secretary, remit the sum so assigned to the treasurers of the unions; and the guardians of each union shall, on receipt of that sum, credit the several electoral divisions with proportions of that sum, according to the net annual value of the property therein.

No. 3.—SCALE of ALLOWANCES to PROSECUTORS and WITNESSES at ASSIZES and QUARTER SESSIONS in IRELAND.

Local Government Board, Dublin,
3rd July, 1882.

SIR,

I am directed by the Local Government Board for Ireland to transmit herewith for your information, copy of an amended scale of allowances to prosecutors and witnesses at Assizes and Quarter Sessions in Ireland, which the Board understand has been sent to Crown Solicitors and Sessional Crown Solicitors, with a request that it may be used in future for that contained in the circular of the 10th April, 1880.

By order of the Board,

D. BANKS, Secretary.

To each Auditor.

[TABLE.

SCALE of ALLOWANCES to PROSECUTORS and WITNESSES at ASSIZES and QUARTER SESSIONS in IRELAND.

Class.	Personal Allowance.				Travelling Expenses.
	Minimum.		Maximum.		
	Per Day.	Per Night.	Per Day.	Per Night.	
	s. d.	s. d.	s. d.	s. d.	
1. Labourers,	2 0	1 6	4 0	2 6	Railway or other public conveyance to be always availed of when practicable. Actual fare paid to be allowed (3rd class by rail). In special cases where the witness is obliged to hire a car for himself the allowance should not exceed 6d. per mile, and half fare returning if on same day. If on a subsequent day a like sum of 6d. per mile. Witnesses proceeding from the same place to use, as far as practicable, the same car.
2. Farmers, Shopkeepers and their Assistants, Commercial and Law Clerks, Artisans, &c.	[illegible]	[illegible]	[illegible]	[illegible]	
*3. Warders and other Gaol officials, except Governors	4s. 6d. per day.		4s. 6d. per night.		
*4. Governors of Gaols and Petty Sessions Clerks.	7s. 6d. per day.		7s. 6d. per night.		Same as above, except that 2nd class fare should be allowed by rail.
5. Merchants, Bank Officials, &c.	5 0	5 0	10 6	10 6	
6. County Surveyors' Assistants, Land Surveyors, &c.	4 0	4 6	10 0	8 0	
*7. Resident Magistrates, and other Government Officials not classed above.	10s. per day.		10s. per night.		Same as above, except that 1st class fare should be allowed by rail.
8. Doctors, Solicitors, Engineers and Handwriting Experts.	21 0	10 0	42 0	10 0	
9. Clergymen, Private Gentlemen, Officers of the Army and Navy, &c.	5 0	5 0	10 0	10 0	

* These payments to be made to *Governors of Gaols and other Gaol Officials* only when the officer is summoned as a witness from some place beyond the vicinity of the Court-house, or attends in charge of prisoners brought up under a writ of habeas corpus as witnesses; and whose duties do not otherwise require him to be in attendance. A *Resident Magistrate* is only to be paid when attending as a witness outside *his district*, and where he is not otherwise required to attend in the discharge of his duties; and a Petty Sessions Clerk when summoned from some place beyond the vicinity of the Court-house.

The allowance to a doctor residing in the town or immediate neighbourhood, in which the trial takes place, should be one guinea, and if detained in Court more than three hours an additional guinea. When summoned to attend as a witness at any other town the allowance should be two guineas for every day he is necessarily detained from home, together with 10s. for each night he is so detained.

The day shall be taken to commence at 6 o'clock, a.m., and end at 6 o'clock, p.m., and the night shall be taken to commence at 6 o'clock, p.m., and end at 6 o'clock, a.m. No allowance to be made for a night's absence from home to any party who could reasonably be expected to reach his or her usual place of residence before 8 o'clock, p.m.

No prosecutor or witness should be allowed expenses in more than one case on the same day.

Should special circumstances exist in any case rendering payment in excess of the scale advisable, such payments can only be made with the sanction in writing of the Attorney-General.

Where witnesses are called upon to give their opinion on matters as to which such opinion is admissible evidence, or where analyses or maps, plans, or models are required, the expenses of such witnesses, or of

No. 4.—Loans from the Commissioners of Public Works in Ireland.

Local Government Board, Dublin,
20th October, 1882.

Sir,

The Local Government Board for Ireland forward to you herewith for the information of the
a copy of the 11th section of the "Public Works Loans (Ireland) Act, 1877," from which it will be seen that every intending borrower is required to send to the Commissioners of Public Works in Ireland, on or before the 31st day of December in every year, a statement of the new Loan, or Instalments of a Loan already granted, which the sender will probably apply to borrow during the then ensuing financial year, commencing on the 1st April.

These statements are to be submitted to the Treasury by the Commissioners of Public Works, with such information as may be necessary for enabling the Treasury to lay before the House of Commons an Estimate of the amount required to be granted for the purpose of Loans by the Commissioners of Public Works, who will not have power, except with the special permission of the Treasury, to decide upon complying with an application for a Loan, or advance any Instalment of a Loan, which has not been included in such a statement as above-mentioned.

The Local Government Board think it right to call attention to this subject in order that where any application to the Commissioners of Public Works for a Loan is contemplated, *the required statement may be sent to those Commissioners* in due time, that is to say, *not later than the 31st December next*, and any failure of the application, owing to non-compliance with the provisions of the Act, may be prevented.

The Board desire at the same time to draw the particular attention of intending borrowers to the necessity of stating *how much of any Loan* will be required in the year ending 31st March, 1884 (the period of the Credit to be taken for the proposed Loans), in order that the Commissioners of Public Works may limit the demand for the year as far as possible, to the requisitions which will actually be made on them.

By order of the Board,
B. Banks, Secretary.

To each Board of Guardians and each Governing Body of a Town in Ireland.

---

obtaining such analyses, maps, plans, or models shall be treated as exceptional, and require the sanction of the Government before being paid.

In cases of illness or inability of any prosecutor or witness to travel without some special means of conveyance, the Court may make such allowance as the justice of the case shall require.

Whenever an interpreter is employed the Court may order him such compensation as may be reasonable, in cases where such interpreters are not paid by salary for the discharge of such duty.

Where a report of proceedings is directed by the Attorney-General the following shall be the scale of charges allowed to the shorthand writer:—

	£	s.	d.
For an attendance not exceeding three hours, . . .	£1	1	0
For each day's attendance, ...	3	3	0
For every 72 words contained in a transcript of the Report, .	0	0	6

For attending in any place out of Dublin there will be added railway fare (first class), or coach fare as the case may be, or if there be no public conveyance available, car fare to and from the place at the rate above stated.

Copy of Sec. 11 of the Public Works Loans (Ireland) Act, 1877, 40 and 41 Vic., c. 47.

11. For the purpose of passing an annual Act of Parliament granting money for the purpose of loans by the Commissioners of Public Works in Ireland, every intending borrower shall send to the Commissioners, on or before the thirty-first day of December in every year, a statement of the new loan or instalments of a loan already granted which the sender will probably apply to borrow during the ensuing financial year; and the Commissioners of Public Works shall as soon as practicable submit all such statements to the Treasury, with such observations thereon and information respecting the same as they may think expedient, and as may be necessary for enabling the Treasury to lay before the House of Commons an estimate of the amount required to be granted for the purpose of loans by the Commissioners of Public Works.

The Commissioners of Public Works shall not, except with the special permission of the Treasury, decide upon complying with an application for a loan, or advance any instalment of a loan, which has not been included in such a statement as above-mentioned.

The Treasury, if they think that after providing for the loans and instalments included in the said statements, or such of them as will actually be advanced, there will be a balance out of the sum granted by Parliament sufficient to meet any loan or instalment not included in the statements, may, if they think fit, grant such special permission, and may grant it conditionally upon the said balance being in their opinion sufficient when the time for the actual payment arrives.

The Commissioners of Public Works, with the consent of the Treasury, may, if they think fit, from time to time make and when made rescind and vary regulations requiring quarterly statements to be sent by the borrowers of the amounts which will be required by such borrowers; and while such regulations, if any, are in force, the Treasury may, if they think fit, refuse to issue in any quarter of a financial year any larger sum than the total of the amounts named in the statements referring to such quarter.

No. 5.—Provisional Orders.—Loans.

Local Government Board, Dublin,
16th February, 1883.

Sir,

The Local Government Board for Ireland enclose herewith a revised copy of the instructions which were forwarded with their instructional circular of the 29th October, 1881, on the subject of applications for Provisional Orders relating to the purchase of lands otherwise than by agreement.

You will observe that the instructions have been revised in several particulars, and especially by the insertion of a paragraph to the effect that where it is only intended to carry sewers or water-mains through lands, such lands should not be included in the petition, or set out in the Book of Reference, as the Board are advised that Sanitary Authorities are empowered by sections 18 and 61 of the Public Health (Ireland) Act, 1878, 41 and 42 Vict., cap. 52 (subject to sections 35, 36, and 37, where these sections apply) to carry sewers and water-mains through lands without a Provisional Order.

The instructions contained in the document enclosed should be carefully perused. Much unnecessary expense in the preliminary proceedings, and subsequent delays and difficulty, will be avoided if the instructions are duly attended to by the Sanitary Authority and their officers, and any professional advisers whom they may employ.

The Board have found that in some instances a misapprehension has prevailed as to the period within which the advertisements and notices prescribed by sec. 203 of the Public Health Act must be issued.

As regards advertisements, the section requires that they shall be published during three successive weeks in the months of September, October, or November; and it is necessary that the three weeks in which the publication takes place should all be included in the same month, whichever of those above mentioned is selected for the purpose.

As regards notices to the owners, lessees, and occupiers of the lands which it is proposed to purchase, they must in all cases be given in the month immediately following that in which the advertisements are published.

The Board have also found that in some cases the deposit of a plan of the proposed undertaking which is required by sub-section (2) of section 203 has not been made until after the advertisement referred to in that enactment has been published. They are advised that the deposit should always be made at such time as to enable the plan to be seen at all reasonable hours at the prescribed place as soon as the advertisement is issued.

The Board may take this opportunity of observing that if the sanitary authority intend to apply for a Provisional Order to enable them to purchase lands compulsorily in connexion with proposed works of sewerage or water supply, some of which will lie outside their district, they will probably find it convenient to satisfy the requirements of sections 35 and 64 of the Public Health Act, when they are issuing the necessary advertisements in respect of the application for a Provisional Order. If this course is taken it will have the effect of preventing the delay which is occasioned at a subsequent stage of the proceedings, in cases where, after the Provisional Order is confirmed, advertisements and notices under the sections in question have to be issued before the works for which the land is required can be commenced. Section 63 should also be complied with where it is intended to construct a reservoir to hold more than 100,000 gallons of water.

By order of the Board,

W. D. Wodsworth, Secretary.

To the Executive Officer of each Sanitary Authority.

Public Health Ireland Act, 1878—Section 203.

Instructions as to Applications to the Local Government Board for Ireland, for Provisional Orders to put in force the Lands Clauses Acts with respect to the Purchase of Lands otherwise than by Agreement.

Petition.

1. The application must be made by a petition, under the seal of the Sanitary Authority containing the particulars required by sub-section 3, of section 203. It must state the lands intended to be taken, in a schedule which should correspond with the Book of Reference mentioned in Instruction 4.

2. The petition should not be presented sooner than fourteen days after the service of the notices which are required to be served under sub-section 2, nor later than 1st February next succeeding the service of the said notices, except for the year 1883, when the time will be extended to 10th March.

Plan.

3. The Petition* should be accompanied by a plan† showing the

* "Petition." This should be written on folio foolscap paper, on one side only, be signed by the chairman of the sanitary authority and countersigned by their executive sanitary officer, and sealed with their seal.

† It is desirable that this plan should be on a scale of not less than one inch to every two hundred feet, so as to be suitable for after proceedings under 14 & 15 Vic., cap. 70, sec. 4, if the Order be issued and confirmed. This plan need not show more of the undertaking than the lands required to be purchased, and not way-leaves.

properties which are to be taken, with a distinctive number marked on each property corresponding to the numbers in the Book of Reference, and coloured so as to distinguish the lands, or lands covered with water, or water proposed to be taken, with the area of each marked in statute acres, roods, and perches.

Book of Reference.

4. The plan should be accompanied by a Book of Reference in duplicate, in which the nature of each property to be taken, the number it bears on the plan, the townland and parish in which it is situate, and the names of the owner, or reputed owner, lessee, or reputed lessee, and occupier should be clearly set out.

Carriage of Sewers or Water-mains.

5. Where it is only intended to carry sewers or water-mains through lands,* such lands should not be included in the petition, or set out in the Book of Reference, as the Board are advised that Sanitary Authorities are empowered by sections 18 and 64 (subject to sections 35, 36, and 37, where these sections apply), to carry sewers and water-mains through lands without a Provisional Order.

Loan.

6. If a loan is required to carry out the purposes in respect of which the lands are proposed to be taken, application for such loan should be made when the petition is presented on the following form:—

"Application by , acting as the† Sanitary Authority, for the sanction of the Local Government Board to a loan of £ for the purpose of at an estimated cost of £ The assessable value of the premises within the district in respect of which this loan is to be borrowed is £ and the balances of all the outstanding loans contracted by the said Sanitary Authority and chargeable on said district, amount to £

"Given under my hand this day of 18

Chairman of the San. Authority.

"(Countersigned), Executive Sanitary Officer."

7. There must be a statutory declaration showing that the requirements of section 203, with respect to advertisements and notices, and the deposit of the plan therein mentioned have been duly complied with. The declaration must be properly stamped, and copies of the newspapers containing the advertisements, and also of the form of notices, and a copy of said plan, with the date of its deposit marked thereon, should be annexed as exhibits. It should specify the manner in which the notices have been served, and so far as relates to these notices it should be made by the person who served them.

8. When the plans and Book of Reference relating to the petition are deposited in this department, duplicates of same must, according to the standing orders, be *at the same time* deposited in the office of the Clerk of the Parliaments in the House of Lords, and in the Private Bill Office in the House of Commons, *but if* the deposit be made after the prorogation of Parliament, and before the 30th day of November, in any year, the duplicates as above must be deposited *on* the 30th day of November. Proof of compliance with the standing orders must be given before the Board will take the petition into consideration.

* By section 2 the term "lands" includes messuages, buildings, lands, easements, and hereditaments of any tenure.

† Urban or Rural, as the case may be.

The following is a copy of the 203rd section of the Public Health Act, 1878, referred to in the above instructions :—

203. With respect to the purchase of lands, or any of the other properties aforesaid (herein included under the term "lands"), by a Sanitary Authority for the purposes of this Act, the following regulations shall be observed ; (that is to say,)

(1.) The Lands Clauses Acts shall be incorporated with this Act, except the provisions relating to access to the special Act, and except section one hundred and twenty-seven of the Lands Clauses Consolidation Act, 1845 ;

(2.) The Sanitary Authority before putting in force any of the powers of the said Lands Clauses Acts with respect to the purchase and taking of land otherwise than by agreement, shall

Publish once at the least in each of three consecutive weeks in the month of November in some newspaper or newspapers circulating in their district, an advertisement describing shortly the purposes in respect of which the lands are proposed to be taken, naming a place where a plan of the proposed undertaking may be seen at all reasonable hours, and stating the denominations and quantity of lands that they require ; and shall further

Serve a notice in the month of December on every owner or reputed owner, lessee or reputed lessee, and occupier of such lands, defining in each case the particular lands intended to be taken, and requiring an answer stating whether the person so served assents, dissents, or is neuter in respect of the taking such lands ;

(3.) On compliance with the provisions of this section with respect to advertisements and notices, and not sooner than fourteen days after the service of the last-mentioned notices, the Sanitary Authority may, if they think fit, present a petition under their seal to the Local Government Board. The petition shall state the lands intended to be taken, and the purposes for which they are required, and the names of the owners, lessees, and occupiers of lands who have assented, dissented, or are neuter in respect of the taking such lands, or who have returned no answer to the notice ; it shall pray that the Sanitary Authority may, with reference to such lands, be allowed to put in force the powers of the Lands Clauses Acts with respect to the purchase and taking of lands otherwise than by agreement, and such prayer shall be supported by such evidence as the Local Government Board requires.

(4.) On the receipt of such petition, and on due proof of the proper advertisements having been published, and notices served, the Local Government Board shall take such petition into consideration, and may either dismiss the same, or direct a local inquiry as to the propriety of assenting to the prayer of such petition ; but until such inquiry has been made no provisional order shall be made affecting any lands without the consent of the owners, lessees, and occupiers thereof.

(5.) After the completion of such inquiry the Local Government Board may, by provisional order, empower the Sanitary Authority to put in force, with reference to the lands referred to in such order, the powers of the Lands Clauses Acts with respect to the purchase and taking of lands otherwise than by agreement, or any of them, and either absolutely or with such conditions and modifications as the Board may think fit, and it shall be the duty of the Sanitary Authority to serve a copy of any order so made in the manner and on the persons in which and on whom notices in respect of such lands are required to be served.

Provided that the notices by this section required to be given in the months of November and December may be given in the months of September and October, or of October and November, but in either of such last-mentioned cases an inquiry preliminary to the provisional order to which such notices refer, shall not be held until the expiration of one month from the last day of the second of the two months in which the notices are given ; and any notices or orders by this section required to be served on a number of persons having any right in, over, or on lands in common, may be served on any three or more of such persons on behalf of all such persons.

[illegible]

[illegible]	[illegible]	[illegible]		[illegible]
		[illegible]	[illegible]	
[illegible]				
[illegible]	[illegible]	—	[illegible]	[illegible]
[illegible]				
[illegible]	[illegible]	[illegible]	—	[illegible]
[illegible]				
[illegible]	[illegible]	[illegible]	—	[illegible]
[illegible]	Do.	Do.	—	[illegible]
[illegible]				
[illegible]	[illegible]	[illegible]	—	[illegible]
[illegible]	Do.	[illegible]	—	[illegible]
[illegible]	[illegible]	[illegible]	—	[illegible]
[illegible]				
[illegible]	[illegible]	[illegible]	—	[illegible]
[illegible]				
[illegible]	[illegible]	—	[illegible]	[illegible]
[illegible]				
[illegible]	[illegible]	[illegible]	—	[illegible]

[illegible]				
[illegible] Town	[illegible]	—	[illegible]	The [illegible]
[illegible] Town	[illegible]	Providing a new pump [illegible]	—	The [illegible]
[illegible]	[illegible]	Supply of water	—	The [illegible]
[illegible]				
[illegible]	[illegible]	Providing a [illegible]	—	The [illegible]
[illegible]	[illegible]	—	[illegible]	The [illegible]
[illegible]				
[illegible]	[illegible]	Providing a pump	—	The [illegible]
[illegible] Town	[illegible]	Supply of water	[illegible]	The [illegible]
[illegible]				
[illegible]	[illegible]	Providing a [illegible]	—	The [illegible]
[illegible]				
[illegible] Town	[illegible]	Providing a pump	—	The [illegible]
[illegible]				
[illegible]	[illegible]	—	[illegible]	The [illegible]
[illegible]				
[illegible]	[illegible]	—	[illegible]	The [illegible]
[illegible]	[illegible]	Providing a [illegible]	—	The [illegible]
[illegible]	[illegible]	[illegible]	—	The [illegible]

[illegible]

[illegible]	[illegible]	[illegible]		[illegible]
		[illegible]	[illegible]	
[illegible]				
[illegible]	[illegible]	[illegible]	—	[illegible]
[illegible]				
[illegible]	[illegible]	[illegible]	—	[illegible]
[illegible]				
[illegible]	[illegible]	[illegible]	—	[illegible]
[illegible]				
[illegible]	[illegible]	[illegible]	—	[illegible]
[illegible]				
[illegible]	[illegible]	[illegible]	—	[illegible]
[illegible]				
[illegible]	[illegible]	[illegible]	—	[illegible]
[illegible]	[illegible]	—	[illegible]	[illegible]
[illegible]				
[illegible]	[illegible]	—	[illegible]	[illegible]
[illegible]	[illegible]	[illegible]	—	[illegible]

APPENDIX D.

TABLES CONNECTED WITH POOR RELIEF AND EXPENDITURE.

No. 1.—A Return (in pursuance of the 29th Section of the Act 10 Vic., c. 31) [illegible] Relieved In and Out of the Workhouse, together with the Receipts in each [illegible] Expenses under Medical Charities, Registration, Sanitary, Burial Grounds, [illegible] the Total Expenditure out of the Poor Rates during the Year.

Part 1.—Return showing the Receipts and Expenditure [illegible]

1.	2.	3.	4.	5.	6.	7.	8.	9.	10.	11.	12.	13.
PROVINCE OF ULSTER.	£	£	£	£	£	£	£	£	£	£	£	£
Antrim.												
Antrim,	[illegible]	[illegible]	[illegible]	[illegible]	[illegible]	[illegible]	[illegible]	[illegible]	[illegible]	[illegible]	[illegible]	[illegible]
Ballycastle,	[illegible]	[illegible]	[illegible]	[illegible]	[illegible]	[illegible]	[illegible]	[illegible]	[illegible]	[illegible]	[illegible]	[illegible]
Ballymena,	[illegible]	[illegible]	[illegible]	[illegible]	[illegible]	[illegible]	[illegible]	[illegible]	[illegible]	[illegible]	[illegible]	[illegible]
Ballymoney,	[illegible]	[illegible]	[illegible]	[illegible]	[illegible]	[illegible]	[illegible]	[illegible]	[illegible]	[illegible]	[illegible]	[illegible]
Belfast,	[illegible]	[illegible]	[illegible]	[illegible]	[illegible]	[illegible]	[illegible]	[illegible]	[illegible]	[illegible]	[illegible]	[illegible]
Larne,	[illegible]	[illegible]	[illegible]	[illegible]	[illegible]	[illegible]	[illegible]	[illegible]	[illegible]	[illegible]	[illegible]	[illegible]
Lisburn,	[illegible]	[illegible]	[illegible]	[illegible]	[illegible]	[illegible]	[illegible]	[illegible]	[illegible]	[illegible]	[illegible]	[illegible]
Armagh.												
Armagh,	[illegible]	[illegible]	[illegible]	[illegible]	[illegible]	[illegible]	[illegible]	[illegible]	[illegible]	[illegible]	[illegible]	[illegible]
Lurgan,	[illegible]	[illegible]	[illegible]	[illegible]	[illegible]	[illegible]	[illegible]	[illegible]	[illegible]	[illegible]	[illegible]	[illegible]
Cavan.												
Bailieborough,	[illegible]	[illegible]	[illegible]	[illegible]	[illegible]	[illegible]	[illegible]	[illegible]	[illegible]	[illegible]	[illegible]	[illegible]
Bawnboy,	[illegible]	[illegible]	[illegible]	[illegible]	[illegible]	[illegible]	[illegible]	[illegible]	[illegible]	[illegible]	[illegible]	[illegible]
Cavan,	[illegible]	[illegible]	[illegible]	[illegible]	[illegible]	[illegible]	[illegible]	[illegible]	[illegible]	[illegible]	[illegible]	[illegible]
Cootehill,	[illegible]	[illegible]	[illegible]	[illegible]	[illegible]	[illegible]	[illegible]	[illegible]	[illegible]	[illegible]	[illegible]	[illegible]
Donegal.												
Ballyshannon,	[illegible]	[illegible]	[illegible]	[illegible]	[illegible]	[illegible]	[illegible]	[illegible]	[illegible]	[illegible]	[illegible]	[illegible]
Donegal,	[illegible]	[illegible]	[illegible]	[illegible]	[illegible]	[illegible]	[illegible]	[illegible]	[illegible]	[illegible]	[illegible]	[illegible]
Dunfanaghy,	[illegible]	[illegible]	[illegible]	[illegible]	[illegible]	[illegible]	[illegible]	[illegible]	[illegible]	[illegible]	[illegible]	[illegible]
Glenties,	[illegible]	[illegible]	[illegible]	[illegible]	[illegible]	[illegible]	[illegible]	[illegible]	[illegible]	[illegible]	[illegible]	[illegible]
Inishowen,	[illegible]	[illegible]	[illegible]	[illegible]	[illegible]	[illegible]	[illegible]	[illegible]	[illegible]	[illegible]	[illegible]	[illegible]
Letterkenny,	[illegible]	[illegible]	[illegible]	[illegible]	[illegible]	[illegible]	[illegible]	[illegible]	[illegible]	[illegible]	[illegible]	[illegible]
Milford,	[illegible]	[illegible]	[illegible]	[illegible]	[illegible]	[illegible]	[illegible]	[illegible]	[illegible]	[illegible]	[illegible]	[illegible]
Stranorlar,	[illegible]	[illegible]	[illegible]	[illegible]	[illegible]	[illegible]	[illegible]	[illegible]	[illegible]	[illegible]	[illegible]	[illegible]
Down.												
Banbridge,	[illegible]	[illegible]	[illegible]	[illegible]	[illegible]	[illegible]	[illegible]	[illegible]	[illegible]	[illegible]	[illegible]	[illegible]
Downpatrick,	[illegible]	[illegible]	[illegible]	[illegible]	[illegible]	[illegible]	[illegible]	[illegible]	[illegible]	[illegible]	[illegible]	[illegible]
Kilkeel,	[illegible]	[illegible]	[illegible]	[illegible]	[illegible]	[illegible]	[illegible]	[illegible]	[illegible]	[illegible]	[illegible]	[illegible]
Newry,	[illegible]	[illegible]	[illegible]	[illegible]	[illegible]	[illegible]	[illegible]	[illegible]	[illegible]	[illegible]	[illegible]	[illegible]
Newtownards,	[illegible]	[illegible]	[illegible]	[illegible]	[illegible]	[illegible]	[illegible]	[illegible]	[illegible]	[illegible]	[illegible]	[illegible]
Fermanagh.												
Enniskillen,	[illegible]	[illegible]	[illegible]	[illegible]	[illegible]	[illegible]	[illegible]	[illegible]	[illegible]	[illegible]	[illegible]	[illegible]
Irvinestown,	[illegible]	[illegible]	[illegible]	[illegible]	[illegible]	[illegible]	[illegible]	[illegible]	[illegible]	[illegible]	[illegible]	[illegible]
Lisnaskea,	[illegible]	[illegible]	[illegible]	[illegible]	[illegible]	[illegible]	[illegible]	[illegible]	[illegible]	[illegible]	[illegible]	[illegible]
Londonderry.												
Coleraine,	[illegible]	[illegible]	[illegible]	[illegible]	[illegible]	[illegible]	[illegible]	[illegible]	[illegible]	[illegible]	[illegible]	[illegible]
Limavady,	[illegible]	[illegible]	[illegible]	[illegible]	[illegible]	[illegible]	[illegible]	[illegible]	[illegible]	[illegible]	[illegible]	[illegible]
Londonderry,	[illegible]	[illegible]	[illegible]	[illegible]	[illegible]	[illegible]	[illegible]	[illegible]	[illegible]	[illegible]	[illegible]	[illegible]
Magherafelt,	[illegible]	[illegible]	[illegible]	[illegible]	[illegible]	[illegible]	[illegible]	[illegible]	[illegible]	[illegible]	[illegible]	[illegible]
Monaghan.												
Carrickmacross,	[illegible]	[illegible]	[illegible]	[illegible]	[illegible]	[illegible]	[illegible]	[illegible]	[illegible]	[illegible]	[illegible]	[illegible]
Castleblayney,	[illegible]	[illegible]	[illegible]	[illegible]	[illegible]	[illegible]	[illegible]	[illegible]	[illegible]	[illegible]	[illegible]	[illegible]
Clones,	[illegible]	[illegible]	[illegible]	[illegible]	[illegible]	[illegible]	[illegible]	[illegible]	[illegible]	[illegible]	[illegible]	[illegible]
Monaghan,	[illegible]	[illegible]	[illegible]	[illegible]	[illegible]	[illegible]	[illegible]	[illegible]	[illegible]	[illegible]	[illegible]	[illegible]
Tyrone.												
Castlederg,	[illegible]	[illegible]	[illegible]	[illegible]	[illegible]	[illegible]	[illegible]	[illegible]	[illegible]	[illegible]	[illegible]	[illegible]
Clogher,	[illegible]	[illegible]	[illegible]	[illegible]	[illegible]	[illegible]	[illegible]	[illegible]	[illegible]	[illegible]	[illegible]	[illegible]
Cookstown,	[illegible]	[illegible]	[illegible]	[illegible]	[illegible]	[illegible]	[illegible]	[illegible]	[illegible]	[illegible]	[illegible]	[illegible]
Dungannon,	[illegible]	[illegible]	[illegible]	[illegible]	[illegible]	[illegible]	[illegible]	[illegible]	[illegible]	[illegible]	[illegible]	[illegible]
Gortin,	[illegible]	[illegible]	[illegible]	[illegible]	[illegible]	[illegible]	[illegible]	[illegible]	[illegible]	[illegible]	[illegible]	[illegible]
Omagh,	[illegible]	[illegible]	[illegible]	[illegible]	[illegible]	[illegible]	[illegible]	[illegible]	[illegible]	[illegible]	[illegible]	[illegible]
Strabane,	[illegible]	[illegible]	[illegible]	[illegible]	[illegible]	[illegible]	[illegible]	[illegible]	[illegible]	[illegible]	[illegible]	[illegible]
Total, Ulster, [illegible]	[illegible]	[illegible]	[illegible]	[illegible]	[illegible]	[illegible]	[illegible]	[illegible]	[illegible]	[illegible]	[illegible]	[illegible]
Total, Ulster, [illegible]	[illegible]	[illegible]	[illegible]	[illegible]	[illegible]	[illegible]	[illegible]	[illegible]	[illegible]	[illegible]	[illegible]	[illegible]
Increase,	[illegible]	[illegible]	[illegible]	[illegible]	–	[illegible]	[illegible]	[illegible]	[illegible]	[illegible]	[illegible]	[illegible]
Decrease,	–	–	–	–	[illegible]	[illegible]	–	–	–	–	–	–

of the EXPENDITURE on the RELIEF of the POOR, and of the TOTAL NUMBERS … UNION in IRELAND, for the Year ended 29th September, 1882; also showing the Superannuation, Cattle Disease (Animals), and National School Teachers Acts, and of Unions during the Year ended 29th September, 1882.

Expenditure. [illegible] (14.)	[illegible] (15.)	Expenditure under the Superannuation Acts. (16.)	[illegible] Cattle Diseases Act … Rate. (17.)	Expenditure under the [illegible] Acts. (18.)	[illegible] (19.)	[illegible] (20.)	[illegible] (21.)	[illegible] (22.)	Valuation of … Sept. 1882. (23.)	Poundage on the Valuation. [illegible] (24.)	[illegible] (25.)	Names of [illegible] (26.)
£	£	£	£	£	£	£	£	£	£	s. d.	s. d.	PROVINCE OF ULSTER. ANTRIM.
895	77	161	22	66	182	–	6,097	440	126,801	1 8	0 10½	Antrim.
[illegible]	21	[illegible]	–	16	42	–	2,1[illegible]	[illegible]	54,[illegible]	0 5	0 11	Ballycastle.
1,2[illegible]	156	246	190	–	156	–	9,979	317	183,782	1 7	1 0½	Ballymena.
[illegible]	65	260	145	110	111	–	4,161	–	83,376	0 7½	1 0	Ballymoney.
4,738	[illegible]	857	64	177	465	6,157	64,092	–	750,[illegible]	1 [illegible]	1 [illegible]	Belfast.
[illegible]	[illegible]	[illegible]	–	69	111	817	4,571	179	169,[illegible]	0 [illegible]	1 [illegible]	Larne.
1,[illegible]	132	941	1	–	738	83	7,816	–	176,879	0 [illegible]	0 10	Lisburn.
												ARMAGH.
2,036	158	367	–	340	394	–	9,181	838	208,617	0 6½	0 6½	Armagh.
1,471	148	148	64	69	319	17	7,786	–	160,243	0 [illegible]	1 1	Lurgan.
												CAVAN.
348	65	170	–	38	66	–	3,970	1,117	60,334	1 3½	1 6½	Bailieborough.
643	36	169	6	18	62	–	3,071	1,989	33,574	1 4½	1 10	Bawnboy.
1,264	24	816	34	32	306	630	9,600	1,061	113,640	1 0	1 7½	Cavan.
[illegible]	41	139	9	–	141	6	3,611	1,619	73,689	0 8½	0 10	Cootehill.
												DONEGAL.
1,078	56	168	–	11	77	–	3,634	697	49,794	0 10½	1 8	Ballyshannon.
742	65	147	11	–	21	–	3,913	1,030	34,536	1 1	1 6½	Donegal.
415	59	69	4	120	28	–	1,694	–	11,375	1 7	3 10½	Dunfanaghy.
[illegible]	77	180	–	60	55	–	3,133	790	30,[illegible]	2 1	2 5½	Glenties.
1,097	87	234	–	–	9	–	4,736	1,498	69,164	1 6	0 9	Inishowen.
685	21	386	4	27	44	–	3,431	612	81,[illegible]	1 7	1 4½	Letterkenny.
519	36	461	21	–	27	160	3,397	2,077	36,971	1 6	1 6½	Milford.
659	65	112	–	97	33	–	3,107	693	60,080	0 11½	1 6½	Stranorlar.
												DOWN.
1,631	182	420	5	77	391	–	6,739	466	168,837	0 7½	0 10	Banbridge.
1,437	160	364	–	83	148	739	6,820	711	177,387	0 6½	0 9½	Downpatrick.
618	64	1,769	1	–	66	–	3,[illegible]	128	63,762	0 6½	1 10	Kilkeel.
1,[illegible]	60	626	–	73	69	784	11,337	2,160	168,630	0 10½	1 4½	Newry.
1,[illegible]	62	600	136	–	161	–	6,[illegible]	739	143,[illegible]	0 [illegible]	1 1½	Newtownards.
												FERMANAGH.
1,537	68	836	58	163	165	150	6,477	831	188,781	0 9	1 8½	Enniskillen.
[illegible]	38	169	6	17	71	630	3,976	572	68,115	0 7½	1 1	Irvinestown.
[illegible]	11	97	–	61	75	–	3,137	650	60,[illegible]	0 [illegible]	1 6½	Lisnaskea.
												LONDONDERRY.
845	160	643	6	–	159	–	6,348	890	162,879	0 6½	1 0½	Coleraine.
[illegible]	61	653	85	70	70	–	5,466	1,354	68,146	0 7	1 0	Limavady.
1,[illegible]	146	346	22	61	165	–	6,[illegible]	788	161,570	0 6	0 10	Londonderry.
611	69	174	19	67	158	–	6,[illegible]	–	93,336	0 8½	1 6	Magherafelt.
												MONAGHAN.
[illegible]	41	68	4	–	73	–	3,449	748	68,[illegible]	1 0½	1 4½	Carrickmacross.
919	64	337	–	–	147	10	4,910	2,146	75,763	0 10½	1 2½	Castleblayney.
686	35	133	–	186	97	–	2,381	419	87,641	0 5	0 9½	Clones.
1,334	89	346	11	30	159	–	4,316	2,130	94,[illegible]	0 7	0 11	Monaghan.
												TYRONE.
379	39	125	–	1	66	–	1,441	768	35,[illegible]	0 9½	1 3	Castlederg.
725	39	241	9	22	91	–	2,928	663	64,[illegible]	0 8	1 1½	Clogher.
763	59	160	34	108	71	–	4,777	2,181	85,677	0 10	1 0½	Cookstown.
[illegible]	73	1,[illegible]	–	65	114	630	6,[illegible]	1,[illegible]	94,[illegible]	0 9	1 4	Dungannon.
[illegible]	77	47	1	–	73	–	2,[illegible]	[illegible]	36,[illegible]	1 0	1 [illegible]	Gortin.
1,[illegible]	81	1,167	–	166	166	–	6,[illegible]	2,[illegible]	94,[illegible]	0 6	1 [illegible]	Omagh.
1,[illegible]	73	1,[illegible]	75	68	125	340	7,[illegible]	630	138,[illegible]	0 10	1 [illegible]	Strabane.
[illegible]	3,784	26,[illegible]	941	3,401	4,637	8,707	300,176	47,196	4,[illegible]	0 10	1 [illegible]	1882, } Total
[illegible]	3,831	25,179	646	3,446	6,546	6,827	293,[illegible]	58,[illegible]	4,[illegible]	0 10	1 [illegible]	1881, } ULSTER.
1,[illegible]	–	1,419	294	–	–	730	9,216	–	18,[illegible]	–	0 0½	Increase.
–	47	–	–	5	611	–	–	1,[illegible]	–		–	Decrease.

[continued.

No. 1.—Part 1.—Return showing the Receipts and Expenditure

Name of County and Union.	Receipts.				[illegible]	Expenditure.						
	[illegible]	[illegible]	[illegible]	[illegible]		[illegible]	[illegible]	[illegible]	[illegible]	[illegible]	[illegible]	[illegible]
1.	2.	3.	4.	5.	6.	7.	8.	9.	10.	11.	12.	13.
PROVINCE OF MUNSTER.	£	£	£	£	£	£	£	£	£	£	£	£
CLARE.												
Ballyvaughan,	[illegible]	[illegible]	[illegible]	[illegible]	[illegible]	[illegible]	[illegible]	[illegible]	[illegible]	[illegible]	[illegible]	[illegible]
Corrofin,	[illegible]	[illegible]	[illegible]	[illegible]	[illegible]	[illegible]	[illegible]	[illegible]	[illegible]	[illegible]	[illegible]	[illegible]
Ennis,	[illegible]	[illegible]	[illegible]	[illegible]	[illegible]	[illegible]	[illegible]	[illegible]	[illegible]	[illegible]	[illegible]	[illegible]
Ennistymon,	[illegible]	[illegible]	[illegible]	[illegible]	[illegible]	[illegible]	[illegible]	[illegible]	[illegible]	[illegible]	[illegible]	[illegible]
Kildysart,	[illegible]	[illegible]	[illegible]	[illegible]	[illegible]	[illegible]	[illegible]	[illegible]	[illegible]	[illegible]	[illegible]	[illegible]
Kilrush,	[illegible]	[illegible]	[illegible]	[illegible]	[illegible]	[illegible]	[illegible]	[illegible]	[illegible]	[illegible]	[illegible]	[illegible]
Scariff,	[illegible]	[illegible]	[illegible]	[illegible]	[illegible]	[illegible]	[illegible]	[illegible]	[illegible]	[illegible]	[illegible]	[illegible]
Tulla,	[illegible]	[illegible]	[illegible]	[illegible]	[illegible]	[illegible]	[illegible]	[illegible]	[illegible]	[illegible]	[illegible]	[illegible]
CORK.												
Bandon,	[illegible]	[illegible]	[illegible]	[illegible]	[illegible]	[illegible]	[illegible]	[illegible]	[illegible]	[illegible]	[illegible]	[illegible]
Bantry,	[illegible]	[illegible]	[illegible]	[illegible]	[illegible]	[illegible]	[illegible]	[illegible]	[illegible]	[illegible]	[illegible]	[illegible]
Castletown,	[illegible]	[illegible]	[illegible]	[illegible]	[illegible]	[illegible]	[illegible]	[illegible]	[illegible]	[illegible]	[illegible]	[illegible]
Clonakilty,	[illegible]	[illegible]	[illegible]	[illegible]	[illegible]	[illegible]	[illegible]	[illegible]	[illegible]	[illegible]	[illegible]	[illegible]
Cork,	[illegible]	[illegible]	[illegible]	[illegible]	[illegible]	[illegible]	[illegible]	[illegible]	[illegible]	[illegible]	[illegible]	[illegible]
Dunmanway,	[illegible]	[illegible]	[illegible]	[illegible]	[illegible]	[illegible]	[illegible]	[illegible]	[illegible]	[illegible]	[illegible]	[illegible]
Fermoy,	[illegible]	[illegible]	[illegible]	[illegible]	[illegible]	[illegible]	[illegible]	[illegible]	[illegible]	[illegible]	[illegible]	[illegible]
Kanturk,	[illegible]	[illegible]	[illegible]	[illegible]	[illegible]	[illegible]	[illegible]	[illegible]	[illegible]	[illegible]	[illegible]	[illegible]
Kinsale,	[illegible]	[illegible]	[illegible]	[illegible]	[illegible]	[illegible]	[illegible]	[illegible]	[illegible]	[illegible]	[illegible]	[illegible]
Macroom,	[illegible]	[illegible]	[illegible]	[illegible]	[illegible]	[illegible]	[illegible]	[illegible]	[illegible]	[illegible]	[illegible]	[illegible]
Mallow,	[illegible]	[illegible]	[illegible]	[illegible]	[illegible]	[illegible]	[illegible]	[illegible]	[illegible]	[illegible]	[illegible]	[illegible]
Midleton,	[illegible]	[illegible]	[illegible]	[illegible]	[illegible]	[illegible]	[illegible]	[illegible]	[illegible]	[illegible]	[illegible]	[illegible]
Millstreet,	[illegible]	[illegible]	[illegible]	[illegible]	[illegible]	[illegible]	[illegible]	[illegible]	[illegible]	[illegible]	[illegible]	[illegible]
Mitchelstown,	[illegible]	[illegible]	[illegible]	[illegible]	[illegible]	[illegible]	[illegible]	[illegible]	[illegible]	[illegible]	[illegible]	[illegible]
Skibbereen,	[illegible]	[illegible]	[illegible]	[illegible]	[illegible]	[illegible]	[illegible]	[illegible]	[illegible]	[illegible]	[illegible]	[illegible]
Skull,	[illegible]	[illegible]	[illegible]	[illegible]	[illegible]	[illegible]	[illegible]	[illegible]	[illegible]	[illegible]	[illegible]	[illegible]
Youghal,	[illegible]	[illegible]	[illegible]	[illegible]	[illegible]	[illegible]	[illegible]	[illegible]	[illegible]	[illegible]	[illegible]	[illegible]
KERRY.												
Cahirciveen,	[illegible]	[illegible]	[illegible]	[illegible]	[illegible]	[illegible]	[illegible]	[illegible]	[illegible]	[illegible]	[illegible]	[illegible]
Dingle,	[illegible]	[illegible]	[illegible]	[illegible]	[illegible]	[illegible]	[illegible]	[illegible]	[illegible]	[illegible]	[illegible]	[illegible]
Kenmare,	[illegible]	[illegible]	[illegible]	[illegible]	[illegible]	[illegible]	[illegible]	[illegible]	[illegible]	[illegible]	[illegible]	[illegible]
Killarney,	[illegible]	[illegible]	[illegible]	[illegible]	[illegible]	[illegible]	[illegible]	[illegible]	[illegible]	[illegible]	[illegible]	[illegible]
Listowel,	[illegible]	[illegible]	[illegible]	[illegible]	[illegible]	[illegible]	[illegible]	[illegible]	[illegible]	[illegible]	[illegible]	[illegible]
Tralee,	[illegible]	[illegible]	[illegible]	[illegible]	[illegible]	[illegible]	[illegible]	[illegible]	[illegible]	[illegible]	[illegible]	[illegible]
LIMERICK.												
Croom,	[illegible]	[illegible]	[illegible]	[illegible]	[illegible]	[illegible]	[illegible]	[illegible]	[illegible]	[illegible]	[illegible]	[illegible]
Glin,	[illegible]	[illegible]	[illegible]	[illegible]	[illegible]	[illegible]	[illegible]	[illegible]	[illegible]	[illegible]	[illegible]	[illegible]
Kilmallock,	[illegible]	[illegible]	[illegible]	[illegible]	[illegible]	[illegible]	[illegible]	[illegible]	[illegible]	[illegible]	[illegible]	[illegible]
Limerick,	[illegible]	[illegible]	[illegible]	[illegible]	[illegible]	[illegible]	[illegible]	[illegible]	[illegible]	[illegible]	[illegible]	[illegible]
Newcastle,	[illegible]	[illegible]	[illegible]	[illegible]	[illegible]	[illegible]	[illegible]	[illegible]	[illegible]	[illegible]	[illegible]	[illegible]
Rathkeale,	[illegible]	[illegible]	[illegible]	[illegible]	[illegible]	[illegible]	[illegible]	[illegible]	[illegible]	[illegible]	[illegible]	[illegible]
TIPPERARY.												
Borrisokane,	[illegible]	[illegible]	[illegible]	[illegible]	[illegible]	[illegible]	[illegible]	[illegible]	[illegible]	[illegible]	[illegible]	[illegible]
Carrick-on-Suir,	[illegible]	[illegible]	[illegible]	[illegible]	[illegible]	[illegible]	[illegible]	[illegible]	[illegible]	[illegible]	[illegible]	[illegible]
Cashel,	[illegible]	[illegible]	[illegible]	[illegible]	[illegible]	[illegible]	[illegible]	[illegible]	[illegible]	[illegible]	[illegible]	[illegible]
Clogheen,	[illegible]	[illegible]	[illegible]	[illegible]	[illegible]	[illegible]	[illegible]	[illegible]	[illegible]	[illegible]	[illegible]	[illegible]
Clonmel,	[illegible]	[illegible]	[illegible]	[illegible]	[illegible]	[illegible]	[illegible]	[illegible]	[illegible]	[illegible]	[illegible]	[illegible]
Nenagh,	[illegible]	[illegible]	[illegible]	[illegible]	[illegible]	[illegible]	[illegible]	[illegible]	[illegible]	[illegible]	[illegible]	[illegible]
Roscrea,	[illegible]	[illegible]	[illegible]	[illegible]	[illegible]	[illegible]	[illegible]	[illegible]	[illegible]	[illegible]	[illegible]	[illegible]
Thurles,	[illegible]	[illegible]	[illegible]	[illegible]	[illegible]	[illegible]	[illegible]	[illegible]	[illegible]	[illegible]	[illegible]	[illegible]
Tipperary,	[illegible]	[illegible]	[illegible]	[illegible]	[illegible]	[illegible]	[illegible]	[illegible]	[illegible]	[illegible]	[illegible]	[illegible]
WATERFORD.												
Dungarvan,	[illegible]	[illegible]	[illegible]	[illegible]	[illegible]	[illegible]	[illegible]	[illegible]	[illegible]	[illegible]	[illegible]	[illegible]
Kilmacthomas,	[illegible]	[illegible]	[illegible]	[illegible]	[illegible]	[illegible]	[illegible]	[illegible]	[illegible]	[illegible]	[illegible]	[illegible]
Lismore,	[illegible]	[illegible]	[illegible]	[illegible]	[illegible]	[illegible]	[illegible]	[illegible]	[illegible]	[illegible]	[illegible]	[illegible]
Waterford,	[illegible]	[illegible]	[illegible]	[illegible]	[illegible]	[illegible]	[illegible]	[illegible]	[illegible]	[illegible]	[illegible]	[illegible]
Total, Munster in [illegible]	[illegible]	[illegible]	[illegible]	[illegible]	[illegible]	[illegible]	[illegible]	[illegible]	[illegible]	[illegible]	[illegible]	[illegible]
Total, Munster in [illegible]	[illegible]	[illegible]	[illegible]	[illegible]	[illegible]	[illegible]	[illegible]	[illegible]	[illegible]	[illegible]	[illegible]	[illegible]
Increase,	[illegible]	–	[illegible]	[illegible]	[illegible]	–	[illegible]	[illegible]	[illegible]	[illegible]	–	[illegible]
Decrease,	–	[illegible]	–	–	–	[illegible]	–	–	–	–	[illegible]	–

of Unions during the Year ended 29th September, 1882—*continued.*

Expenditure.								[illegible]	Valuation on [illegible] 1882.	Poundage on the Valuation.		Names of Unions and Towns.
[illegible]	[illegible]	[illegible]	[illegible]	[illegible]	[illegible]	[illegible]	[illegible]			[illegible]	[illegible]	
14.	15.	16.	17.	18.	19.	20.	21.	22.	23.	24.	25.	26.
£	£	£	£	£	£	£	£	£	£	s. d.	s. d.	**PROVINCE OF MUNSTER.**
												CLARE.
[illegible]	[illegible]	[illegible]	–	[illegible]	[illegible]	[illegible]	[illegible]	[illegible]	[illegible]	[illegible]	[illegible]	Ballyvaghan.
[illegible]	[illegible]	[illegible]	[illegible]	[illegible]	[illegible]	–	[illegible]	–	[illegible]	[illegible]	[illegible]	Corrofin.
[illegible]	[illegible]	[illegible]	[illegible]	[illegible]	[illegible]	–	[illegible]	[illegible]	[illegible]	[illegible]	[illegible]	Ennis.
[illegible]	[illegible]	[illegible]	[illegible]	[illegible]	[illegible]	–	[illegible]	–	[illegible]	[illegible]	[illegible]	Ennistymon.
[illegible]	[illegible]	[illegible]	[illegible]	[illegible]	[illegible]	–	[illegible]	–	[illegible]	[illegible]	[illegible]	Kildysart.
[illegible]	[illegible]	[illegible]	[illegible]	[illegible]	[illegible]	–	[illegible]	[illegible]	[illegible]	[illegible]	[illegible]	Kilrush.
[illegible]	[illegible]	[illegible]	[illegible]	[illegible]	[illegible]	–	[illegible]	[illegible]	[illegible]	[illegible]	[illegible]	Scariff.
[illegible]	[illegible]	[illegible]	[illegible]	[illegible]	[illegible]	–	[illegible]	[illegible]	[illegible]	[illegible]	[illegible]	Tulla.
												CORK.
[illegible]	[illegible]	[illegible]	–	[illegible]	[illegible]	–	[illegible]	[illegible]	[illegible]	[illegible]	[illegible]	Bandon.
[illegible]	[illegible]	[illegible]	–	–	[illegible]	–	[illegible]	[illegible]	[illegible]	[illegible]	[illegible]	Bantry.
[illegible]	[illegible]	[illegible]	[illegible]	[illegible]	[illegible]	–	[illegible]	[illegible]	[illegible]	[illegible]	[illegible]	Castletown.
[illegible]	[illegible]	[illegible]	–	[illegible]	[illegible]	–	[illegible]	[illegible]	[illegible]	[illegible]	[illegible]	Clonakilty.
[illegible]	[illegible]	[illegible]	[illegible]	[illegible]	[illegible]	–	[illegible]	[illegible]	[illegible]	[illegible]	[illegible]	Cork.
[illegible]	[illegible]	[illegible]	[illegible]	[illegible]	[illegible]	–	[illegible]	[illegible]	[illegible]	[illegible]	[illegible]	Dunmanway.
[illegible]	[illegible]	[illegible]	–	[illegible]	[illegible]	–	[illegible]	[illegible]	[illegible]	[illegible]	[illegible]	Fermoy.
[illegible]	[illegible]	[illegible]	[illegible]	[illegible]	[illegible]	–	[illegible]	[illegible]	[illegible]	[illegible]	[illegible]	Kanturk.
[illegible]	[illegible]	[illegible]	[illegible]	[illegible]	[illegible]	–	[illegible]	[illegible]	[illegible]	[illegible]	[illegible]	Kinsale.
[illegible]	[illegible]	[illegible]	[illegible]	[illegible]	[illegible]	–	[illegible]	[illegible]	[illegible]	[illegible]	[illegible]	Macroom.
[illegible]	[illegible]	[illegible]	–	[illegible]	[illegible]	[illegible]	[illegible]	[illegible]	[illegible]	[illegible]	[illegible]	Mallow.
[illegible]	[illegible]	[illegible]	[illegible]	[illegible]	[illegible]	–	[illegible]	[illegible]	[illegible]	[illegible]	[illegible]	Midleton.
[illegible]	[illegible]	[illegible]	[illegible]	[illegible]	[illegible]	–	[illegible]	[illegible]	[illegible]	[illegible]	[illegible]	Millstreet.
[illegible]	[illegible]	[illegible]	[illegible]	[illegible]	[illegible]	–	[illegible]	[illegible]	[illegible]	[illegible]	[illegible]	Mitchelstown.
[illegible]	[illegible]	[illegible]	[illegible]	[illegible]	[illegible]	–	[illegible]	–	[illegible]	[illegible]	[illegible]	Skibbereen.
[illegible]	[illegible]	[illegible]	[illegible]	[illegible]	[illegible]	–	[illegible]	–	[illegible]	[illegible]	[illegible]	Skull.
[illegible]	[illegible]	[illegible]	[illegible]	[illegible]	[illegible]	–	[illegible]	–	[illegible]	[illegible]	[illegible]	Youghal.
												KERRY.
[illegible]	[illegible]	[illegible]	[illegible]	[illegible]	[illegible]	–	[illegible]	–	[illegible]	[illegible]	[illegible]	Cahirciveen.
[illegible]	[illegible]	[illegible]	[illegible]	[illegible]	[illegible]	–	[illegible]	[illegible]	[illegible]	[illegible]	[illegible]	Dingle.
[illegible]	[illegible]	[illegible]	[illegible]	[illegible]	[illegible]	–	[illegible]	–	[illegible]	[illegible]	[illegible]	Kenmare.
[illegible]	[illegible]	[illegible]	[illegible]	[illegible]	–	–	[illegible]	[illegible]	[illegible]	[illegible]	[illegible]	Killarney.
[illegible]	[illegible]	[illegible]	–	[illegible]	[illegible]	–	[illegible]	[illegible]	[illegible]	[illegible]	[illegible]	Listowel.
[illegible]	[illegible]	[illegible]	[illegible]	[illegible]	[illegible]	–	[illegible]	–	[illegible]	[illegible]	[illegible]	Tralee.
												LIMERICK.
[illegible]	[illegible]	[illegible]	[illegible]	[illegible]	[illegible]	–	[illegible]	[illegible]	[illegible]	[illegible]	[illegible]	Croom.
[illegible]	[illegible]	[illegible]	–	[illegible]	[illegible]	–	[illegible]	[illegible]	[illegible]	[illegible]	[illegible]	Glin.
[illegible]	[illegible]	[illegible]	[illegible]	[illegible]	[illegible]	–	[illegible]	[illegible]	[illegible]	[illegible]	[illegible]	Kilmallock.
[illegible]	[illegible]	[illegible]	[illegible]	[illegible]	[illegible]	–	[illegible]	[illegible]	[illegible]	[illegible]	[illegible]	Limerick.
[illegible]	[illegible]	[illegible]	[illegible]	[illegible]	[illegible]	–	[illegible]	[illegible]	[illegible]	[illegible]	[illegible]	Newcastle.
[illegible]	[illegible]	[illegible]	[illegible]	[illegible]	[illegible]	–	[illegible]	[illegible]	[illegible]	[illegible]	[illegible]	Rathkeale.
												TIPPERARY.
[illegible]	[illegible]	[illegible]	–	[illegible]	[illegible]	–	[illegible]	[illegible]	[illegible]	[illegible]	[illegible]	Borrisokane.
[illegible]	[illegible]	[illegible]	–	[illegible]	[illegible]	–	[illegible]	[illegible]	[illegible]	[illegible]	[illegible]	Carrick-on-Suir.
[illegible]	[illegible]	[illegible]	[illegible]	[illegible]	[illegible]	–	[illegible]	[illegible]	[illegible]	[illegible]	[illegible]	Cashel.
[illegible]	[illegible]	[illegible]	[illegible]	[illegible]	[illegible]	–	[illegible]	[illegible]	[illegible]	[illegible]	[illegible]	Clogheen.
[illegible]	[illegible]	[illegible]	[illegible]	[illegible]	[illegible]	[illegible]	[illegible]	[illegible]	[illegible]	[illegible]	[illegible]	Clonmel.
[illegible]	[illegible]	[illegible]	–	[illegible]	[illegible]	–	[illegible]	[illegible]	[illegible]	[illegible]	[illegible]	Nenagh.
[illegible]	[illegible]	[illegible]	[illegible]	–	[illegible]	–	[illegible]	[illegible]	[illegible]	[illegible]	[illegible]	Roscrea.
[illegible]	[illegible]	[illegible]	[illegible]	[illegible]	[illegible]	–	[illegible]	[illegible]	[illegible]	[illegible]	[illegible]	Thurles.
[illegible]	[illegible]	[illegible]	[illegible]	[illegible]	[illegible]	–	[illegible]	[illegible]	[illegible]	[illegible]	[illegible]	Tipperary.
												WATERFORD.
[illegible]	[illegible]	[illegible]	–	[illegible]	[illegible]	–	[illegible]	[illegible]	[illegible]	[illegible]	[illegible]	Dungarvan.
[illegible]	[illegible]	[illegible]	–	[illegible]	[illegible]	–	[illegible]	[illegible]	[illegible]	[illegible]	[illegible]	Kilmacthomas.
[illegible]	[illegible]	[illegible]	[illegible]	[illegible]	[illegible]	–	[illegible]	[illegible]	[illegible]	[illegible]	[illegible]	Lismore.
[illegible]	[illegible]	[illegible]	[illegible]	[illegible]	[illegible]	[illegible]	[illegible]	[illegible]	[illegible]	[illegible]	[illegible]	Waterford.
[illegible]	[illegible]	[illegible]	[illegible]	[illegible]	[illegible]	[illegible]	[illegible]	[illegible]	[illegible]	[illegible]	[illegible]	1882, } Total, Munster.
[illegible]	[illegible]	[illegible]	[illegible]	[illegible]	[illegible]	[illegible]	[illegible]	[illegible]	[illegible]	[illegible]	[illegible]	1881, } Total, Munster.
[illegible]	–	[illegible]	[illegible]	[illegible]	–	[illegible]	[illegible]	[illegible]	[illegible]	[illegible]	[illegible]	Increase.
–	[illegible]	–	–	–	[illegible]	–	–	–	–	–	–	Decrease.

[*continued.*

No. 1.—Part 1.—Return showing the Receipts and Expenditure

Names of Counties and Unions.	Receipts.				[illegible]	Expenditure.						
	Amount of Poor Rate lodged.	Parliamentary Grant.	[illegible]	Total Receipts during the Year, exclusive of Bank Balances.	[illegible]	In-Maintenance.	Out-Relief.	[illegible]	[illegible]	Salaries and Rations of Officers.	All other Poor Law Expenditure.	Total Expenditure.
1.	2.	3.	4.	5.	6.	7.	8.	9.	10.	11.	12.	13.
PROVINCE OF LEINSTER.	£	£	£	£	£	£	£	£	£	£	£	£
CARLOW.												
Carlow,	10,379	876	281	10,480	482	4,860	3,260	64	[illegible]	1,782	1,866	11,261
DUBLIN.												
Balrothery,	7,236	632	765	8,607	–	1,651	1,316	77	–	878	744	4,886
Dublin, North,	48,858	9,823	6,415	65,512	–	38,860	4,369	770	18	3,915	3,829	52,425
Dublin, South,	74,218	8,746	6,880	82,754	–	37,184	6,268	684	620	6,607	12,834	60,361
Rathdown,	16,873	1,329	367	16,860	–	6,187	926	110	–	1,432	4,087	14,148
KILDARE.												
Athy,	12,288	730	136	13,187	697	4,472	1,948	17	8	888	1,117	8,678
Celbridge,	7,410	418	37	7,878	83	1,971	1,707	15	13	753	1,028	8,866
Naas,	10,123	895	488	11,506	480	3,404	2,760	36	187	1,185	888	8,868
KILKENNY.												
Callan,	9,563	441	8	10,024	224	3,836	1,031	80	30	957	748	4,888
Castlecomer,	4,346	376	52	4,774	418	1,627	707	–	–	745	624	3,873
Kilkenny,	11,686	838	258	12,782	321	4,330	7,041	11	8	1,387	1,077	14,833
Thomastown,	6,195	388	84	6,615	944	1,878	948	15	8	620	838	3,915
Urlingford,	3,289	397	68	3,711	–	1,748	715	80	–	536	530	3,367
KING'S CO.												
Edenderry,	6,647	634	1,442	8,023	179	1,863	684	40	–	640	848	4,071
Parsonstown,	6,825	683	101	6,971	235	3,310	440	35	5	714	830	4,870
Tullamore,	8,640	633	79	9,373	639	3,475	2,338	65	5	886	685	7,579
LONGFORD.												
Ballymahon,	4,178	303	8	4,860	783	1,414	371	28	8	688	464	2,883
Granard,	7,174	751	43	8,988	1,778	2,137	2,408	33	39	813	1,383	6,738
Longford,	8,461	453	116	6,888	1,646	2,867	1,279	44	30	771	1,088	6,048
LOUTH.												
Ardee,	6,886	376	184	7,739	648	3,880	1,657	49	38	715	667	6,886
Drogheda,	9,879	761	828	10,868	285	3,241	2,863	65	4	864	868	6,896
Dundalk,	7,864	685	578	8,753	416	3,880	2,330	111	–	926	789	6,194
MEATH.												
Dunshaughlin,	4,762	418	627	5,765	–	1,278	1,684	15	–	835	519	3,880
Kells,	8,873	643	88	8,894	630	2,834	1,616	47	77	697	869	4,381
Navan,	8,697	638	85	8,851	131	2,643	5,762	8	–	818	787	8,280
Oldcastle,	4,634	405	65	5,080	1,150	1,627	827	66	160	586	686	3,576
Trim,	7,132	334	836	7,891	640	2,265	2,388	81	88	788	642	6,071
QUEEN'S CO.												
Abbeyleix,	4,875	468	21	6,888	380	1,643	841	33	18	676	707	4,876
Donaghmore,	6,988	377	88	4,888	804	1,611	401	83	–	880	468	3,887
Mountmellick,	8,334	789	717	10,180	2,180	3,334	2,467	60	–	886	1,080	8,169
WESTMEATH.												
Athlone,	8,873	709	849	8,474	1,476	3,334	1,067	68	8	747	778	8,812
Delvin,	3,687	188	65	4,040	146	1,884	877	84	–	480	838	3,677
Mullingar,	11,888	549	144	12,861	150	8,880	6,446	80	286	1,080	1,488	10,184
WEXFORD.												
Enniscorthy,	8,808	780	28	9,615	538	3,578	7,331	16	–	811	988	7,880
Gorey,	3,746	888	88	4,560	519	1,673	579	3	36	644	889	3,577
New Ross,	9,348	617	19	10,108	640	4,321	3,308	66	81	844	1,314	9,688
Wexford,	8,635	680	87	9,417	163	3,336	1,337	63	–	968	1,487	8,838
WICKLOW.												
Baltinglass,	6,167	688	17	6,787	378	2,918	1,180	8	–	700	1,083	6,118
Rathdrum,	10,678	838	33	11,117	697	3,448	5,171	66	–	1,088	1,448	7,838
Shillelagh,	4,178	349	74	4,888	339	2,117	97	74	–	549	688	3,383
Total, Leinster { 1880	457,391	29,836	19,462	456,667	10,877	169,843	69,869	2,728	1,461	41,287	46,838	341,683
Total, Leinster { 1881	380,846	28,867	18,734	457,888	10,466	163,880	72,372	4,166	1,194	43,314	43,612	337,364
Increase,	17,828	–	1,166	47,795	–	3,889	–	–	267	806	3,616	8,674
Decrease,	–	431	–	–	171	–	2,873	575	–	–	–	–

of Unions during the Year ended 29th September, 1882—*continued.*

Expenditure. [illegible]	[illegible]	[illegible]	[illegible]	[illegible]	[illegible]	[illegible]	[illegible]	[illegible]	Valuation on [illegible] Sept. [illegible]	Poundage on the Valuation. [illegible]	[illegible]	Names of Counties and Unions.
14.	15.	16.	17.	18.	19.	20.	21.	22.	23.	24.	25.	26.
												PROVINCE OF LEINSTER.
£	£	£	£	£	£	£	£	£	£	s. d.	s. d.	CARLOW.
1,[illegible]	[illegible]	877	8	[illegible]	169	–	11,618	[illegible]	128,[illegible]	1 0¾	1 0½	Carlow.
												DUBLIN.
1,370	41	[illegible]	–	225	887	–	9,471	–	90,[illegible]	0 10½	1 4	Balrothery.
4,[illegible]	630	[illegible]	377	261	8,169	97	63,[illegible]	–	[illegible]	2 0	2 [illegible]	Dublin, North.
2,[illegible]	816	890	165	1,016	7,[illegible]	–	77,[illegible]	–	897,[illegible]	1 [illegible]	2 [illegible]	Dublin, South.
2,[illegible]	135	1,209	[illegible]	482	878	–	19,[illegible]	–	[illegible]	1 [illegible]	1 [illegible]	Rathdown.
												KILDARE.
1,[illegible]	58	780	31	96	285	–	11,[illegible]	1,087	111,[illegible]	1 [illegible]	1 11½	Athy.
687	35	159	31	50	371	–	7,[illegible]	197	115,[illegible]	1 [illegible]	1 [illegible]	Celbridge.
1,421	40	423	223	85	257	–	11,119	–	160,[illegible]	1 1½	1 [illegible]	Naas.
												KILKENNY.
[illegible]	80	216	15	226	116	–	7,[illegible]	240	72,[illegible]	1 6	1 11½	Callan.
470	87	301	–	98	42	246	4,473	917	32,634	2 [illegible]	3 6	Castlecomer.
1,[illegible]	81	263	–	209	136	–	11,746	617	100,390	2 [illegible]	2 4	Kilkenny.
528	37	210	13	98	110	–	4,730	116	68,988	1 1	1 4½	Thomastown.
810	19	150	26	–	84	–	4,311	–	43,740	1 [illegible]	1 3½	Urlingford.
												KING'S CO.
1,201	41	291	15	160	116	95	6,[illegible]	3,089	83,110	0 10½	1 6½	Edenderry.
1,[illegible]	66	317	6	61	191	–	8,[illegible]	854	107,943	0 7½	1 7	Parsonstown.
497	90	256	65	90	189	–	9,923	931	93,130	1 5½	2 1½	Tullamore.
												LONGFORD.
751	36	179	60	88	103	–	4,077	1,107	62,691	1 6	1 2½	Ballymahon.
1,143	35	190	12	10	124	–	8,[illegible]	2,[illegible]	80,[illegible]	1 [illegible]	1 11	Granard.
[illegible]	45	824	47	–	187	–	6,[illegible]	1,[illegible]	69,[illegible]	1 10	2 [illegible]	Longford.
												LOUTH.
[illegible]	33	218	6	87	163	–	6,784	678	96,[illegible]	1 1½	1 4½	Ardee.
1,[illegible]	71	260	91	59	[illegible]	–	10,418	[illegible]	188,[illegible]	1 [illegible]	1 6	Drogheda.
1,[illegible]	[illegible]	817	–	–	169	–	7,[illegible]	1,[illegible]	187,188	1 1½	1 6	Dundalk.
												MEATH.
[illegible]	83	165	–	–	451	–	4,[illegible]	–	185,[illegible]	0 [illegible]	0 11½	Dunshaughlin.
763	[illegible]	159	10	40	132	269	7,811	896	76,801	1 0	1 1	Kells.
[illegible]	[illegible]	180	42	188	141	976	7,897	360	89,[illegible]	1 [illegible]	1 1½	Navan.
651	[illegible]	117	1	115	126	–	4,810	781	80,[illegible]	1 [illegible]	1 [illegible]	Oldcastle.
[illegible]	[illegible]	207	27	85	317	220	7,718	720	142,[illegible]	1 1	1 8	Trim.
												QUEEN'S CO.
789	31	880	17	69	87	17	6,[illegible]	804	67,850	1 7½	1 6½	Abbeyleix.
318	11	188	8	161	61	64	7,769	337	41,102	1 5	1 1½	Donaghmore.
1,[illegible]	98	853	30	857	134	–	10,176	2,[illegible]	108,[illegible]	1 7	1 11½	Mountmellick.
												WESTMEATH.
1,967	83	347	66	118	111	–	8,[illegible]	1,[illegible]	89,121	1 11	1 6½	Athlone.
479	82	147	–	10	101	–	3,[illegible]	881	60,[illegible]	1 [illegible]	1 [illegible]	Delvin.
1,[illegible]	78	329	69	198	128	–	14,[illegible]	[illegible]	148,[illegible]	1 [illegible]	1 7	Mullingar.
												WEXFORD.
1,[illegible]	61	860	12	66	162	–	9,[illegible]	829	133,731	1 [illegible]	1 8	Enniscorthy.
757	45	220	8	–	166	–	4,[illegible]	380	80,467	0 10	1 1½	Gorey.
1,327	195	[illegible]	81	70	10	–	11,[illegible]	83	104,[illegible]	1 [illegible]	2 [illegible]	New Ross.
1,677	91	374	82	–	[illegible]	–	9,[illegible]	183	105,[illegible]	1 6	1 [illegible]	Wexford.
												WICKLOW.
880	37	156	127	8	117	–	6,437	875	73,762	1 4½	1 9	Baltinglass.
1,[illegible]	11	447	120	48	90	–	10,[illegible]	775	120,[illegible]	1 [illegible]	1 7	Rathdrum.
[illegible]	87	[illegible]	84	247	83	–	4,[illegible]	[illegible]	50,[illegible]	1 4½	1 [illegible]	Shillelagh.
17,[illegible]	3,083	14,697	8,751	6,051	39,765	1,[illegible]	438,075	21,[illegible]	1,791,[illegible]	1 5½	1 10	1882. } Total,
17,[illegible]	3,[illegible]	13,878	[illegible]	[illegible]	[illegible]	1,179	[illegible]	[illegible]	1,[illegible]	1 5½	1 10	1881. } LEINSTER.
140	–	[illegible]	148	119	–	71	[illegible]	[illegible]	14,771	–	–	Increase.
–	179	–	–	–	3,849	–	–	–	–	–	–	Decrease.

[*continued.*

No. 1. Part I.—Return showing the Receipts and Expenditure

Names of Provinces and Unions.	Receipts.					Expenditure.						
	Amount of Poor Rate Lodged.	Parliamentary Grant.	[illegible]	Total Receipts during the Year, exclusive of Seed Rate.	Seed Rate Lodged.	In-Maintenance.	Out-Relief.	[illegible]	[illegible]	Salaries and Rations of Officers.	All other Poor Relief Expenditure.	Total Poor Relief Expenditure.
1.	2.	3.	4.	5.	6.	7.	8.	9.	10.	11.	12.	13.
PROVINCE OF CONNAUGHT.	£	£	£	£	£	£	£	£	£	£	£	£
Galway.												
Ballinasloe,	[illegible]	610	[illegible]	[illegible]	4,941	[illegible]	112	32	–	[illegible]	[illegible]	[illegible]
Clifden,	[illegible]	[illegible]	[illegible]	[illegible]	–	1,1[illegible]	1,[illegible]	[illegible]	–	[illegible]	[illegible]	[illegible]
Galway,	[illegible]	341	310	7,0[illegible]	[illegible]	[illegible]	[illegible]	150	[illegible]	1,[illegible]	1,[illegible]	[illegible]
Glennamaddy,	[illegible]	[illegible]	–	[illegible]	[illegible]	[illegible]	[illegible]	–	[illegible]	[illegible]	[illegible]	[illegible]
Gort,	[illegible]	[illegible]	16	4,0[illegible]	[illegible]	[illegible]	[illegible]	[illegible]	[illegible]	[illegible]	[illegible]	[illegible]
Loughrea,	[illegible]	421	[illegible]	[illegible]	1,1[illegible]	[illegible]	414	[illegible]	[illegible]	[illegible]	[illegible]	[illegible]
Mountbellew,	[illegible]	[illegible]	[illegible]	[illegible]	1,[illegible]	[illegible]	114	[illegible]	–	[illegible]	[illegible]	[illegible]
Oughterard,	[illegible]	[illegible]	[illegible]	[illegible]	–	[illegible]	[illegible]	[illegible]	–	[illegible]	[illegible]	[illegible]
Portumna,	[illegible]	[illegible]	14	[illegible]	[illegible]	[illegible]	107	[illegible]	–	[illegible]	[illegible]	[illegible]
Tuam,	[illegible]	[illegible]	110	[illegible]	[illegible]	[illegible]	1,[illegible]	[illegible]	[illegible]	[illegible]	[illegible]	[illegible]
Leitrim.												
Carrick-on-Shannon,	[illegible]	[illegible]	[illegible]	[illegible]	1,[illegible]	[illegible]	[illegible]	[illegible]	[illegible]	[illegible]	[illegible]	[illegible]
Manorhamilton,	[illegible]	417	[illegible]	[illegible]	1,101	[illegible]	[illegible]	14	–	[illegible]	[illegible]	[illegible]
Mohill,	[illegible]	[illegible]	10	[illegible]	[illegible]	[illegible]	[illegible]	[illegible]	[illegible]	721	[illegible]	[illegible]
Mayo.												
Ballina,	[illegible]	[illegible]	[illegible]	[illegible]	[illegible]	[illegible]	[illegible]	[illegible]	–	[illegible]	[illegible]	[illegible]
Ballinrobe,	[illegible]	[illegible]	110	[illegible]	[illegible]	[illegible]	[illegible]	[illegible]	17	761	[illegible]	[illegible]
Belmullet,	[illegible]	[illegible]	[illegible]	[illegible]	[illegible]	[illegible]	[illegible]	16	–	[illegible]	[illegible]	[illegible]
Castlebar,	[illegible]	[illegible]	61	[illegible]	[illegible]	777	[illegible]	[illegible]	–	[illegible]	[illegible]	[illegible]
Claremorris,	[illegible]	[illegible]	[illegible]	[illegible]	[illegible]	[illegible]	[illegible]	[illegible]	4	[illegible]	[illegible]	[illegible]
Killala,	[illegible]	[illegible]	6	[illegible]	[illegible]	716	[illegible]	–	–	911	[illegible]	[illegible]
Newport,	[illegible]	[illegible]	[illegible]	[illegible]	[illegible]	[illegible]	[illegible]	30	–	[illegible]	[illegible]	[illegible]
Swinford,	[illegible]	[illegible]	[illegible]	[illegible]	[illegible]	[illegible]	[illegible]	[illegible]	[illegible]	[illegible]	1,[illegible]	[illegible]
Westport,	[illegible]	[illegible]	[illegible]	[illegible]	[illegible]	[illegible]	[illegible]	[illegible]	–	[illegible]	[illegible]	[illegible]
Roscommon.												
Boyle,	[illegible]	287	172	[illegible]	[illegible]	[illegible]	[illegible]	[illegible]	[illegible]	[illegible]	[illegible]	[illegible]
Castlerea,	[illegible]	471	[illegible]	[illegible]	[illegible]	[illegible]	[illegible]	[illegible]	[illegible]	[illegible]	[illegible]	[illegible]
Roscommon,	[illegible]	107	[illegible]	[illegible]	[illegible]	[illegible]	[illegible]	[illegible]	[illegible]	721	[illegible]	[illegible]
Strokestown,	4,710	[illegible]	37	[illegible]	[illegible]	[illegible]	1,[illegible]	[illegible]	[illegible]	417	[illegible]	[illegible]
Sligo.												
Dromore West,	[illegible]	810	[illegible]	[illegible]	[illegible]	[illegible]	[illegible]	4	4	410	410	[illegible]
Sligo,	[illegible]	[illegible]	[illegible]	[illegible]	[illegible]	[illegible]	1,[illegible]	36	–	[illegible]	1,[illegible]	[illegible]
Tobercurry,	[illegible]	410	[illegible]	[illegible]	[illegible]	[illegible]	[illegible]	[illegible]	–	[illegible]	[illegible]	[illegible]
Total, Connaught { [illegible]	[illegible]	[illegible]	[illegible]	141,[illegible]	[illegible]	[illegible]	17,[illegible]	[illegible]	[illegible]	[illegible]	[illegible]	[illegible]
Total, Connaught { [illegible]	[illegible]	[illegible]	[illegible]	[illegible]	[illegible]	[illegible]	[illegible]	[illegible]	[illegible]	[illegible]	19,[illegible]	[illegible]
Increase,	1,[illegible]	–	–	–	31,[illegible]	–	–	[illegible]	[illegible]	–	–	–
Decrease,	–	[illegible]	[illegible]	[illegible]	–	[illegible]	[illegible]	–	–	[illegible]	[illegible]	[illegible]

SUMMARY OF

Ulster,	[illegible]	[illegible]	[illegible]	[illegible]	[illegible]	[illegible]	[illegible]	[illegible]	[illegible]	[illegible]	[illegible]	[illegible]
Munster,	[illegible]	[illegible]	[illegible]	[illegible]	[illegible]	[illegible]	[illegible]	[illegible]	[illegible]	[illegible]	[illegible]	[illegible]
Leinster,	[illegible]	[illegible]	[illegible]	[illegible]	[illegible]	[illegible]	[illegible]	[illegible]	[illegible]	[illegible]	[illegible]	[illegible]
Connaught,	[illegible]	[illegible]	[illegible]	141,[illegible]	[illegible]	[illegible]	17,[illegible]	[illegible]	[illegible]	[illegible]	[illegible]	[illegible]
Total, Ireland, { [illegible]	[illegible]	[illegible]	[illegible]	[illegible]	[illegible]	[illegible]	[illegible]	11,[illegible]	[illegible]	[illegible]	[illegible]	[illegible]
Total, Ireland, { [illegible]	[illegible]	[illegible]	[illegible]	[illegible]	[illegible]	[illegible]	[illegible]	[illegible]	[illegible]	[illegible]	[illegible]	[illegible]
Increase,	[illegible]	–	–	[illegible]	[illegible]	[illegible]	–	–	[illegible]	[illegible]	[illegible]	[illegible]
Decrease,	–	[illegible]	[illegible]	–	–	–	[illegible]	[illegible]	–	–	–	–

of Unions during the Year ended 29th September, 1882—*continued.*

Expenditure. 14.	15.	16.	17.	18.	19.	20.	21.	22.	23.	Poundage on the Valuation. 24.	25.	Names of Provinces and Unions. 26.
£	£	£	£	£	£	£	£	£	£	s. d.	s. d.	PROVINCE OF CONNAUGHT.
												GALWAY.
[illegible]	47	[illegible]	45	26	[illegible]	-	[illegible]	[illegible]	[illegible]	[illegible]	[illegible]	Ballinasloe.
[illegible]	21	[illegible]	[illegible]	56	[illegible]	-	[illegible]	-	[illegible]	[illegible]	[illegible]	Clifden.
[illegible]	75	[illegible]	[illegible]	112	113	-	[illegible]	[illegible]	[illegible]	[illegible]	[illegible]	Galway.
[illegible]	[illegible]	[illegible]	[illegible]	[illegible]	[illegible]	-	[illegible]	-	[illegible]	[illegible]	[illegible]	Glennamaddy.
[illegible]	[illegible]	[illegible]	[illegible]	44	14	-	[illegible]	[illegible]	[illegible]	[illegible]	[illegible]	[illegible]
[illegible]	44	[illegible]	[illegible]	97	101	-	[illegible]	[illegible]	[illegible]	[illegible]	[illegible]	Loughrea.
[illegible]	[illegible]	[illegible]	[illegible]	-	[illegible]	-	[illegible]	[illegible]	[illegible]	[illegible]	[illegible]	[illegible]
[illegible]	[illegible]	[illegible]	-	[illegible]	[illegible]	-	[illegible]	-	[illegible]	[illegible]	[illegible]	Oughterard.
[illegible]	[illegible]	[illegible]	[illegible]	-	[illegible]	-	[illegible]	[illegible]	[illegible]	[illegible]	[illegible]	Portumna.
[illegible]	[illegible]	[illegible]	[illegible]	117	[illegible]	-	[illegible]	[illegible]	[illegible]	[illegible]	[illegible]	Tuam.
												[illegible]
[illegible]	[illegible]	[illegible]	[illegible]	[illegible]	[illegible]	-	[illegible]	[illegible]	[illegible]	[illegible]	[illegible]	[illegible]
[illegible]	[illegible]	[illegible]	[illegible]	[illegible]	[illegible]	-	[illegible]	[illegible]	[illegible]	[illegible]	[illegible]	[illegible]
[illegible]	[illegible]	[illegible]	[illegible]	[illegible]	[illegible]	-	[illegible]	[illegible]	[illegible]	[illegible]	[illegible]	[illegible]
												[illegible]
[illegible]	[illegible]	[illegible]	[illegible]	[illegible]	[illegible]	-	[illegible]	[illegible]	[illegible]	[illegible]	[illegible]	[illegible]
[illegible]	[illegible]	[illegible]	[illegible]	[illegible]	[illegible]	-	[illegible]	[illegible]	[illegible]	[illegible]	[illegible]	[illegible]
[illegible]	[illegible]	[illegible]	-	[illegible]	[illegible]	-	[illegible]	-	[illegible]	[illegible]	[illegible]	[illegible]
[illegible]	[illegible]	[illegible]	-	[illegible]	[illegible]	-	[illegible]	[illegible]	[illegible]	[illegible]	[illegible]	[illegible]
[illegible]	[illegible]	[illegible]	[illegible]	-	[illegible]	-	[illegible]	[illegible]	[illegible]	[illegible]	[illegible]	[illegible]
[illegible]	[illegible]	[illegible]	-	[illegible]	[illegible]	-	[illegible]	[illegible]	[illegible]	[illegible]	[illegible]	[illegible]
[illegible]	[illegible]	[illegible]	[illegible]	[illegible]	[illegible]	-	[illegible]	-	[illegible]	[illegible]	[illegible]	[illegible]
[illegible]	[illegible]	[illegible]	[illegible]	[illegible]	[illegible]	-	[illegible]	[illegible]	[illegible]	[illegible]	[illegible]	[illegible]
[illegible]	[illegible]	[illegible]	[illegible]	[illegible]	[illegible]	-	[illegible]	[illegible]	[illegible]	[illegible]	[illegible]	[illegible]
												[illegible]
[illegible]	[illegible]	[illegible]	[illegible]	[illegible]	[illegible]	-	[illegible]	[illegible]	[illegible]	[illegible]	[illegible]	[illegible]
[illegible]	[illegible]	[illegible]	[illegible]	[illegible]	[illegible]	-	[illegible]	[illegible]	[illegible]	[illegible]	[illegible]	[illegible]
[illegible]	[illegible]	[illegible]	-	[illegible]	[illegible]	-	[illegible]	[illegible]	[illegible]	[illegible]	[illegible]	[illegible]
[illegible]	[illegible]	[illegible]	[illegible]	[illegible]	[illegible]	-	[illegible]	[illegible]	[illegible]	[illegible]	[illegible]	[illegible]
												[illegible]
[illegible]	[illegible]	[illegible]	[illegible]	[illegible]	[illegible]	-	[illegible]	[illegible]	[illegible]	[illegible]	[illegible]	[illegible]
[illegible]	[illegible]	[illegible]	[illegible]	[illegible]	[illegible]	-	[illegible]	[illegible]	[illegible]	[illegible]	[illegible]	[illegible]
[illegible]	[illegible]	[illegible]	[illegible]	[illegible]	[illegible]	-	[illegible]	-	[illegible]	[illegible]	[illegible]	Tobercurry.
[illegible]	[illegible]	[illegible]	[illegible]	[illegible]	[illegible]	-	[illegible]	[illegible]	[illegible]	[illegible]	[illegible]	1882, Total, Connaught.
[illegible]	[illegible]	[illegible]	[illegible]	[illegible]	[illegible]	-	[illegible]	[illegible]	[illegible]	[illegible]	[illegible]	1881, Total, Connaught.
-	-	[illegible]	-	-	[illegible]	-	-	[illegible]	-	-	-	Increase.
[illegible]	[illegible]	-	[illegible]	[illegible]	-	-	[illegible]	-	[illegible]	[illegible]	[illegible]	Decrease.

PROVINCES.

14.	15.	16.	17.	18.	19.	20.	21.	22.	23.	24.	25.	26.
[illegible]	[illegible]	[illegible]	[illegible]	[illegible]	[illegible]	[illegible]	[illegible]	[illegible]	[illegible]	[illegible]	[illegible]	Ulster.
[illegible]	[illegible]	[illegible]	[illegible]	[illegible]	[illegible]	[illegible]	[illegible]	[illegible]	[illegible]	[illegible]	[illegible]	Munster.
[illegible]	[illegible]	[illegible]	[illegible]	[illegible]	[illegible]	[illegible]	[illegible]	[illegible]	[illegible]	[illegible]	[illegible]	Leinster.
[illegible]	[illegible]	[illegible]	[illegible]	[illegible]	[illegible]	-	[illegible]	[illegible]	[illegible]	[illegible]	[illegible]	Connaught.
[illegible]	[illegible]	[illegible]	[illegible]	[illegible]	[illegible]	[illegible]	[illegible]	[illegible]	[illegible]	[illegible]	[illegible]	1882, Total, Ireland.
[illegible]	[illegible]	[illegible]	[illegible]	[illegible]	[illegible]	[illegible]	[illegible]	[illegible]	[illegible]	[illegible]	[illegible]	1881, Total, Ireland.
[illegible]	-	[illegible]	[illegible]	[illegible]	-	[illegible]	[illegible]	[illegible]	[illegible]	-	-	Increase.
-	[illegible]	-	-	-	[illegible]	-	-	-	-	[illegible]	-	Decrease.

No. I. Part 2.—Return of the Number of Persons who received Poor Relief during the Year ended [illegible] September, 1862, together with the Expenditure for Provisions, [illegible], and Clothing of Workhouse Inmates during the Year, and the average Weekly Cost per head in the Workhouse.

PROVINCE OF ULSTER

Antrim.

Armagh.

Cavan.

Donegal.

[illegible]

[illegible]	[illegible]	[illegible]	[illegible]	[illegible]	[illegible]	[illegible]
[illegible]	[illegible]	[illegible]	[illegible]	[illegible]	[illegible]	[illegible]

SUMMARY OF PROVINCES.

No. 2.—Classification of Persons Relieved in the Union Workhouses in Ireland, during each of the Half Years ended 25th March and 29th September, 1852, respectively.

	Classes of Persons Relieved in the Workhouses.	No. in the Half-year ended 25th March, 1852.	No. in the Half-year ended 29th September, 1852.
	Able-bodied and their Children.		
1	Adults, Married Couples, Males,	4,573	4,395
2	Adults, Married Couples, Females,	4,373	4,595
3	Adults, Other Males,	59,773	57,637
4	Adults, Other Females,	28,685	26,031
5	Children under 15, of Able-bodied Inmates, Illegitimate,	6,293	7,761
6	Children under 15, of Able-bodied Inmates, Other Children,	18,574	23,115
	Not Able-bodied.		
7	Adults, Married Couples, Males,	793	869
8	Adults, Married Couples, Females,	791	869
9	Adults, Other Males,	26,859	25,763
10	Adults, Other Females,	19,131	21,719
11	Children under 15, Of Parents not able-bodied being Inmates, Illegitimate,	810	706
12	Children under 15, Of Parents not able-bodied being Inmates, Other Children,	1,538	2,253
13	Children under 15, Orphans, or other Children, relieved without Parents,	8,596	9,403
	Lunatics, Insane Persons, and Idiots.		
14	Adult Males,	1,467	1,589
15	Adult Females,	2,063	2,724
16	Children under 15,	119	108
17	Total number of Males,	93,655	93,282
18	Do. Females,	55,072	65,223
19	Do. Children under 15,	37,630	42,948
20	Grand Total,	185,017	201,363

No. 3.—CLASSIFICATION of PERSONS RELIEVED out of the WORKHOUSES in UNIONS in IRELAND, during each of the Half Years ended 25th March and 29th September, 1882, respectively, including Persons relieved in Blind and Deaf and Dumb Asylums.

	Classes of Persons Relieved.	Number in the Half-year ended 25th March, 1882.	Number in the Half-year ended 29th Sept., 1882.
1	Blind Persons maintained in Asylums, — Males,	120	114
2	— Females,	168	178
3	Deaf and Dumb Persons maintained in Asylums, — Males,	231	[illegible]
4	— Females,	191	181
	Total,	710	699
	RELIEVED UNDER 10 VIC., C. 31, SEC. 1.		
5	Adult Males permanently disabled by old age or infirmity,	8,390	8,879
6	Families of Adult Males under heading 5, — Wives,	4,499	4,170
7	— Children under 15,	2,365	2,578
8	Adult Males relieved in cases of their own sickness or accident,	7,028	7,660
9	Families of Adult Males under heading 8, — Wives,	5,261	5,036
10	— Children under 15,	15,704	16,768
11	Adult Women permanently disabled by old age or infirmity,	17,093	17,749
12	Children under 15, of Women under heading 11, — Legitimate,	472	453
13	— Illegitimate,	24	21
14	Adult Women relieved in cases of sickness or accident,	4,166	4,650
15	Children under 15, of Women under heading 14, — Legitimate,	2,724	3,316
16	— Illegitimate,	168	140
17	Able-bodied Widows, having two or more legitimate children dependent on them,	3,936	4,193
18	Children, under 15, dependent on Widows under heading 17,	13,450	14,177
19	Lunatics, Insane Persons, and Idiots, — Males,	41	60
20	— Females,	48	67
21	— Children under 15,	69	75
	Total,	85,437	91,185
	PERSONS RELIEVED UNDER 10 VIC., C. 31, BUT NOT UNDER SEC. 1.		
22	Adult Males, married or single, relieved on account of want of work,	13	163
23	Families of Adult Males under heading 22, — Wives,	17	19
24	— Children under 15,	23	37
25	Able-bodied Women, — Unmarried,	—	30
26	— Widows not relievable under sec. 1,	1	1
27	Children of Women under headings 25 and 26, — Legitimate,	—	—
28	— Illegitimate,	—	—
	Families Relieved without Husband or Father.		
29	Husband or Father in Gaol, — Wives,	48	64
30	— Children under 15,	164	142
31	Husband or Father on service in Army or Navy, — Wives,	—	—
32	— Children under 15,	—	—
33	Deserted by Husband or Father, — Wives,	1	8
34	— Children under 15,	5	16
35	Orphans and children relieved without either parent,	—	10
36	Number of persons relieved provisionally, and not included in the foregoing,	3,809	4,208
	Total,	4,096	4,701
37	Number of persons relieved under 11 & 12 Vic., c. 47, sec. 4, and 44 Vic., c. 4, sec. 2, and not included in the foregoing,	485	1,878
38	Orphans or Deserted Children out at Nurse under sec. 9 of 25 and 26 Vic., c. 83,	3,501	3,639
	Grand Total (Nos. 5 to 38 inclusive),	92,479	99,778

No. 4.—Summary of Returns from Clerks of Unions, showing for each Province, and for all Ireland, the Number of Persons admitted to the Workhouses during the Year ended 29th September, 1882, distinguishing the Number admitted in Sickness; also the Number of Births and Deaths in the Workhouses during the Year.

Provinces.	Number of Persons admitted during the Year.						No. of Births in the Workhouse during the Year.	No. of Deaths in the Workhouse during the Year.
	Number admitted in Sickness.				[illegible]	Total number admitted during the Year.		
	[illegible]	[illegible]	[illegible]	Total number admitted in Sickness.				
Ulster, . .	1,7[illegible]	1,[illegible]	[illegible]04	9,4[illegible]	53,7[illegible]	63,[illegible]46	4[illegible]	2,[illegible]
Munster, . .	[illegible]	15,77[illegible]	[illegible]	[illegible]	[illegible]	[illegible]	[illegible]	[illegible]
Leinster, . .	1,787	16,711	793	19,261	100,[illegible]	113,[illegible]	[illegible]	[illegible]
Connaught, . .	[illegible]	4,[illegible]	[illegible]	6,[illegible]	16,19[illegible]	71,[illegible]	1[illegible]	[illegible]
Total, Ireland,	7,274	44,631	2,672	54,615	236,161	291,[illegible]	1,[illegible]	10,[illegible]

No. 5.—Summary of Returns showing for each Province, and for all Ireland, the Number of Sick Persons who received Medical Treatment in the Workhouse Hospitals and Fever Hospitals, during the Year ended 29th September, 1882.

Provinces.	Under treatment at the commencement of the Year.				New Cases.				Total Cases treated in Hospitals during the Year.			
	Fever or other [illegible]	Other Diseases.	Accidentally Injured.	Total.	Fever or other [illegible]	Other Diseases.	Accidentally Injured.	Total.	Fever or other [illegible]	Other Diseases.	Accidentally Injured.	Total.
Ulster, . .	13[illegible]	[illegible]	[illegible]	3,[illegible]	[illegible]	17,[illegible]	[illegible]	[illegible]	[illegible]	[illegible]	[illegible]	[illegible]
Munster, . .	[illegible]	[illegible]	1[illegible]	[illegible]	4,[illegible]	[illegible]	1,[illegible]	31,[illegible]	[illegible]	[illegible]	[illegible]	[illegible]
Leinster, . .	[illegible]	[illegible]	167	[illegible]	[illegible]	[illegible]	[illegible]	[illegible]	[illegible]	[illegible]	[illegible]	[illegible]
Connaught, . .	[illegible]	1,76[illegible]	[illegible]	1,[illegible]	[illegible]	[illegible]	[illegible]	7,[illegible]	[illegible]	[illegible]	[illegible]	[illegible]
Total, Ireland,	27[illegible]	[illegible]	[illegible]	[illegible]	[illegible]	[illegible]	[illegible]	[illegible]	11,[illegible]	[illegible]	[illegible]	[illegible]

No. 4.—Statement (in pursuance of Sec. 29 of 12 & 13 Vic., c. 103) relative to the Audit of Union Accounts;—(in continuation of Statement in Tenth Annual Report of the Local Government Board (Ireland), 1882, Appendix D., No. 7).

I. Date up to which the Unions have been audited.

The Accounts of all the Unions have been audited up to [illegible] March, [illegible], except those of [illegible]; and up to [illegible] September, [illegible], except those of [illegible], and [illegible].

II. Sums disallowed or found due on Audit of the Accounts of Unions in Ireland, up to 29th September, 1882, and whether recovered or by means of Recovery from the Parties charged.

Union.	[illegible]	[illegible]	Amount [illegible]	Whether paid or by means of Recovery.	[illegible]
			£ s. d.		
[illegible]	[illegible]	[illegible]	[illegible]	Paid.	[illegible]
"	[illegible]	[illegible]	[illegible]	Paid.	[illegible]
Antrim	[illegible]	[illegible]	[illegible]	[illegible]	[illegible]
Athy	[illegible]	[illegible]	[illegible]	Paid.	[illegible]
"	[illegible]	[illegible]	[illegible]	Paid.	[illegible]
[illegible]	[illegible]	[illegible]	[illegible]	Paid.	[illegible]
"	[illegible]	[illegible]	[illegible]	Paid.	[illegible]
[illegible]	[illegible]	[illegible]	[illegible]	Paid.	[illegible]
[illegible]	"	[illegible]	[illegible]	Paid.	[illegible]
Callan	"	[illegible]	[illegible]	Paid.	[illegible]
"	"	"	[illegible]	Paid.	[illegible]

Sums disallowed or found due on Audit.

[illegible]	[illegible]	[illegible]	[illegible]	[illegible]	[illegible]
"	"	"	[illegible]	[illegible]	[illegible]
"	[illegible]	[illegible]	[illegible]	Not paid	[illegible]
"	"	"	[illegible]	Not paid	[illegible]
[illegible]	[illegible]	[illegible]	[illegible]	Paid	[illegible]
[illegible]	[illegible]	[illegible]	[illegible]	Not collected	[illegible]
[illegible]	"	[illegible]	[illegible]	Not collected	[illegible]
"	"	"	[illegible]	Not collected	[illegible]
"	"	"	[illegible]	Not collected	[illegible]
[illegible]	"	[illegible]	[illegible]	Not recovered	[illegible]
"	"	"	[illegible]	Paid	[illegible]
[illegible]	"	[illegible]	[illegible]	Not paid	[illegible]
[illegible]	[illegible]	[illegible]	[illegible]	In course of recovery	[illegible]
"	"	"	[illegible]	Paid	[illegible]
[illegible]	[illegible]	[illegible]	[illegible]	Paid	[illegible]
[illegible]	[illegible]	[illegible]	[illegible]	Not paid	[illegible]

[illegible]	[illegible]	[illegible]	[illegible]	[illegible]	[illegible]
[illegible]	"	[illegible]	[illegible]	Paid.	[illegible]
"			[illegible]	Paid.	
"	"	"	[illegible]	[illegible]	[illegible]
[illegible]	"	[illegible]	[illegible]	Paid.	[illegible]
[illegible]		[illegible]	[illegible]	Paid.	[illegible]
"	[illegible]	[illegible]	[illegible]	Not yet paid.	[illegible]
[illegible]	[illegible]	[illegible]	[illegible]	[illegible]	[illegible]
"	[illegible]	[illegible]	[illegible]	[illegible]	[illegible]
"	"	"	[illegible]	[illegible]	[illegible]
"	"	"	[illegible]	[illegible]	[illegible]
"	"	"	[illegible]	[illegible]	[illegible]
"	"	"	[illegible]	[illegible]	[illegible]
[illegible]	"	[illegible]	[illegible]	[illegible]	[illegible]
[illegible]	[illegible]	[illegible]	[illegible]	Paid.	[illegible]
"	[illegible]	[illegible]	[illegible]	Not yet [illegible]	[illegible]
"	"	"	[illegible]	Paid.	[illegible]
[illegible]	"	[illegible]	[illegible]	[illegible]	[illegible]
"	"	"	[illegible]	[illegible]	[illegible]
[illegible]	[illegible]	[illegible]	[illegible]	Paid.	[illegible]
"	[illegible]	[illegible]	[illegible]	Paid.	[illegible]

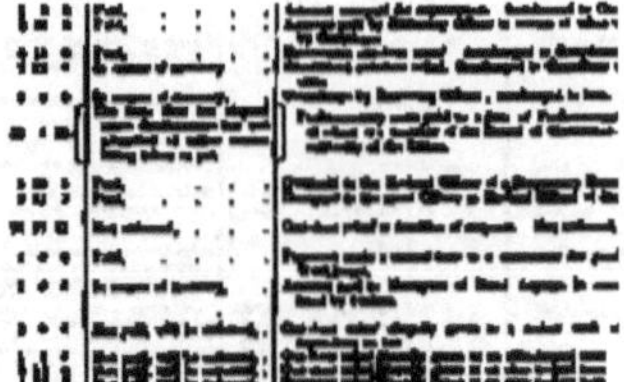

[illegible]

[illegible]	Pressure and infirmity of body and spirit	[illegible]	[illegible]	[illegible]
[illegible]	Permanent [illegible] of body	[illegible]	[illegible]	[illegible]
[illegible]	Infirmity of body	[illegible]	[illegible]	[illegible]
[illegible]	Old age	[illegible]	[illegible]	[illegible]
[illegible]	[illegible] of body	[illegible]	[illegible]	[illegible]
[illegible]	Do.	[illegible]	[illegible]	[illegible]
[illegible]	Old age	[illegible]	[illegible]	[illegible]
[illegible]	Infirmity of mind and body	[illegible]	[illegible]	[illegible]
[illegible]	Old age	[illegible]	[illegible]	[illegible]
[illegible]	Do.	[illegible]	[illegible]	[illegible]
[illegible]	Infirmity of body	[illegible]	[illegible]	[illegible]
[illegible]	Do.	[illegible]	[illegible]	[illegible]
[illegible]	[illegible] infirmity of mind	[illegible]	[illegible]	[illegible]
[illegible]	Old age and [illegible]	[illegible]	[illegible]	[illegible]
[illegible]	Old age	[illegible]	[illegible]	[illegible]
[illegible]	Infirmity of body	[illegible]	[illegible]	[illegible]
[illegible]	Do.	[illegible]	[illegible]	[illegible]
[illegible]	Do.	[illegible]	[illegible]	[illegible]

[illegible]	[illegible]	[illegible]	[illegible]	[illegible]	[illegible]	[illegible]	[illegible]
[illegible]	[illegible]	[illegible]	[illegible]	[illegible]	[illegible]	[illegible]	[illegible]
[illegible]	[illegible]	[illegible]	[illegible]	[illegible]	[illegible]	[illegible]	[illegible]
[illegible]	[illegible]	[illegible]	[illegible]	[illegible]	[illegible]	[illegible]	[illegible]
[illegible]	[illegible]	[illegible]	[illegible]	[illegible]	[illegible]	[illegible]	[illegible]
[illegible]	[illegible]	[illegible]	[illegible]	[illegible]	[illegible]	[illegible]	[illegible]
[illegible]	[illegible]	[illegible]	[illegible]	Do.	[illegible]	[illegible]	[illegible]
[illegible]	[illegible]	[illegible]	[illegible]	Do.	[illegible]	[illegible]	[illegible]
[illegible]	[illegible]	[illegible]	[illegible]	[illegible]	[illegible]	[illegible]	[illegible]
[illegible]	[illegible]	[illegible]	[illegible]	[illegible]	[illegible]	[illegible]	[illegible]
[illegible]	[illegible]	[illegible]	[illegible]	[illegible]	[illegible]	[illegible]	[illegible]
[illegible]	[illegible]	[illegible]	[illegible]	[illegible]	[illegible]	[illegible]	[illegible]

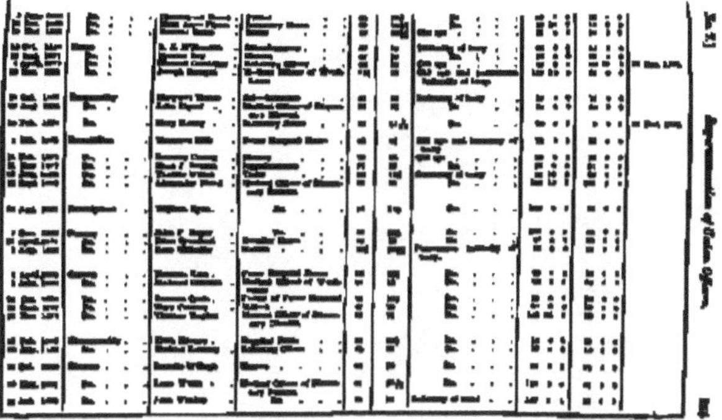

[illegible]

No. [illegible]—[illegible] Officers' Superannuation.—Statement of Allowances under the Superannuation Acts in force during any portion of the year ended 29th September, [illegible]; showing also the cases in which the Allowances had terminated during the year. (In continuation of Statement in the Tenth Report under Local Government Board (Ireland), [illegible], Appendix D, No. [illegible])—continued.

[illegible]	Union	Name of Officer	Office	Age	[illegible]	Cause of Retirement	[illegible]	Annual [illegible] Allowance	[illegible]
							£ s. d.	£ s. d.	
[illegible]	[illegible]	[illegible]	[illegible]	[illegible]	[illegible]	[illegible]	[illegible]	[illegible]	
[illegible]	Do.	[illegible]	[illegible]	[illegible]	[illegible]	[illegible]	[illegible]	[illegible]	
[illegible]	Do.	[illegible]	[illegible]	[illegible]	[illegible]	Do.	[illegible]	[illegible]	
[illegible]	Do.	[illegible]	[illegible]	[illegible]	[illegible]	[illegible]	[illegible]	[illegible]	
[illegible]	[illegible]	[illegible]	[illegible]	[illegible]	[illegible]	[illegible]	[illegible]	[illegible]	
[illegible]	Do.	[illegible]	[illegible]	[illegible]	[illegible]	[illegible]	[illegible]	[illegible]	
[illegible]	[illegible]	[illegible]	Clerk	[illegible]	[illegible]	[illegible]	[illegible]	[illegible]	
[illegible]	Do.	[illegible]	[illegible]	[illegible]	[illegible]	[illegible]	[illegible]	[illegible]	
[illegible]	[illegible]	[illegible]	[illegible]	[illegible]	[illegible]	Do.	[illegible]	[illegible]	
[illegible]	[illegible]	[illegible]	[illegible]	[illegible]	[illegible]	Do.	[illegible]	[illegible]	[illegible]
[illegible]	Do.	[illegible]	[illegible]	[illegible]	[illegible]	Do.	[illegible]	[illegible]	
[illegible]	[illegible]	[illegible]	[illegible]	[illegible]	[illegible]	[illegible]	[illegible]	[illegible]	
[illegible]	Do.	[illegible]	[illegible]	[illegible]	[illegible]	[illegible]	[illegible]	[illegible]	
[illegible]	Do.	[illegible]	[illegible]	[illegible]	[illegible]	Do.	[illegible]	[illegible]	
[illegible]	[illegible]	[illegible]	[illegible]	[illegible]	[illegible]	[illegible]	[illegible]	[illegible]	
[illegible]	Do.	[illegible]	[illegible]	[illegible]	[illegible]	Do.	[illegible]	[illegible]	
[illegible]	[illegible]	[illegible]	Clerk	[illegible]	[illegible]	[illegible]	[illegible]	[illegible]	
[illegible]	Do.	[illegible]	[illegible]	[illegible]	[illegible]	[illegible]	[illegible]	[illegible]	

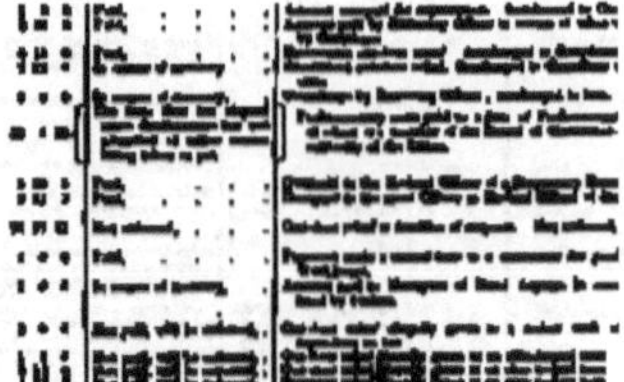

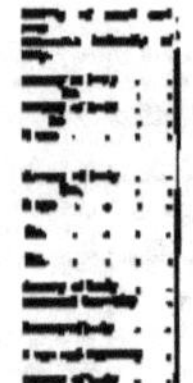

[illegible]	Union.	Name of Officer.	Office	Age	[illegible]	[illegible]
[illegible]	[illegible]	[illegible]	[illegible]	[illegible]	[illegible]	Old age and infirmity
[illegible]	[illegible]	[illegible]	[illegible]	[illegible]	[illegible]	Do.
[illegible]	Do.	[illegible]	[illegible]	[illegible]	[illegible]	[illegible]
[illegible]	Do.	[illegible]	[illegible]	[illegible]	[illegible]	[illegible]
[illegible]	Do.	[illegible]	[illegible]	[illegible]	[illegible]	Old age and infirmity [illegible]
[illegible]	[illegible]	[illegible]	Do.	[illegible]	[illegible]	[illegible]
[illegible]	Do.	[illegible]	[illegible]	[illegible]	[illegible]	[illegible]
[illegible]	[illegible]	[illegible]	[illegible]	[illegible]	[illegible]	[illegible]
[illegible]	Do.	[illegible]	[illegible]	[illegible]	[illegible]	[illegible]
[illegible]	[illegible]	[illegible]	[illegible]	[illegible]	[illegible]	Do.
[illegible]	[illegible]	[illegible]	[illegible]	[illegible]	[illegible]	Do.
[illegible]	Do.	[illegible]	[illegible]	[illegible]	[illegible]	Do.
[illegible]	[illegible]	[illegible]	[illegible]	[illegible]	[illegible]	Do.
[illegible]	Do.	[illegible]	[illegible]	[illegible]	[illegible]	[illegible]
[illegible]	Do.	[illegible]	[illegible]	[illegible]	[illegible]	[illegible]
[illegible]	[illegible]	[illegible]	[illegible]	[illegible]	[illegible]	Do.
[illegible]	Youghal	William C. [illegible]	[illegible]	[illegible]	[illegible]	Do.
[illegible]	Do.	[illegible]	[illegible]	[illegible]	[illegible]	Do.
[illegible]	Do.	[illegible]	[illegible]	[illegible]	[illegible]	Old age
[illegible]	Do.	[illegible]	[illegible]	[illegible]	[illegible]	[illegible]

APPENDIX E.

TABULAR RETURNS IN CONNEXION WITH RELIEF UNDER THE MEDICAL CHARITIES ACT.

(NOTE.—In this series of Tables, the Unions are classed in the Counties and Provinces in which the chief or central place of the respective Unions is situate; but many of the Unions comprise parts of more than one County or Province. The total of Population and Area of the Unions in the respective Counties and Provinces, as arranged in these Tables, will not, therefore, agree with the summaries of those Counties and Provinces in the Census Returns. An Alphabetical Index List of the Dispensary Districts is annexed (No. 8), showing the name of the Union in which each District is situate, and referring to the table and page in which the particulars relating to each District are to be found.)

STATEMENT of ALTERATIONS in DISPENSARY DISTRICTS in Unions in Ireland (arranged in Provinces and Counties) according to the Orders issued in pursuance of sec. 6 of 14 and 15 Vic., cap. 68 :—(*since the completion of Table No. 1, Appendix E, in Tenth Annual Report of the Local Government Board*).

NAME OF UNION.	NAME OF DISPENSARY DISTRICTS.	No. of Electoral Divisions [illegible]	Population, 1881.	Area in Statute Acres.	Poor Law Valuation.	[illegible]	[illegible]	Number of Apothecaries [illegible]	Number of Midwives.	Date of Order.
Column 1.	2.	3.	4.	5.	6.	7.	8.	9.	10.	11.
PROVINCE OF ULSTER.					£					
COUNTY OF ANTRIM.										
ANTRIM, .	Connor, .	–	–	–	–	18	–	–	–	20th Feb., 1882.
COUNTY OF DONEGAL.										
BALLYSHANNON,	Ballyshannon, .	–	–	–	–	26	–	–	–	23rd June, 1882.
LETTERKENNY,	Manorcunningham,	–	–	–	–	–	–	–	1	17th May, "
COUNTY OF DOWN.										
NEWRY, .	Newry, .	–	–	–	–	29	–	–	–	3rd Aug., 1882.
COUNTY OF TYRONE.										
COOKSTOWN, .	Cookstown, .	–	–	–	–	25	–	–	–	6th June, 1882.
PROVINCE OF LEINSTER.										
COUNTY OF DUBLIN.										
NORTH DUBLIN	North City, .	–	–	–	–	–	–	1	–	30th June, 1882.
COUNTY OF KILDARE.										
NAAS, . .	Rathmore, .	–	–	–	–	–	–	–	1	15th May, 1882.
COUNTY OF MEATH.										
OLDCASTLE, .	Ballyjamesduff,	–	–	–	–	–	–	–	1	26th Aug., 1882.
"	Crossakeel, .	–	–	–	–	–	–	–	1	" " "
"	Oldcastle, .	–	–	–	–	–	–	–	1	" " "
"	Virginia, .	–	–	–	–	–	–	–	1	" " "
COUNTY OF WEXFORD.										
ENNISCORTHY,	Oulart, .	–	–	–	–	30	–	–	–	13th April, 1882.
"	Ferns, . .	–	–	–	–	–	–	–	1	25th July, "

STATEMENT of ALTERATIONS in DISPENSARY DISTRICTS—*continued.*

NAME OF UNION.	NAMES OF DISPENSARY DISTRICTS.	[illegible]	Population, 1881.	Area in Statute Acres.	Poor Law Valuation.	[illegible]	[illegible]	[illegible]	[illegible]	Date of Order.
Column 1.	2.	3.	4.	5.	6.	7.	8.	9.	10.	11.
PROVINCE OF LEINSTER—*continued.*										
COUNTY OF WICKLOW.					£					
RATHDRUM, .	[illegible], .	–	–	–	–	–	–	–	1	21st June, 1882.
PROVINCE OF CONNAUGHT.										
COUNTY OF MAYO.										
BELMULLET, .	Bangor, .	–	–	–	–	11	–	–	–	16th May, 1883.
" .	Knocknalower,	–	–	–	–	13	–	–	–	" " "
COUNTY OF SLIGO.										
TOBERCURRY, .	Tobercurry, .	–	–	–	–	–	–	–	1	20th June, 1882.

SUMMARY OF DISPENSARY DISTRICTS, ACCORDING TO TABLE No. 1, APPENDIX E OF PREVIOUS REPORT, AS ALTERED BY THE FOREGOING TABLE UP TO THE 25TH MARCH, 1883.

PROVINCES.	Number of Unions.	Number of Dispensary Districts.	Number of [illegible]	Population, 1881.	Area in Statute Acres.	Poor Law Valuation, [illegible]	[illegible]	Number of Apothecaries.	Number of [illegible]
Column 1.	2.	3.	4.	5.	6.	7.	8.	9.	10.
						£			
ULSTER, .	44	211	873	1,743,075	8,462,291	4,220,444	225	6	64
MUNSTER, .	50	206	1,023	1,331,115	6,067,743	3,416,233	270	21	43
LEINSTER, .	40	205	845	1,278,989	4,876,918	4,741,291	229	14	184
CONNAUGHT, .	29	99	693	821,037	4,393,085	1,400,442	114	3	54
Total, Ireland,	163	721	3,444	5,174,836	20,819,925	13,691,431	833	41	284

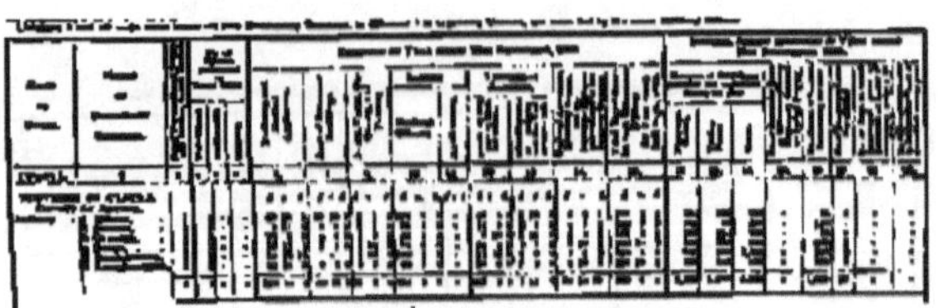

[illegible]

[illegible]

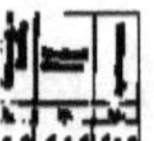

[illegible]

No. 8.—[illegible] [illegible], with the [illegible], and [illegible] of [illegible] [illegible] affording, in the several [illegible]—continued

[illegible]

[illegible]

[illegible]

[illegible]

[illegible]

[illegible]
[illegible]

[illegible], with the [illegible], and [illegible] of [illegible] afforded, in the several [illegible]—continued

[illegible]

[illegible]

[illegible]

[illegible]

[illegible]

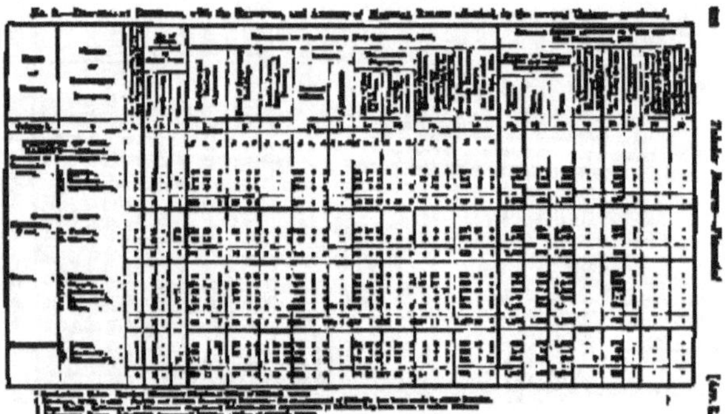

SUMMARY OF PRELIMINARY TABLE, No. 1.

[illegible]

No. 3.—General Summary of previous Tables, in Provinces:—containing, 1. Dispensary Districts formed under § 6 of the Medical Charities Act, 14 & of Dispensaries, Officers, &c.:—2. Financial Statement; showing the 1881, to 29th September, 1882:—and 3. Relief Return; showing the Home, respectively; the Number of Cases in which Tickets for Medical Vaccination performed; Number of Cases of Dangerous Lunatics certified; year ended 30th September, 1882.

Names of Particulars in foregoing Tables.	Ulster.		Munster.	
Column 1.	2.	3.	4.	5.
Statistics of Unions and Districts:				
Population of Unions, in Provinces,—1881,	. .	1,743,970	. .	[illegible]
Area of Unions and Dispensary Districts, in statute acres,	. .	5,483,201	. .	[illegible]
Poor Law Valuation of Unions, in Provinces,—1882,	. .	£4,[illegible]	. .	£3,[illegible]
Number of Unions,	. .	44	. .	[illegible]
" Electoral Divisions,	. .	879	. .	[illegible]
" Dispensary Districts,	. .	214	. .	[illegible]
" Dispensaries or Dispensary Stations therein,	. .	227	. .	[illegible]
" Medical Officers authorized to be appointed for Dispensary Districts,	. .	233	. .	[illegible]
" Apothecaries,	. .	3	. .	[illegible]
" Midwives,	. .	44	. .	[illegible]
Expenditure in Year ended 29th September, 1882:—	£		£	
Medicines and Medical Appliances,	8,0[illegible]	. .	5,104	. .
Rent of Dispensary Buildings,	2,407	. .	[illegible]	. .
Books, Forms, Stationery, Printing, and Advertising,	351	. .	[illegible]	. .
Salaries of Medical Officers,	24,570	. .	23,[illegible]	. .
" Apothecaries,	390	. .	[illegible]	. .
Vaccination Expenses,	5,00[illegible]	. .	5,[illegible]	. .
Fuel, Attendance, and Incidental Expenses,	3,175	. .	[illegible]	. .
Total Expenditure in year ended 29th September, 1882,	. .	£44,989	. .	£44,[illegible]
Relief Return, and Duties of Medical Officers for year ended 30th September, 1882:—				
Number of Cases attended on Dispensary Tickets,	118,600	. .	121,7[illegible]	. .
" " on Visiting Tickets,	64,[illegible]	. .	51,776	. .
Total New Cases in the year,	. .	183,215	. .	173,[illegible]
Number of Cases in which Tickets for Medical Relief were cancelled in the year,	. .	186	. .	57
Number of Cases of Vaccination under Medical Charities Act in the year,	. .	61,021	. .	68,[illegible]
Number of Cases of dangerous Lunatics certified in the year,	. .	308	. .	[illegible]
Number of Patients attended in Bridewells or Houses of Correction during the year,	. .	26	. .	103

STATISTICAL STATEMENT; showing the number of Unions, Electoral Divisions, and
15 Vic., c. 68; the total and average Population, Area, and Valuation; Number
Expenditure under the Medical Charities Act for the year from 29th September,
Number of Cases of Medical Relief afforded at the Dispensary and at the Patient's
Relief have been Cancelled by the Dispensary Committee; the Number of Cases of
Number of Patients attended at Bridewells or Houses of Correction, &c.; during the

LEINSTER.		CONNAUGHT.		TOTAL for IRELAND.		AVERAGES. Per Union.	Per Dispensary District.	Per Medical Officer.
6.	7.	8.	9.	10.	11.	12.	13.	14.
. .	1,270,[illegible]	. .	521,061	. .	6,174,916	81,747	7,177	5,404
. .	4,876,018	. .	4,392,066	. .	20,319,[illegible]	127,730	24,210	—
. .	£4,791,891	. .	£1,360,452	. .	£13,901,661	£94,078	£10,142	—
. .	40	. .	20	. .	153	—	—	—
. .	942	. .	590	. .	3,444	21	5	4
. .	205	. .	99	. .	721	4	—	—
. .	325	. .	144	. .	1,093	7	—	—
. .	529	. .	114	. .	838	6	—	—
. .	14	. .	8	. .	41	—	—	—
. .	134	. .	24	. .	254	2	—	—
£		£		£		£ s.	£ s.	£ s.
7,034	. .	4,507	. .	27,767	. .	170 6	38 10	34 7
2,079	. .	1,258	. .	5,530	. .	33 6	11 17	—
421	. .	160	. .	1,187	. .	4 18	1 11	—
26,250	. .	12,163	. .	95,308	. .	541 0	123 0	106 19
1,452	. .	163	. .	8,781	. .	—	—	67 7
2,610	. .	2,597	. .	14,774	. .	59 3	20 4	—
7,135	. .	1,267	. .	16,003	. .	86 14	21 13	—
. .	£47,289	. .	£21,937	. .	£169,098	£775 18	£250 11	—
139,770	. .	55,288	. .	420,298	. .	2,540	507	523
60,462	. .	18,010	. .	164,843	. .	1,154	263	239
. .	200,232	. .	73,278	. .	515,139	3,774	838	763
. .	80	. .	66	. .	698	—	—	—
. .	84,340	. .	33,017	. .	169,826	816	194	164
. .	611	. .	147	. .	1,617	—	—	—
. .	17	. .	13	. .	158	—	—	—

No. 4.—Vaccination:—Summary of the Number of Persons Vaccinated in the Workhouses and Auxiliary Establishments of the several Unions in Ireland, by the Medical Officers of those Institutions; and of the Number Vaccinated in the several Dispensary Districts, by the Medical Officers of Dispensaries under the Medical Charities Act, in the Year ended 30th September, 1882:—abstracted from Returns made by the respective Medical Officers.

Provinces.	No. Vaccinated in Workhouses by Medical Officers thereof.			No. of Cases Vaccinated by Medical Officers of Dispensary Districts.	Total Number returned in Columns 4 and 5.	Provinces.
	Successful Cases.	Unsuccessful Cases.	Total.			
1.	2.	3.	4.	5.	6.	
Ulster, . . .	581	19	600	[illegible]	51,401	Ulster.
Munster, . . .	364	16	380	33,547	34,027	Munster.
Leinster, . . .	457	8	460	44,240	44,700	Leinster.
Connaught, . . .	168	8	176	23,917	24,003	Connaught.
Total, .	1,450	48	1,498	[illegible]	154,241	

No. 5.—Number of Cases of Scarlatina, Smallpox, and Fever, reported by Medical Officers of Dispensaries in Ireland, as having been attended in the Quarters ended 31st December, 1881, 31st March, 30th June, and 30th September, 1882.

Provinces.	Quarters ended	Scarlatina.	Smallpox.	Fever.
Ulster, . .	December 31st, 1881, . .	238	78	598
	March 31st, 1882, . .	213	170	618
	June 30th, 1882, . .	199	56	459
	September 30th, 1882, . .	170	11	443
Munster, . .	December 31st, 1881, . .	254	28	971
	March 31st, 1882, . .	151	58	1,057
	June 30th, 1882, . .	131	31	891
	September 30th, 1882, . .	96	19	814
Leinster, . .	December 31st, 1881, . .	166	—	483
	March 31st, 1882, . .	249	4	482
	June 30th, 1882, . .	194	1	407
	September 30th, 1882, . .	233	2	297
Connaught, . .	December 31st, 1881, . .	97	8	314
	March 31st, 1882, . .	65	9	357
	June 30th, 1882, . .	9	—	358
	September 30th, 1882, . .	9	—	308
SUMMARY.				
Ireland, . .	December 31st, 1881, . .	755	114	1,864
	March 31st, 1882, . .	669	241	2,304
	June 30th, 1882, . .	588	94	2,109
	September 30th, 1882, . .	507	32	1,763
	Total, ...	2,354	479	8,389

No. 6.—INDEX LIST of DISPENSARY DISTRICTS; with NAMES of UNIONS in which they are situate, and REFERENCES to PAGES in which the Districts are to be found in the Appendix.

Ballyshannon.

Names of Dispensary Districts.	Unions in which situated.	Reference to Page	Reference to Page
		Page	Page
Binghamstown,	Belmullet,	-	[illegible]
Blackrock and Stillorgan,	Rathdown,	-	[illegible]
Blackwatertown,	Armagh,	-	[illegible]
Blanchardstown & Castleknock,	North Dublin,	-	[illegible]
Blarney,	Cork,	-	[illegible]
Blessington and Ballymore,	Naas,	-	[illegible]
Boherbuoy,	[illegible]	-	[illegible]
Borris,	Carlow,	-	[illegible]
Borris-in-Ossory,	Donaghmore,	-	[illegible]
Borrisokane,	Borrisokane,	-	[illegible]
Borrisoleigh,	Thurles,	-	[illegible]
[illegible]	Roscrea,	-	[illegible]
Boyle,	Boyle,	-	[illegible]
Bray and Rathmichael,	Rathdown,	-	[illegible]
Bridewell,	Athlone,	-	[illegible]
Bridgetown,	[illegible]	-	[illegible]
Bridgetown,	Wexford,	-	[illegible]
[illegible]	[illegible]	-	[illegible]
Broadway,	Wexford,	-	[illegible]
Brookeborough,	Lisnaskea,	-	[illegible]
Brosna,	Tralee,	-	[illegible]
Broughshane,	Ballymena,	-	[illegible]
Bruff,	Kilmallock,	-	[illegible]
Bruree,	Kilmallock,	-	[illegible]
[illegible]	Kilkeel,	-	[illegible]
[illegible]	Loughrea,	-	[illegible]
Buncrana,	Inishowen,	-	[illegible]
[illegible]	Kilmacthomas,	-	[illegible]
Burt,	Londonderry,	-	[illegible]
Bushmills,	Coleraine,	-	[illegible]
Buttevant,	Mallow,	-	[illegible]
Caher,	[illegible]	-	[illegible]
Cahir,	Clogheen,	-	[illegible]
Cahirconlish,	Limerick,	-	[illegible]
Caledon,	Armagh,	-	[illegible]
Callan,	Callan,	-	[illegible]
Camolin,	Gorey,	-	[illegible]
Cannaway,	Macroom,	-	[illegible]
Cappawhite,	Tipperary,	-	[illegible]
Cappoquin,	Lismore,	-	[illegible]
Carbury,	Edenderry,	-	[illegible]
Carlingford,	Dundalk,	-	[illegible]
Carlow,	Carlow,	-	[illegible]
Carndonagh,	Inishowen,	-	[illegible]
Carney,	Sligo,	-	[illegible]
Carrick,	Glenties,	-	[illegible]
Carrickbyrne,	New Ross,	-	[illegible]
Carrickfergus,	Larne,	-	[illegible]
Carrickmacross,	Carrickmacross,	-	[illegible]
Carrick-on-Suir,	Carrick-on-Suir,	-	[illegible]
Carrigaholt,	Kilrush,	-	[illegible]
Carrigaline,	Cork,	-	[illegible]
Carrigaline,	Kinsale,	-	[illegible]
Carrigallen,	Mohill,	-	[illegible]
Carrignavar,	Cork,	-	[illegible]
Cashel,	Cashel,	-	[illegible]
Castlebar,	Castlebar,	-	[illegible]
Castlebellingham,	Ardee,	-	[illegible]
Castleblayney,	Castleblayney,	-	[illegible]
Castlecomer,	Castlecomer,	-	[illegible]
Castlederg and Killeter,	Castlederg,	-	[illegible]
Castledermot,	Athy,	-	[illegible]
Castle Finn,	Strabane,	-	[illegible]
Castlegregory,	Dingle,	-	[illegible]
Castle Island,	Tralee,	-	[illegible]
Castlemaine,	Tralee,	-	[illegible]
Castlemartyr,	Midleton,	-	[illegible]
Castleplunket,	Castlerea,	-	[illegible]
Castlepollard,	Delvin,	-	[illegible]
Castle Quarter,	Ballymoney,	-	[illegible]
Castlerea,	Castlerea,	-	[illegible]
Castlereagh,	Belfast,	-	[illegible]
Castleshane,	Monaghan,	-	[illegible]
Castletown,	Abbeyleix,	-	[illegible]
Castletown,	Castletown,	-	[illegible]
Castletown,	Croom,	-	[illegible]
Castletown,	Newry,	-	[illegible]
Castletown Geoghegan,	Mullingar,	-	[illegible]
Cavan,	Cavan,	-	[illegible]
Celbridge,	Celbridge,	-	[illegible]
Charleville,	Kilmallock,	-	[illegible]
Church Hill,	Ballyshannon,	-	[illegible]
Churchhill,	Letterkenny,	-	[illegible]
Clane and Timahoe North,	Naas,	-	[illegible]
Clara,	Tullamore,	-	[illegible]
Claremorris,	Claremorris,	-	[illegible]
Clarina,	Limerick,	-	[illegible]
Clashmore,	Youghal,	-	[illegible]
Claudy,	Londonderry,	-	[illegible]
Clifden,	Clifden,	-	[illegible]
Clogh,	Ballymena,	-	[illegible]
Cloghan,	Parsonstown,	-	[illegible]
Clogheen,	Clogheen,	-	[illegible]
Clogher,	Clogher,	-	[illegible]
Cloghjordan,	Borrisokane,	-	[illegible]
Clonakilty,	Clonakilty,	-	[illegible]
Clonaslee,	Mountmellick,	-	[illegible]
Clonavaddy,	Dungannon,	-	[illegible]
[illegible]	Mount Bellew,	-	[illegible]
Clondalkin,	South Dublin,	-	[illegible]
Clonelly,	Irvinestown,	-	[illegible]
Clones,	Clones,	-	[illegible]
Clonmany,	Inishowen,	-	[illegible]
Clonmel & St. Mary's,	Clonmel,	-	[illegible]
Clonmellon,	Delvin,	-	[illegible]
[illegible]	Macroom,	-	[illegible]
Clonroche,	Enniscorthy,	-	[illegible]
Clontarf and Howth,	North Dublin,	-	[illegible]
Clonygowan,	Mountmellick,	-	[illegible]
[illegible]	Oughterard,	-	[illegible]
Clough,	Downpatrick,	-	[illegible]
Cloyne,	Midleton,	-	[illegible]
Coagh,	Cookstown,	-	[illegible]
Coal Island,	Dungannon,	-	[illegible]
Coleraine,	Coleraine,	-	[illegible]
Collon,	Ardee,	-	[illegible]
Collooney,	Sligo,	-	[illegible]
Comber,	Newtownards,	-	[illegible]
Cong,	Ballinrobe,	[illegible]	[illegible]
[illegible]	Antrim,	[illegible]	[illegible]
Cookstown,	Cookstown,	-	[illegible]
[illegible]	Limerick,	-	[illegible]
Coolaney,	Tobercurry,	-	[illegible]
[illegible] and [illegible]	Shillelagh,	-	[illegible]
Coole,	Granard,	-	[illegible]
Coolgreany,	Gorey,	-	[illegible]

[continued.

[continued.]

[continued.

DUBLIN: Printed by ALEX. THOM & Co., 87, 88, & 89, Abbey-street,
The Queen's Printing Office.
For Her Majesty's Stationery Office.

DIAGRAM

SHOWING THE FLUCTUATIONS FROM WEEK TO WEEK IN THE NUMBER OF WORKHOUSE INMATES IN IRELAND.

DIAGRAM

SHOWING THE FLUCTUATIONS FROM WEEK TO WEEK IN THE

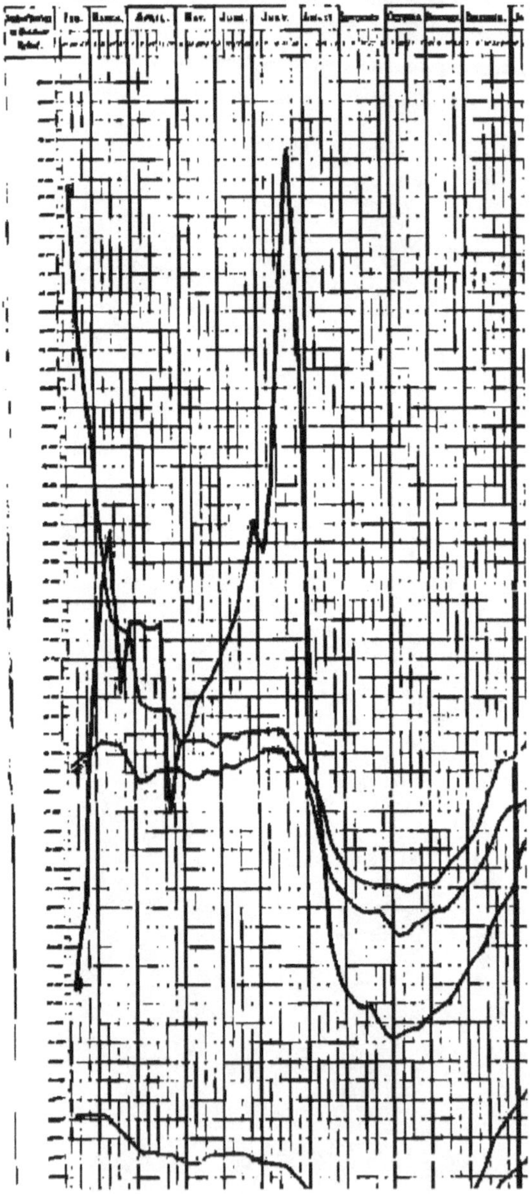

Feb. | March. | April. | May. | June. | July. | August | September | October | November | December.

www.ingramcontent.com/pod-product-compliance
Lightning Source LLC
Chambersburg PA
CBHW031020120726
47905CB00007B/1984

* 9 7 8 3 7 4 2 8 0 6 1 3 0 *